THE BLIND AND THE CAGED

To Dawnita

Just because I have not come
to visit doesn't mean I have
forgotten... I remember the pain
vividly. (Just a joke.. Don't tell Dr. K)

Best Wishes
&
Enjoy

Jeremy Fulmer

8/28/02

EXIMUS / PRINE

THE BLIND AND THE CAGED

Jeremy Fulmore

Writer's Showcase
San Jose New York Lincoln Shanghai

The Blind and the Caged

Writer's Showcase
an imprint of iUniverse, Inc.

For information address:
iUniverse, Inc.
5220 S. 16th St., Suite 200
Lincoln, NE 68512
www.iuniverse.com

ISBN: 0-595-23253-1

Printed in the United States of America

How could I think of devoting this work to anyone else (if I know what's good for me) than my loving wife Manuela. Somewhere around chapter four I asked her to take a look at the previous chapters for fear my characters lacked depth. She was hooked, and put me on a chapter churning schedule that I dare not exceed. Many books never get finished, it helps to have someone anxiously awaiting. Just another form of support I can be grateful for.

Contents

Preface . . . . *ix*

Chapter 1   A Question of Sanity 1

Chapter 2   The Enigmatic Dr. Prine 15

Chapter 3   Eternal life 31

Chapter 4   Hanging by a Thread 49

Chapter 5   Choose Wisely 61

Chapter 6   Reborn Kings 73

Chapter 7   In Preparation of the Day 85

Chapter 8   Blonde beauty 97

Chapter 9   Testament of Power 113

Chapter 10   That Woman Again 123

Chapter 11   Deviant Renegades 133

Chapter 12   Trust of a Stranger 147

Chapter 13   The interview 153

Chapter 14   Silence 161

Chapter 15   The Pristine Case 173

Chapter 16   Serena the Throne 183

Chapter 17   Dorothy's Secret 191

Chapter 18   The Shooter 205

Chapter 19   Invitation to Disaster 217

Chapter 20   Miracle Sunday 231

Chapter 21   Parable of the Wicked 245

Chapter 22   The Angels Come to Play 259

Chapter 23   Gathering Thoughts 273

Chapter 24   Falling Apart 285

Chapter 25   The Angelic Council decides 297

Chapter 26   What Rameci Has Done 313

Chapter 27   Jack's Revelation 325

Chapter 28   A Life Changing Decision 339

Chapter 29   Save the Children 353

Chapter 30   Secret of the Rhine 367

Chapter 31   Prine vs. Rameci 381

Chapter 32   Dr. Bonney's Journal 395

Preface

Those that believe in God often wonder what Heaven is like. The thought even crosses the minds of those who do not believe. Pondering thoughts of a higher power has crossed the minds of us all. If not, you are probably incapable of rational thought. Billions of people occupy the earth, and there are almost that many opinions of what "a higher power" means to them. It revolves around a familiar term we have all come across in our lifetime; an idea called faith. That is the basis for determining whether you live this life following religious beliefs or as an atheist. Each religion has its own means of reaching the holy pinnacle. Some are simple, and others are as complex as Thermonuclear Physics. But I am not here to exalt nor denigrate any one belief, religion, or preference. The book was founded on a question; If Hell was created for Lucifer and his followers, what would it mean for us if he did not sin against God? If you think this question has no relevance then think again. If Heaven did not have a rebellion, would Hell have been created for us humans? We would have sinned regardless if Hell existed or not. Who would be the "evil" leader…Adam? It is apparent to me that we, as human beings, are caught in the middle of something beyond us. Even when you look in the book of revelation the underlying message is that it is not our fight. The Angels of Heaven and the Angels of Hell will fight. We…will await the outcome. Angels: they were the first to live in Heaven, and the first to occupy Hell. Yet throughout most of religious text there is no definitive description of their impact or story. This series is in no means an attempt to fill in the gaps, or provide answers. It is purely a work of fiction about a subject we give little thought. Who are these beings and what is their purpose? What are their beliefs, and what are they fighting for?

Acknowledgements

There are times when even the most mentally secure individual needs a little positive reinforcement; and some of us need it more than others. I had many questions about my approach to writing as well as my writing style. In the fall of 2000 I decided to take an English class at the College, for one last test. I decided to go "Incognito," and not disclose any of my previous attempts at writing. I would live or die by the reaction of the professor and my peers to my writing. At the time this book had only the first chapter completed and it had been put aside for several months. The first piece I had written was read aloud as an example of writing at the College level. Since this is the finished product I guess you know how the rest turned out, but there is someone in particular I wish to acknowledge. Michele Demoss-Coward teaches part-time at the College of Southern Maryland and it was her class I had enrolled in. If it were not for her positive comments about my writing I am not sure this book would have ever been written.

CHAPTER 1

A Question of Sanity

An incredibly eerie feeling came over Felix Revner as he turned into the parking lot of the nursing home. Anxiety or possibly guilt, from his current state of mind it was too difficult to determine. He was not looking forward to this. The guilt of being accused of turning his back on the family, of being out of touch with the real world, or just not caring enough. His mother, Gertrude, could do that to people. She was capable of verbally dismantling the strongest, most confident individual, and have them doubt their own existence.

Felix was neither strong nor secure, he was rather passive. The perfect child for a mother like Gertrude, at least she thought. Until he found the strength to put her out of harms way and into this nursing home. Mainly, out of *his* way. But still there are visits like these, when Felix must pay his respects to the woman who raised him. And he has to face the built up aggression she carries—at least two months worth. Where, in that time, she makes him regret he had even been born. Then again, that *is* why Felix sent her to the nursing home in the first place.

At fifty-one years of age Felix was no great success. As the manager of a large department store he earned a decent living. Nothing at all like he imagined he would years before. For now, Felix was content with biding his time until retirement. A small achievement compared to his father who had built up a considerable amount of wealth before he retired. Felix brushed his salt and pepper hair away from his face and he thought about his children, one in particular who was not there, his oldest daughter Cindy.

Gertrude was a very strong and domineering mother figure, as time went by her mental faculties began to deteriorate. Now, her personality remains the same, and her actions make her a serious risk to her safety, and the safety of those around her. This makes her very uncomfortable to be around, especially for Felix her youngest son who put up with her for most of his life.

"Honey…Felix, honey." Sitting next to Felix, the soft comforting sound of his wife Elise's voice snapped his mind back to the task at hand. "Felix, are you ready?" Hesitating slightly, Felix slowly shook his head, trying to reassure his wife, and maybe even himself, that he was ready.

"Can we get out now," screamed Brigitte from directly behind the driver's seat. Brigitte was the younger of Felix's two teenage daughters. A bit on the heavy side, and quite impatient, the energetic fourteen year old flung the door open violently, causing the whole car to rock as the door contacted the stop and almost slammed shut again. "You watch that attitude young lady," said Elise in a stern voice. The soft and reassuring voice she displayed with her husband quickly became a voice of discipline.

"This is not the time to start with me." The stern Austrian accent and a glare from Elise's beaming eyes quickly brought the rowdy teenager under control. "Now," she said, "when we see your Grandmother I want you to be on your best behavior. You will be respectful, but most of all do not bring up the details of your sister, Cindy. There will be a lot of other adults there who want to see your grandmother, so you just show your love and then you can step back out of the way or wait in the lounge or something. I don't want you to be in the room too long, Okay." Brigitte started shaking her head disparagingly, as if she heard the speech several times before, but only after her mother turned away.

"Don't worry Mom, I'll look after Brigitte," Sandy the elder of the sisters spoke. "We just want to say hi to grandma." Sandy, unlike her younger sister, was slender and ladylike. Both sisters were fairly attractive but Sandy's more pleasant demeanor made her the favorite among the neighborhood boys. Her unique charm mystified boys as young as three years old as they sought to gain her attention for something as innocent as a smile. Her mother Elise was looking toward Sandy to take responsibility when they went inside. It was clear, Sandy was more of a leader like her mother, but Brigitte only saw her sister's cooperation as *sucking up*. As they exited the car Brigitte rolled her eyes in disgust, and whispered under her breath, "butt kisser!"

Felix Revner, the third son of Gertrude, still didn't know what to expect of his mother. Distractions have a way of settling a nervous situation, his daughter Brigitte's outburst temporarily took his mind of the dreaded meeting, but the uneasiness soon returned, and Felix was more nervous than ever. If he could only be like his older brother Phil, he thought. Felix was always afraid of confrontations, which made life with his mother a mild form of torture. Phil, on the other hand, loved a challenge, and was not afraid to say exactly what he thought. Exactly what Gertrude would be thinking, Felix had no idea, except he knew the subject would be focused around his eldest daughter, Cindy Revner.

All thoughts were on Cindy, an innocent twenty-two year old girl missing for over eight months now. She is the oldest daughter of Felix and Elise. As in most missing person cases, the longer the person goes missing the greater the chance that person will not be found alive. All of her belongings were left behind, her grandmother continues to pay rent on Cindy's one bedroom apartment. The place is kept intact, very little was disturbed, which Felix believes will help investigators find clues, if they ever need to revisit the apartment. Cindy owned a small business where she sold custom jewelry and T-shirts; that was also found abandoned. Phone records turned up nothing unordinary, her voice mail contained one message, which turned out to be a dead end, and her neighbors claim there was nothing out of the ordinary about her life.

Except at the bank, one teller claimed she tried to make a large deposit, but got spooked when a large line began to form behind her, and quickly left. The teller has no idea exactly how much money Cindy had with her, she estimates it was well into the thousands. Once investigators got wind of this, their enthusiasm for the case stalled.

People disappear all the time, and most do not want to be found. This was the tag, which was thrown on Cindy. Investigators began asking questions of a secret life, something only close friends would be aware of, anything to support the theory that she disappeared on her own terms. Nothing of that nature was found either. For the family however, not knowing takes its toll on all concerned. Suspicion and doubt, loom in the minds of investigators, who oppose the claims of Cindy's virtue and innocence.

Foul play must be the cause of her disappearance. Her grandmother Gertrude is a firm believer of that. Of course this does not make Felix feel any better, his daughter was weeks away from returning home. She had just told her mother she was tired of California and was ready to move back east. Felix remembered telling Cindy to take her time with the decision, and that she had her whole life ahead of her. Now he wishes he could go back, if he could, he would fly out to California personally, hug her as if he were never letting go, and bring her back home.

"Do you think Phil is here already?" His wife, realizing Felix had drifted into a state of reverie tried to gain his attention. "I hope so Elise," Felix replied. "You know how mom can be sometimes, it would sure make things a lot easier if he was here. If I only knew how she would take the news, she...she could cause a scene. Accuse me...accuse of everything..."

"Don't think about it so much Felix." Elise turned toward Felix, ensuring her eyes met with his and gave him a reassuring gaze. "We will get through this, somehow. You can believe me." Felix did believe her, and the four of them exited the car and made their way to the nursing home entrance.

Through their twenty-seven years of marriage there have been many times where he thanked God for a woman like Elise. Today, he had one more reason to give thanks. He was going to make it through today, maybe slightly bumped and bruised, but he would survive. Felix took a deep breath, gave his wife a reassuring nod, and pressed the elevator button. The elevator was rather large for a nursing home, with dark wood grain colored background and soft lighting. Silence, as the group rode the elevator all the way to the sixth floor.

As the elevator door opened, the atmosphere was common for that of a nursing home. As it was every other time they came to visit their beloved grandmother. Filled with loneliness, family members who felt cast aside. The somber mood of the elderly, feeling useless and discarded. Forgotten members of society, whose time has passed. Some who spent their entire lives giving, until they were unable to, who has now become a burden on those whom they had dedicated their lives to. They now live among themselves, cherishing the memories of the past, to help ease their suffering.

Except when it came to visitors, fresh young faces always seemed to liven the mood. As the family walked toward the room their grandmother now called home, other elderly residents looked on with interest. Curious heads turned to see the visitors and where they were going. Felix slowed as he approached his mother's room, hoping to hear the familiar voices of his other brothers within the room. This would make his entrance all the more easier, the thought of being the first to arrive was too much for him to bear.

He heard the voice of someone already in the room. Good, he thought, this would help him and his family to slip in casually and blend in with the other visitors.

"You can't go off on some kind of vengeance trip mom, the police have nothing." Felix recognized the voice as his brother Phil. "It stinks, I know, but they have to do their job." Phil had the voice of a leader, not too overpowering, but direct and to the point. There was a frustrated tone to Phil's voice this time. Felix did not have to hear the beginning of the conversation to know what they were talking about. Next, came the voice of his mother, Gertrude. "That sumbitch will pay, you mark my words. I will see to it!" Her voice was old and crackling, the obvious emotional stress, and old age, has changed the sound slightly. Her Georgian accent however, still came through crystal clear, and the conviction in her words was still evident.

Gertrude may have sounded like an old woman; just an old woman with the voice of someone you did not want to mess with. "No one treats one of mine like that, not one of my own. This family may have tried to forget about me, lock me up in here, but I still have a say."

"Now mom," said Phil who was clearly trying to settle his mother down, "nobody locked you up anywhere. You need to realize you are an 80 year old woman with special needs and we don't have the time."

Phil made a mistake when he said that.

"You make time!" Gertrude was spitting and coughing as she almost came out of her bed. "I raised all you damn kids and this is what you do to me! Toss me aside like garbage. Well we will see, my angel friend will be here soon and you'll see. I'm not the crazy one. You all think I'm crazy cause I spent all your money right? Well it wasn't your goddamn money to begin with. Your father gave that money to me. And before I die I will spend it as I damn well please." Felix began to hear sniffling, as if someone was crying. Now, in a crackling voice, Gertrude struggled to control her emotions with her last statement. "I'mmm yyyour mother dammit!"

Felix took a deep breath, it had begun and it was not about to get any better. This was his cue, to face his fears and help his brother out. Felix tightened his lower jaw and threw his shoulders back until his posture was one resembling confidence. Trying to reassure himself of inner toughness, he looked his family over, making eye contact with each one and giving a nod of approval like a military commander preparing his troops for battle. He then turned toward the open doorway and led his family into the room.

Felix's mother Gertrude, was still crying. Her chin draped to her chest, she jerked her body with every breath like a five-year-old over-exaggerating for attention. A white linen gown was all she wore and it had about as much style as the bed sheets she slept on. Her long stringy gray hair hung freely across her shoulders. She was not concerned with how she looked, and knowing visitors were coming, she did not make an attempt to show herself presentably. For an old Southern woman of her economic stature, this behavior struck Felix as odd.

The room was small and not in the least bit cozy. It felt more like a hospital room than a home. Even hotel rooms were more hospitable than this one. The tiny dwelling barely fit the five of them, there were chairs, and even they were uncomfortable to sit on. The atmosphere conveyed a lack of personal attachment, someone stayed there but no one called it home.

The room was painted off white. The furniture consisted of two chairs, both antique wooden chairs, with a pastel color designed cushion. A corner lamp and one window supplied lighting for the room, with pink pull curtains as the only means of blocking the sunlight. The bed, of course, was the only comforting piece in the room. Directly under the window, the queen sized adjustable bed was tilted slightly upward. There lied Gertrude; she had stopped crying now, the flow of tears were still evident on her pinkish hued cheeks.

Gertrude focused her attention on her new visitors. Felix did not know what to think of his mother as she gazed at him. Her eyes were glassy and unfocused. She looked in his direction, but did not acknowledge his presence. Just as Felix opened his mouth to say something, his two girls ran out from behind him, eager to see how their grandmother was doing. As if a light switch was turned on, Gertrude immediately snapped out of her trance like state, visibly embarrassed, trying to quickly wipe the tears from her face. She put on a fake smile for her grandchildren and pretended as if nothing was wrong.

Gertrude wondered how much the children knew about the horror that faced the family, how much they overheard, and how much Felix had told them. In all, she acted like a true grandmother and welcomed the children as if they were the only concern in the world.

"Ah, my lovely grandchildren. How are you girls holding up?"

"We are doing great grandma, despite all the secrecy," Brigitte said, as she turned toward her father. Elise could have strangled her youngest daughter for making such a comment, especially after being cautioned about good behavior. Felix did not appreciate the statement either. "Come girls," replied Gertrude, "I know you came to see how old grandma was doing, so sit right her next to me so I can talk to you lovely girls."

The girls sat on opposite sides of the bed; they began telling their grandmother all they had done since the last visit. Sandy began first, "I'm nervous about going into that new private school. Starting high school last year was scary enough."

"They're shipping you away because of all the boys that hang around all the time," said Brigitte. "They think that would keep her concentrating on her studies more by sending her to an all girls private school, but I heard the girls there are even more boy crazy than the girls at regular schools."

"And what about you," said Gertrude, "aren't you going also?"

"No not me!" Brigitte replied "I don't have a problem with studies."

"And why don't you share the same problem as your sister? As charming as you are, the boys must be chasing you around too?"

The ever so mouthy youth was silenced; taken by surprise at her grandmother's sarcasm. A quick snicker came from one of the three adults standing behind her. Brigitte turned around immediately to see which one caught a chuckle at her expense. By that time all three were looking in different directions and acted as if they had not heard a thing.

The girls continued to tell their grandmother all that was going on in their lives for ten minutes. Gertrude encouraged them to include all the details. Then Gertrude told the girls she wanted to discuss other things with just the adults, "You do understand, don't you?" Gertrude looked at Sandy. "Of course grandma," said Sandy.

She immediately walked toward her sister, gently grasping her arm. "Brigitte, its time to take a little walk to the lounge area."

"Where all the old people hang out," snapped Brigitte. "They always want to talk to me an' stuff. They always say 'Why, you look just like *my* granddaughter,' and 'Gertrude is so lucky to have such fine grand children.' It's so boring! I rather stay here with...Owww!" The gentle grasp Sandy had on her arm began to tighten. "Let's go!" Brigitte was heard mumbling her displeasure all the way out the door.

Gertrude watched as the girls left through the doorway, her smile disappeared as the girls moved out of sight. "Now, how do you suppose you were going to talk to me with those two hanging around?" Gertrude was furious. "Is that what you are doing now, hiding behind those children?" Everyone in the room was astonished. Gertrude was known to be vicious and attack with no warning, but this was uncharacteristic.

"Was I supposed to leave them home? I thought you wanted to see them? But it doesn't matter mother, If I left them home, you would have criticized that as well."

"If you were this nurturing of *all* of your children, Felix, we would not be here under these conditions in the first place." She was referring to his eldest daughter Cindy.

In a fury Felix left the room, he was tired of being the victim of his mother's tirades. He stood outside for only a minute when his brother Phil walked up beside him.

"Mother has not been the same since she heard the news. The nurse on this floor is worried about her mental well being. Says she keeps talking of strange men coming to visit. There is one man I am worried about, the FBI Agent, Jack Ward. For some strange reason he believes her cockamamie stories about that religious guy being behind Cindy's disappearance. And she has also been speaking of a messenger coming to deliver vengeance…or something like that."

"The FBI believes her?"

"Hard to believe isn't it," Phil responded. "Apparently they wanted this guy for some time now, and they're looking for any reason to investigate him." Felix could not believe anyone actually took the ramblings of an impious and senile old woman seriously, especially the FBI.

"Let's go back inside and talk to her some more. I want to know what she is up to."

"Wait," Phil said, "the nurse told me other things about mother's behavior, which leads me to believe she is on her last days. I know you have been thinking of telling her exactly how you feel about her, but due to the recent developments, now might not be a good time. The nurse said that in situations like this the important thing is to treat her like everything is normal. I always talk to her like that. If you start, that might be enough to agitate her condition. So try to be easy on her will you?" Felix neither agreed nor refused to cooperate. Both men reentered the room to see Elise by Gertrude's bedside.

"I was just trying to settle things down," said Elise. "Your mother tells me Cindy called her shortly before she disappeared." Elise gave the men a condoning wink.

"I think you should hear her out. She has something interesting to tell you."

"Hell no, I ain't telling them a damn thing!" Gertrude exclaimed boisterously, "those bastards won't believe me anyway! They just want to get a hold of my money, and hope I don't spend too much more of it before I die. But I'm not ready to die yet. I tell those young doctors that all the time. They are not like the ones from my time."

"What are you talking about now mother?"

"Have you paid attention to anything I've been saying?" Gertrude continued, "I'm talking about people walking all over you, taking advantage of everything they can. You kids still have not learned a thing have you?"

"Not everyone is out to get you mother," Felix stated, after being silent for so long. The brashness of his statement intrigued the elderly woman, she did not expect this from Felix. "Oh, growing a backbone are we…now that I can barely move? The smell of blood is in the water, and I guess you feel safe now that I have broken my hip and cannot move freely. Well, lets see how far your new bravery takes you. Are you ready to tell your wife and children the truth? Hopefully, this is why you brought them here with you today."

Felix had a dreadful feeling in his gut. Did Gertrude know he told Cindy to make sure she was ready to come home, and not make an impetuous decision? Does she suspect that if Cindy left swiftly like she wanted to, that she would be among them right now? Guilt began to invade his thoughts. Phil, noticing his brother was stalling, came to his aid. "That's enough mom, what's done is done. It is time for the healing to begin."

"Healing begins with justice," said Gertrude, "and the authorities have not a clue. I have to point them in the right direction."

Gertrude paused to grab a sip of water from the end table. "I have hired a private investigator, he has been on my payroll for years. In case of an emergency he has been given specific instructions. I gave him this order over fifteen years ago, that upon my death, he would carry out the instructions. But, I'm afraid it cannot wait that long. He is carrying out my instructions as we speak."

Both Felix and Elise were in shock, and Phil was outraged. "What! Are you insane?"

"That is still your mother Phil," said Elise, trying not to let things get too far out of control.

"That's okay Elise," Gertrude responded, "at least I know he stands up for himself." *This was Gertrude's way of taking another cheap shot at Felix.* "This investigator has found something very near and dear to me. Something that people more esteemed than I wished they could know before they died. Believe me, I will have my justice."

They did not know what to think of their dear mother's proclamations. Only that she needed help. "Mother," Phil questioned, "does this have anything to do with the $50,000 a year salary you have been paying to this *Jeff Arnold* person, for the past fifteen years?" Gertrude and Felix were both equally shocked that Phil knew this, but for different reasons.

"I knew you were checking on what I did with my money, but it is none of your business." Felix confirmed, from his mother's reaction, that what Phil said was true.

Why Phil kept this hidden from the rest of the family had Felix bewildered. "I had this Arnold person checked out," said Phil, "he's a drunk! He has no other clients, his family has left him, and his business would have failed if it wasn't for you."

"That..." Gertrude responded with a smile, "is because he carries a tremendous burden on his shoulders. One shared with me, but he is loyal to the core. He did not even tell his own family for fear of being ridiculed. He carried this secret to his grave. He may be still breathing, but he is buried in a drunken grave. He refuses to believe the truth, even after he has seen it with his own eyes. His weary load will soon be lifted; he is going to face his tormentor as we speak...As I said earlier, I will have my justice!"

CHAPTER 2

The Enigmatic Dr. Prine

1303 Mulberry Place, a small house located in the middle of a fairly new subdivision in Northern Virginia. The neighborhood children were all playing outside on this fine Saturday afternoon. The area was quite peaceful, a serene, picturesque view of the perfect community. From a parked car, the aging investigator Jeff Arnold sat, waiting for just the right time. Perhaps when his nerve was up and his hands stopped shaking. His line of work was indeed dangerous. Jealous husbands and wives, and of course people who did not want to be found. Jeff knew this to be the case at the Mulberry residence. And people who do not want to be found were not known to give warm welcomes.

As he sat in his 1986 Monte Carlo, Jeff remembered how he got to this point. Many years ago, when he was the best in his field, a woman walked into his office and promised to make it worth his while financially, if he would dedicate himself to a certain case. Jeff paused from his thoughts to take a swig of whiskey. Nothing like Jack Daniels straight to calm the nerves, he thought. He perched his lips on the bottle, and threw his head back quickly. When you have been drinking like Jeff has, straight whiskey no longer burns. It is just a soothingly, numb feeling on the way down the throat.

"Hey, what are you doing mister?"

Startled, Jeff jumped as he turned toward the partially open passenger window.

A small boy sitting on a bicycle was curiously looking in. Jeff gave a sigh of relief. "You shouldn't be sneaking up on people like that kid." He tried to hide the bottle between his legs but did not do a very good job.

"Are you from Jehovah's Witness or something? They come around here a lot, except they don't sit in the car and drink before they knock on the door."

Jeff looked down at the bottle tucked between his legs and smiled. "You must be on stakeout," the boy continued. Jeff's smile quickly vanished.

"Yep, just like in the movies," said the boy. "Cops drink all the time, even on duty. Then they start beating on peoples heads with that Billy club."

"I'm not a cop kid."

"My friend lives in that house right there." The boy pointed to the house that Jeff was watching. "He has all kinds of video games. So what did he do? Are you going to call for back up?"

Jeff immediately came to the conclusion this youngster was too smart for his own good. Lying would have been fruitless. "I am here to serve a letter," said Jeff.

"You mean a subpoena," said the young inquisitor. Jeff was dumbfounded; the boy looked no older than eight years old.

"No," Jeff replied, "this is just a letter."

The kid watched Jeff carefully for about three seconds, then replied, "Yeah, I believe you. You look too raggedy to be an officer of the court, and they don't drink so much either. See ya!"

Jeff watched as the young boy hopped back onto his bicycle and hastily peddled away. Peculiar way to start a morning, Jeff thought to himself. It was now or never, the fifteen-year-old job had now come to an end. Jeff put down the half empty bottle of Jack Daniels, grabbed the sealed envelope, and headed toward the front door. As Jeff walked he looked for some sign of movement inside the dwelling, but saw none.

That was not a good sign. It is when all is quiet, that there is everything to fear. Jeff had been in this business long enough and escaped many close calls to realize that—drunk or sober. The direct approach is the most successful method, he stood at the front door and rang the doorbell. Within a few seconds a man opened the door. He was an African-American male, around his mid twenties. He stood wearing a pair of brown silk pajama pants and had a toothbrush in his mouth.

He had the features most men would die for, and a body to match. Carved like Michelangelo's David, he stood impatiently waiting for Jeff to speak. "Hello, I am looking for a gentleman named Elijah Morales. I was told he could be found here." Jeff held the sealed envelope in one hand, where the man could visibly see it. He did not appear to be panicking which Jeff figured was a good sign.

The man looked down on the aging investigator, and then tilted his head at a slight angle as if he were thinking. Thinking of his next move perhaps? Jeff had done his homework, he may have his problems, but he was a thorough investigator. He knew this man that stood before him was named Walter Prine, a professor of Psychology at the University. That is the name he goes by now. Before that it was Frank Knoll and prior to that Elijah Morales. Those were just the latest in a long string of alias's…the trademark of someone who does not wish to be found.

"Your name is…" the man inquired. "Jeff Smith" the investigator replied. "Jeff, I am Dr. Walter Prine, pleasure to meet you. Would you like to come in? I want to discuss where you obtained that letter of yours." *Hell no*, Jeff thought to himself. He was already scared at what his eccentric employer; Gertrude Revner had told him about this guy. And after chasing him around for fifteen years he was beginning to believe it. "No need," said Jeff, "the letter is from an old friend of his."

At that moment the young boy on the bicycle pulled up behind Jeff. "It's okay dad, this guy is some kind of private investigator or something," said the boy. "I just don't know why he drinks so much; he must have a lot on his mind." Dr. Prine was amused. "So, you have spoken to my son before you came to the door? What questions did you ask him?" Jeff looked toward the boy to bail him out of a most uncomfortable situation. "Please," the doctor continued before Jeff could find an answer, "I have to know where you got that letter." Jeff turned to look at the young boy once more, who simply shrugged his shoulders in response. Dr. Walter Prine held the door open, made a welcoming hand gesture, and waited for Jeff to enter. Reluctantly, he entered the doctor's home.

The home did not look like much from the outside, but inside it was elegantly decorated. There were several antique pieces that covered several tables and over the fireplace mantle. Jeff looked on in interest, although Jeff was no collector, the rarity of the items displayed had a story all its own. Jeff had the luxury of examining the artifacts without intrusion as Dr. Prine changed into something more suitable for entertaining guests. Jeff stood the entire time, the truth being, he was reluctant to sit down. He did not want to get too comfortable, no telling when he would have to make a quick exit. Just then Dr. Prine's son walked in. "Would you like something to drink?"

"A coke would be fine," Jeff replied. The boy went into the kitchen and quickly returned with the drink.

"Before you go," Jeff inquired, "how did you know I was a private investigator?" The boy paused for only a second. "It's the only thing you could be I guess." The little boy scampered out of view and simultaneously Dr. Prine reentered wearing a dark colored shirt, a pair of jeans, and round wire rimmed glasses, which he was not wearing earlier. It gave him a more distinguished look.

"You met young Lexington outside, did you?" Dr. Prine was referring to his son. "He is quite intelligent for a boy his age," Jeff replied.

"He is almost nine years old, and already too smart for me to handle. Are you enjoying your drink?"

Jeff did not touch his beverage. "Sorry, I was admiring some of your pieces. They look like rare works of art." "They are! Most are from ancient civilizations; rare pieces of mysticism and ancient power long forgotten by more civilized man. Do you follow many works from ancient history?"

"No, none at all," Jeff replied.

"Many of it is just folk lore, but interesting none the less. Take this for example, it is my favorite piece."

Dr. Prine led his unwilling guest over to the mantle where there was an old, knurled, wooden stick. It had a large round shape at one end and pointed at the other. It was only twenty inches long and looked no different from any other strangely shaped piece of wood found among the brush. Yet, Dr. Prine treated it with reverence. "This is from the Mayan civilization. There is a story behind this object. The people who created the perfect calendar, and in turn were able to predict future events with accuracy. Some believe they had discovered a means of accessing a higher power and subsequent abuse of that power led to their demise."

"The Mayan civilization was wiped clean without a trace. But here is a story about this object translated from an archeologist. An esteemed, king who was considered very wise was in possession of this object. He was married to a beautiful woman, her radiant looks and alluring personality made her the envy of all women. She adored the attention she received and feared most of all, losing her attractiveness to age. After years of pleading with her wise husband, asking if there was something the gods could do, he revealed this staff. He warned her, there is a reason to all of nature's rules, but she did not care. He performed a ritual with the staff, and when it was over told his wife she would age no more.

"As the years went by, she discovered the spell worked as her husband said it would. Her husband, her children, and her friends all aged as time went on. They began to become old and started passing away. She began to see death on a regular basis, her children and grandchildren, dying of sickness, war, and old age. Soon she could not tell her family who she was any more. A great grandmother, who looked as if she were twenty, was too severe for the normal mind to handle. So she had to leave her place of birth and venture out on her own. There, she discovered extreme loneliness, her beauty remained, but no one was in awe any more.

"She was a freak, an abomination; wherever she went she had to be careful not to get too close to anyone, not to have too many friends, and not to love anyone. It was too painful, whomever she loved died eventually. And when the pain of loss became too great she tried to end her own life. It did not work, she tried again and again, and still she lived on. Severely depressed and confused, she desperately returned to the Mayan culture where she was raised. She returned, hoping there would be someone left who still knew the ancient ways of power and could reverse her spell. But she was faced with more sorrow, as there was nothing left but the erected monuments of that once great civilization. She cried for five years and finally wrote her story among the ruins. The mysterious staff was laid beside it. She will return every one thousand years in hope that someone wise is the old ways will end her sorrow."

After finishing, Dr. Prine gently laid the piece back onto the mantle.

"Interesting story," said Jeff, after sipping his drink. "I appreciate your hospitality, but I am afraid I have to leave."

"First, I wish to know about the letter."

Jeff was about to drop the letter and make his way to the door. He could not understand his feeling of helplessness about the whole situation. Jeff had never been enticed into a person's home like this before, especially one whom he intended to deliver a message to. He only agreed because the boy, Lexington, would be present. And Lexington seemed to be so well behaved and sincere, that nothing could possibly go wrong while he was around.

Except now Jeff was beginning to question his own rationality. The sickening feeling in Jeff's stomach became overwhelming, alcohol and fear, did not mix well. The aging detective's body began to reject the early morning cocktail onto the floor of the doctor's living room. Lexington came running down the stairs after hearing the distinctive sound someone regurgitating. "Oh—gross!!"

"Thank goodness I have hardwood floors," Dr. Prine said jokingly. "Help me clean this up son. And you Jeff, you are definitely staying now. You owe me after heaving all over my collectibles."

Who knows why Jeff stayed, possibly because he felt obligated, or maybe to put an end to his fifteen year job. The certainty of the situation was that he was tired of wondering, Jeff wanted answers. It took about ten minutes to clean up. Dr. Prine moved his guest into another room in the house. There he gave Jeff a glass of water and a towel, sat him down in a comfortable chair, and began to talk. "When I saw the letter, and you mentioned that name, I knew this day would come."

"What are you running from doctor, or are you really a professor at all?"

"To answer the second question," said Dr. Prine, "Yes. I worked hard for my degree and earned every bit of it. To answer the first question is slightly difficult. Ten years ago, if you had come to the door the way you did today, I would have snapped your neck like a twig and thrown your body among the rubble. You were right to be afraid."

Jeff was startled at the nonchalant tone of the doctor's voice.

"You entered my house because you trusted my son obviously. If so, you have great instincts. My life has changed since then, since the birth of my son. And I am also tired of running." Since Dr. Prine was laying it all out on the table Jeff decided to speak about the letters origins. "That letter was given to me many years ago," Jeff said, "with specific instructions on when and how to deliver it. I have no idea of its contents. I do not want to give away its author for fear of their safety. I was hired to track you down and keep tabs on you until the day arrived when I would reveal myself. The call to do that came last night and as promised I performed my duty without question."

"How long have you been following me?"

"Over fifteen years."

A long pause followed, as Dr. Prine thought hard about what that meant.

"So, you know all about me?"

"Yes I do," Jeff responded.

Dr. Prine poured himself a drink, Smirnoff and juice. "There was a time when identities were easy to buy, Jeff. A person was not required to have a social security number until they were eligible to work. All that was needed was a birth certificate. Today, identities are tracked from the day you are born, and every country in the world is using some kind of system to track its occupants. Soon, they will use DNA logged in a central computer somewhere, tricking the system to create or steal identities will become almost impossible in the near future. Unless you find some underachieving computer hacker to do the dirty work for you. And after that they might put a bar code on your ass, and Lojack chips in your brain, to track your every move or something."

Dr. Prine paused momentarily to take a long drink. "Anyway, you know only what I want you to know about me. The information you gathered so far is too outlandish for the average mind to comprehend. No one would believe you."

"I have no idea what you are talking about," said Jeff.

"You don't?" Dr. Prine walked over to where Jeff was sitting. He leaned down and got within four inches of the private investigator's face, looking directly into his eyes.

"Then Jeff…Why are you so afraid?"

Jeff heard footsteps approaching from down the hall, followed by the sound of a car horn. He thought he heard a car horn earlier, but was too engaged in the professor's conversation to be distracted. "The cab is here," said Lexington.

"Good, I cannot have the investigator driving through my neighborhood in his current condition," said Dr. Prine.

"What about my car?"

"It will be safe right where it is. By the time you make it back here I trust you will be sober. Pleasure meeting you Jeff Smith."

Dr. Prine escorted Jeff outside his home and into the awaiting taxicab. He handed the driver a fifty-dollar bill and instructed him to take Jeff to the Ramada Hotel on the other side of town.

The enigmatic Dr. Prine returned to his home, and to the letter, now resting on his coffee table. "Who is Elijah Morales?" his son asked.

"Someone I knew a long time ago." Dr. Prine picked the letter off the table and began to read it. When he was done, he walked over to the phone and began dialing. "Yes, this is Walter Prine. I will be unavailable to teach this summer…There is a family emergency I must take care of…Yes, I understand. I was speaking to Patrick Nell recently, he may be able to fill in…Of course, and I will be back for the fall semester. This is a sensitive matter and my family needs me…Yes, I will call the minute I return. Thank you, Goodbye."

He grabbed his glass of Smirnoff and juice and drank what was remaining in one big swoop. "I misled you earlier son, what I meant when I said Eli Morales was someone I knew a long time ago—this was a name I used to go by. The letter is really addressed to me." Lexington understood and did not seem offended by his father's beguiling word play. "We must always rely on each other," said Dr. Prine.

"Integrity is a big part of trust, I want you to know I will always be there for you and I'm sorry if I tried to fool you." Lexington was far more intelligent that most children his age. He understood what his father was trying to tell him. "That's okay Dad."

"Good—looks like we are going on a trip," said Dr. Prine.

"Where are we going?"

"To visit an old friend in Connecticut."

Prine, as he preferred to be called, arrived at the Wiltshire Nursing Home in Connecticut with his son Lexington, two days after receiving his letter. Lexington really did not know what to think of his father's unusual actions. Since his visit from the private investigator, Walter Prine seemed compelled, for reasons unknown to Lexington, to travel to this location. It was late June in Connecticut and the weather was just starting to heat up, but still considerably cooler than Northern Virginia was. The father and son duo entered the lobby of the home and sought directions. Prine told his son to wait for him in the lobby and he would return soon.

Lexington sat patiently by himself, there were no other people in the room. He kept himself entertained by watching the television, until two teenage girls entered the room. The younger was quite loud and immediately let her presence be known. The other sat directly across from him. The two girls were Brigitte and Sandy, the daughters of Felix Revner. Brigitte, in her usual boisterous style began to voice her displeasure at being sent to the waiting area once again.

"Every time we come here we get kicked to the curb and sent to the waiting room."

"This place was not meant for young people like ourselves," Lexington interjected. Brigitte raised her eyebrows in disbelief, apparently irritated the young boy would attempt to strike up a conversation with her. "You have to forgive my sister," said Sandy, "she doesn't have any manners to begin with. My name is Sandy and the brat over there is Brigitte."

"Brat? I'm tired of being here. We've been coming every other day for a week and every time we have to come out here and sit."

"As you can see," Sandy said sarcastically, "she is just thrilled to death." Lexington loved Sandy's sense of humor.

"That's understandable; it's quite boring out here. I am here with my father and my name is Lexington."

"What a well-spoken young man you are. How old are you Lexington?"

"I am almost nine years old. But people tell me I act a lot older."

"Yes, you do!" said Sandy, amused at young Lexington's attempts to be impressionable. "Are you visiting family here?"

"Nope, my father is here visiting an old friend."

"Well we are here visiting our grandmother," Brigitte interjected. "But we hardly get to see her at all, just *this* room."

"Parents always keep secrets from their kids. It's like some kind of parental code or something," Sandy added.

"All they have been doing is whispering," said Brigitte, "then yelling, and after that they start fighting. This time it is just our mother and us. I thought we would get a chance to stay in the room since it was just us girls this time but nooooo."

"Give it a rest," Sandy insisted. "I am worried about grandmother. I know she smiles and tells us she is happy to see us, but something is different. I'm certain there is more going on than they are telling us."

"Secrets," Lexington stated, "are sometimes a means of protection. Sometimes it is better that we don't know. Problems that adults go through are serious and we don't need to worry like they do. I rather have fun. Even though they are wrong about us, they don't think we can handle it. We can...they show their love for us by shielding us."

Brigitte raised her eyebrows once again. "Who are you? Some pint sized philosopher? Where did you come up with that crap? I'm tired of being left in the dark. I want to know what is going on like everybody else." Lexington shrugged off Brigitte's shrewd comments and tried to turn his attention to Sandy.

Sandy tried not to let her concern over her grandmother's condition upset her. From what she overheard, her grandmother is in her final days and getting delusional. For the last decade Gertrude has been spending an extravagant amount of money, mostly on charity and volunteering her time as a missionary. Both her grandmother and grandfather, Charles Revner went wherever help was needed, physically and financially for the past thirty years. Charles Revner died thirteen years ago. Now, her grandmother has given up helping, she stopped caring, and has given up on mankind. Her faith in people has withered until it is no more. Her first grandchild is missing and she fears the worst. She feels all of her praying, all of her charity, all of her time, has served nothing. She feels abandoned and betrayed. Gertrude believes it is because of something she did years ago and she plans on correcting that mistake.

That is all Sandy knows of the situation involving her grandmother, the rest is blurred due to family members arguing and falsely accusing each other. A tear began to form in Sandy's eye as she remembered how this all started, she remembered her older sister Cindy, and how they all wish she would return. If this is what their parents were hiding from them they were right to do so. Cindy was loved dearly; there was no brighter personality in the entire family than Cindy Revner. Even the seemingly insensitive Brigitte, would sit in Cindy's old room and cry uncontrollably, wondering if she would ever see her older sister again.

Sandy quickly cleared her eyes and tried not to think about her eldest sister. Lexington went into the next room to get a snack from one of the machines with the change his father had given him. He returned with a bag of chocolate chip cookies, his favorite. He sat across from Sandy, where he had been sitting before, and began eating. This time Brigitte paid a little more attention to Lexington than previously, chocolate chip cookies were her favorite also.

"So, who is it your father came to see, Lexington? Maybe our grandmother knows him? We can ask her the next time," said Sandy.

"My father did not tell me, but I got a peek at the letter he kept reading. The name of the man is Dr. Clifford Bonney. He is a psychiatrist that works here or something."

"Bonney? Why does that sound so familiar?" Brigitte scratched her head.

"That's our great-grandfather," Sandy replied. Brigitte was too young to remember her great-grandfather. And Sandy only remembers because she recently wrote a school report on her family tree. "But he is no longer alive Lexington. I think he used to work here part-time."

Sandy could not help but think her eccentric grandmother was involved in this somehow. *Grandmother, what have you done*, she thought.

Noticing Sandy was occupied with other thoughts Brigitte took it upon herself to initiate the conversation.

"Lexington," she asked "who is your father, and what does he do?"

Elise thought it best she pay Gertrude a visit without the boys—Gertrude's sons. A nice woman to woman talk was known to work wonders in getting to the root of what was troubling the ailing grandmother. Elise had a lot of respect for her mother-in-law. Although she could be a bit callous, Elise knew deep down that Gertrude's heart was in the right place. She was a woman who was family oriented, all of Gertrude's actions was done with the family's best interest in mind. It was shocking to hear her speak of vengeance, the decent Christian woman that she was. Her life was dedicated to giving; now it seems her tone has changed.

Felix, her son, believes Gertrude was loosing her mind, but Elise was not ready to believe that just yet. Cindy was the love of Gertrude's life, especially after her husband died. To have that snatched away without a trace is a lot for an old woman to handle.

Elise sat in silence and watched Gertrude; the elderly woman stared at the ceiling. She did not blink or even acknowledge someone else was in the room for five minutes. Until, while still staring elsewhere, she began to speak to Elise.

"I did everything required of me Elise. Everything good and decent people should. Why should I suffer such heartache before I die? I don't deserve this." Elise searched for words of comfort, but did not come up with much. After all, it is the tragedy involving her daughter, in which Gertrude was referring to. "I never dreamed something like this would ever happen to us," Elise finally responded. "Dream," said Gertrude. "Yes, it is all like a dream. I am waiting for someone to wake me up and tell me that was all it was. I'm too damn old to believe that lie though."

Gertrude sat up, the silver hair once draped along side her face was swept back into a ponytail. She grabbed a mirror from the nightstand and began to apply makeup.

"Mother Gertrude," said Elise "there is another issue I wish to discuss. One that is very sensitive also, the nurse made reference to you no longer attending the church services. She thought with your background, in times like these, you would be the one leading the prayer groups instead of discouraging them."

"I cannot pray right now," said Gertrude, "I am afraid I might be talked out of doing something."

"What is it, you think you are going to do?"

"I know you think I am crazy, I had this secret for close to fifty years. The whole time I tried to convince myself it was not true, because if I believed it…I *would* be crazy. There are things about this world that you do not understand and I have no time to explain it to you now. Whatever you think of me, that's just fine, I am not out to win anyone over."

"I want to know what this crazy secret is Gertrude." The stern Austrian woman was blunt and to the point, it was a trait Gertrude admired.

"Well you are in luck Elise. I believe that crazy secret just walked past that door. Would you be so kind as to direct him in here?" Elise looked toward the door, there was no one there.

"He is down the hall, honey."

Elise followed Gertrude's request without question, her curiosity had gotten the best of her. From what she could tell her mother-in-law was sane. She spoke like a woman with an enormous amount of stress plaguing her mind, with one delusional, furtive idea of life being something it is not. This is the closest anyone in the family has gotten to finding out what Gertrude has been mumbling under her breath. She just seemed to be speaking in riddles. But she just implicated another person in her cryptic babble, a person now roaming the halls of the nursing home. Elise would find out whether this person was real or not.

CHAPTER 3

Eternal life

Elise thought there was nothing to it; she would find this person whom Gertrude was referring, and expose him for the phony he was. Elise already knew there would be someone visiting Gertrude today. She overheard Gertrude speaking to the private investigator on the phone two days ago. Elise planned to surprise Gertrude and her guest; she planned on staying there all day if she had to. Stimulated by Gertrude's shroud of mystery regarding this stranger, Elise took off down the hall after him. She turned the corner just in time to see a figure dart into a room to the far-left corridor. It was the office of the resident psychiatrist. She hurried toward the room as the door closed; cautiously she turned the knob and entered.

Looking from behind, the larger Dr. Prine dwarfed the five-foot tall Elise. He turned around as she entered the room behind him but thought nothing of being followed.

Prine looked around the empty waiting room section of the office. He then walked over to what appeared to be the secretary's desk. It was a small black and silver desk, contemporary office furniture design, with a single, six drawer file cabinet located behind it. Prine was a stickler for neatness and admired the secretary's sense of organization.

Scanning the visible documents without upsetting anything, he found the information he was looking for. *Tuesday office hours: 2pm to 4pm.* He looked at his watch, the current time was 11:35 a.m. The business hours the Doctor kept was longer than Prine was willing to wait.

Elise instinctively acted as if she were looking for the same information while trying to get a closer look at Dr. Prine. She was not as inconspicuous as she thought. Noticing eyes were continuously upon him, Prine tried to be semi-social with small talk.

"It looks as if the Psychiatrist won't be in for another two hours," Prine said to Elise.

"Oh well, I guess I will have to come back later," Elise responded. "I wanted to know how my mother was doing with her sessions. Is that what you are here for?"

"No," Prine blurted. "I'm here to locate and old friend, one that used to work here."

Prine thought that bit of information about the psychiatrist not returning for a few hours would get rid of the inquiring woman, but she continued to nose around. Her impudence was upsetting Prine, he wanted to get at that file cabinet, but that woman just would not leave.

Elise began to wonder if there really was a connection between he and Gertrude. After being so close, she absolutely, had to know. "What is it you do for a living sir?"

"I am a professor of Psychology, I teach at the University in Northern Virginia," he replied.

"The reason I am asking," said Elise, trying to look as innocent as she could, "is because my mother-in-law saw you walk by her room and told me you remind her of someone. And she insisted I go and see if you were really that person she thinks you are. Being a professor of psychology and all, I am sure you can understand why I just had to make it look like I was listening to her, or else I would never hear the end of it."

"I guess I can understand that." There was brief silence as they both stood, apparently waiting for the other to leave the office.

Then Elise came up with another idea. "Sorry, to bother you once again—I know this is awkward, we really do not know each other, but you would be doing me a great favor by doing this. Could you come with me—back to my mother-in-law's room? I need for her to see for herself, that you are not who she thinks you are?"

Perturbed by her incessant company, especially when he had other things on his mind, Prine tried to suppress his displeasure. "Who does she think I am? You can just tell me and I will let you know one way or the other." Prine appeared unwilling to play the woman's game. Elise, on the other hand, was not backing down.

"That is irrelevant; whenever she gets unreasonable like this, the only way to shut her up…is to show her up! This won't take long and I promise afterward I will leave you alone."

He did not have much of a choice since she put it that way. Dr. Prine was not thinking of hanging around until the psychiatrist returned. "I can only stay about five minutes."

"That is just fine," replied Elise. "She is back in room 622, come on, I will take you there."

As she walked back down the corridor with Dr. Prine, Elise was so excited she could barely stop talking. "You don't know what this means to me. She can be so difficult in her ways. Stubborn, she just goes on and on and never drops an issue until she beats it into the ground. She would have made life hell for us for the next three days if I couldn't get you to do this." If the mother-in-law was anything like her, Prine thought, he would be in for a long day. He was right on both accounts.

Prine slowed as he passed the room directly before Gertrude's. He had an uncanny sense of detecting when a person was at the end of their life. Harold Franklin was the man in the room next to Gertrude. Harold had no tubes, no life support, no monitors attached to his body. From all outward indications he was a healthy old man—his situation was not unique. Harold had simply lost the will to live. His room was empty; he had not had visitors in over three months. Alone and lonely, he simply decided his time was done. The mind is more powerful than most people give credit, and once the mind has decided a fate there is nothing in the world that could stop it.

Prine looked into the open room and made eye contact with the elderly man. Harold's glassy eyes confirmed it for Prine. Harold raised his left hand and held it in the air for a few seconds, his suspended hand shook uncontrollably. Acknowledging the old man's gesture, Prine gave Harold a nod and whispered something, wishing him luck on his journey.

"It's the next room over," said Elise. "Remember, my mother-in-law? You can stand in the doorway if you are uncomfortable with entering."

"No," Prine replied. "Let's go."

Led by Elise, Prine followed his new acquaintance into Gertrude's room. Gertrude was unexpectedly bubbly, and full of life. Elise could not believe her eyes. This new behavior confounded Elise. Dr. Prine stood erect, waiting for Gertrude or someone to tell him there was a mistake and he could go. Except Gertrude was not in the least interested in doing so. She was seated upright in her bed, and curtailed her excitement enough to speak.

"My, what a fine specimen you are!" Elise could not believe her innocent mother-in-law just said that. "Come over here so I can get a good look at you."

Prine looked to Elise to intervene, she remained tight-lipped and motioned Prine to do as Gertrude requested. This was not what Elise had expected and curiosity had the best of her. Prine confidently walked over to the side of the bed, Gertrude carefully examined his body as he stood just a few feet away. She extended both of her arms and motioned Prine to put his hands inside hers. Her wrinkled, knobbed hands held his as best she could, as she looked through the bottom half of her bifocals. Then she looked over the tops of her glasses at his face again and released her grip on him. "You can go now," she said. Prine took a step toward the door. "Not you," said Gertrude. "I am talking to my daughter-in-law! This doesn't concern you Elise. You can wait in the lobby with your children if you wish. I have a lot of catching up to do with this young man."

"I'm sorry ma'am," Prine finally interrupted. "I came as a request by your daughter-in-law. The truth is I have no idea who you are."

"Maybe you don't, but I am the one you are looking for. My name is Gertrude Revner."

Prine still had no idea who she was, but the name was one he recognized. "I don't think you have any idea what you are talking about," he said.

"The reason you are here—does this have anything to do with the letter you are carrying around?" That was all Prine needed to hear, apparently she did know something. Elise had already delayed him getting information once before by nosing around the psychiatrist's office, Prine was not going to be interrupted any longer. He did not try to be subtle, as it was time for one of them to leave. He walked over to Elise and kindly escorted her out of the room.

"Mama Gertrude, I'm not leaving you in here alone with this strange man!"

"You don't have a choice," said Gertrude, "neither one of us want you in here right now. Go call Felix if you have a problem with it!" The door was then closed and locked, with Elise on the outside looking in. Flabbergasted, Elise would take Gertrude's advice. *She ran toward the pay phones in the lobby.*

The small room and all of its uncomfortable furniture were a challenge to anyone looking to relax. Prine made the best of it, he grabbed the chair to sit and then stretched his feet onto the step Gertrude used to assist in getting in and out of bed. Gertrude waited until he was comfortable before she began.

"What shall I call you?"

"My name is Dr. Walter Prine. I prefer to be called Prine."

"Okay…Prine! Would you like something to drink?"

"No thanks. I take it that you knew Dr. Clifford Bonney in some way?"

"Of course, he was my father," she replied. "And you knew Elijah Morales?" Prine thought carefully before he responded. "I knew him well." Gertrude looked confused then she smiled coyly.

"Elijah Morales and my father had a special relationship way back in the early 1900's. Would you like to hear the story?" Prine did not respond, so Gertrude continued.

"My father was working at a psychiatric hospital in Louisiana. It was said the government was connected somehow, but that rumor was later dispelled. It was just that the state of Louisiana didn't give a damn about what happened at those facilities, so the doctors were free to do some strange and unorthodox things to their patients. Well, deep in the lower levels, where they keep the most dangerous and vicious criminals, was our boy Elijah Morales. How he got there was another story; he was such a danger to himself and others that they simply just kept him locked in a padded cell and never tried any kind of therapy.

My young father, being the rebel that he was, had been given the task of trying to treat Elijah. Elijah ranted of being cursed, that he was a demon, and he was being punished, by walking the earth for all eternity. Isn't that the damnedest thing you ever heard Dr. Prine?"

Prine sat motionless; the story interested him in more ways than one. Gertrude could see by his reaction that Prine did not find the story unbelievable and he had her full attention. Gertrude cleared her throat and continued. "My father had tried for several months to connect with Elijah in order to treat him successfully. He only became frustrated in the process. There was another doctor who consulted with my father on his difficulty. Since the state did not regulate the treatment of mental patients back then, this doctor recommended my father stop wasting his time. His methods were more brutal than my father wished to perform, but after speaking with him on several occasions he convinced my father to incapacitate Elijah within an inch of his life. Then they could properly examine him without risk of being injured. Poison was the best method, and no one would ask questions. My father's associate even provided the poison, a plant seed known as Ricin. It was mixed in with his food and piled into his feeding dish. That night my father checked to make sure all of the food was consumed and it was.

"They practiced very crude methods back then and my father fell victim to their inhumane practices. Elijah Morales was considered a permanent fixture there. They wanted to cut him open and perform a lobotomy. That way they could run tests to try and understand how his body could be so resilient, but they could not subdue him. Drugs, starvation, dehydration, electrocution—he would appear to be incapacitated until someone entered the cell, and it would be lights out for that poor unfortunate soul that was coerced into going in. Poison was tried on Elijah before, my father was unaware at the time he administered the near-fatal dosage. It did not work before, and it did not work when my father did it. After seeing it with his own eyes my father could not conceive a person could be resistant to drugs like Elijah was. This haunted my father, the words that Elijah mumbled haunted him also. He could not understand what Elijah was saying, it sounded like some other language. Elijah would repeat it in a pattern, over and over.

"My father, did not agree with conventional methods of psychiatry at the time. He thought that Elijah would be a perfect candidate to try new methods, which he was developing. His technique was to find the world—the state of mind in which the patient existed—and slowly bring him into reality. The hardest part to determine was to understand where Elijah's mind had gone. My father listened to him everyday, trying to piece together the strange language he spoke, and worked on understanding the English meanings to his rambling.

"He drew charts and graphs, flow charts, and thousands upon thousands of notes. He took his work to language experts in hopes that they could help him crack the code of this strange dialect. For four years, it drove my mother crazy, as my father worked on breaking the language barrier. Who knows why my father spent so much time on Elijah. It was evident he was obsessed with the psychotic mystery of the subject. Finally on April 23rd he was able to connect with a single word. My father said the words 'Ko din tah'…it stood for *Heaven*."

Gertrude held a captive audience of one, as Prine sat and listened. "This was a phenomenal breakthrough. Elijah believed someone understood his pain and began speaking more of his strange dialect. My father began to take notes once more. Six more years of therapy before my father had Elijah speaking English all the time. His therapy accelerated, and through my father's new break-through techniques in psychiatry, he was able to piece Elijah Morales's thoughts back together. Enough so that he could start the second phase of therapy and Elijah could finally come out from behind the cage.

My father was heralded in the psychiatric community, his colleagues who thought he was obsessed with an insurmountable task was now singing his praise. It took him twelve years of his career, but he finally felt his job was worthwhile. Then things went sour. The head psychiatrist, maybe driven by jealousy, still wanted Elijah for his initial experiment. Elijah was still such a superior physical specimen that the head psychiatrist wanted him studied. Now that he was no longer a menace, he thought the task was attainable. My father was not notified—they tried to take Elijah—it failed and Elijah escaped."

"I have a feeling you knew all of this already Dr. Prine," said Gertrude.

"Yes…it was still interesting hearing the story again."

Gertrude smiled once more. "I may be old, but I am no fool. Jeff, the private investigator I hired, said you told him of a Mayan legend and that you have several antique and occult artifacts."

"I am fascinated by the supernatural," Prine said.

"We are all looking for answers, it is where you look that counts. If you help me, I will show you where you can find the answers you seek." Prine did not hesitate to take her up on her offer. "Keep talking…"

"There was something unordinary about Elijah Morales, perhaps this is why my father was so interested in him in the first place. The supernatural was definitely enshrouded around Elijah, what he spoke in that native tongue of his was secrets, secrets to the next life. Secrets to power we have yet to understand. Maybe he had it all figured out and somehow he was silenced, by taking his mind from him—I really do not know the truth. For the rest of his natural life my father worked on deciphering what Elijah Morales had said. I am in possession of over 1,000 pages of translated text. I will give these pages to you if you help me with my problem."

Prine rose to his feet and paced around the room. His mind consumed in heavy thought, calculating his next move. Still determined to carry out the charade to the end if he had to. This woman knew more than he cared for anyone to know and she held the key to his deepest desires. The frail old woman waited patiently for an answer. Prine would tip his hand and reveal what he had revealed to no one else. "Do you mind if I ask you a serious question?"

"Not at all," Gertrude responded.

"Why go through all of this trouble?"

"I thought this was something you were interested in Dr. Prine. I am simply making a deal."

"Enough that you would risk your own life?"

"I am in my final days. I have nothing to fear," she said.

"And your family? You just put them all at risk. If you know all about me like you claim you do, you would have never let me near them."

"You are a man of honor. If you had killed in the past it was only to protect yourself. You are in no way threatened by me, Elijah. It is time to end this. I told you I am no fool."

Prine was agitated by the woman's trickery. "You just called me Elijah!"

"That's right," said Gertrude.

"I would be over 100 years old if I were him, and in worse shape than you right now!"

"You *are* well over 100 years old," she continued, "maybe even 1000 years old. Not even you know when you were born do you. Probably all you can remember is the past eighty years or so." Prine's breathing increased; his heart rate also increased at a steady rate. He was angry, but tried not to show it. "I am afraid nature would disagree with you old woman," he said finally, "how do you explain my body? It has not aged."

"You are the one who told the story about the Mayan princess. I believe you hold reverence to that tale because it parallels your own life. Somehow you came across the secret of eternal life!"

This feeble, elderly woman was delivering her theory with such brashness and gallantry; she practically dared him to deny it. Prine took a step back; he had the look of disbelief on his face. He then began to laugh hysterically. "Do you know how crazy that sounds," he asked, to which she responded.

"Then why are you here?"

"Because, I came across knowledge that I thought would be valuable to me," said Prine. "I took care of Elijah for years and when he died I stole his identity, that's all. It all sounded like some sort of myth to me, but if there was just the possibility of it being true it was worth checking out. After all of this, I merely find a senile old woman with an over active imagination. I want to see this book of yours, after listening to your theories I suspect it is just as worthless as you are."

The unbreakable Gertrude raised an eyebrow at that one. "Worthless is it? You came a long way for worthless. Worthless is what you might find at a garage sale. People don't normally travel great distances for garbage. You have a letter dated fifteen years ago about a patient in a mental hospital and here you are. Sure—for years I wondered if it were true. That's why I had an investigator track you down and keep up with your every move. I spent a small fortune wondering if there was any truth to my father's lifelong obsession. I know there was a possibility of it being true because of the information gathered about you. I can appreciate its value, and today I know it was all true. Indeed, I do know how crazy it all sounds. That's why I can be confident. There is only one other person in existence who would risk the ridicule of chasing that myth. Only one person who would have an idea about the journal's content. Only Elijah would have shown up here today."

"If I were Elijah, I would not need the journal of an unorthodox psychiatrist. As you said, the knowledge was Elijah's to begin with."

"Elijah has no identity of his true self. That was how his sanity was restored. He was given a new identity a new life. This was my father's method of treatment. He figured Elijah's mind was damaged, so he was given a new one. Not physically, only psychologically. But in order to do that, all of the bad or disconcerting information had to be purged and replaced with new information. His secrets were too much of a burden on his conscience, so he was given a life he could handle. Now I see that was not entirely true. I figure you obtained the knowledge of eternal life, rendering your body immune to poisons, disease, and mortal injury. Completely self sufficient, with no need of food or water to sustain itself. You then violated some sort of code, or were not supposed to have that knowledge to begin with, and you were punished by the Gods. They scrambled your mind and forced you to roam the earth for all eternity."

"You are a sick woman," said Prine, "a very sick woman. You know what is contained in this journal. Then why haven't you used it? The fountain of youth—you would be rich beyond your wildest imagination. The world would be at your feet, and you would be able to enjoy it for as long as you desire. Tell me, how could you pass that up, and then offer it to me?"

"I have it," said Gertrude, "but I dare not look at it. There is a natural order to things, those who upset that balance are doomed. You are the proof of that. You heard of the expression 'careful what you wish for,' that phrase was coined after centuries of experience. You want that journal, not because of eternal life; you want your life to be over. You wish to reverse the curse and become mortal again. You've seen enough death, more pain, slavery, torture, incest, rape, murder, treachery, sorrow, and ignorance than you can handle. Time passes, but man's precarious ways remain the same. That is why I know I can trust you Dr. Prine. The crimes of man disgust you and you have seen enough, I posses the answer to your sorrow."

Prine paced along the perimeter of the room. For Prine the charade was over.

"You are a tough woman Gertrude, and smarter than I gave you credit…I am who you say I am!"

It was all true, this was the reason he changed identities. All he could remember of his meager beginnings was Gertrude's father, Dr. Clifford Bonney befriending him. Then he remembered the doctor's suspect betrayal over seventy years ago. There were certain things Prine felt he needed to know, things this journal might reveal. Prine looked down at his hand and began to rub the unique dimple shaped wound on his left hand. It was the only scar on his whole body and was located on the knuckle of his middle finger. With his other hand, he massaged the rough outer edge of the scar; then it hit him. That must be how Gertrude knew it was him, by the mark on his left hand.

People normally do not take supernatural occurrences seriously, they try to explain it through some circumstance of nature. It is usually no more than titillating conversation at parties and urban legend horror novelties for frat houses. Taken seriously by only the eccentric and often dangerous members of society. However, Gertrude knew with conviction about him. She was in complete control, and the turning over of the journal came with one stipulation.

"Now that we have that settled Prine, I would like you to do something for me. There is a family member who is near and dear to me that is missing. I want you to find her for me."

"Let me guess, the police have no leads. They believe she does not want to be found. After six months the likelihood of foul play becomes increasingly probable…correct? I have no experience in things like this. Why don't you use your hotshot private investigator, Jeff? He obviously is extremely talented."

Gertrude responded, "Jeff is burned out after chasing you, and the police already think Cindy does not want to be found, so they stopped looking. On the issued of foul play I am positive that is what we are facing."

"You think she is dead?"

"Common sense says yes, but my heart is screaming no," replied Gertrude. Gertrude began sobbing, the callous old woman had a soft spot after all, Prine noticed. "I told the police where to look, I don't have any credibility with them so they don't pursue it. Cindy, my grandchild, told me she was coming home with something I might be interested in. I shared with her, the story about you, and my father's journal when she was young. It fascinated her to no end, I am afraid she made an enemy. Shortly after telling me she was returning home, she was never heard from again."

"Why do the police think she does not want to be found?"

"There was an issue about her depositing, a large amount of money shortly before she disappeared or something. But I know that isn't right, I can tell the difference," said Gertrude.

"Why do you need me?"

"There are elements of the supernatural that others might not appreciate. Let's face it, they would find it *damn* hard to believe. Have you heard of…*The Miracle?*"

"Performed by the Reborn Kings Ministry, of course I have," said Prine. "Everyone in the modern world knows about it."

"Cindy's drivers license was recovered from a rental vehicle, rented by one of the members of the church."

"BOOM, BOOM, BOOM!"

A loud banging came from the door. There was a small glass window about ten inches square, cut into the door. The face of Felix Revner was plastered against the glass. He could see his mother and another man talking inside. "Open this door!" shouted another voice. It was Phil; both brothers had come to see the stranger their mother was talking to. Through the door window they saw their mother point toward them. Prine walked over to the door, and the brothers got to take a good look at him, right before he closed the small privacy blinds that covered the opening.

"Who the hell is that?" Phil could not believe Prine would have the audacity to keep them out of their mother's business. They were concerned for her safety—and maybe they were just a tad bit nosey—but they did not deserve to be treated like *children*.

"I told you," said Elise, "his name is Dr. Prine. He is a professor at some university." As the three huddled outside Gertrude's room Brigitte, the youngest of Felix and Elise's daughters, joined them.

"Is it time to go yet? We are getting bored out there," said Brigitte.

"Can't you see we are having an adult conversation here? I would like for you to go back, to the waiting room and wait for us there."

The brothers were still conversing among themselves, Brigitte could not make out what the fuss was about, so she began walking back to the waiting room as her mother instructed. About fifty feet away Brigitte heard them mention the name Prine. She recognized the name immediately and concocted a mischievous idea within seconds.

"Mom," she said, "is that Dr. Walter Prine in there with Grandma?"

Elise was perplexed, "How did you…"

The brothers began arguing with each other regarding their mother's condition. And whether it was safe to have her in there with a strange person, she had met only moments before. Elise quickly walked to where Brigitte was standing, they talked for a minute, and then she joined Brigitte on her journey to the waiting room. She thought not to disturb the boys, as they seemed to be preoccupied in other discussions. Elise decided to sneak off, with Brigitte, and talk to the young man in the waiting room without them.

Lexington was engaged in a crossword puzzle, with help from the beautiful Sandy of course. He tried not to impress her with his over-average intelligence, as she insisted on helping him. The atmosphere was fairly quiet until Brigitte and her mom entered into the room and walked directly to her daughter and the young man named Lexington. Elise acted as innocent as she could while addressing her daughter Sandy, who was sitting next to her real target.

"Hello, Sandy," Elise said with the utmost virtue.

"Are we ready to go?"

"Not yet," said Elise as she watched Lexington. "Who is your friend?"

"Don't you think you are over-doing it on the charm mother?" Brigitte's snide comments came naturally for the sturdy fourteen-year-old.

Elise could not believe after all the warning she had given her youngest daughter, that she still had the audacity to behave rudely. Lexington was a classy young man and made up for Brigitte's interruptions.

"My name is Lexington Prine," he replied to Elise.

"Pleasure to meet you Lexington."

"Oh skip the formalities Mother," insisted Brigitte once more, "She wants to know why your father has come 300 miles to see our grandmother? She wants to know who he is and what he does? We all want to know what business he has with our grandmother!" As the pulsing vein in Elise's forehead increased robustly, the unmindful Brigitte, had no idea she just came within an inch of being dragged out of the nursing home by her hair.

"What is going on mom?" Sandy was perplexed by her mother's behavior.

"I was just concerned for grandma, that's all," Elise replied, "You know what? I will sit right here with you all, and wait until they are done in there."

That provoked an agitated sigh from Brigitte, to which her mother replied forcefully, "…and I'll deal with you later, Brigitte!"

Elise made herself comfortable in the seats adjacent to theirs. It seemed longer, only ten minutes had gone by. With everyone waiting for Dr. Prine to enter the waiting room; it seemed each person had his or her own reasons.

Finally the graceful, doctor walked into the waiting room. The seriousness of his expression discouraged anyone from asking questions. Lexington rose as if previously rehearsed, he waived goodbye to the girls, and he and his father quickly exited the building. The walk through the parking lot was where Lexington decided to break the ice and talk about his visit to the nursing home.

"There were people back there that wanted to meet you, dad. They froze after you came out. Even that loud mouthed Brigitte didn't say a thing."

"It was probably better they didn't son. Everything they would want to know they could find out through Gertrude. They might even have a new respect for her, the hardest thing for them would be to trust her."

"On the letter, it said you were going to see a person named Clifford Bonney. I guess that turned out to be Gertrude's father."

Prine was initially stunned his son was so attentive to his surroundings; he was not stunned for long. For his son, things like that was common practice, amazing feats of deduction and drawing conclusions. He could deduce correctly, from the most diminutive of clues, ever since he could speak. It was ashamed his mother was not alive to revel in her son's brilliance.

Prine maneuvered his way through the parked cars to find his. He removed his keys from his pocket and unlocked the door. His thoughts quickly turned from pride to concern. Honoring the wishes of Gertrude and hunting down her missing grandchild would be no easy task. Although he had never met Gertrude before today, he felt compelled to find the answers regarding Cindy's disappearance.

The razor sharp mind of young Lexington would come in handy. The two buckled in and adjusted their seats for the long ride home. This was the way Prine preferred to travel whenever possible, it gave him more time with his son. The only person he truly felt attached to, his own flesh and blood. Since his wife died, Prine felt the two of them grow closer than ever before. Right now, Lexington was the only person who would accept him unconditionally for who he was.

"Once we get home we need to pack our bags. We are going on a trip to California. We will probably be gone for about three weeks, maybe longer. But first, I need to make a pit stop. I have an appointment to see an FBI agent in D.C."

"Can we go to the Zoo afterward," asked Lexington. "The last time I went with the school, the tigers all stayed inside and they rushed us to the buses before I could check on them again."

"Sorry son, as much as I would like to, I cannot take you to this meeting with the agent."

Prine began to think about Gertrude and her situation, the timing did not seem right. The private investigator mentioned he had been following Prine for fifteen years. Yet, Cindy has been missing for only seven or eight months. Why has she suddenly decided to reveal her knowledge about him now? Prine felt as if he were being manipulated by this seemingly clever and frail old woman. With that into consideration, Prine was still willing to take the risk in order to get his hands on the journal. This journal might contain the answers Dr. Prine has sought for as long as he could remember. He was no average man. Gertrude knew this also. However strange it might seem, Dr. Walter Prine decided he would play this out to the end.

CHAPTER 4

Hanging by a Thread

The stereotypical California day is sunny, not too hot, not too humid, picturesque blue skies, with an occasional cool breeze from the coast. The perfect climate controlled weather, a haven for the outdoors type. The coast was a place untouched by warm and cold fronts, high humidity, and wind streams that affect the rest of the country. Whatever the current temperature trends the nation suffered, the California coast remained unscathed; immune and unblemished, to write its own laws. Nature had its ways but California was the exception.

For most of the year this holds true, but there is a down side. Where nature is excluded from gradual change, it often makes up by extreme measures. Floods, mud slides, earthquakes, and raging fires are all part of the Californian elemental repertoire. If you emphasize pleasure over risk, this is the place to be, at least that was how Marie Carthon felt.

For her, there was no place like it in the world. All she needed was a warm sun and a serene wooded trail to escape from the troubles of everyday life. A long run was more than exercise it was a moment of peace. Early morning before the kids would wake for school, before she would have to hurry to work, Marie could be found running along the trails behind her small subdivision.

The morning started out like most of the others, she got dressed in her white T-shirt and white shorts with green reflective trim, put on her blue Old Navy ball cap, and let her long black hair hang out the back in a ponytail. Marie did not have the traditional runner's frame; thin and wiry, her legs were slightly muscular and complimented her toned physique. She stretched inside her house every morning before heading outside to minimize drawing attention to herself. As a mother of two boys, she did not want them to worry about her. The woods could be a dangerous place to be stranded, so she was cautious before entering alone.

Her husband, who thought the early morning was best for last minute sleep, had suggested weeks before that she change her routine if she insisted on going so early. Marie took all of these things into consideration each time she went running, the answer was still the same. She preferred not to break the invigorating routine for starting her day. She would be alert when running, but was not going to take so many precautions that it would take away from her enjoyment. She thought about all of these things as she stretched, exactly as she had given it thought the day before. When she was all warmed up Marie stepped outside and headed down to the trail.

The sun had just broken over the horizon, the morning dew still present on the grass outside her home. It was neither too humid nor chilly, but it felt damp enough that goose bumps began to form on her arms. Marie rubbed her hands across her arms quickly, to create friction in an attempt to warm herself. It was not happening fast enough, so she decided to start her run from her front door instead of walking to the woods first.

She started slowly running down her walkway, turning left at the sidewalk for about 200 yards, then a sharp right across the street to the beginning of the wooded trail. This was her normal start point, right next to the green park bench. She dashed by the entrance and began to pick up pace on the trail. The lights that were positioned on the main trail were close enough that it aided in lighting the dirt trail for about the first 500 yards.

The soft orange hue from the sun provided the additional light, enabling her to see clearly throughout the entire course. The wooded trail was where Marie got close to nature, her athletic shoes pounded on the earth as she strode along. About five minutes into her run she noticed a shoe, in the shrubbery, off to the right side of the trail. She thought nothing of it as there is often trash and other things left behind from the inconsiderate pedestrians who have little to no respect for nature.

Winding trails were a real challenge to Marie; she chose this one because of its steady and progressive incline. Her ponytail danced from left to right with each stride. She could feel her thighs begin to burn; she pushed herself harder on the inclines. There was a sharp right turn ahead—pacing herself—she timed her strides perfectly and powered right into the turn.

Marie stepped on something and turned her head to see what it was. It was a small object—probably a watch. Another turn to the right; now was the time she would psyche herself for the forty-five degree incline just 100 yards ahead. Rhythmical breathing, ponytail dancing, and the pounding sound of her feet hitting the ground, this is how she gained the mental energy to overtake this steep obstacle. She got closer with each stride, and counted down in her head, 'Three–Two–One,' her left foot hit the base of the hill and with a mighty thrust she charged upward. The tips of her shoes dug into the hillside, instinctively she swung her arms for balance. Her thighs began to burn even more as she pushed forward.

Excitement began to overtake her, the end was in sight. The peak of the incline was the halfway point of her run, the path leveled off for half a mile then came the decline as the path circled around to the starting point. The trees masked the magnificent view of the city from there, but city life was the farthest thing from her mind.

Her shoes steadily pounding the dirt path—she glanced at her watch in an effort to keep pace. When Marie lowered her arm she noticed about five feet off the ground, hanging off a tree limb to her left, was a woman's blouse. The ends of the lime-green blouse flapped gently in the soft breeze. It looked fairly new; the elements had not soiled it, so it had to be put there recently.

Off in the distance, directly behind the blouse, she thought she saw what looked like jeans lying on top of the fallen leaves. Initially she thought nothing of it, probably a young couple going for a romp in the woods, but after running a few feet past the blouse Marie wondered if there was someone in need of help. That would be foolish, she thought, she was just as vulnerable. Marie thought to keep going. When she reaches her home she would call the police to investigate.

Other thoughts crossed her mind. If there were someone in need of help, would it be too late. A liberated woman like Marie could not bear the thought that a member of the womanhood may be calling out for help that never arrives. There were mostly trees on that side of the trail; she could see a good 200 yards radius. There were no shrubs or brush to hide in, if she walked serpentine through the trees, she would be able to see if anyone was hiding behind one.

The sun had risen rapidly since she started her run, beams of sunlight was now shining through the trees. Attached to her waist was a small, but loud, 110-decibel siren. Pulling a small pin activated it. Her husband gave it to her for protection. The siren would attract attention if she were ever attacked. Marie removed the device from her waist with her left hand and inserted her right index finger into the ring securing the pin.

She headed toward the jeans lying off in the distance, weaving through the trees and scanning the area for danger. The crunching of the dry leaves beneath her feet and dead tree limbs assured she was not sneaking up on anyone. No surprises, the thought of startling someone sneaking around was not in her best interest, she decided to warn whomever might be out there. "Hello," she screamed as loudly as she could. "I found some clothes on the trail. Are they yours?" There was no response.

With each step her feet sunk into the compost of leaves and dead branches, she wandered further from the beaten path. Ducking in and out of trees, until she reached the pair of blue jeans on the ground. Looking a complete 360 degrees, she saw nothing besides the blouse, indicating the direction she would walk to get back to the trail. Marie lowered herself into a squatting position to examine the jeans. Keeping her head level to spot anyone who may be approaching her, she reached blindly with her hands and probed the jean pockets for some form of identification.

Besides for a few dollars the pockets were relatively empty. "*Snap!*" came a sound from behind her, she spun her head to the left and peered over her shoulder. It sounded like a tree branch snapping. She stood to get a better view of the surroundings; there were no other sounds. Marie tried to quiet her breathing in an attempt to hear better, the sounds of the Forrest were still. No birds, no crickets, no squirrels, besides what little noise she made, this area of the woods was ominously silent.

The sounds of nature could never easily be silenced. Only after detecting natural predators, or extreme danger, would the indigenous beasts become frightened into being silent—the sixth sense animals seemed to possess that humans did not. Then again the threat had to be serious enough to affect *all* of them; from the ground to the treetops.

Nervous fear began to enter her mind; her eyes darted around in their sockets. It was time for her to leave, except she was in the beginnings of an anxiety attack. The task at hand was to try and calm herself. She held the small siren up in one hand, the sound of silence was too much for her to bear.

She pulled the pin and the high pitched siren pulsed, filling the air with its warning. She held the alarm in front of her as she spun around completely, ensuring the sound traveled in all directions.

After twenty seconds she inserted the pin back into the sound device. Her ears were still ringing, she looked down at the jeans and decided she had enough excitement for one day.

Marie located the green blouse still hanging from the branch off in the distance and headed straight toward it. Her feet crunched the dried leaves and brush as she walked back, this time she did not weave in and out of the trees. Her plan was to exit as expeditiously as possible. Toward the midway point, Marie heard someone call out. "Hello," he said. She froze instantly.

Walking along the wooded path in front of her, she saw a man in white robes. Marie could see a long cane in his right hand—apparently a walking stick. "Don't move," he said, "people put all kinds of traps out here. They hunt illegally. I heard this awful noise and decided to see what the problem was." That last statement put her slightly at ease, if he responded to the siren then the device did its job.

Marie watched him as he moved forward, extending the white walking stick in front of him, feeling out obstacles as he walked. "Are you blind?" asked Marie, and instantly felt ridiculous after saying it.

"Yes, in an unfortunate accident a long time ago. I'm over it now. Getting in touch with nature helped me overcome my handicap." Marie started to move forward to assist the man. "No," he insisted, "believe me I am quite capable. And it is very dangerous for you out here."

"I run here all the time. I saw some clothes off in the woods, I thought someone was in trouble," she said. When the strange man got close enough she examined him carefully. His eyes remained closed the whole time; he tilted his head left and right as if listening carefully to his surroundings.

His robes were nothing like she had seen before. It was a very stylish, fine cloth garment with white silk trim. It remained impeccably clean even as he tromped through the tree limbs and brush. He had long white pants made from the same material and Japanese style flip-flop sandals. He was tall, around six-foot-three, with long straight black hair similar to her own. He stopped within fifteen feet of her position. "I believe you should go that way." He motioned over to her left. "I know of the troubles in this place. That is your path to safety. You should have never wandered off the main road."

"I just wanted to help…you are starting to scare me," she said.

"You were already scared, but you decided to try and make a difference. To help, if you could. Most people ignore what goes on around them; for survival they look the other way. It was quite noble of you; I will handle it from here."

Marie was not going to stay another minute; she started to move through the trees in the direction the man had instructed.

"Watch your step!" It was too late. The soft wet ground had caught her attention. After going from crunching dried brush, to mushy, moistened leaves, it was hard not to notice. There were red streaks of bloodstains covering her white and blue tennis shoes.

The leaves were soaked in a concentrated area covering about a three-foot diameter. She did not think it was blood; she did not want to believe it. When she decided to wander off the path, she was thinking of the worst possible scenarios where someone might require her help. In her wildest imagination, she had no idea she would find just that.

In disbelief, Marie retreated from the blood soaked area beneath her feet, when she felt an object hit the brim of her ball cap. She instinctively looked up and a drop of blood fell and hit her left thigh. "Oh my God!" she said as she looked overhead. Up about thirty-five feet in the air, on a tree limb was a woman. Wearing nothing but her undergarments. She was tied by the ankles and hung upside down from the branch.

Blood had stained several parts of the tree trunk as it was blown off course by the wind on its way to the earth. Her body had small cuts made to the surface of her skin. The most notable feature was that her head was missing. She had been decapitated; blood dripped from the open neck where the head used to be. Her arms hung down lazily and limp. The body flinched suddenly, adding terror to the already morbid image.

"That was a reflex reaction of the muscles," said the blind man. "Quite common actually. I am sure she is dead," he added.

Marie trembled in fear; she began repeating hysterically. "Oh my God! Oh my God! Oh my God!" When suddenly interrupted by the blind stranger.

"God…is too busy for you woman. He is too busy for me…too busy for us of all." Marie stepped back blindly, looking upward until she backed into a tree. What has she gotten herself into? All she could think of was running until she could run no more. Marie looked strangely back at the blind stranger; there was a certainty to his actions.

He knew the body flinched. He did not open his eyes; he must have sensed it. He knew too much about what was going on. Had he contacted the police already? He could not be a part of this, could he?

"Did you know about this already?" she asked.

"Yes I did."

"Did you notify the police?"

"No, I did not," he said. Trembling against the tree, Marie's face strained to hold back the tears. Why? Was the question she wanted to ask, but was afraid to. She was afraid that the stranger would say he did not call the police, because he was somehow involved. She knew she was in trouble. That sixth sense that animals seem to possess…well, humans have it also. Just by the time they realize it, it is often too late.

"Do you have a family?" asked the blind man. "Loved ones?"

Marie answered by starting to cry.

"That's too bad."

♣   ♣   ♣

After returning home from Connecticut, Dr. Prine headed to Clibel's restaurant in Washington D.C. He regrettably, could not take his son Lexington with him this time, he got a hint of what the conversation would be about from Gertrude. She set up the meeting between the two. Prine had never met the agent before, his name was Jack Ward, a forty year old field agent from Sarasota, Florida.

Gertrude was persistent enough to find someone in the agency that would believe her, and not just anyone either. Jack Ward was highly regarded among his peers, truly skilled at what he did. Gertrude promised she would help him on a case he was working on by convincing him the two were related. The missing person case involving her granddaughter Cindy Revner, and the case he was currently pursuing.

Clibel's Restaurant was on 19th street, right off Constitution Avenue. D.C. traffic was congested as always during the weekday, something Dr. Prine was accustomed to. He left his home in plenty of time to compensate for the expected delays. The scheduled meeting time was 11:30 a.m. Prine arrived first and told the Host to direct the agent over to his table when he arrived.

He seated himself in a booth near the rear of the restaurant away from wandering eyes and ears. A petite brunette waitress wasted no time in coming over and introducing herself. "Hi, I'm Joy. I will be your waitress this morning. Can I get you something to drink while you decide?" Prine noticed she did not have a pencil and pad. Waitresses now go through some sort of memorization training where it is no longer required to write things down.

Interesting he thought, so long as she gets the order right. He is an extremely picky eater. "I would like a Mocha to start…and there is another guest coming. I won't order anything else until he arrives."

"Very well, I will be back with your Mocha in a minute." She briskly walked off in the direction of the kitchen. The restaurant was filled with businesspeople and young college kids, a good mix of culture, which was common for the area.

He watched the door as people steadily poured in for lunch. A gentleman with a dark gray business suit began speaking to the Host—she pointed in Prine's direction. Dr. Prine raised his hand instinctively and smiled. Jack Ward was an average sized man, five foot eight, medium build. He appeared to be in great shape. The sides of his hair was just turning gray, he combed it back, and had some type of styling gel to keep it in place. Jack had a dark olive complexion; he apparently made sure he made his tanning sessions each evening. Dr. Prine stood as the agent approached the table, extending his hand upon introduction. "Jack Ward? Pleasure to meet you, I am Walter Prine."

"Yes, Gertrude told me all about you. Persistent old hag isn't she?" Jack suddenly realized he let that slip out, without knowing his guest's relationship with Gertrude. Jack was a lively fellow who liked to tell it like it is. He reminded Prine of the tough street cops he seen on television…Baretta, in fact.

"Don't worry," said Prine. "She was a pain in the butt with me too." This brought a sly grin to Jack's face.

"Hell, we are all going to be there one day. How old are you?"

"Thirtyish." Prine said confidently.

"I just turned forty, two weeks ago. Have you ordered yet?"

"Only a Mocha. Here she comes with it now."

The waitress, Joy, energetically bopped down the aisle with Prine's drink and places it in front of him. "I see your guest has arrived. Can I get you anything?" she asked.

"Nothing fancy like this guy, just a plain old coffee," Jack replied.

"Okay, I'll be back in a minute," she said, with a big smile on her face, as she hurried back to the kitchen.

"Now that's more my speed right there," said Jack, referring to the tight-bodied waitress. "Are you married Walt?" That struck a nerve with Dr. Prine, not the question of marriage, but Jack addressed him by his first name, which he absolutely loathed.

"My wife died a few years ago—and just call me Prine from now on."

"Sorry to hear that…Prine. I'm divorced; it became final eight months ago. Now I'm starting over. The dating game is a strange place to be at my age." Joy, the waitress, returned with Jack's coffee, she poured the first cup and placed the carafe onto the table. Jack's eyes wandered freely, examining the young waitress thoroughly. An embarrassed Dr. Prine decided it would be best if he placed his order first.

"I would like a double cheeseburger, on a *grilled* roll with lettuce, mayo and mustard, two dill pickles on the side, french fries *and* onion rings, a small order of macaroni salad, and a glass of water with my meal," said Prine.

"Whoa, cowboy. I'm glad I'm not picking up the tab. I'll have a BLT on rye, sweetheart. That's it for me." She repeated everything they said to ensure she got it right and then hurried back to the kitchen to place the order. "She's good," said Jack. "She didn't even write any of it down."

"The real test is when she brings out the food," Prine replied.

"Yeah, well I bet your side of the tab that she gets it all right."

"You have yourself a bet, Jack." What power, a great set of legs and a big smile from a beautiful woman have over men, Prine thought. It is something men never grow out of.

"Alright Prine, time to get down to serious business. Gertrude says that you might be able to help us, that you are an expert at profiling certain people. The type of person we are after is part of a very powerful religious group. He has millions of followers and it is growing by the day. And when I say millions I mean global. His power does not end with the United States. We have people that work for the bureau that are experts in their field, but not one, who is also an expert in the occult—if you get what I mean. Now, this is not technically a cult, it is a respectable Christian type Ministry, however, there is an occult type of attraction, that steadily gathers followers to his ministry, that has us concerned. With you being a professor of Psychology and an expert in the occult, Gertrude felt you were the perfect man for the job. I am talking about the Reborn Kings Ministry, and its top man, Reverend Roland Stark."

CHAPTER 5

Choose Wisely

Roland Stark was the head the most recognizable ministry in the world, the Reborn Kings. He was second only to the Pope when it came to religious Icons. For him to be involved in the disappearance of Cindy Revner was almost inconceivable. "How is he involved with Cindy Revner?" asked Prine.

"The only thing we have is Cindy's drivers license. It was found in a rental car. One of the attendants found it and noticed she was not registered to drive the vehicle. It was registered by 'the Kings,' and the person registered to drive the vehicle was Roland Stark. The attendant never saw him, of course one of his people picked the vehicle up for him and returned it."

"And everyone involved was questioned. Why do you still suspect him?" asked Prine.

"Cause I don't like him and I didn't like the answers I got. No one remembers who drove the vehicle, no one even heard of Cindy Revner, and his millionaire partner keeps using his political muscle to keep us away."

"You don't have much evidence against him if politics can keep the FBI at bay."

Jack sipped his coffee, he now knew Prine had an idea of crime investigation and bureaucratic influence. Maybe this would be a good pairing after all. He had nothing to loose. Jack actually had more against the religious leader than he disclosed, but he had to ensure Prine would not hinder the investigation.

Jack planned on filling Prine in on all the evidence on a need to know basis. Prine passed the first test, now he wanted to see just how close the charming professor could get to the organization. Perhaps he may discover something they overlooked. Besides there was the other investigation Jack was involved in. He needed someone like Prine to handle the charismatic functions of the investigation.

The vibrant waitress, Joy, returned with their food, to Prine's surprise everything they ordered was delivered as instructed. Jack winked at the professor for confirmation.

"If there is anything else I could get you just let me know," said Joy.

"Just put everything on one tab and hand it to my friend over there." Jack said with a sly smirk on his face. "My new friend is feeling extra generous today." Joy busily hurried off again.

Jack went back to business, "I will set you up with everything you need Dr. Prine. Whom ever you want to interview, just let me know."

"I thought you said no one was sure *who* drove the vehicle…the one that the girl's license was found in…I'm confused on what I can do." Jack put his sandwich down, and laid out a plan, he needed Dr. Prine for a very specific line of investigation.

"There are details in the organization that we need information on. If you weren't in a cave for the last five years, you should be familiar with 'The Miracle Ceremony' they perform once a year. This is a private investigation—somewhat illegal on my part—but I think it is relevant to this case. I want you to look into the ceremony, its participants, and anyone else that might be close enough to give you information. They gain millions of members each year because of this 'Miracle' they perform. If it is a hoax I want to know about it.

This is why you are here professor, only someone extensively familiar with how cults and mass hypnosis works can get in and expose these guys for what they are. If it is legit, I will get on my knees and beg for forgiveness. But if they are deceiving people, then there is the possibility they would go to extreme measures to cover it up. Do you get what I'm saying Prine?"

Prine understood fully, this was a unique opportunity for him. He was always intrigued with the Reborn Kings and the chance to get close to the organization was an offer he would not turn down. He had his own reasons, he was hoping to gain insight into his own unique situation. "So when do I start?"

"That's what I like to hear; a motivated individual." Jack handed Prine an 8x10 envelope, inside it had plane tickets and a list. "Here is a list of people who were involved with the ministry during the past five years. Some are still active, some have moved on. You can work the list in whatever order you see fit, that part I will leave entirely up to you. If anyone asks, you don't work for me...got it? In a couple of weeks we will meet to compare notes. If..."

Jack was distracted and reached down to his belt. It was his cellular phone; he had it on vibrator mode. "This is Jack...Got it, I'll be there momentarily." Jack grabbed his half-eaten BLT and prepared to leave. "My number is in there too, Dr. Prine. If you need anything give me a holler. Good luck!"

Once again, the sound of silence terrorized Marie Carthon. The image of what she once considered the most precious part of the day, her morning run, has forever been changed due to the horrid turn of events. The married, mother of two, who resided a few miles away, had gone out for her morning run when she came upon the grim scene. A young woman's body swung directly overhead, from a tree branch, thirty-five feet in the air. Hanging by what appeared to be a thin white thread.

Decapitated and lifeless, the body swayed back and forth, dripping blood onto the leaf covered foliage below. Standing just a few yards away was a blind stranger. Who he was exactly? She did not know, nor did she care. Of the two of them, he was the calm one, despite being fully aware of the dreadful circumstances. She began to suspect the blind man was somehow involved in this wicked display of violence.

Although hard to believe, he seemed to know all about the crime in question. He even attempted to steer Marie away from the scene before she discovered the carnage overhead. She feared this man's friends would be back any minute and her fate would be the same as the woman above. "Run in a more public place, where people are around", her husband said constantly. She had not figured anything of this nature could ever happen to her.

This is the fatal last thought of most victims, that they will be smart enough, quick enough, and alert enough. That they would never let themselves get caught in a predicament where their life might be taken. In a city with millions of people, Marie prayed to see just one pedestrian haplessly strolling down the trail, and aware enough to notice her peril.

But that was a fantasy, a desperate wish made by a woman who wondered if she would ever see her two sons again. In the year she has been running this path, other pedestrians occupying this trail were few and far between. It was the solitude she enjoyed that got her ready for the day ahead. Already today there have been more people than she cared to see, one alive and one dead. Right now, it was the live one she was deftly afraid of.

"What a unique situation," said the blind man, "you found my friend here in the trees. I tried to keep you away; you were too persistent I guess." Marie fought with her sanity as thoughts of self-condemnation took over mind. She had trouble discerning if this was actually happening. Her thoughts kept reverting back to her family, and if she had chosen to do things differently, she would be with them right now.

She wished she could go back in time, back to this morning. Then she would have chosen to ignore the alarm, and in the alternative time line in her mind, she would be home in bed, with her husband's arms wrapped securely around her. But now is not the time to play "what ifs." She wants to live, long enough to learn from her mistake. And for that she has to take control, *right now*!

The calm, broad shouldered stranger stood tall and continued to quiz Marie Carthon. "My friend up there has not finished draining yet. It is unfortunate you came by when you did. Another hour and my work would have been done, your interference has me puzzled on what I should do next."

"Y-Y-You can l-let m-m-me go." Her shaken voice uttered, she could hardly feel her lips due to the numbing affect fear had upon her.

"Why, because I cannot see you? You can see me just fine, and you will tell everyone all about me. You will tell them what I look like and what I have done. Are you asking me to take a risk like that? All so you can return to your pitiful life?"

"I-I-I-I will say no-th-thing," and she shook her head emphatically.

"No, I am afraid that is not good enough. I can smell your fear. A fearful person will say anything to preserve their existence. Then the minute they felt safe, they would tell the world their story. You would do just that. Then it would force me to kill you and all of your loved ones later. It would be easier to take care of you now and not go through the trouble later."

"I'm-not-lying! Please I want to see my sons; I want to see my husband. My family needs me. I-I-I won't risk putting them in danger, I swear." The blind man tilted his head to the side, interested in what Marie had to say.

"Swear? What will you be willing to swear?"

"The life of my family! If I say anything, I swear."

He thought for a second.

"Not good enough! It's just more work for me." The blind man took a step forward—Marie screamed.

"Stop! No, No!!" she desperately cried.

"What is it now?"

Marie fought with anxiety to gain her composure. Over to the left, she saw the green blouse hanging from a tree branch. She knew the path lay directly behind it. The blind man was carefully feeling his way through the brush toward her. She had to think fast.

"If I get away, I can't make that same promise of silence." He tilted his head to the side again, intrigued by what Marie had to say this time.

"So you think you can get away? You plan on running?" The blind man broke out in a chuckle.

She knew if she ran she could escape him. "I am in shape, I run everyday, I know these woods like the back of my hand. You are wearing a robe and you are blind. You won't be able to find me if I do." The humorous grin quickly left the strange man's face.

"Shame when a woman as cocky as yourself cannot get away from a blind man even when her life depends on it. I know women like you and I will call your bluff. Deep down you are just dainty pieces of flesh ready to urinate all over your trousers in the face of mortal danger. You can run and keep pace when you are calm, but right now you are panting so hysterically you can hardly keep yourself from hyperventilating. Try running now that you know I will be right behind you, waiting for you to slip on the dry leaves, or make a wrong turn. Try running knowing that one wrong move and you will be dead. Run, if you have the guts to stand up for yourself, or get on your knees and beg for your life. I have already decided I will let you go *if* you do one of those things. Which one should you do? Well…let's just hope for your sake you make the right decision. So what is it. Choose wisely, your life depends on it. Do you run, or do you get on your knees and beg. You have thirty seconds."

The alarm went off again; the high pitch beeping of the radio alarm clock on his bedside nightstand was the sound most men dreaded waking up to. Marcus strained to focus his eyes, checking the current time to see if he could hit the snooze button one more time. His queen sized comfort-luxury mattress urged him to stay put, unfortunately his boss did not share the same enthusiasm for him sleeping in.

So the morning ritual begins and Marcus stares at the white ceiling of the master bedroom. "I need a job closer to home." He mumbles with his dry and crackling morning voice. He flips over on his side, pulls the covers over his shoulder, and closes his eyes, going over in his mind how good it would feel if he could only get one more hour of sleep. As if in shock, both eyes spring wide open, he realizes it is time to get out of bed.

Throwing the covers off, he sits up and hangs his legs off the side of the bed until his feet gently touch the carpet of his bedroom floor. Hunched over in poor posture he gathers the strength to hoist himself onto his feet and lumbers toward the bathroom. Marcus fumbles to find the light switch and turns it on. He squints as the bright bathroom lights burn his eyes until he can get accustomed to them. He turns and looks back out the bathroom and around the bedroom. With a puzzled shrug of his shoulders he put the toothpaste on his toothbrush and begins to brush his teeth.

He is feeling better now, although still not eager to face the morning rush hour. Marcus starts the water to his shower and gets undressed. After removing his watch he realizes something, his wife is running behind schedule. Marie should be back by now? She better hurry or *she* will be late.

Marie's heart pounded beneath her chest; the pressure echoed through her body. The stress was immeasurable, she had already made a bad decision, and it was the reason she stood before the blind man. Now, if she chose wrong she would be killed.

"Ten seconds," said the man, informing her of the time that had elapsed since his offer. Run or surrender, should she fight or should she cower. Her original decision was to run. It is what came natural to her; it made the most sense. There are trees; the terrain is uneven. It has leaves and brush scattered about. There is no way possible this blind man should be able to catch her. He is playing some game, a mind game. He is using the frightening scene above to intimidate her.

Her ability to think clearly has been impaired due to the excess of adrenaline flowing through her body. It must be what was keeping her there. It must be the reason she is talking to him now instead of doing what is natural and running for safety. He cannot be alone, that would be impossible. He must have friends, but where are they? Are they hiding somewhere in the woods just waiting for her to run by?

"Twenty seconds." Something told her to drop to her knees and plead for her life. She stood and did nothing. Marie could not bear the thought of guessing incorrectly. The things that she held precious in life; the people she endeared were just a few miles away. She decided to go to them.

"Thirty!"

In an instant she ran; slipping on the leaf covered surface with her first step, she regained her balance and dashed toward the hanging blouse near the dirt trail. She found it extremely hard to breathe or concentrate. Her thoughts were a blur; tree branches scratched and tore at her flesh as she ran by them. Focused on the green blouse that inched closer and closer, she ran toward it, weaving in and around the wooded obstacles before her.

Tears began to flow from her eyes, partly from horror and partly from the sting of the forest's twigs lashing at her body as she ran. Every ounce of nervous energy she could gather pushed her closer to the dirt path. The green blouse, which hung before the dirt trail, was now in plain sight fifty yards ahead. Suddenly, from her right she heard sounds…footsteps. It was the familiar sound of someone running through the woods, tromping on dried leaves and foliage.

The sound of scurrying footsteps was closing in on her to the right. She turned her head quickly to see who it was—it was the blind man. His nimble feet flashed in-between the wooded obstacles, he was at an angle to intercept Marie before she reached the path and he was closing in fast.

"NNNNOOOO!!!!!" she screamed, as she could not believe what she was seeing. She stopped running and stared intensely at the blind man who now also stopped. Marie shook her head vigorously in disbelief. "*It's impossible, impossible!*" she shrieked. At the top of her lungs she cried, "*this isn't real, this is some kind of dream! You're not real! THIS ISN'T FUCKING HAPPENING!*" The blind man smiled and began walking toward her, he reverted back to how you think a blind man would walk through the forest. Care was taken with each step as he slowly felt his way around each tree. He was mocking her.

"Don't you take another step you bastard!" she screamed. This only provoked him into making a sprint straight toward her. Marie screamed at the top of her lungs and took off running again, this time running at an angle slightly to the left of the blouse. The swift blind man zipped through the trees with ease crossing directly behind Marie then continuing over to her left. Marie changed course again and was bawling loudly like a three-year-old child. She gave up focusing on any one-reference point; she was now trying to escape by any means necessary.

After grossly underestimating her pursuer, she was running wilder than ever. Without a reference or a compass the trees in the forest all look the same, she could have been running in circles for all she knew. Through spider webs and those annoying thorn vines that grow out of the ground, she ran. Lacerating her flesh and frustrating her, but not enough to stop her. She pulled the pin from the siren alarm she had in her left hand. She talked to herself, screamed, yelled "fire," anything to make noise, anything to attract attention to herself, while running.

She heard the swift steps of the blind man closing in on her to the left; she threw the siren alarm over her shoulder in his direction. Temporarily distracted and unaware of her surroundings, Marie failed to see a low tree branch and ran directly into it. The branch caught her directly on the bridge of her nose, jerking her head back violently. She momentarily lost her balance but continued to run. With all the adrenaline flowing through her system she hardly felt it, however she broke her nose on impact. Blood began to stream out of her nostrils; she was light headed…she did not stop!

The sound of swift footsteps hitting the ground became closer and closer, Marie wailed uncontrollably. The woods became denser; she was entering a part of the woods she was unfamiliar with. She had no idea where she was and she did not care. She felt the presence of someone directly behind her left shoulder, she fought with the idea of turning to look. Marie ran until the urge was overwhelming, she then turned to look over her left shoulder. There she saw running stride for stride with her was the blind man, his face was less than six inches away from hers.

He stuck his cane out in front of her in an attempt to trip her up. Marie tried to knock it away with her left hand. She abruptly changed direction again to the right; Marie looked over her shoulder to see where he was. This time he was even closer and his eyes were not closed. Marie stared directly into nothingness of the black glossy surface where his eyes should have been. She screamed once more before she lost her footing and fell.

There was a steep decline to the park surface, and Marie tumbled end over end, slamming into trees on the way down. Her feet continued to move as if she were running even when they were off the ground. She did not loose consciousness, although she contacted several trees and large rocks with tremendous force. Resilient, she bounced to her feet and found herself a few feet from the main path of the park, where she started her run this morning, less than 200 yards away from home.

The sun was now brightly lighting the sky, people were out and about, ready to start the day. She continued running and screaming, off the wooded area, onto the concrete path, past the park bench, and across the street. She was still making enough noise where several of the passing cars had already seen her and stopped accordingly. A man in a red Mustang convertible honked the horn, agitated at how she carelessly stepped out in front of his car. But that did not stop her from running into another car, falling over the hood, and continuing on to the other side of the street. She continued running wildly through the complex toward her house until a neighbor recognized her—torn and battered—and decided to call 911.

Marie ran to the front door of her house and turned the knob, it was locked. She frantically fumbled around looking for her keys and then began to beat the door. Her husband, who had been getting dressed for work, hurried to the door and opened it. Marcus had to look only once to realize something traumatic had happened to his wife. The bloody nose and torn clothes, along with cuts and bruises all over her body said it all. "Oh my God. What happened to you?" he said. Marie ran inside and grabbed Marcus, holding her husband like she never had before. "Call the police," she said, "Call the police!" Marcus turned to close the door. "What happened?" asked one of their sons. All the commotion had awakened him. "Nothing son, go back to bed," the father insisted.

"Is mommy okay?"

"Yes, she is fine son go back in your room okay. Please son!" Marie curled up in a fetal position on the living room couch and watched the door. Her husband, visibly shaken by his wife's condition, picked up the phone and dialed the police.

CHAPTER 6

Reborn Kings

The dream was always the same—it begins in a majestic field of tall grass that stretched out to the east as far as the eye can see. The terrain was filled with several hills and when the wind blew the tall grass made waves like the ocean. To the west was a large valley and to the north was a forest of tall pine trees. Birds could be found gliding in the wind high overhead and soothing echoes of a massive waterfall from the south filled the air with nature's sweet sounds. A truly peaceful scene, except this dream was anything but peaceful. It is the reoccurring dream of the enigmatic Dr. Prine, and he finds himself running. Running over the hillside through the tall grass toward the pines to the north. He is being pursued. Over what? He is not clear. All he knows is that there are many of them. He is being hunted like game.

His primary objective is to get to the woods, he knows inside there is a safe haven, it is his means of escape. As he turns to look for his pursuers he discovers they are gaining ground. Running with force, they are determined to catch him in the open fields, they know, as he does, if he reaches the woods he will escape them. The men were all extremely athletic. They wore armored chest plates and silver bands across their forearms and biceps. They chased with certain tenacity; this was their opportunity. The feeling in the air was retribution; this was no ordinary chase. They wanted blood, Prine did not know, and was not concerned, with why they were after him, he was simply desperate to get away.

Prine strained to maintain his pace, and was immensely frustrated with his inability to escape the men with ease. He knew he was faster, much faster than those chasing him. So why were they still gaining on him? Prine focused on what was wrong with his body. The symptoms then began to reveal itself. He was injured. Yes, his whole body was covered with bruises. He must have been in a massive battle. He may have been victorious, but now he was on the run.

Prine struggled to recall the location of this place, or the reason for the battle. It could possibly be just a representation of what really happened. The mind fabricating various details in an attempt to tell a story. But it felt real enough to Prine; this may have actually occurred. With each stride his pursuers gained ground, Prine assesses the speed at which he was traveling, the distance to the woods, and the rate at which his attackers were closing in on him. He will not make it in time. He decides to make a last stand, he stops and prepares to defend himself.

About fifty men or more quickly surround him; the brave warriors' chest armor reflected shimmering sunlight off of its polished surfaces. Despite being gravely outnumbered Prine felt confident; the panic-stricken faces were on the men who surrounded him. They waited patiently for their leader to come into the center of the circle. The men parted, leaving him a clear entrance into the arena.

Leading the charge was a muscular man with brown curly hair. He wore a golden chest shield and a white Scottish styled kilt. His arms were bear and showed off his massive physique. He was of fair skin in contrast to Prine's dark brown complexion.

The leader had no weapon, none of them did. Several of the warriors were bruised and bloodied, they looked valiant even though they were not victorious in the previous battle. You could tell from the feeling in the air that this time the battle was to the death. Prine could not explain his overconfidence in the face of such overwhelming odds, but he knew he was up to the task. The leader spoke out in a commanding voice. Prine did not recognize the language but he somehow understood what was said. "You were ordered to leave this place, you and your kind can no longer occupy this area," the leader stated in so many words.

"We are superior," said Prine, "we will not yield…ever!"

"Stand down Morningstar, or you will be destroyed!" the leader insisted. The dialogue was quickly over as he realized their disagreement had escalated to the point of being fruitless to argue over. Each one knew what the dispute would come down to in the end.

Prine prepared for battle, the group's leader did not wait long before he gave the order to attack, and they did. The men charged in a coordinated assault and Prine met them head on. Once the fighting began Prine felt different, he became stronger. A sensation flowed through his body, which could only be described as extreme euphoria. This feeling of nirvana flowed through his veins as he was overcome by intense energy. One by one members of the small army began falling under Prine's attacks. He felt the incredible rush of adrenaline his bone crushing attacks had produced.

Although they were loosing, Prine admired their valor, he felt proud to be a part of these elite warriors, even though they were now on opposite sides. Their ranks began to diminish, but as each one of them fell they took a little piece of Prine with them. Prine's body began to feel the effects of their blows also. The battle began to even out, punishing blows, exhaustion and fatigue took its toll on Prine's awesome physique. Just then two more warriors came over the hilltops, Prine recognizes them, but their names escape him. He cannot recall who they were, but he does remember that these warriors have strength superior to his.

In his present state, defeating them will be no easy task. He raises his left fist before his face and shows off the incredible weapon built into his own body. An eight-inch spike that extends from the knuckle of his middle finger, with every punch the extended spike becomes a most deadly appendage. He figures he must have been using it all along, because it is covered in blood. The spike's rough and jagged surface was extremely painful for anyone who happened to be caught on the wrong end of it. The once brave warriors lying at Prine's feet could attest to that.

The two new, elite warriors to the scene seemed to be aware of the dangerous physical weapon built into Prine's body and were prepared. They moved unlike the others, they were much faster. Prine struggled to keep up with their movements. Being constantly one step behind he was quickly subdued. Prine had not even landed one blow against these two warriors.

Prine was pinned face down in the tall grass, wounded and in extreme pain. The elite warriors began asking him questions, they spoke in the strange language the others did, this time Prine did not understand anything they said. They questioned him repeatedly, but Prine refused to answer. With his face pressed down in the tall grass Prine could hardly see the bright sword one of the warriors drew from it's sheath.

His arm was outstretched and his vision impaired, but the slicing pain was unmistakable, as with one swift motion Prine's bone spike was removed at the base of the knuckle with the warrior's sword. The intense pain had Prine screaming through gritted teeth. He spoke to them in their native language and was sure he used invectives to describe his displeasure.

They had toyed with him long enough and Prine sensed the end was near. He felt the cold steel touch the base of his neck three times as the warrior lined up the next blow with his magnificent weapon. For Prine, it was pointless to resist, but in the foreground echoed a familiar noise from the south—battle cries. There were those who sought to punish the mighty warriors for invading their land. Prine's friends were coming to his defense.

The two elite warriors let go of Prine and prepared for their new challenge. Prine was no longer pinned down but there was no more fight left in his weary body. Dizziness kept him from maintaining his enthusiasm for battle. He lay there as the cavalry came to his defense...afterward everything fades to black.

Prine had this dream many times before, this time it was on the plane ride over to California. Sitting next to him, calmly reading a book was his son Lexington. He was unaware of his fathers troubling visions as he flipped the page. But the visions left Prine psychologically depleted, especially when the wound on his left hand was a physical indication that there was some truth to the dream. He sympathetically felt the pain of the severed appendage each time the dream occurred.

The concave shaped wound was a constant reminder of his torment. That is why Prine wants the prized journal that Gertrude covets. The journal her father kept of his patient Elijah Morales, a.k.a. Dr. Walter Prine. If her father figured out the dialect through constantly interacting with Prine and consulting with language experts, then the key to uncovering what the elite warriors were asking him would also be there. His mind must be suppressing the comprehension of this exotic dialect for a reason.

The mind usually does this to avoid some sort of emotional duress or extreme physical pain. The secret to Prine's existence must be encoded in this strange language. He hopes to recapture his knowledge of days past. It should explain who he was and how he got there. The mysteries of the supernatural often had some sort of power contained in the written or spoken word. These words would unlock the secrets of the universe. Where ordinary men would rise to become extraordinary simply by having the knowledge to power at their beckoning.

To Prine, his current condition symbolized some sort of abuse of that power and the key to unlocking that portal lies in deciphering his dreams. Why were the warriors chasing him? Their character seemed dogmatic—they wanted to punish him for something. And he was powerful, more powerful than he is right now. Those men who attacked him were not enemies he did not recognize—he knew them. Although he could not recall their names he felt an affinity with them, like a brotherhood of some sort. He was one of them, but who were they?

Once Prine knew the answer to that, he would be able to move on. Prine looked down at the small bag of honey roasted peanuts sitting on the flimsy tray table in front of him. The silver foil bag had been ripped open and all its wonderful contents were gone. The roasted peanuts were the most favorite part of the whole plane ride for Prine. In the time he chose to sleep, his son had eaten all of his peanuts, and since his father put up no resistance, he ate Prine's also.

A growing boy needs his food, especially if he is going to be like his father. Even though Prine was no where near as strong as he was in his dream, as improbable as it might seem, he was still stronger than any other man he has ever met. And the competition does not even come close. Dr. Prine was unique, in every facet conceivable, and he was anxious to get this thing started.

The Reborn Kings ministry was the most diverse and controversial ministry of its time. Its spiritual healing sessions have stunned and perplexed medical experts and scientists. Followers of 'the Kings' claim Roland Stark has a direct link to the almighty God. "Impenetrable," was the word used by Jack Ward to describe his stronghold on the religious community. If the Roman Catholic Church had not been the icon for so many years, the Reborn Kings would have easily replaced it as the most recognizable religion in the world. They have nothing to hide, when it comes to general inquiries and College interviews.

Answering questions from the FBI was different. Prine had easily set up appointments with a few members of the ministry by telling them this was research for a theology lecture. Prine ensured he showed poise when talking to anyone associated with the Kings, to minimize suspicion. A wrong decision on his part might end up being catastrophic towards gathering information. They operated in a tight group network and once the word gets out about a specific person or organization trying to discredit the ministry, they instantaneously blackball that person.

With one word from Roland Stark, Prine's interviews could be over before it started. It was imperative Prine be cautious from the beginning. One of the first people on his list was a woman who has gone through the ultimate ceremony of spiritual and physical healing. "The Miracle," as it was called, is held once a year. A person is selected to reenact the incredible ritual of divine power. A woman named Mary Beth Reynolds was the first to experience this miraculous phenomenon. Prine was eager talk to her about her experiences. It was the mysteries of the supernatural that got his blood flowing. He was getting goose pimples from all the excitement. *When is this plane going to land?*

"Life is good," it seems like a tired cliché, but there were no better words to describe the life of Roland Stark. He was the religious leader and founder of one of the most successful Ministries in history. People of every nation were busting through the doors to be a part of his diverse congregation. He is the man who possesses the water of purity and followers witness a most intriguing event.

All other religious artifacts and tales of divine intervention fail to hold a candle to what Roland can do with ordinary water. And Roland revels in excitement knowing he is responsible for delivering so many people into the light. He has brought the poor, the ailing, the hungry, and countless others wanting to experience the power of

God, to the "Hall of Kings" in California. The hall houses roughly 30,000 people, he holds a sermon every Sunday and there is standing room only each week.

The Hall of Kings was a huge dome similar to the ones used to play football games. There was a large altar in the center of the arena, with four ten-foot columns around the outer edges. A huge podium sat on the ground level to the right of the altar. The altar's gold laced columns and ivory tabletop was hand crafted from Italy and weighed over 2,000 pounds each. Behind the altar, at the rear of the arena floor was a large entrance leading to the lower levels of the stadium. The stairs behind the center stage podium descended underground and were twenty feet wide, enough room for the whole choir to enter at one time. Each Sunday countless members of Roland's entourage would seemingly rise up from the ground behind the altar to start the service.

Security was always in abundance, guards could be seen everywhere directing traffic by showing people to their seats. With the amount of people attending each sermon crowd control was a real issue. The security guards resembled secret agents, they used small hand held radios and wore ear pieces to ensure they heard over the crowd noise. Camera crews were stationed at several points around the arena, they could often be seen performing visual and audio checks since the sermon was broadcast. This was a major production and the revenues generated reflected that.

What propelled this moderate, ordained minister named Roland Stark to such great heights in the world of religion? A tragic event that turned into a miracle, which happened to be captured on live television. Before that Roland had no more than five thousand followers. He was on his way to becoming famous, but had nothing more to offer than many of the other ministers in his field.

He had a local channel in Ohai, California broadcast his show once a week. Roland had a bit of flair when he delivered his sermon, he used an embarrassing handicap to his advantage. He had severely overactive glands, which caused him to sweat excessively. With the energy he expounded on each word, and the showmanship he used to deliver his message, the sweat just added to the theatrics. Making it appear he was overworking himself.

This was not done purposely of course, Roland was an energetic speaker. All the sweat just gave the appearance of over exertion when he delivered his message, and the diehard Christians of Ohai loved him.

"What is going on now?" said Roland, grabbing a towel and heaving it across the room. "People are in no type of urgency around here. I have a performance to do. God's word needs to be delivered. You people don't seem to understand that." Roland was in his dressing room in the lower levels of the arena. The make up artists had to put up with his bickering every week. Despite this being a regular occurrence, it did not make it any easier for the young woman trying to apply foundation to his face.

The excessive sweat Roland produces will make his face light up like a Christmas tree beneath the lighting around the altar. She was simply doing what she was hired to do.

"Hurry," Roland insisted, "I have a sermon to rehearse and several other things I must do. Colleen, please explain to her the value of expedience."

Roland was speaking to Colleen Rigetti, his female assistant. She had a special way of dealing with Roland few people dared to emulate.

"Shut up and keep still." She said, "This is something you just have to get used to."

The make up artist loved the way Colleen put Roland in his place. She would have done it herself if her job were not on the line. "Roland, everything is in place and we are right on schedule. Your choir has just finished warming up. You have your sermon on the prompters if you need them—the stage security is in place. And you have plenty of towels," said Colleen.

"How can you say I am on time when this woman is still trying to doll me up!" Roland did a double take when he looked at the makeup girl; she raised her eyebrows at his last comment. Apparently she felt it was impossible to make him look any better. He did not have the right tools to begin with. Roland was of a husky build with fair skin and dark brown hair. He had a large stomach that represented his love of eating and lack of exercise.

He was not an attractive man and he did not try to be. He had large bushy eyebrows that needed to be trimmed once a month, the network insisted on it, and was always conscious of his sweaty condition. Whenever he could he wore light colored clothing to try and hide the perspiration soaking through his garments. His boisterous ways made him difficult to work with, but when he preached he was a sight to behold. The only outward sign of his success was a huge four-carat ring he wore on his right ring finger.

"The purification of unrighteous people cannot wait on make up Colleen," Roland began again. Colleen smirked slightly and knew when he got like this there was no stopping him until he got his way. She gave the make up girl a nod. "That's enough, thank you," she said. The make up artist swiftly gathered the items in her case and left the room.

"I need my water Colleen, make sure I have plenty of water up there. I get parched under all those lights. And when you get the ice make sure it is made from bottled water. The cubes you brought me last week were stale. I gagged right in the middle of my sermon. Did you see that? That would have been embarrassing. People would have seen me regurgitate the Holy Spirit all over the altar."

"If you say so," answered Colleen. "Now that you chased the make up girl out of here let's check on the choir and see if they are ready."

Upstairs, in the Hall of Kings arena, thousands of people were making their way to their seats. Camera crews worked rapidly to perform last minute visual and audio checks before show time. The security guards kept their composure while dealing with the massive crowds. Discourteous people scurried toward the front, trying to get as close to ground level as possible, in hopes to get chosen by Roland to participate in the coming event. That event was the seventh anniversary of the Miracle.

The lucky person chosen would appear on national television and receive the full power of God by drinking his divine water. Many faith healers have come and gone, but Roland remains. What makes Roland so special is that he has one thing on his side the others have not—documented medical and scientific evidence that his healing is authentic. Irrefutable evidence, examined and documented, studied and debated. The end result is that he saved a woman's life by having her drink from the water blessed on his altar.

CHAPTER 7

In Preparation of the Day

Seven years ago during one of Roland Stark's sermons, in the little town of Ohai, California, an enraged member of the congregation brandished a firearm and shot a young woman. No one knew why this man had gone to such extremes as to bring a firearm into church and fire five rounds into the crowd. The perpetrator was never caught despite having the entire event captured on film. The lens angle was bad and the camera was never able to get a good picture of the assailant's face, but what they did catch on film was the greatest spiritual event ever filmed.

The victim, Mary Beth Reynolds, lied on the cold tiled floor of the church. The gunshot wound was to her lower abdomen, her eyes rolled back as she fought to stay conscious. Blood pooled across the tile floor and panicked members of the congregation were confused on what to do. Roland ran over immediately and the crowd gave way so that he could be with the woman until the ambulance came, or in the worst case scenario, to administer her last rights if necessary.

Roland was handed a glass of water, the glass he usually drank from during his sermons. He put the glass to Mary Beth's lips and she took a small sip. It was just enough to wet her lips, then Roland delicately pulled the glass away. With a shaken voice, Mary Beth asked for more water. Roland held the glass as she drank; she drank until it was all gone.

She said, it made her feel better, and the grimacing expression of pain soon left her face. She began talking and tried to express to Roland how great she was feeling. That was when Mary Beth reached down and pulled up the blood soaked blouse exposing her wound, except there was no wound to be found. The wound had healed, the blood had stopped flowing, and her strength was returning. The camera zoomed in on the area where the bullet ripped through her body, but the only hole left was the one on her blouse. To the hundreds of bystanders in the immediate area it was instantly called a miracle.

When the ambulance arrived they were astounded. They were answering a call for a potentially fatal gunshot wound to the abdomen, and they found Mary standing on her feet, wearing a blood soaked blouse. They searched other members of the congregation for someone else who may have been shot. Someone who was near Mary, in all likelihood that person was in a state of shock, and did not realize they had been injured. That person could have possibly been bleeding on Mary Beth and she believed it was her blood.

The ambulance crew came up with nothing; no one else had so much as a nosebleed. After hearing the eyewitness accounts from the congregation the ambulance crew decided to whisk Mary Beth away to the hospital as a precautionary measure. Members of the television crew began to suspect it was all a hoax. A scheme dreamed up by Roland and his group to boost ratings. So the team grabbed their cameras and followed the ambulance to the emergency room.

When the camera crew arrived at the hospital Mary Beth was being examined. The doctors gave her a full check up, they checked her blood pressure and heart rate. Everything was normal. Next, they drew blood, sent it to the lab to get analyzed, and took x-rays of Mary's the chest area. She was given a clean bill of health. The doctor heard Mary as she told her story about what happened and he tried to convince her of the improbability of what she believed happened. The doctor explained to Mary Beth how the trauma of simply hearing gunshots could play tricks on the mind, followed by the sight of blood, and that was all she would need to sympathetically feel the pain of injury.

The doctor's deduction made perfect sense to him and it would have all been concluded as one elaborate hoax if it were not for the doctor reexamining the chest x-ray. There he saw a small object that should not have been there, a small spot on the left side of her body. It turned out to be a .38 caliber slug pressed into the back of her left kidney. He immediately called for Mary Beth to be taken surgery.

During the emergency operation, the surgeon had the opportunity to properly examine her inner organs. There was severe scar tissue in the area of the lodged bullet; the scar tissue showed evidence of an object traveling through the body, at high velocity, to the point where the bullet was eventually removed.

The doctor's report had concluded the only way scar tissue could have developed to the internal organs is by an object passing through it. And the bullet recovered was determined to be that object. When the camera crew interviewed the doctor, shortly after surgery, and filmed the doctor's reaction to Mary Beth's mysterious bullet, they knew this was a major story. The video of the gunshot, and footage of interviews with doctors and staff, was sold to a major network and broadcast nationwide.

The reporter dubbed the piece "The Miracle," and the label stuck to this day. Roland Stark and the Reborn Kings Ministry have been on the rise ever since. The divine healing water was something Roland did not expect, but God continued to shine his light on the ministry each year. The anniversary reenactment of "The Miracle" takes one person from the congregation and blesses them with the divine healing water.

People continued to gather into the Hall of Kings, one week before the Miracle Ceremony. One person out of 30,000 would be picked to receive next week's ultimate blessing. It was said to be the embodiment of God's power among the King's congregation. What greater reward would there be than to receive it.

The Hall of Kings had three sublevels below the main floor. The levels were mainly used for utilities; it was the central location for most of the power and communications systems for the facility. The service elevator at the northern end of the building was the primary means of reaching the lowest basement level, B3. That level consisted mainly of hallways and miles of conduit.

However, there was one room on the basement floor, in the center of one of its many hallways, which was of particular interest. The room was twenty by twenty feet and on the wall adjacent to the main door were 150-television monitors. The monitors just about covered the entire wall. Each monitor had several cameras wired to receive inputs, and the Hall of Kings was equipped with an elaborate video system with over 400 cameras. There was not a square foot of the facility that could not be monitored by a camera somewhere. A large and extremely complicated control board sat in front of the monitors and sitting in front of the board was a lone figure.

He watched ceaselessly, switching between cameras, as hoards of people flowed into the place of worship above. His brown eyes shifted from monitor to monitor, cautiously scanning the congregation. This was an elaborate security system, except it was not a part of the standard security. This was a private system installed by one of the original donors, whose funds helped to build the arena; a sophisticated businessman named Jericho Black.

Jericho manned the boards personally, few others knew about the room on level B3 or what was in it. Those who did know dared not to touch, or even enter the room, without his permission. Jericho hated surprises and his primary concern was safety. One of his most coveted possessions was Roland Stark, the Reborn Kings leader.

Business has been good for Jericho since he and Roland teamed up and he wanted to keep it that way.

Jericho looked on, continuing to watch as each person entered the arena and found their way to their seats. Jericho paused on monitor #28; he fingered the controls on the panel without taking his eyes of the monitor. He zoomed the camera in on a petite redheaded woman, and panned the controls following her for several yards. His fingers expeditiously worked the control board as she went out of view on monitor #28 and he switched her image over to monitor #119. There he was able to get a better look at her.

She looked around thirty years old and wore large round glasses. She had short curly hair and wore a pink sundress. The woman appeared to be alone and from the way she looked around the arena, this was her first time here. Jericho worked his mastery of the board, switching from camera to camera watching her every move. After around fifteen minutes the woman in the pink sundress finally found her way to her seat. She seemed nervous and she had good right to be. Besides this being her first time at the Hall of Kings ministry she was being watched by the ominous Jericho Black. Jericho picked up a small black phone at the edge of the control board. The phone had no key pad or dial. Upon picking up the receiver the phone dialed a number instantly. The phone was answered on the other end after only one ring.

"Petite redhead in seat C177, section David," said Jericho. After-ward he lowered the receiver back onto the phone.

Up on level B1, the choir was wrapping up on their warm up ses-sion and the rest of the entourage began positioning themselves to take stage. Roland Stark, minister of the Reborn Kings, is already beginning to sweat. Colleen works frantically to keep him as calm as possible before the sermon begins. A member of the television crew approached them at the bottom stair of the altar entrance. "Okay everyone," the man announced, "We will be ready in two minutes. Reverend Stark, are you ready?"

"This is what I was born to do son. We are all ready."

A silver haired man in a black suit slowly made his way up the stairs to the altar entrance. He walked around the altar to the podium on the right. Once he stepped up to the microphone, he reached into his jacket pocket and pulled out a pair of reading glasses. The hum of thirty thousand people started to silence as the elderly gentleman readied himself to speak.

He opened the massive Bible which had been laid on the podium and started the service. "Good Morning Ladies and Gentleman on this fine Sunday morning, this is a most glorious occasion. Anytime you have this many people assembled in one place to receive God's blessing it is a splendid occasion. Our own Reverend Roland Stark has a wonderful message he wants to bring to you—a divine gift from above. He wants you to know the Lord as he does. He wants to share with you inspiration and the comfort of knowing you are loved. And that God exists, today and forever, within each of us."

The sound system came alive as the choir began singing while they emerged from the stairs leading the way up to the altar. Fifty choir members flooded the altar as they walked toward the elevated station that they sang from. Following behind, the energetic Roland Stark took the stage. His overactive sweat glands began to kick in under the intense heat of the lights. With a handkerchief in hand, Roland made his way over to the elderly gentleman who gave him his introduction and whispered something in his ear. Then he gave the man a big hug and began dancing around the pulpit, pointing into the stands, screaming over the volume of the choir in the background saying, "God loves you."

Colleen, his assistant, imagined Roland probably told the elderly gentleman his introduction was not grand enough and that he should work on it. She stood near the top of the stairs, out of view before fading in the background. It was hard work dealing with a man like Roland. He was pushy, temperamental, opinionated, and overbearing. However, once he began to deliver the word of God, he was a new man, and she was astonished at the transformation he made every Sunday. She wanted to stay and see the service first hand, but she was a 'behind the scenes' girl. Today, she had an important job; getting the person selected for next week's Miracle ceremony to the stage; from wherever he or she was seated. In an arena of this size that was no small task.

Flushing, Queens—In a small one-bedroom apartment just off Queens Boulevard lived William Richardson, a petty thief with a malicious nature. William was currently on parole after serving three years on an assault charge. The apartment was rented in his aunt's name and it had a clear view of the busy shopping center on Queens Boulevard. Lessons for William did not come easy, shortly after being released he began hanging with the wrong crowd again. Actually, there was no way to stop it. He was the wrong crowd, and he corrupted any unfortunate soul he befriended.

His two sidekicks, Thad Voight and July Matlow were also in the apartment with him. Of the small group of ex-con's, William may have been the leader, but he was not the brightest. That honor belonged to Thad. Thad was a twenty-seven-year-old man that once had the potential for a bright future, but his love for the fast life took his career down another path. Like many criminals, life in lockup gives one time to reflect. Thad was released from prison just three months ago and was at odds with himself over whether he should see his old friend William.

Against the wishes of his girlfriend July, here he was, together with his old friend William and discussing matters of criminal intent. Thad stood by the window in silence; the television was blaring away in the background. The noise did not bother Thad at all, he was in his own little world. He was wondering about things most people wonder about, happiness, security, and a sense of belonging.

None of us fully understand any of it—why our bodies pull us in different directions at the same time. How each of us take different paths, but still we all want the same things. Rarely do we realize at the time how one moment can change our futures forever. We all make hundreds of decisions each day, yet all it takes is *one* decision to change the course of our lives.

This may be one of those moments Thad thought. William was undoubtedly a negative influence, but being an ex-con himself, he felt he had no right to be critical. Trouble often rears its ugly head when you least expect it. In the life that Thad Voight chose to live death is a common fate. When staring death in the face the mind goes through different stages: denial, depression, bargaining, anger, and finally acceptance. Thad is only twenty-seven yet he is already in the acceptance stage. No one else in the room has the foresight to put any thought into their future actions except Thad. Just being in the room with William gave the atmosphere an ominous feel. Something about this meeting would mark the beginning of the end of Thad's life and he knew it. If Thad had anything of worth he would have no one to leave it to. What was most troubling to Thad was the thought of when he died, no one would miss him. That was why he got hooked up with William in the first place.

Thad kept thinking of taking his girlfriend by the hand and walking of out the door, leaving William alone with his twisted ideas of mischief, but he was frozen. His girlfriend July Matlow was the most innocent of the trio. This is why Thad really regrets meeting his old and troublesome friend. July was loyal to Thad and would follow him wherever he went; too much in love to go against his wishes, or else she would see what a horrid man William was and would leave the two behind.

Love and loyalty would be her downfall, Thad thought. That would be her life changing decision, if she only had the foresight to know. July was a cute twenty-two year old girl from Kansas. She met Thad at the laundry mat not too long after he was released from prison. The two grew close over time and now they are inseparable. Thad stared through the paned glass window and made his decision. When the time came he would save July. She does not deserve to end up like them. The hands of fate already had a firm grasp of William and Thad; he would not let July fall to the same. Thad's thoughts were interrupted, it was time for William to lay out his plan for destruction.

"What the hell is so interesting out that window Thad?" William asked.

"Nothing...but life itself," Thad replied.

"Ha-Ha, how poetic. Now get over here, we have more important things to discuss. Have you seen this?" William slams a newspaper on the kitchen table. The headlines read "Miracle Sunday Count-down." Thad glanced with a shallow stare at the headlines, then returned his attention outside the window. "Yeah, I seen it," said Thad.

"Get over here Thad, this is important!"

"Stop talking to him like he is some kind of dawg. You treat my man with some respect," said July with a southern accent, coming to Thad's defense.

"Believe me sweetheart that's the only way to get this man back to reality sometimes. Now come on Thad, we gotta do something about this. This man has gotten away with this crap for too many years."

Thad removed himself from the window and took a seat at the kitchen table across from where William was seated.

"See this, See this," said William pointing to the headlines and scratching his sandy blonde goatee. "This is a slap in our face—Mir-acle Sunday. It turned into some freakin' sideshow. You know this wasn't supposed to happen."

"Damn," said July interrupting once more, "I know you are gonna start blamin' my man once again. 'Thad if you hadn't missed,'" she said mimicking William like a school child.

"You better get control of your woman Thad!" said William in an agitated voice. "I don't know you all that well and you don't know me girl." The two were involved in a stare down. Thad motioned to July to leave the room.

"This doesn't involve you. Go wait in the living room," said Thad. She left the room at Thad's request, but in the small apartment the next room over was still within earshot of their conversation. To annoy William even further she turned on the television and increased the volume.

William lit up a cigarette; "It's time to hit 'em where it hurts. I thought about it while I was in the joint. All those years they enjoyed their fat and happy success and we get nothing. Where is our credit, huh? Well I got something in mind that will blow the roof off of that Ministry. And we're gonna hit them big time." William began tapping the article with his index finger as he spoke, reemphasizing his point. "There is gonna be a full house next week"

"If you are planning anything for next week forget it," said Thad. "There will be the tightest security imaginable. People from nations all over the world will be there. This is like the Super Bowl of religion."

"Your not getting scared like the last time, are you Thad?"

The comment touched a nerve with Thad, it was a subject he did not with to discuss…with anyone. An internal conflict within that Thad did not fully understand. Things that men like William could *never* understand.

"Anyway buddy, you were lucky I was there to cover your ass," said William. Funny, Thad does not remember it that way. From his viewpoint he was left to carry out the dirty deed on his own and he escaped with William nowhere in sight. Thad remembers that day as the luckiest day of his life.

"You say that as if Thad owes his life to you," July said to William, muting the volume on the television. "I just don't take you as the type to save anyone's ass but your own."

"You need to go back to Oprah and stay out of this. You may have been *told* what happened but you weren't there."

"Why don't you tell me your version William. Tell me exactly what you did in all this. How did you cover his ass?"

"This is good! I am so glad you don't trust me sweetheart, because I don't want you with us in the first place."

"Tough, I'm with Thad. Where he goes, I go!"

Thad decided to change the course of the conversation. It was time to see exactly what the twisted mind of William had in store for the trio. Then he would decide what to do about July and how far he was willing to take her. Thad and William were involved in the first Miracle and from all indications they would also be involved in the last.

"So what's your plan William?"

"That's my boy Thad. Just like the good old days."

CHAPTER 8

Blonde beauty

"Sleeping in" on occasions was once thought to be a healthy practice. People need relief from the everyday stress associated with life. Lately, attitudes toward this idea have changed and men find themselves waking up early to catch the fresh morning dew. At least the men of Sun Valley, Nevada feel that way. In this neighborhood early risers receive a special treat, not for fear the world would pass them by—just one female in particular. Every morning glistening in the warm sun, the men of Sun Valley were treated to visions of long tanned legs stretched out by the poolside.

The classic girl next door fantasy would run through their salacious little minds. The community pool was located in the center of the neighborhood and most of the homes had a clear view of the poolside activities. It was designed that way so parents could monitor their children from their homes instead of being out in the torrid sun. But the men used that design in community safety to gaze at the shapely beauty of Sun Valley.

Her long blonde hair was tied in a ponytail and flowed down to the small of her back. At six foot two she was as graceful as a gazelle, most women that size were disproportionate, even a bit clumsy, but not Serena...she was perfect.

Serena Capistrano, attracted attention wherever she went because of her size and beauty, she tried to escape to this retreat and be inconspicuous. For her that was next to impossible, she captivated the interest of every man who graced her presence. But time was running short for the men of Sun Valley. They recently received word she would be leaving them today to return to California. The men were enjoying one last look before they said their good-byes. For the men of Sun Valley their early morning treat would be gone forever. For the women, she could not leave fast enough.

After an hour of sun bathing the leggy beauty stood and stretched. She gathered her belongings and waved goodbye to the people watching her from the homes overlooking the pool. The homes were far enough away where she could not see anyone observing her, but she knew they were there. She always knew. Before heading back to her home she stopped momentarily at the shower station to cool off.

"Playing around again are you?" came a voice from the other side of the pavilion. A man, impeccably dressed, was standing just a few feet away from the showerhead. He was a well-built man wearing a maroon Italian business suit with black leather loafers.

Serena turned on the shower and stepped under the cool flowing waters acting as if his presence was of no surprise. "Are you here to counsel me, Raphael? If not I wish you would consider adapting to the surroundings. No one dresses like that around here," she said.

"I have expensive taste and something you know little about...style! Besides you walk around wearing *that*? Telling me what *I* wear is attracting attention? You may have to reevaluate your competence as a field agent Serena. I believe you are getting sloppy."

"You are starting to annoy me Raphael. What is it you want?"

"The council is going to meet in a couple of days. I just wanted a report of what is happening. Hopefully in between your sun bathing sessions you were able to get some actual work done."

"Everything is fine Raphael, just fine. There is absolutely nothing to report." Raphael was becoming annoyed with her insolent tone.

"You work for me Serena, don't you forget what I can do to you. You need to appreciate the importance of your mission and what it means for you personally."

"Don't you mean to say what it means for the council? You can try to act as if you are doing a great service but I know the truth. A step up on the competition is all you are after Raphael."

"Then let's hear what our competition is doing! I know you have something for me, I can sense it."

The cool water of the outdoor shower was on a timer—it shut off automatically. Serena took one hand and ran it down the length of her hair, squeezing out the excess water. She looked down at Raphael, who was a few inches shorter, her green eyes piercing his. This was neither a move of seduction nor intimidation, this was how she looked at everyone she took serious. "There is something happening to the west…on the coast. A young boy with incredible intelligence is headed there as we speak. He shows promise, I would love to work with him—test him to his full potential."

"Is that all you have Serena?"

"Of course not, you hired me for a reason; because I am good. It looks like the boy's father is about to get mixed up with our old friend Nukial. And you know how he does not like to have surprises thrown at him."

"What is the father like? Is he on our side?"

"It is too early to tell Raphael, besides the real story is how long Nukial can carry on his charade without arousing the suspicion of people like us."

"Are you heading over to the coast now Serena?"

"I was wrapping things up here and on my way, before you interrupted me."

"Keep me informed as soon as you get there. I guess what you have will do."

Raphael took out a pair of sunglasses he had in his left jacket pocket, placed them on his head and turned back behind the pavilion from which he came. Serena began to see Raphael as a real nuisance, but there was not much she could do at the time. For now it was important she got on that plane to the West Coast. Her main point of interest was not Nukial, but the boy prodigy, something about him attracted her full attention. Serena's gut instincts were seldom wrong.

❧   ❧   ❧

The FBI was normally not welcomed to a crime scene, especially when local authorities are the first on the scene. The invasion did not sit well with regular Police Officers. College bred pretty boys throwing their weight around just because some bureaucrat deems it necessary for the Feds to get involved. Officers take pride in protecting people. They take pride in their ability to hunt, catch, and convict bad guys. Local officers do not like being left out of the problems that plague their streets. And when a vicious pattern of crime occurs, to their chagrin, they are often pushed aside.

Jack Ward knows what it is like to be on the cold end of the welcoming committee. He is able to disguise his discomfort by using his abrasive, streetwise personality. Nonetheless, it is his job, and he was put on this case because he was good at catching serial killers. Jack was guided up a steep incline in the wooded area of the park just off the dirt trail. A local female officer led him to the scene, Jack tried to make small talk, but she was not too receptive to his advances. Jack held a small silver thermos in his right hand as he ascended the trail. He took his thermos full of coffee wherever he went, it was a part of him. He could not function without coffee nearby—even on the grimmest of crime scenes.

"Officer Envy, I hope this isn't too much further. I think I'm getting a nosebleed up here," Jack said wittingly.

"It's not too much further sir."

"Sir? You make me feel like an old man. Don't let this salt and pepper hair fool you. I still got plenty of kick left in me."

"Then you shouldn't have a problem making it to the crime scene." Jack had no comeback for that comment.

"Listen, how many of these crime scenes have you been on?" asked Jack.

"About fifty or so. But for this particular murder this is only the second one."

"How big an area does the crime scene usually cover?" Jack knew the answer, he just wanted to see how well the other Officers followed the case.

"Around twenty feet or so."

"Well, our boy must be getting sloppy." Jack pointed to a small piece of fiber hanging from one of the thorned branches nearby. "Looks like someone came running through here in a hurry."

Jack had Officer Envy mark the location of the torn fibers, he then directed her to continue on to the main scene. "Where there any clothes in the area of the crime scene?" he said.

"No, I hear from the previous cases the clothes were found in a nearby Dumpster. Neatly folded and free of any blood."

"You have been doing your homework. I bet you want to be the one who catches this jerk too. I know the feeling; this guy is especially slippery. He is neat, clean, and very disciplined. I should not be discussing the case with you, you know. It's against the rules. You know why I decided to tell you about it?"

"I figured you were trying to impress me enough to get into my pants."

"Am I that obvious?" Jack said jokingly. Jack looked off into the distance. The tree branches in this area was high enough to allow a person to see 200 yards or so. Hanging upside down by the ankles, Jack saw the body of a woman. Her lifeless arms swung back and forth; her pale body was covered only by her underwear.

"This looks like our guy!" Jack announced as he approached the scene. Local and State Officers were repulsed at the sight of the agent, and made it a point to get out of his way, as previously instructed by their superiors. Jack's motto in these situations is "ignorance is bliss," and he was totally oblivious to the Officers' cold treatment.

"Agent Ward? I am Captain Jeffries. Anything I can do to help you with your investigation just let me know." Captain Jeffries had direct orders to be cooperative—it was in his best interest.

"Yeah, I guess you can help me by telling me how the hell he got that girl all the way up there," said Jack.

"I believe he hoists the body up there with some sort of pulley system. He throws a line over the branch and pulls the body upward. He then climbs the tree and secures the body at the top."

"That's good, except we can never find any rope fibers on any of the nearby branches that could be used to lift her. With the weight of the body and the friction caused by the rope rubbing on the tree bark there should be debris all over the place."

Jack reexamined the crime scene; you could not tell if he was giving instruction on how to properly investigate a scene or showing the Officers on the scene why they were out of their league. He noticed the how the victim's severed head added to the grizzly scene; the pool of blood stained leaves lied directly below. "Notice the issue of when the head was severed, because of the initial blood pattern, the head had to be severed from up there." Jack pointed to the body in the tree.

"How could you be certain?" asked the Captain. "Forensics!" said Jack. Jack had the advantage of science, forensics, and examining the previous crime scenes of this killer on his side. The reports of the blood stain patterns suggest the blood fell from a distance—a height of thirty to forty feet. Reports also suggest the person was hung upside down while alive, possibly for twenty four hours or more, before being decapitated. This aided in completely draining the blood from his victims. All previous victims were found the same way, with little to no blood left in their bodies.

"He hangs them there like a slab of beef, draining the blood," said Jack. "Like all serial killers, the point is to get inside their minds. If you can find out what they are thinking you can catch them. See…right now we have a hard time with this because we don't understand. Once we find out why, we will know who is doing this."

Jack's little display of arrogance did nothing to gain friends with the local Officers. They took his feeble display of crackpot investigating and ignored it thoroughly. They were all competent at investigating, perhaps it was bad judgement on Jack's part; he was just trying to break the ice.

"What about that piece of fibers you found on the way up here," said Officer Envy. Jack had not forgotten, the other scenes were completely clean. When Officer Envy mentioned the clue found on the way up Jack went right to work. He stood approximately ten feet from the blood soaked leaves under the body and turned 360 degrees. He paused with his hand on his chin and began to walk southwest.

Most of the Officers on scene began to point and giggle, "What does he think he is doing?" But a few Officers were intrigued enough to follow Jack. Jack's head scanned back and forth examining the wooded surroundings as he walked. Jack made a slight turn to the left and began weaving in and out of trees. He stopped and knelt down, looking closely at the wooded foliage before standing and continuing on. Jack changed directions again, several Officers were still following close behind, including Officer Envy. Jack walked directly to a particular tree and stood for several seconds, "Blood Sample!" he yelled. Officer Envy ran forward with a kit, equipped with the necessary tools for gathering evidence.

Jack pointed to a small spot of blood located on the tree trunk. Officer Envy began to gather a sample and Jack continued on. The word was circling back among the Officers, by radio, that Jack was on to something. Other interested Officers began to follow the entourage led by Jack. Soon Jack came across the piece of fiber stuck on the thorned branches he discovered earlier. Another Officer gathered the fiber as evidence and Jack continued to examine the terrain once again. Jack seemingly began to walk in circles, wandering back three or four times until he came to a huge decline. The hill was greater than a forty-five-angle drop and extended down about one hundred feet. Carefully Jack climbed down the hill, past the huge rocks and debris until he came to a clearing near the park's entrance. Jack walked through the park out onto the main path and began to look around the neighborhood. A smile came to his olive colored cheeks.

"They got away." Jack said, "Someone got away."

❦   ❦   ❦

Serena Capistrano traveled alone. She arrived on the warm California coast within a few hours. She had several pieces of luggage she needed to retrieve at the baggage claim and headed to the lower level of the airport. Slowly, the baggage was placed on the conveyor belt and Serena waited for her luggage to pass through. A middle aged African American woman walked up and stood next to Serena. She did not seem interested in the luggage as it passed by, she was only interested in Serena. "I have something for you," she said. The woman handed Serena an envelope, which was filled with several items. She also handed Serena keys to a rental car and directions to where she was staying. "Is it all set up?" asked Serena. "Yes, everything is in place as instructed Ma'am," the woman answered.

Serena never took her eyes off of the conveyor belt, she hated for her luggage to be misplaced or mishandled and was eager to collect her belongings. Bag after bag rode by and Serena began to get impatient. The woman who handed Serena the envelope grabbed the first baggage handler that came by and began questioning him. "Is that all the luggage for this flight?"

"No, there is more on the way." The handler answered, "It should be out in just a minute."

"We need those bags now!" the woman insisted. "I want you to go in the back and ensure me they are working as diligently as possible to get our luggage out in a timely manner."

"I am sure they are ma'am."

"I want you to make sure!" the woman screamed. She began to cause a scene. Other people who were waiting to get their baggage heard the woman clearly. People started wondering what the commotion was all about. "Look, do you see this woman?" she continued, pointing toward Serena. "Do you know who this woman is? It wouldn't be wise to let her wait." Serena tried to calm the woman down. "It's okay," said Serena. "I can wait like everyone else." A few minutes later Serena's baggage came out.

"I'll get that for you," said another baggage handler. He quickly came up from behind and loaded the bags onto a dolly. "Where can I take this for you Ma'am," said the handler.

"Take it out to this car," and Serena threw him the keys. He hurried on his way to perform Serena's request. Both Serena and the woman made their way out the airport terminal entrance and to the pick up area. The car was parked and unattended in the front of the airport terminal entrance and no one seemed to care. The terminal police walked by the vehicle several times without incident. Serena stood beside the car as the bags were loaded into the trunk. "Did you enjoy the flight?" asked the woman.

"Yes, but you don't need to do all of this for me." Serena was referring to the special treatment she received.

The handler closed the trunk after the bags were loaded and made his way to the driver's door. He held the door open for Serena and she climbed inside. It was a beautiful late model sedan, fully loaded, with an electric moon roof. Serena started the engine and paused to gather her thoughts. She pulled out the envelope's contents and placed them on the passenger's seat. She started to examine the contents, but someone tapping on the passenger's window interrupted her—it was the woman who gave her the information. Serena pressed the button to roll down the window. The woman spoke.

"The boy and his father will be arriving on flight 226 in about two hours. They will be coming to see me and I will direct them to you. You will get to meet them sometime tomorrow."

"That will be fine," said Serena

"The boy's name is Lexington."

"I know him well, you don't have to say another word." The woman was visibly shaken that she possibly upset Serena in some way. It was like walking on eggshells, the woman thought carefully before she said anything.

"It is okay," said Serena, "I am one of the good guys remember. You will be rewarded for your service, I will see to it personally." The woman could hardly conceal her joy. "Thank you ma'am. Praise the Lord, Praise the Lord."

Serena pressed the button again to raise the passenger's side window. The woman walked away overjoyed at what Serena had told her—and she should be. She was given implicit instructions, which she carried out to the letter. Serena had the opportunity she had waited for. For over three years she wanted to meet the boy prodigy, Lexington Prine. Since he amazed the crowd at the National Junior Math and Science competition, Serena had been a secret fan of his. But her admiration went much farther than that, she means to test him for a special reason.

Although Lexington did not win the competition years back, she recognized a familiar trait. A specific pattern to his thought process, which had gone unnoticed even on the genius level. Serena planned to test young Lexington, for reasons known only to her. Getting by the boy's father was another issue. He was sort of an intellectual himself. Dr. Walter Prine could possibly be reasoned with—if he were told someone was testing his son in the name of science, but she did not want anyone to know what she was doing.

The doctor might get suspicious and decide to check into Serena through credible sources, which she did not have. The file said Dr. Prine was proud of his son and watched over him constantly. There was more than enough information tracking Lexington since his birth to the present. And Serena was so ensnared with Lexington's information that she failed to notice the lack of history on Dr. Prine. The impeccable network, which gathered the information for her, had made a fatal flaw. They were so involved with the subject they failed to be concerned with his protector. Serena would soon discover that it was the enigmatic Dr. Prine, in which she should have focused her attention on. However grave the oversight, she had a plan and she was determined to make it work.

Jack Ward's skill was remarkable, at least that is what some of the Officers who witnessed his romp though the woods thought. Others who saw his tracking skill of gathering evidence dismissed his findings as luck. However, he was able to gather two vital bits of information. The blood found on the tree was not of the victim, who has yet to be identified, and the fiber was something they could track to a particular piece of clothing later if they needed to. The information was analyzed at a forensics lab and forwarded to Jack. The woman retrieved from the tree had been taken to the lab also. There they searched the body methodically looking for clues, anything they could use to find the killer.

Any evidence that might lie on the surface of the skin, or under the fingernails, was searched. This information was used along with clues about the woman's body type, age, and how she died. It was forensics' job to piece together what they could, to paint a clear picture of her final moments. Maybe some of that information may come in handy in the future. For now the information was stored and filed in a report. To the common observer there was not much to go on. The physical evidence was limited in what one could do—without knowing the identity of the woman. And there was no other evidence belonging to another human being present. Absolutely no physical evidence that could be linked to the other victims—no hair, no fibers.

Jack was not falling into the trap of the same old crime scene. There was a new element to the scene, one which the seven other murders of the same fashion did not have—a survivor. Many Officers thought Jack was nuts, that he found circumstantial evidence of someone in the woods and that evidence could have been there long before the murder took place. But Jack believed in his instincts, he learned to trust what his mind was telling him.

When he stood at the bottom of the park entrance, Jack thought to browse the neighborhood to see what he could find. After speaking with a few people he was informed of a woman who was hit by a car after leaving the park early one morning. The woman apparently was so hyper she continued to run after suffering a few broken ribs. Another person who witnessed the accident reported the woman ran into the car and she did not appear to hit it hard enough to cause the damage she sustained. Jack took all of the eyewitness reports and neighborhood gossip networks and came up with a name—Marie Carthon. She had just returned from the hospital after keeping her there a few days for observation. From the doctor's report, Marie suffered no broken ribs—just severely bruised, numerous scrapes and bruises, and a fractured nose. Shortly after returning home the Carthon's was paid a visit by the inquiring agent.

"Good Morning," said Jack after the door was cracked open slightly. "I was wondering if I might have a word with you." Jack was trying to be as polite as possible in order to get through the front door. He held up his badge as a sign of good faith.

"What is that? A Federal badge? An FBI agent?" said Marcus Carthon, Marie's husband.

"I understand your wife had a nasty accident out here a few days ago. I was wondering if I could speak to her about some of the details involving her accident."

"Did my wife do something wrong? I would like to know what this is all about if you don't mind. She is quite shaken up and on medication for her injuries. It just is not a good time."

"Then I will return," said Jack, displaying his streetwise accent, with the paperwork needed to speak with her legally." Jack was very serious, he was hoping the gravity of his tone would convince Marcus that this was an urgent matter—it did.

"What did she do?" asked Marcus, concerned that his wife was in some sort of trouble.

"She did nothing wrong Mr. Carthon. I have reason to believe she witnessed a murder."

"Murder?" Marcus looked back toward the rear of the house wondering if his wife was awake—wondering if what the agent was saying was true.

"I think this is the time when you let me in." Jack was anxious to get the questioning underway.

Marcus stepped aside and let the FBI agent inside the house; he motioned him to take a seat in the living room. Jack sat on the baby blue loveseat, located directly in front of the living room's bay window. Marcus closed the door, and circled around the large glass coffee table and sat on the sofa adjacent from Jack. "Would you like something to drink?" said Marcus.

"Coffee!"

"Sorry, we don't drink coffee."

Jack figured something was wrong with anyone who did not drink coffee. "Then whatever you got," Jack said quickly. Marcus left the room and returned a few minutes later with a bottled beverage. A non-carbonated, all natural flavored drink. 'Health nuts.' Jack thought to himself.

"So could you call your wife, Sir? This should only take a minute."

"She is in the bedroom resting. First, I would like to talk to you if you don't mind." Jack waited patiently to hear what Marcus had to say. "Now," Marcus continued, "you come here saying she might have witnessed something—a murder. I just want to know how you were able to single her out—how you came to this conclusion. You see my wife—she has not mentioned anything about a murder. The accident has taken a lot out of her. Her problems go deeper than the injuries she sustained in the accident. She has not spoken since that day, not a word…to anyone." This quickly got Jack's attention. "She goes in for therapy a few days from now, if she does not come around. The doctor's figure she went into shock after the accident."

"I am afraid Mr. Carthon, she may have been in shock long before she was hit by that car."

Marcus Carthon fought to make sense of it all, he did not have to think for long. Jack's theory about his wife possibly being a witness to a murder made more sense about her strange behavior than being hit by an automobile. Confronting his wife with this discovery was now a major concern of his. Marcus was no psychiatrist, but he figured whatever she saw must have been serious enough for her to suppress it. Despite his own conclusion, Marcus wanted to push the agent into giving more information.

"What evidence do you have to support your theory Agent…"

"Ward, just call me Jack Ward. Leave the 'agent' stuff out please." Jack took a sip of his health drink, he raised his eyebrows indicating the drink was quite tasty before returning it to the table. "I spoke to your wife's doctors; they considered the points of impact which occurred to her midsection and concluded that she sustained multiple periods of impact. Meaning there was more than one blow. She had to have been thrown against another object or car to have all of those injuries on various locations of her body. Eyewitness accounts say she was not thrown anywhere she was on the hood of the car momentarily before getting up and running away. One witness claims your *wife* was the one who ran into the car. She had scrapes and bruises, which covered over ninety percent of her exposed skin. The angles of the scrapes indicate she was upright and moving forward. A person who is propelled across the ground from impact sustain scrape patterns in only one direction. Then, there is the number of thorns and dirt that was cleaned from her wounds, unless the hood of that car looked like a thorn bush, I'd say she was running through the woods. Through brush, not on any trail."

"So, my wife was running, she always runs every morning."

"That morning your wife ran through the foliage and thorn bushes, ran into a tree, and fell down a steep decline to the park entrance. Not only that, she got up ran into a car, got up again and continued to run until she was home. That sounds to me like a person who saw something they wasn't supposed to see—a person who was running for her life. We have blood and clothing samples we would like to analyze at the lab and I am almost positive they belong to your wife. So here is the deal, your wife will cooperate with our investigation…period! I have been after this bastard for almost a year and this is the first big break I've got."

For Marcus, hearing the agent analyze the details of his wife's injuries put things in perspective. Reluctantly, Marcus conceded, "I believe you Jack, but it is of no use. My wife does not speak anymore. She is a scared little mouse that was once a brave independent woman."

"And getting hit by a car doesn't cause a person to retreat into a shell does it, Marcus?"

"I guess not."

"This is against normal procedure, but I am going to tell you what she saw. Maybe you can help her recover if you know what has got her so…spooked. But I am not doing this just for you, this is also for the investigation's sake. The second your wife is speaking I want to know. Here, this is a business card from a well-known Psychiatrist from the east. He will be in town a few days. If you are not satisfied with the progress of your doctor's this guy will come out at the government's expense." He handed Marcus the business card of Dr. Walter Prine. "Now Marcus, I want you to listen carefully. Eight murders in over eleven months, and no one has even gotten a look at the guy, until now. I believe you wife was the first to survive, and she paid with her ability to communicate. Fortunate for me the condition is not permanent. The crime scenes usually look like this Marcus; a body suspended thirty feet in midair. Hanging by the ankles…"

As Jack disclosed the details of the murder Marcus began to fear for the safety of his family. He knows the madman is still out there, and if his wife saw him, the murderer also possibly knows what *she* looks like.

CHAPTER 9

Testament of Power

"I have been blessed," said Roland Stark, religious leader of the
Reborn Kings. It was an hour into the service, the perspiring prince
of the pulpit continued to deliver his message on the Sunday before
the big ceremony. Roland, in extravagant style captivated the congregation. He had a method of delivering the word of God, which few
could match and the excitement of the events to come held the
crowd in anticipation. The person selected for the seventh Miracle
ceremony celebration will soon be announced. Every one in the
audience was a potential participant, but only one out of the thirty
thousand would be selected. However the odds were even smaller
than that.

Since the original Miracle, the uneventful shooting of Mary Beth
Reynolds, all of the subsequent participants have all been women.
This had not been done purposely, at least as far as the congregation
knew. It was designed as a lottery, a game of chance. Roland
declared, "this way the hand of God would pick the next person to
receive his blessing." On this Sunday, when the people entered the
Hall of Kings, they were asked to fill out the back of their ticket stub
and place it into a holder.

There were hundreds of large cylindrical tubes, which contained the stubs, located all around the complex. These were also carefully guarded by security to prevent tampering. The stub contained the seat number in which each person was expected to sit. During other sermons, people would often change seats or move to other parts of the hall, but not today. Sitting in any other seat, but their own, might cause them to miss out on the greatest gift God could bestow on modern man. Even with the lottery concept, women have been the benefactors of the previous ceremonies.

The hundreds of cylinders, which contained the stubs, were gathered and its contents poured into one large glass container. The huge glass ball filled with the ticket stubs was now beside the altar. With the patient crowd eagerly awaiting whom the next Miracle participant would be, Roland prepared to pick from the thousands of hopefuls.

"There is an overwhelming feeling of joy which sweeps over me every time I am prepared to channel God's loving grace to one of you," said Roland. "I feel honored that a lowly preacher like me could ever be worthy of such a gift. That's me being humble if the rest of you haven't figured that one out yet." That drew a small chuckle from the crowd.

"Yes, I talk about humility all the time because it's not me. I am not the one performing the miracles. I am a mere instrument, a tool in which God uses to do what he does. Listen—look at me—if I were doing the healing, the first thing I would do was to make myself look pretty. Then I would make it so I could climb a flight of stairs without draining two gallons of sweat out of my body." The congregation was in uproar.

"So you see, it is not me. And when you came here you did not come to see me. You came to witness the awesome gift of God, I just happen to be standing here. Since you cannot see God—and if you did your mind would not be able to comprehend what you were seeing—then God sends me in his place. Anyway, you all know that. I just want to make sure you understand it. Because it is much bigger than me, the picture is so big you can't even frame it. The vision is so great our feeble little minds cannot grasp the concept. The only thing that matters is that we love and appreciate our God, and that we live life by his law."

The congregation broke out with scattered "Amen" all across the arena. "Enough of that, now on to the blessed event. I will let the hand of God operate though my hands to pick the Miracle person."

Roland walked over to the huge glass ball that was filled with thousands of ticket stubs of potential benefactors. There was a large silver handle on the side, a crank type handle used to shuffle the contents. Roland grabbed the handle firmly and began to turn it several times. The ticket stubs tumbled within the huge glass dome. After a couple of spins he released the handle and let the contents settle. That little bit of exertion had Roland's brow covered with sweat again. He took the handkerchief from his left jacket pocket and wiped it across his forehead before continuing.

A large man, who was positioned on the rear of the altar, helped Roland remove the door of the dome and placed it over to the side. "Lord, guide my hand as you see fit." While facing the congregation, away from the dome container, Roland reached in and picked a single ticket stub. He then handed it to the large man at the rear of the altar so he could be a witness. Roland looked at the stub once again and prepared to read the name and seat number of the ticket.

"I'm sorry—I know you men have been eagerly awaiting the moment when one of you would be picked to receive God's glory. There is a reason God does these things, but I guess he sees someone who is in desperate need of his blessing and that person is another woman." A hum befell the crowd as they awaited the name of the young lady selected. "Seated in the David section, in seat C117 is a woman named Sheryl O'Connor."

People seated all around the David section turned to see who was sitting in seat C117, the rest of the people in the arena began to applaud. Sheryl O'Connor, the woman in the pink sundress, had her face partially covered by her hands, she still could not believe Roland Stark called her name. Thousands of faces focused in on her; the experience was overwhelming. She did not expect much when she arrived at the Hall of Kings, this was her very first time. A friend, who felt she might need it, gave the ticket to her. Sheryl had just gone through a nasty and emotional divorce and was in serious need of social support.

The stress she endured over the past six months was affecting her performance at work. She was withdrawn and her future was looking bleak. Sheryl was not one for religion. If her life was not in such disarray she would have passed on the ticket. Now she was about to make history as the seventh person to receive the miracle healing water.

It was stunning how quickly security moved in on her location. It seemed like they were moving in her direction the minute it was announced. One of the security members held his outstretched hand out Sheryl to take. "There you go sweetheart, follow security. They will escort you to the stage," said Roland over the microphone.

Sheryl nervously grabbed the hand of the security member and made her way through the aisle. Hoards of people left their seats and began to flood the level's entrances, they wanted to get a closer look at the person chosen by God to receive his blessing. More security guards began to assemble in the David section; they wanted to ensure Sheryl made it to the altar in a safe and speedy manner. Eight security guards total surrounded Sheryl, the lead guard got on a radio and informed the others when they were ready to move. The routine had been carefully sequenced as to what route they would take and what support they would need from the other guards.

When everything was in place they began to move. Sheryl felt like a celebrity, the guards quickly ushered her down the hallways and to the lower level's special elevator. The lead guard got on the radio again, this time informing the rest of the team that they were safely in place. After a few seconds the elevator door opened, the four members of security up front entered the elevator with Sheryl. The four in the rear did not enter, but turned around to guard the elevator door. The elevator took the group to the basement level, B1, where they were set to enter the main floor from the entrance at the rear of the altar.

Colleen Rigetti, the assistant of Roland Stark waited at the elevator entrance of level B1. When the elevator door opened she went right to work. The four security members exited the elevator first and behind them was Sheryl O'Connor, apprehensive and intimidated. "Hello Sheryl, you are surely blessed. My name is Colleen Rigetti, I am an assistant to the Reborn Kings organization. Please don't be nervous, I know how scary this all might seem. But you are about to receive a glorious gift, one that I can only imagine. You will be part of an elite group of people who were chosen to receive this. Only six people before you, indeed you are a special person. So relax, and welcome the shower of blessings God is about to bestow upon you."

Colleen walked Sheryl down the long hallway to the altar entrance. They paused at the bottom step while Colleen pointed to the thousands of people above. A few people on the highest levels facing the altar could see two people at the bottom step ready to enter the stage. Sheryl was in awe of the huge crowd, "Just walk up the stairs and may God bless you," said Colleen. Sheryl tried to control her short shallow breaths before she climbed the steps to the altar, but decided every minute she delayed made it that much harder on her. Sheryl then gathered herself and ascended the stairs to the altar.

Roland waited patiently for the young woman to emerge from the altar's entrance. Cheers from the congregation announced her arrival. After reaching the top stair she walked directly over to Roland in the middle of the altar.

"God has chosen, my brothers and sisters. He has spoken and the word of God travels great lengths. It passes by every ear, some might not want to hear it, but it passes by. This young woman Sheryl O'Connor will be tested—not by God—but by the media, by doctors and nurses, by her family, and by anyone else whose goal is to prove that God does not exist. For one week she will be put through tests of faith until, on Miracle Sunday, when her burden will be lifted. The attention she gets will be relentless, camera crews will be following her around. There will be physicians brought in to test her physically and mentally. People wanting favors of her, long lost relatives popping up out of the woodwork—just to say they know her—looking to benefit from her vigilance. With God's help she will persevere, she will rise up on the final days and God will reward her loyalty with his holy gift. Come here Sheryl."

Roland held out his hand and Sheryl stepped closer. "Are you scared?" he asked. Sheryl's thoughts were scrambled, but she managed to respond. "Just a little."

"Good, nothing worthy comes without trials. This feeling of despair is a good feeling. It is a feeling that you will remember when the pain is gone and has faded away. You will remember how it plagued you, how it limited you. And you will feel exalted when God lifts that burden from your shoulders and you will scream alleluia, alleluia, ALLELUIA!"

The congregation began to cheer and celebrate. The choir began to sing and Roland began dancing around the altar. Sheryl stood in one spot apprehensively clapping her hands in the middle of the altar. She wondered what Roland meant by trials, after all, she was already nervous enough. She was frightened because she really was not a religious person. She believed little of God in any shape or form. She was out of place and extremely uncomfortable with just being there, not to mention being selected to be the participant of next week's ceremony.

Sheryl felt lost around these people, she had nothing in common with them. Their behavior was strange; the only object she treated with reverence was a six pack of beer. They were all a bunch of boring geeks and they were foolish to think she could be considered one of them…Upon reflection, she realized she could play this for all it's worth. The media would put this Miracle to the test and for the highest bidder she would expose these people for what they were. But what if it is all real, she thought. What if he truly could heal the ailments of the body? How would she treat them then?

Roland danced uninhibited around the altar, Colleen could tell he was enjoying himself and was filled with excitement. Inspired by the Holy Spirit, Roland danced over to the huge ball filled with ticket stubs, grabbed a handful, and threw them across the altar. He continued dancing without a care in the world, the roar of the congregation was exhilarating and fed Roland's enormous energy. One of the stage workers for the arena saw a lone ticket stub fall off the altar and onto the arena floor. He was in charge of lighting and so he was out of view to the rest of the congregation. He walked over toward the stub and attempted to pick it up, he was looking to keep it for a souvenir. Although it was slightly out of his reach, the man was persistent. He finally stretched his arm far enough through the barred fence to reach it. Overjoyed with his prize, the lighting worker put the stub in his pocket for safekeeping. He returned his attention to the altar and to his work when something began to bother him. Although he only glanced at it once something told him to take another look at it.

He reached back into his pocket and pulled out the ticket to examine it. All looked normal, the seat number of the ticket was "David section, seat C117." This was the winning ticket drawn, he thought to himself. What luck! This ticket is valuable—a rare find. He wondered what a rich eccentric entrepreneur would offer for the seventh Miracle selection ticket, picked by Roland Stark himself…except, Roland grabbed *these* tickets from the glass dome afterward, and threw this one along with other tickets.

To prove its validity he had to get his hands on one of the other stubs. That way there was no reason to dispute its authenticity. He began looking around under the stage for another one. "There must be several that fell down here," he whispered to himself. The lighting worker pulled out his handy flashlight from his pants' pocket and shined it under the arena's altar. There, some twenty feet away, he saw another stub. He quickly surveyed the surrounding area as what was the best way to retrieve it.

Looking through his worker's pouch he found a roll of waxed string he used to secure the lighting wires. He attached a small pair of needle nose duckbill pliers to the string and tossed it in the direction of the ticket, being sure to hold the other end of the string tightly. The first throw was too far to the right, he tried to manipulate the error by pulling the string over slightly as he drew it in—it did not work. He drew the string with the attached pliers completely in before trying again.

This time his throw was right on line but landed a few feet behind the ticket. This was no real problem, as he began to draw in his second attempt, the pliers passed over the ticket stub and carried it about halfway before sliding from under the pliers.

His eyes widened as he saw the ticket. He shined his flashlight directly on it—he was not hallucinating. Unsure of what to do, he realized he had to have that ticket. No one would believe him otherwise. He prepared the pliers for another throw, his excitement affected the toss and he missed the mark by a few feet. Before he could try again he was interrupted.

"Hey," came a loud voice from behind. One of the security guards for the arena was approaching. "What are you doing under there?" the guard asked. "I-I was trying to get my pliers. I dropped it under there," said the worker as he pointed behind the gated section under the altar.

"You can't be here. For security reasons I am going to have to ask you to leave this area," said the guard. "Sure, right away. I have my pliers now anyway." The worker pulled the remaining waxed string and held up the pliers for the guard to see. Quickly, he shoved the pliers and string back into his worker's pouch and rushed out of the area. The security guard observed the worker carefully for strange behavior and walked over to the gate to check it out. Peering through the bars he saw the ticket stub, even from where he was standing he could read the ticket, "David section, seat C117."

"There is a slight problem on the main level," said the security member over the radio. "A worker beside the altar was interested in grabbing a ticket stub. One of the stubs from the dome."

"What?" said the voice on the other end. It was Jericho Black, business associate of Roland. Jericho was on one of the sublevels of the Hall of Kings, level B3, in his private surveillance room. The millionaire and President of Black Inc. liked to keep a personal watch of his interests. In this room he could keep track of every square inch of the Hall of Kings. Those who were trusted enough to know about the room say he has a fetish with cameras. Others think his patterns resemble someone who is on the lookout of something more ominous.

Paranoia or pleasure, one thing is for certain, he is almost as obsessed with watching monitors as he is with watching his money. Jericho worked his magic on the control board, selecting the camera at the side of the altar and locating the guard. He then panned around the arena and saw the assorted ticket stubs scattered across the altar. "Damn it! Send a crew to clean up those ticket stubs, I want that altar secured and the remaining tickets in that dome burned…got it."

"Yes sir."

"Where is that worker now and what is he wearing?" asked Jericho.

"He is about five foot five, one hundred and seventy pounds, brown hair, brown eyes, with a mustache and beard, and wearing the standard industrial type uniform with a yellow sports jacket. He was heading to the main level entrance."

Jericho took that information and began backtracking with the cameras, searching for the elusive worker. Five minutes into his search he located a man who fit the description on the second level of the arena. "There he is. I will take care of this myself," said Jericho. He stood up from behind the monitors and left the room.

CHAPTER 10

That Woman Again

The long trip to the West Coast was exhausting for Prine and his son. Compounded by the loss of luggage at the airport made for a catastrophic start to their trip. Nothing was going right. The reservation for the rental car was lost, Prine had to settle for an economy car, and he got lost on the way to the room. Prine put the tab on the FBI, so he did not mind the cost. He was going to take full advantage if someone else was going to pay for it.

Prine reserved an apartment instead of a hotel, his preference was room and privacy, two things the common hotel did not supply. He found a place in Ventura County, which rented by the month. The monthly rate was slightly inflated of course, but then again it was not coming out of his pocket book, so what did it matter. The apartment complex had a beautiful garden and common area, complete with a pool and a place to work out. The common area was designed to resemble thirteen century Spanish architecture and had a small fountain in the middle of the courtyard.

There were two levels to the apartment complex and all entrances had a balcony overlooking the courtyard. The place had a feeling of warmth and community spirit. Prine was pleased that he took the advice of a friend to stay here. Besides this is where Prine arranged for a babysitter. Lexington could not go with him on some of these interviews. The woman, who was to watch Lexington, lives in this apartment complex, and came highly recommended by one of Prine's colleagues back on the east coast.

Prine made his way to the lobby to find the landlord, he was interested in getting his keys and retreating to the bedroom for a few hours before doing anything else. Then he could contact the airport with his new number in case they find his baggage quickly.

"This place has become quite popular lately," said the jovial man behind the counter. "I am Mr. Tibby. I am the landlord of this place." Mr. Tibby was a middle-aged man with a peculiar sense of organization. Everything had its proper place and was best not to be disturbed. If an object was not exactly where he left it he could tell instantly.

Kids and adults who knew his obsession with organization would often nudge one of the carefully arranged items on his counter to see if he would notice. It would take less than one second for him to spot the misplaced item and subsequently throw a fit. In his mind was an outline of each item and where it is placed, which only he could see. An object displaced by only a fraction of a millimeter would send him over the edge. It was best not to touch anything that belonged to him. The thing to remember about Mr. Tibby was to keep your hands at your sides at all times.

"As you can see this is a lovely place to live and we would like to keep it that way. You guys look like good people, so I know we will have no problem out of you two." Unfortunately, Lexington had not been briefed on Mr. Tibby's manner and Lexington grabbed a small trinket off the counter.

"That's right," said Prine. "We are simply here on business…well at least I am. And my son is well behaved."

Lexington put the item back, but not before getting the evil eye from Mr. Tibby.

"I'm sure he is a fine boy," said Mr. Tibby, readjusting the trinket to its proper position. "How will you be paying for this?"

"Charge!" said Prine, as he proudly pulled out the credit card supplied to him by the FBI. Sometimes there is nothing more satisfying than spending someone else's money.

After checking in Prine took what little luggage he had, which was one carry on bag, up to the apartment. Lexington also had one bag that contained the essentials, a few shirts and toiletries. They had a second floor apartment near the corner of the complex. With one smooth motion Prine pushed the key into the lock and opened the door. The spacious apartment was fully furnished and its style resembled the same taste of Spain the outside was fashioned after.

The living room extended a full thirty feet to a sliding glass door on the other end. In between was a hallway, which led to the bedrooms. There were two bedrooms, one for each of them, each with an entrance to the master bathroom. Off to the left of the living room was the kitchen. Where the cooking area lacked in size, it made up for in the dining area. It also came equipped with a breakfast bar.

The whole living area was designed in earth tones, several shades of tan and ivory graced the apartment walls and floors with its colors. Lexington walked through the rooms before returning to his father with the results of the inspection. The apartment met his approval.

"This is great dad, my room and yours share the same bathroom. My room is big, this is much better than getting a hotel room," said Lexington.

"Which room were you looking at? The biggest room has got to be mine. So don't even think about taking up that bathroom until I take a hot shower and a nap."

"Okay, then I will go outside. I want to see the area." Being a father, Prine had a look of caution on his face regarding Lexington wondering around on his own.

"Stay around the apartment complex, don't go near the pool, and keep away from strangers!!" Prine got the last word out just as Lexington scurried out the door. He wondered if it was safe to let his son wander about, he would give him fifteen minutes before going to look for him. For now, Prine was looking forward to that shower.

Being the inquisitive young man he was, Lexington wasted no time in becoming familiar with his new surroundings. His first stop was to explore the pavilion and exercise room. There had to be a candy machine in there somewhere. Maybe even some other kids to play with. Lexington entered and immediately spotted Mr. Tibby, the landlord. He was such a phony that Lexington decided to steer clear of that guy, unless he was with his father.

Around the counter he went, being extremely careful not to catch the attention of Mr. Tibby until he was clear. Before he knew it Lexington was in the exercise area, there was no one working out. An empty weight room was of no interest to him, so he decided to move on. Out of the weight room and over to the left was another point of interest—video games. Lexington was always fascinated with the games, but never had much opportunity to play them.

He only had one dollar with him and thought about spending it on the games. There was no place he could get change besides back at the main counter, and that meant dealing with old Mr. Tibby. He was not going to do that, he had to think; what do I do now? As he turned he spotted a candy machine, it was exactly what he was looking for in the first place. Great…the machine took dollar bills, so if he chose an item which was less than a dollar, and the machine gave him change, he would have enough for the video game. Imagine that, he could have his cake and eat it too. Brilliant plan, Lexington thought to himself.

He quickly moved over to the candy machine and scanned its contents—nothing more than fifty cents or else he would not have enough for the game. There he found a bag of cookies, which was exactly fifty cents. He took the dollar out of his pocket and carefully fed it into the slot. The soft hum of the electric motor sucked the dollar out of his hand and into the machine. Lexington pressed the button for his precious cookies; the large circular screw turned and dropped the cookies to the bottom. The sound of two coins also being dropped was heard as it landed into the coin container.

Everything was working out great, he got his cookies and was now on his way to the video machines. On the way back, the noticed something he had overlooked previously. Between the rooms was a view to the pool out back, there was no one there, except for one woman who was lying on a lounge chair. He was extremely disappointed at his first encounter with exploration, there were no other kids anywhere to be found.

Mr. Tibby must have scared them all away he figured. With his phony smile, so exaggerated it looked like his eyes were closed, as he strained to keep his face in that position. He could best be described as an uptight prude and no kid wants to be near someone like that. Well, at least Lexington has the video game.

There were three games, one of which was a fighting game. This was the one he wanted to try. He was normally to engulfed in books to live like a normal kid, this was his first attempt at acting his age. After a quick rundown of the controls Lexington dropped both coins into the machine and pressed start. Lexington smashed the buttons and slammed the joystick left and right; he was really getting into it. Before he knew it one of his lives had been taken.

"Round two" the machine announced and faster than the first, another life was gone. This is much harder than it looked, he thought, as round three commenced. Lexington's hands moved faster than ever across the buttons, he even moved his whole body—as if that would help. But to no avail, his third life was taken and the game was over. The time elapsed since he pressed the start button was less than one minute.

That was not satisfying at all, he wanted a rematch. The next time he would let the game have it. If only he had more money. "Those machines are a waste of time," said a voice from behind. Lexington turned around to see who it was. It must have been the lady who was lying out by the pool. She was dressed in a long cherry-red terry cloth robe and flip-flops. She was much taller now that she was standing, than she first appeared to be…and very pretty.

"But if you insist on wasting your time, I guess I couldn't refuse such a handsome young man. Would you like to play again?" Lexington was taken by surprise and did not know what to say; he remained quiet. "I guess you are not supposed to talk to strangers right? My name is Serena, I just moved in here and I am trying to get to know my neighbors. So far you are the only one I have seen. Even though you are small that doesn't make you less of a person does it? You are still my neighbor—anyway that's okay. You don't have to say a thing, I understand. I will just put these two quarters over here and walk away. After that you can do whatever you want."

This was fantastic, Lexington thought, but tried to hide his excitement as best he could. Serena took the two quarters in her hand, placed them on the video game and walked away just as she said. She turned the corner and headed out the main entrance. "Have a good day Miss Capistrano," said Mr. Tibby as she passed by.

Lexington returned his attention to the video game and the two quarters on top. He cautiously removed the coins from the top of the game and inserted them into the slot. He waited another minute before hitting the start button, just in case the woman decided to return. When everything looked safe he started the game. This time Lexington was doing much better—at least he thought he was. There was however, one lingering thought about the woman who left him the money. He could not shake the feeling that he saw her somewhere before.

A woman like that was hard to miss. As he continued to play he also thought about something a little stranger, while she was standing there talking to him he could not get over how good she smelled. He did not say a word. Partly because he could not believe one person could smell so favorably. It was better than a bouquet of roses or a perfumed fragrance. The delightful scent made him feel…good!

✤   ✤   ✤

Late Sunday evening, the atmosphere around the Hall of Kings was quiet. The chairs were empty, the lights dim, and the decibel level was back to zero. Immediately after the service Roland headed straight for the shower and a fresh change of clothes. One of his assistants even suggested that he have an intermission where he could change in between the service, but that sounded absurd to Roland's ears. How could you explain to God that you are taking a break just to change into something fresh? That idea was quickly shot down.

After the shower, Roland came back out to meet Sheryl, who remained in the lounge beside the dressing rooms. All of the choir and people who worked behind stage were there to meet her and give her support. There was a family type atmosphere among the Kings personnel and they welcomed Sheryl into the fold as one of their own. They gave her a small ribbon that each of them wear during the service as a sign of strength and unity. If times get too tough she could look at her collection of ribbons and be reminded that she was not alone.

The shower of support was an unfamiliar feeling for Sheryl. The people seemed to be genuine, but she still did not know what to make of them. She was so used to people with ulterior motives that she was constantly looking for the scam. She did not let her guard down once, giving them only bits of information about herself.

The only people permitted down on level B1 were people who were part of the service. After a couple of hours people said their good-byes and began to return to their families. Soon after, there was only a small group of people left, Roland, Sheryl, Colleen, and one of Roland's main bodyguards.

"So how are you feeling?" Colleen asked Sheryl. "Are you ready to return to the world?"

"I still can't believe I was chosen. This is incredible, but yeah, I'm ready to go home. I can't wait to call my mom."

"Believe me," said Roland, "your mother already knows. So do all of your friends, past and present, your relatives, people you don't want to know, and people you *never* want to know. This is going to be a trying time for you. We learned all of this from the previous miracle participants. Fame is like a drug that everyone wants to get his or her hands on. It will change people, unfortunately it will change the way you look at others. The sad part of this experience is upon receiving God's precious gift, you will find out who your friends really are. Your enemies will expose themselves also. And it will all revolve around you, camera crews will hunt you down and steal your privacy. There will be interviews, phone calls—going to the store to get a gallon of milk will feel like a covert operation. In time it will all pass, and your life will be back to normal...in a sense. Except, what you discover about yourself, and others, will be with you forever. But there is one thing you must remember in all of this—the creator has chosen you for a reason. You must honor his lesson and value the trials he puts you through. You may not agree with them, but in the end you will discover his purpose. And you will be forever stronger."

Those words spoken by Roland echoed in Sheryl's mind as she made the five-hour drive back to her home in Nevada. She had seen a small glimpse of what was to come when she was taken out a secret entrance to her car, bypassing the media camped out on the Hall of Kings grounds. She was driving a rental car; one of the guards already spotted the media secretly monitoring her car in the parking lot. Someone must have a friend in the police department and ran the tags of all the remaining cars in the lot. Colleen decided they would pay to rent her a car until next week, she had already been through enough for one day and needed some time to herself.

When Sheryl arrived at home all was normal, from the way Roland was talking she expected people to be there waiting for her to return. She lived in a small yellow rambler on a quarter of an acre lot. A small community complex, like so many in Nevada, where she lived for most of her life. Unbeknownst to Sheryl, Colleen had sent a member of security to her home earlier to keep an eye on things. He had chased all of the local media and crews from her property hours earlier.

The security member was now waiting across the street in a parked car until the morning, when he would introduce himself. Upon entering her home Sheryl felt secure and went straight to her bed to unwind. That was where she realized what Roland had spoke of had already begun. The message machine on the nightstand next to her bed was full. *She would get a total of thirteen more calls before morning.*

CHAPTER 11

Deviant Renegades

Although she was not personally interviewed, it did not take long for word to spread about the person picked for the seventh annual Miracle ceremony. By that evening, word of Sheryl O'Connor's selection had graced the pages of the evening news. The local media gathered a ton of information in a short amount of time and Sheryl's life was already on public display. The price of fame was having an instantaneous effect on her life.

There were three people, in particular, that was especially interested in who, and where, Sheryl O'Connor was—William Richardson, Thad Voight, and July Matlow. The three had been plotting a means of revenge against the Reborn Kings organization. They were somehow involved with the religious group in the past and are now focused on destroying the organization in its greatest hour. William had been released from prison just a short time ago, during his time in lock up he saw the success of Roland Stark and was overcome with jealousy.

Thad, the only level headed one of the group wished to change his corrupt ways, but his path is headed back toward disaster. The minute he agreed to meet with his old friend and fellow felon. So long as he associates himself with characters like William things will always be the same, and he knows this. The small one bedroom apartment in Flushing, Queens, was where the trio met. They had been together in that apartment for nine hours.

July had went out to get the late edition of the news paper. The three were plotting their next move against the Kings. Their method of destruction was through an innocent, unsuspecting woman named Sheryl O'Connor.

"It's about time you showed up. I was beginning to think something might have happened to you. It wouldn't have bothered me any if something had happened, I would have just liked to know where to collect your corpse," said William to July, who had just returned with the paper. "Don't worry," she replied "when it's my turn to go I will be sure to take you with me." The two of them did very little to conceal their dislike for each other.

"Just hand over the paper please, we are running short on time and I need to get my plans together," said William. All was quiet while William scanned the paper searching for any bit of information that might be useful toward achieving his devious plot. "Here it says she lives in Nevada." He read through the article again, just to make sure. "It does not mention where in Nevada!" William shouted. "Well it doesn't matter! We all take turns driving, the trip should take no more than a few days if we do that. We need to be in Nevada by Thursday at the latest."

"What?" said Thad, July did not find his plan amusing either. "We are driving to Nevada, just like that." Thad remarked, "Without knowing where this woman lives, without a decent plan. We are just driving thousands of miles and then we are going to figure out the rest later—is that right? I heard enough William, it's time to come up with something better."

William wasn't surprised by Thad's remark about his plan, after all he knew Thad well. Thad was a thinker, and it was an insult to have him follow an idea that appeared to be thought up in a spur of the moment. Somehow he had to convince his buddy that it was a well-conceived plan, even if it was not. William calmly lit a cigarette and attempted to instill some confidence in his two accomplices.

"I am your friend Thad, you and I go way back. You know I would never do anything stupid that would endanger you and that woman of yours. Look, I have a plan—a great plan. One I have been thinking out for years. We can't let the Reborn Kings get away like that. You and I were there from the beginning—there are some things that need to be taken care of personally. There are some plans that we can discuss openly, and some that need to be discussed in private. I will let you in on the big picture when we have time later. Right now is not a good time, I know she is your girlfriend, but she was not with us when it all went down the first time."

William was now referring to July. "She can come with us, but the final plan just includes the two of us, and it is better if she does not know a thing. In case the cops pick her up she can't be pinned as an accomplice. You don't want her to get in trouble anyway. For pete's sake trust me, but we need to get a move on, time is precious in this operation and we have to move fast." Although still apprehensive, William's speech convinced Thad to go along with the idea. Thad did not want July to be involved, but knew she would go anywhere he went. The less she knew the better off she was.

"Okay, what do we need before we go."

"First, we need cash, it's going to be an expensive trip." William took one last drag from his cigarette and then extinguished it. "I wouldn't ask any of you to put up your own money, you know that's not my style. Besides I doubt if you have any money anyway, not like the dollars I am after."

"So what do you suggest?"

William was getting so excited he had to light up another cigarette before he could explain. "Check it out, there is an illegal card game I know about. I visited it a couple of nights ago and checked it out. It is not controlled by the mob or anything, it is just some school kid making bucks on the side. In a house out in Rockaway—he's got some muscle out there—but they are still just college kids. They'll probably shit in their pants when real thugs come rollin' through. We roll quick and we roll hard, grab the cash and head straight to Nevada." William gave them time to absorb the information.

"What do you think we'll take?"

"A few grand tops, it's a small operation."

"What weapons will we be packing?"

"The kind that scares young kids…big ones. Pump action twelve gauge and I'll carry the Mac 10."

"Casualties?"

"Only if they get stupid…now's the time to turn back, people. Speak now or forever hold your peace."

William loved to say that before every mission. There were no objections. "Copasetic—let's roll!"

Far Rockaway, two a.m. early Monday: the neighborhood outside was peaceful, inside the party was just starting. Gambling was in full swing in the private household on the corner of Merle street and Lincoln avenue. Word had spread about the late night black-jack—and to more than just the local college kids. Working class family men were also known to frequent this place, for it's seclusion and for it's professional flair. The whole basement was converted into a classy gambling establishment, complete with drinks and a bargirl. Because of their popularity with the locals in the neighborhood they did not fear any threat from within. What they did not factor was word getting out of the neighborhood about their private little busi-ness. Although they considered themselves prepared for any negative situation that they might encounter, they were not prepared for the visit they were about to receive from three people *outside* their neighborhood.

The house was a two story, three bedroom home with a finished basement. People wishing to gamble entered from the side entrance, which led directly to the basement. There was a bright spotlight that was pointed in front of the door that was turned on to check out people they were not familiar with. First time visitors usually got a thorough look-over before they were allowed to enter. All of these details were carefully calculated by William and company before they got there, the perfect distraction for this job was July. With her standing there, the person behind the door would be more inclined to open without many questions.

Chris Atlas was a student at Queens College, this high stakes blackjack entrepreneur grew up on Long Island. The desire to escape from under the roof of his parent's home brought him out here to Far Rockaway. Life on his own granted him the freedom to expand his horizons and do things he would not have had the opportunity to do under the watchful eye of his father. The card game had humble beginnings and started out small, just a few friends from the school and some neighborhood dads, but in time opportunity and greed got the best of Chris.

His failing grades were a direct reflection of his change of priorities as Chris looks to take his new business to another level. The greater the success, the greater the risk, if he had paid enough attention to his studies he would have came across this age-old principle and would have been prepared. Like so many young people, Chris believed that he would not suffer the same misfortune others have. That others who attempted this type of illegal business and got busted were careless, stupid, or just unlucky and he did not fall into any of those categories.

With youth comes the arrogance of invincibility, Chris was one who believed his new endeavor would last forever. He believed he had taken all the proper precautions to protect himself from the authorities and from thieves. Little did he know how easy it was, for those who wanted what he coveted, to send his little empire toppling to the ground. A fatal flaw of the human mind; no matter how smart you are, the true fools of the world are those who believe "it will never happen to me."

The gambling house on the corner in Far Rockaway had three exits, one in the front of the house, one to the side and one at the rear. The rear entrance was at the kitchen, the front went to the living room area, and the side entrance was where the stairs to the basement lied. One of the strong arms who guarded the establishment stood behind the side door entrance, the other was a presence at the card table, and the third was responsible for watching the front and rear entrances. The guy who watched the front and rear was there looking for any suspicious circumstances, primarily watching those who came in for the card game and looking for any type of police surveillance.

Every five minutes the guard would turn his attention to either the front or the rear entrance. The group bought themselves a pair of night vision goggles, which was used to check out the yard at night. There were no phone lines active at the residence; they exclusively used cellular phones as the primary means of communication. The greatest security feature of the establishment was a four-inch thick steel door at the foot of the basement. If anything went wrong the steel door would supply a sufficient amount of time to clean up and get rid of the evidence if a raid was to occur.

The effectiveness of all those safety measures, no matter how cleverly they were planned, are poor once the human factor is calculated into the equation. The people responsible for guarding against disaster have lost focus, the everyday routine has left them complacent. The strong arm behind the door rarely screens the customers as hard as he once did. The person watching the game was getting involved in the outcome instead of watching for trouble, and the person watching the front and rear entrances rarely took the time to look for more than three seconds.

If all were doing their jobs two weeks ago they would have spotted William Richardson. When he was there they would have noticed his interest was not in the game at all. They would have noticed his questions were going beyond the normal small talk. That he was just acting like an inquisitive idiot to thwart suspicion. They might have even noticed how William was studying the characteristics of the steel door at the foot of the basement. Last year, Chris and his crew would have picked up on all of these details and would have handled William accordingly. But a year of having to deal with nothing but drunken customers, angry at losing their grocery money, has left Chris and his group dull. They lost their edge—when they needed it the most.

Chris was running the table as he usually does; the house was doing well, pulling in a good seventy percent of the money being thrown around the table. There were four people at the table, two college students and two men from the neighborhood. "Eighteen, do you take a hit or you want to hold?" Chris asked one of the men at the table. "I'll hold," he replied.

"Okay," Chris flipped over the remaining house card; it was a seven of spades. "Sorry guy, you were smart to hold though. It just didn't pay off this time." Chris prepared to set up a new round when the buzzer at the side of the table went off. He grabbed a small hand held radio he kept on his waist. "What is it?" The voice on the other end was the guy at the side entrance. "There is a woman out here, she wants to play. Says she heard about the game from Sherry."

"Sherry Rosenburg?" said Chris, "The one who lives down the block? Is Sherry with her?"

"No, she's by herself."

"By herself?" said Chris. "What the hell is a girl doing out at this hour by herself?"

"I don't know. She looks drunk, or high…or both."

"What does she look like?"

"She's a looker. She's wearing a black mini. Nice pair of legs too."

"A drunk girl in a mini wants to play blackjack at two o'clock in the morning. What the hell, I'll take her money if she wants to give it. What do you say fellas, we could use some company." The guys at the table had no objections. "Let her in."

The door opened and the sound of high heels coming down the stairs were heard by the guys at the blackjack table. Chris reached under the table and buzzed the steel door at the bottom of the stairs, it opened and in walked July Matlow. The smell of alcohol immediately hit the noses of everyone in the room. She doused a glass of vodka on her body, like cologne, before she got dressed to enhance the effect—but not a drop went in her mouth—she needed all of her senses at 100%. She began to survey the room; it was easy to do it when you were acting drunk. Her head swayed back and forth looking all around as she pretended to be impaired.

"Is there a spot at the table for me?"

"Of course," said Chris, "come on over here and sit down. We're getting ready to start another round." They made room for her in the middle of the table, the bargirl had the evening off, so she was the only female in the room. Chris took a long hard look at her before he started the next hand—then he dealt.

"Take a hit...excuse me. We are all on first name basis in here. Your name is?"

"Kathy," she said.

"Alright Kathy, do you want a hit?

"I'll hold," she said. Her cards totaled sixteen.

Chris thought he had a live one, but when the hands all played out everyone was busted trying to top sixteen. "This round goes to the lady. Kathy, way to get things started," said Chris.

The chain of events has already begun, William and Thad started three houses to the left of the gambling residence. They began hoping fences and entered the yard of the Chris Atlas' home on the opposite side of the basement door entrance, there they sat and waited. Thirty minutes after she walked through the door July began showing signs of extreme nausea, she was faking of course, but she got the desired affect.

"Hey Kathy," said Chris, "This is an expensive table. If you are not feeling well I would appreciate it if you went to the bathroom." A frustrated Chris turned to the guard in the room. "Show her to the bathroom," he commanded, and the guard did as instructed. July stumbled on her way to the bathroom, gagging every few steps just to make it convincing.

She entered the restroom and closed the door behind her. Once inside she pulled out a piece of paper from her purse, it was a layout of the bathroom. It also gave detailed wiring for the steel door, which ran through the bathroom. The wiring ran above the drop ceiling, she removed her shoes and climbed up onto the sink. It was an old-fashioned type sink, there was no cabinet underneath, just the basin and a leg attached to the bottom, which went to the floor. She had to be careful because she was not sure the sink would support her. She cautiously maneuvered herself on the sink and raised the ceiling tile. Just as the diagram outlined there was a small wire bundle running across the top. She pulled out a pair of wire cutters from her purse and prepared to cut the wiring.

"RUAAAAHHH!" As loud as she could, she made sounds like she was regurgitating, as she simultaneously cut the wires. There was a large arc, which singed the wire cutters, causing July to momentarily lose her balance. "Are you all right in there?" said a voice from outside the door. It was followed by sounds of laughter from the guys at the card table. "Yes, I'm fine," she said.

Quickly she replaced the ceiling tile, climbed down from the sink, and threw the items back into her purse. After putting her shoes back on she flushed the toiled and turned the bathroom light off—then on—three times.

William and Thad were lying on the ground outside the bathroom window. It was a frosted glass window with welded bars on the outside. They could see movement, but did not know that it was July until they got the signal. "Time to do it, Thad." The pair of William and Thad ran around to the other side, being careful to avoid being detected as they went around back. They got themselves in position to make a charge at the door. Now they would wait again for the door to open.

In the bathroom, July sprinkled water on her face and dragged her fingers across it smudging her makeup. She took a look in the mirror to she if she looked nauseous enough, then she opened the door. "This is not good guys," she said.

"You look terrible Kathy. It might be time to call it a night."

"No I'll be okay, really. I just need some water." July began gag as if she were going to vomit again.

"I insist you go! Get some rest, you can come back tomorrow night." Chris was more concerned about his expensive card table than her health. "Show her out Steven." July panicked momentarily as the guard grabbed the doorknob before Chris could buzz the door to unlock it. He began to open it a split second before Chris pushed the button, but it was so close that he did not notice.

He held the door open for July and wished her a safe trip home. July continued the act. She lumbered up the stairs to the door leading outside. At the top of the stairs, the large man had her wait beside him; he looked out the peephole before opening the door and saw no one. July began gagging once more, judging from how terrible she looked from when she first arrived, he hurried to open the door before she made a mess in the entrance way. The area behind the door was extremely confined and the smell of puke would be too much for him to endure for the rest of the night.

"I'm alright," July claimed, "I can't leave yet, I lost too much money." She attempted to head back down the stairs. The scene was a familiar one and the large man grabbed July by the arm. "Time to go!" he said. "Playtime is over, you need to sleep this off." He held July firmly under the arm with one hand and opened the door with the other. On the other side William Richardson greeted him with the Mac 10, the barrel pointed a few inches from his face.

"Release the lady big guy, she's not your type." William and Thad wore rubber gargoyle Halloween masks to disguise themselves. This also gave the pair a more menacing look to their victims. William wore the green mask, Thad wore the dark gray one. Quickly, Thad handed July a small handgun and she dashed up to the kitchen area to find the man patrolling the rear entrance. Thad ran down the stairs to the steel door. There was a camera that monitored the stairwell, but it went down so fast that neither Chris nor the guard had time to react. Before they knew it the steel door was open and Thad had all of them pinned in one spot.

If the guard were doing his job properly he would not have been standing around the table, making it difficult for Thad to corral them all together. But Thad had the clear advantage, he could see everyone in the room without turning his head.

"You, big guy. Take your weapon out slowly and drop it on the ground. *Everyone at the table—on the ground—lying on your stomach*...NOW!" Thad ran up to the guard, making him take a good look down the barrel of the twelve-gauge pump shotgun. "If that punk behind the counter makes a wrong move, you die—it's that simple." Thad moved the barrel from the guard's face and pressed the cold steel against his chest. "Walk backwards behind the table to where the money is." He followed Thad's commands without question.

All was going as planned down stairs, fear had set in and the calculated attack caught them all by surprise. Upstairs, a dainty female with runny makeup was holding a young cocky male at bay with a small caliber handgun...that was a problem.

July Matlow was not intimidating at all, she found her target in the kitchen. He was just getting ready to find out what the commotion was about when July stormed in brandishing her weapon. July stood about five foot three and only 110 pounds, the man she was watching was a good 100 pounds heavier and had an attitude. He used to patrol the tables, but was kicked upstairs because of this brashness with the customers.

He suspected everyone and everything. His personality was one thing William did not factor. Those wanting to play blackjack rarely saw the man responsible for the rear and front entrances. William knew only of his patterns, not of his temperament. Putting the responsibility on July, to handle a guy like that, was a mistake.

The black smudges of runny mascara made July look like a woman who did not have it all together. Appearance is everything in a job like this, when victims believe they can take control of the situation it usually spells disaster for the attacker. The arrogant male was about to make a move, then decided he would talk to July in an effort to catch her off guard. She made him sit in a chair while she stood to his left, waiting for the word to leave.

"You guys do this all the time? Rob others of their hard earned money." July did not respond, she chose to concentrate on what she was doing. "You will never make it out of here you know. There are all kinds of security measures; the call has already gone out. Our boys will be combing this place in a minute with all kinds of artillery. You have no idea who you are messing with. Your little plan got you in, but it will not get you out—at least not in one piece."

July knew he was bluffing, the way the layout of the place was drawn out to perfection, she knew William, as obnoxious as he was, had did his homework. There would be no one to come and rescue these boys and all this man was doing was attempting to distract her. "Look," the man continued "I will tell them to take it easy on you when they get here. I'll tell them you were confused, lovesick, and scared; then they probably won't kill you. But you...have to show me you are a good little girl and give me your gun."

This was when July began to suspect she had someone who was not willing to cooperate. She had to think, and fast, before it got out of hand. "If anyone comes to that door—even a Girl Scout selling cookies," she said to the man, "I will *bleed* you all over the kitchen floor." July had no problem being tough, she just hoped her line was effective.

Two minutes had gone by, July's words had no affect on the frightening the young man. He was too much of a chauvinist, and too cocky, to take a threat from a woman seriously. From the way she handled his questions, he believed that if he demanded the weapon forcefully, she would not fold under pressure. But even if she did not yield the weapon, with his speed, he thought he could get to her, before she could get off a shot.

He tactically shifted his eyes toward the kitchen entrance making it appear as if he just saw someone walk by. When July looked in the same direction he made a break for the gun. July recovered in time and pulled the trigger, shooting charging man in the jugular vein. He instantly dropped to his knees, clutching the right side of his neck. Blood oozed through his tightly pressed fingers, as the look of shock at what just happened, branded his face with a blank expression. After seeing what she had done, July quickly made her way to the side door entrance.

"I'm getting the car," she said as she passed William. William, still pointing his weapon at the man occupying the side door entrance decided to tone things down.

"In a minute I am going to let you go see how your buddy is doing. Don't think about running out to follow us. This gun will put more of a hurtin' on you than what she is carrying," said William to the man he held at bay.

Thad was almost done collecting the money when he heard the shot. There was a frightful look on the faces of everyone in the room. Thad was also surprised; behind the mask no one could tell. He quickly blurted a line to regain control of the room. "Sounds like you have someone upstairs that isn't too smart. None of you will make that mistake I'm sure."

Chris put the last of the cash inside the bag that Thad supplied and put it on the card table. "Okay, the rest of you hit the deck. It's all over now, those of you who played nice, your reward is your life." When Chris was lying on the floor, Thad grabbed the bag and dashed up the stairs. "Done," he said to William as he passed by. "You go take care of your buddy now…Go!" William scooted out the door closing it behind him. William ran out to the front where July was waiting in the car, he jumped in the back and they sped off.

A car was stolen just for the job. They drove the stolen car three blocks to where Thad's car was parked. Thad took a spray bottle of bleach and sprayed the door handles, steering wheel, and anywhere else they might have touched thoroughly, took all of their belongings, changed cars, and left the scene.

CHAPTER 12

Trust of a Stranger

In his furnished apartment near Venice California, Dr. Walter Prine, a professor of psychology, waited patiently for Wilma Florence to arrive. She was the babysitter scheduled to look after his son Lexington. Prine was ready to go on his first interview in an attempt to gather information for Jack Ward, a FBI agent in charge of investigating the disappearance of Cindy Revner. The mystery of Cindy is of particular interest to Prine because her grandmother, Gertrude, possesses a piece of documentation Prine is eager to get his hands on—a journal of immense importance.

So far the journey has been less than thrilling for Prine and his son. Prine was hoping that would all soon change. The woman he was about to interview was Mary Beth Reynolds, who had her own tale of the supernatural. The original miracle, where a woman was shot and had miraculously healed, was Mary Beth's story. Her notoriety had faded somewhat due to time—she was old news now. However, Gertrude convinced the FBI that the true mystery Mary Beth Reynolds holds inside her has yet to be revealed. That Mary Beth holds the key to uncovering secrets, about Gertrude's missing grandchild, and a series of murders revolving around the Reborn Kings Ministry.

Gertrude's knowledge of strange phenomena does not stop with Mary Beth, she revealed to Prine that she knew about *his* unbelievable history. That she knew Prine was a patient of her father's in the early 1900's and despite nearly a century of time which has elapsed since then, Prine was just as young and healthy as a twenty year old man. Until now, Prine thought this secret was his alone. He fought hard to keep this enigmatic fact hidden from others. He tires from running and wishes to learn more about his true nature and origin. Especially since the addition of his son became the most significant part of his life. Prine knows he has secrets, secrets that he keeps hidden from his own mind.

Gertrude's father's journal is the object Dr. Prine feels is the key to leading a normal life, to possibly undo what has been done. A curse handed to him for crimes of betrayal or insolence—at least that is what Prine *thinks*.

4:00 p.m. in the afternoon, Prine tries desperately to get a hold of the woman who is supposed to watch his son for the day. He slams the phone receiver down with a loud bang, no one is answering at her apartment. Frustrated, Prine knows he is running out of time. He is scheduled to meet Mary Beth Reynolds at 6:00 p.m. sharp at her home in Santa Barbara and does not know how she will respond to him being late.

"Damn," screamed Prine, visibly angry. "I have no idea what this woman looks like. I can't leave you with a total stranger I know very little about. At least I wanted to talk to her for a little while before I left, now I can't even trust her to be responsible—what a day."

"I can watch myself, "said Lexington," I will read this book and go to sleep at 8:00 p.m. After I eat a big bowl of ravioli."

"You can't be serious. Me...trust *you* to go to bed on time?" There was a knock at the door; Prine went to open it. He looked up at the tall blonde figure standing in the doorway and was momentarily speechless.

"Hello, Dr. Prine, I am Serena Capistrano." Lexington recognized the voice but could not see her due to his father standing in the way. He maneuvered his way in-between the door and his father to take a closer look. Yes, it was the woman who left him the money to play another game at the pavilion. How lucky could he be if she was the babysitter?

"I am a good friend of Wilma Florence," said Serena. "She sent me here to give you the unfortunate news of her father passing away. She had to go to Missouri to handle the arrangements, she will be gone for two weeks." What else could go wrong? Prine sighed, disappointed upon hearing the news. "I'm sorry about her father. Thanks for stopping by," said Prine.

"I'm not stopping by. She asked me if I could baby-sit for her. I didn't have anything planned so I said—sure."

"What did you say your name was again?"

"Serena Capistrano, I am studying to become a teacher."

Serena knew all about Prine and his son. The best way she could figure to get Prine's immediate attention was to pick an occupation that he could relate to, the same occupation, which would interest his son also.

"Really?" said Prine; the response was just as Serena expected. "California is known for its excellent Colleges. The field is very rewarding despite what it may appear on the outside." Prine was letting his guard down, his first instinct was to turn down the offer, but there was something about her that he liked. He did not know why, his overprotective nature, especially when it came to his son, was beginning to erode. Besides he had important business to attend to.

"Aren't you running late?" said Serena, she must have read his mind. "Wilma said I should be here before 4:00 p.m."

"Normally, I would run out the door, but in this case I must be cautious. You must understand this is my first time here, I don't know anyone. I went off the reference of a friend and hired Wilma, now I find out she won't be available. Then you show up at the door. I meet you for the first time. I am just not ready to walk out the door and leave my only son with a stranger in a strange place."

The phone rang, Lexington pried himself from eavesdropping on his father's conversation to answer it. "Dad, it's someone on the phone for you. She says her name is Wilma Florence." Prine left the door open as he went toward the kitchen to get the receiver. The phone was not a cordless one, in a furnished apartment cordless phones would turn up missing too often.

"Yes, this is Dr. Prine...She is right here—yes, she told me about your situation. I am sorry to hear about your father, I send my condolences to you and the family...Serena told me she would be happy to watch Lex, I just wanted to make sure she is whom she says. I don't want to be known as a bad parent and leave my son with someone I know nothing about...Yes, she did begin to tell me about herself, and she seems like a fine young woman...Okay Wilma, thanks for calling, I understand—when you got the news you had other things on your mind—perfectly understandable. Okay, goodbye."

Prine hung up the phone and walked back toward Serena, who was standing in the doorway. "Come on in Serena, I guess I don't have much of a choice. I need to get a few more things, I also need to give you my cell phone number. Give me a hand in the back will you Lexington." Prine motioned for his son to follow him to the bedrooms. Lexington was too busy, delighting in the heavenly fragrance Serena wore, to notice his father's attempt to get him in private. "Lexington!" He called again, and Prine was heard the second time.

Lexington followed his father into the room, Prine closed the door behind. "Listen son, do you feel comfortable with this woman? If not I will find some other way to get the interview done. This is a total stranger and I don't want you to feel like I forced this person on you." Lexington heard what his father was saying and tried to hold back his excitement. You could not pick out a better babysitter than

Serena, he still had not told his father about the episode at the pavilion. She did not mention to Prine that she meet Lexington at the arcade either, which made her even *cooler* in Lexington's eyes.

"No Dad, I like her. I think I am going to have fun."

"Just save your excitement until I am out of the door," Prine responded. Prine opened the bedroom door and prepared to leave the apartment. "Serena, it is official, you have the job. My only request is that this young man be to bed at 8:00 p.m., other than that you two can do whatever you want. The number to my cell phone is on the kitchen counter—make yourself at home. I just got here, so food in the fridge is minimal. There is also twenty dollars in the jar over there if you want to order out." Prine looked at his watch one last time. "I have to go, give your dad a hug and I will see you later." Prine said his good-byes and headed out the door.

"Eight o'clock? I think that bedtime is too early for you, what do you think, Lexington?" She's cool, dad's one rule and she is breaking it already.

Serena had her long blonde hair in a ponytail, Lexington wondered if it was her shampoo that was giving off such an inviting scent. He eased closer to Serena and slyly attempted to smell her hair. She turned around at the last minute.

"What are you doing?" she said.

"Nothing."

CHAPTER 13

The interview

The years after the accident were good to Mary Beth Reynolds, and her humble estate in Santa Barbara was a clear indicator of that success. Although she is not a household name like she used to be, she still attracts attention, and is the center of many debates. 'Miracle or Hoax' whichever you choose, it usually sparked a provocative discussion. At the center of it all stood Mary Beth, a woman whose life was instantly transformed in a matter of seconds. From shooting victim, to being healed, to celebrity, she endured it all.

Seven years have passed since she was fighting for her life on the church floor, after being shot in the abdomen by one of the congregation. Then the mysterious healing waters said to be touched by God, touched her lips and healed her wounds. Dr. Walter Prine was no stranger to the supernatural and was always interested in 'The Miracle' story. But he was driven by his own desires, the need to discover secrets of his own mysterious phenomena.

Through uncovering Mary Beth's secrets, he hoped to gain insight into curing his own unique dilemma, and he sought to try by going where many have gone before—straight to the source.

Mary Beth was used to the attention, talk shows and church appearances, over 1000 different interviews. Then throw in the doctors' examinations and scientific research, in which she was examined and probed a hundred times more. For uncovering the mystery of phenomena one must start with the purity of innocence—that means from the beginning. Although it may seem like a dead end, Prine had to start with Mary Beth, there was no other alternative.

With her fame and the attention dwindling slowly she might not resort to the years of 'programmed' responses to his questions. At least that is what Prine was hoping for. The media frenzy was hooked on the latest member of the miracle family, Sheryl O'Connor. Her life was now on public display and would be for another year—until the eighth miracle member was named.

But Prine did not want the distraction of what was currently going on with the latest miracle member to interfere with Mary Beth's interview. He made a mental note not to mention any of what was currently going on to Mary Beth. He wanted her full attention reflecting what happened in her own unique experience.

The miracle frenzy turns into a media circus. But her life, besides the occasional interview, has pretty much returned to normal. A funny thing happens when a normal life turns to fame, then over time returns back to normal. When people are clawing into your life—you crave peace and privacy. When normalcy has returned you miss the attention.

When the call came from Dr. Prine, to interview Mary Beth for college research, she was willing to oblige. He still had to go through a manager to reach her, and what he was able to accomplish with one phone call would have been impossible five years ago.

Prine pulled up to the enormous home of Mary Beth, the ex-insurance claims adjuster had done well for herself. Luckily, Prine's interview was considered a charitable contribution to an institute for higher learning or he would have been slapped with a healthy interview fee. Despite leaving the apartment late, he arrived at Mary

Beth's on time. The forty-one year old brunette came out to greet Prine dressed in comfortable blue jeans and a white blouse. She looked fabulous, unlike when she was slightly overweight seven years ago. Being constantly in the public eye, dental work, plastic surgery, and a personal trainer was a must, especially when people donate the money for it.

"I was expecting someone older." Said Mary Beth, "Professors are usually someone with a few more years under their belt."

"Thank you, I will take that as a compliment." Prine responded.

Prine usually tries to dress "casual-professional," he wore a red polo shirt with navy blue khakis. His small round wire rim glasses added a look of intelligence, though the glasses were for looks only. His eyesight was perfect, beyond that of normal standards. The look of sophistication is what Prine was after, and his clothes were carefully selected to produce that effect.

Dr. Prine greeted Mary Beth properly and shook her hand at the front door. "I hope you don't mind me coming out to meet you. I just thought you would like a tour of the place before the interview." Prine looked around the manicured garden surrounding the house. "I don't mind if you do." He replied.

Mary Beth escorted Prine around the property, pointing out all of the modifications done to the home and garden since she bought the place four years ago. They settled around back to the patio, this was where the interview would take place. Mary Beth was a very charming woman and a marvelous host. Prine wondered how often she had done this; she seemed to be acting from routine.

Prine pulled out a small tape recorder and placed it on the patio table. "This is Dr. Walter Prine, I am here with Mary Beth Reynolds. Seven years ago she was shot in church by a member of the congregation and was miraculously healed. Now she tells her story." Prine positioned the recorder between the two of them and started the questioning.

"What were you doing that morning before you arrived at the church?"

"The morning was like any other morning, nothing especially particular. As you may already know, it was my first time going to the church. I really didn't believe in any higher power at the time. I went because a friend asked me to go."

"Your friend's name is…"

"Dorothy, Dorothy Clark, she worked at the insurance agency with me. She often told me how happy she was and that she was doing God's work, but I just don't see insurance as the profession of saints." Mary Beth found her last line mildly humorous and began to chuckle. "Insurance is sometimes a dirty business—back to the morning of the service; I was sitting in church next to Dorothy. The great reverend Roland Stark began to speak and I felt as though he was speaking to me. Like no one else was in the room, and his words began to have a profound affect on my life. Just sitting there I felt the Holy Spirit begin to lift me…"

"And turn my soul upside down." Prine ended her sentence mockingly. Mary Beth was offended, "Do you want to hear my story or not," she said. Prine turned off the tape recorder.

"Exactly…I want to hear your story, but not the same way you have been telling it for the past seven years. I already know that story. I read it hundreds of times before. I am not interested in the programmed responses you have given through countless interviews. I want to know exactly how you felt. The thoughts that were going through your mind, even the smallest, most insignificant ones. Actually that is all I want, I want an account of the things you feel were insignificant. The details you believe did not matter."

This caught Mary Beth totally off guard, she dealt with rude interviewers before, ones that ridiculed and badgered her. But she was always allowed to tell the story her way. Prine knew this, he did his homework and noticed the story and phraseology she used was always the same. Maybe not everything was the same word for word, but the phrases she used were all similar.

Breaking her routine would get her to think; it would force her to try and recall different things about what went on that day. From that he was hoping he would have something new to go on. "So what kind of research is this for Dr. Prine?" she asked with a shaken voice.

"This is research into how many details the human mind can retain after severe trauma or extraordinary physical phenomena. You just happen to be the perfect subject because you experienced both circumstances." Prine was used to making up all types of studies in psychology, this one he improvised at a whim.

"You really don't care about the spiritual aspect?"

"That's a minor detail as far as my research is concerned. I really want to know seemingly insignificant details."

"You don't want to know about the water…Roland Stark…or the miracle?"

"Those are not important. Only if they play into my research, and if that information is pertinent I will let you know."

Prine started the tape recorder again, Mary Beth was surprised, and slightly confused, but decided she was going to give Prine what he wanted.

"Let's start with why you decided to go to the ministry with your friend. What changed your mind about the church?" Prine asked. Mary Beth thought hard for a few seconds. "Be honest, the first thing that comes to mind, I want you to tell me."

"I did not want to go at all," Mary Beth responded, "I thought if I went just once, Dorothy would get off my back. She was pushy and I just wanted it known that I went once. Then I could honestly tell her I did not like it."

"Did you like it?"

"The preacher, Roland, was entertaining—he had some good things to say but I don't think I would have went back. Not if I did not get shot."

"So you were simply going at the request of a friend."

"Yes."

"Where did you sit and why did you sit there?"

"We sat in the middle pews on the right side of the church, about ten to twelve rows from the front. I was looking to sit somewhere further back. It was Dorothy who wanted to sit there. She said it was her normal seat—something about being able to see Roland clearly from there. Once the sermon began she was right. It was a clear view to the altar where Roland spoke. I think it was the angle of the pews that allowed a clear view, with no heads obstructing the view."

"You could see him and he could see you clearly, Right?"

"Yes, in the small church it was the best seat in the house. I don't think too many people realized it."

"So, now you were seated and the service began. Roland Stark was talking and doing his thing. When do you suppose you began to get into what he was saying and take the service seriously?"

"I didn't I just kept thinking, when will this be over, maybe I can still catch the game. Then some psycho began screaming in my ear behind me, there was some loud banging sounds—around five of them, and then my side felt like someone took a hammer and slammed it into my gut. Oh, I forgot—when the guy was screaming I turned around to see what was going on, there was a whole lot of movement and it was a blur, but I was facing the back of the church when one of the bullets hit me. Everybody hit the floor, I just hit the ground harder than the rest of them."

"Tell me, what thoughts went through your mind when you realized you were shot?"

"After I felt the pain, there was a period that I began to believe it wasn't too bad. I don't know if I was just getting accustomed to the pain or I was just going numb. There was a panicked frenzy throughout the church, people running for the exits—I remember seeing them scrambling for the door. Others were confused and some were angry that something like this could occur in the house of the Lord. I thought the same thing, what kind of place is this? There were a few people brave enough—or concerned enough to see if anyone needed help. Of course Roland Stark was one of them. Ten or fifteen people were all around me, one man thought quickly and removed his shirt, and he applied pressure to my wound. He began telling me everything was going to be okay, I remember looking in the face of everyone who remained—I could tell everything was not okay. Roland knelt beside me and assisted in applying pressure to my wound. I did not believe in God back then—as I saw Roland I began to wish there was a God. The pain began to fade even more, I felt out of it, like if I was on drugs—I wasn't my self."

"You said you looked around at the faces of those who remained, where was your friend Dorothy?"

"I did not see her, she said she ran off to get help. She was shaken up by the accident—she's the one who brought me there. I would be disturbed also if the roles were reversed."

"Go to when you received the water."

"I was so out of it, I don't remember what went on directly before drinking the water. The next thing I know I was feeling invincible and everything was better. My wound, which was there a minute ago, had vanished. For your research, I am sorry I can't recall more accurate details of what was going through my mind. It was a very traumatic experience."

"That is a normal response, the mind begins to shut the body down to preserve life. My research measures how much the mind shuts down and to what degree of memory one can expect to retain in situations like this."

"Because it was so blurry, I keep a tape from the local television station who recorded it. It truly is amazing when you watch it on tape. Would you like to see it Dr. Prine?"

"I would love to."

Mary Beth led Prine inside the den; there was a large screen television inside. Dr. Prine sat on the couch across from the television until she returned with the videotape. She played the tape and Dr. Prine witnessed many of the accounts Mary Beth related in her interview. By the time the camera focused on who was doing the shooting, it just caught a glimpse of him before he ran out of the church.

The man who applied the tourniquet and Roland Stark was coming to lend a hand. Prine thought about her friend Dorothy and decided to ask something more about her. "Point out where Dorothy is now," he said. Mary Beth responded, "She will be coming in to the top of the screen any minute now." When Dorothy entered the picture Mary Beth paused the tape to point her out.

"There she is, wearing the white dress." She came into view with another man following directly behind her. Prine figured this was the help she said she was going to find. Mary Beth continued the tape, Prine focused on what was going on around Mary Beth. He was hoping for some new insight into explaining exactly what happened. Prine saw something interesting and asked Mary Beth to rewind the tape once more, to the point where Dorothy returned with help.

She rewound the tape and replayed it as Prine instructed. It was not much to go off of, it was just a feeling. Something about Dorothy and the man she brought to help—the man was the one who handed Roland the water.

"Your ordeal, must have strengthened Dorothy's faith in God, she must be overjoyed."

"Actually, she has withdrawn. I don't know if it was jealousy or envy. She does not speak to me anymore...now the roles are reversed. All I want to talk about is how great God is and she does not."

"One last question, who is that gentleman that handed Roland the water."

"That is Jericho Black, President of Black Inc. He actually produces the Reborn Kings telecast."

"Thank you, Mary Beth, It was a pleasure."

CHAPTER 14

Silence

Marie Carthon witnessed the unspeakable—while on a morning run through the park, she saw a headless woman hanging from the trees. Perhaps what was more chilling than this grizzly scene, was the man who she suspects performed the brutal act. She stumbled onto his prize and found herself in peril, as she suddenly became the hunted in his twisted game. By sheer will alone she was able to get away.

Marie's family and friends care and support her, but they do not know why Marie is as traumatized as she is. She has not explained to them what really happened, she has not told anyone. Since that day Marie has not spoken a word, *to anyone.*

Her life is on hold and no one can figure out exactly why. Most of the neighborhood believes it was because a car hit her as she crossed the street. She was hysterical, but few noticed that she was in that condition before being hit. One person who was observant enough to ask the right questions was the FBI agent, Jack Ward. Jack visited the home of Marie Carthon after he examined the information obtained from the scene, coupled with eyewitness accounts and doctors reports about Marie's accident. His gut feeling had told him

Marie was running scared and she saw far more than she cared to tell.

Marie is on temporary leave from her job and her family is worried about her. She appears to be on the verge of a break down. Her husband Marcus was told by FBI agent Jack Ward, that his wife may have witnessed a murder, and now Marcus has come to the same conclusion the agent has. Although his wife remains silent, the severity of her condition leans toward an incident more serious that an automobile accident. But Marcus struggles to find the truth. With his wife speechless and unwilling to cooperate, he feels helpless and frustrated.

Marcus was running out of ideas, he wanted an instant fix—he does not understand the process will take time. He wanted to know what happened, so he scheduled an appointment with a psychiatrist—at their physician's request. Marcus has more than his speechless wife on his mind, Jack Ward had warned him of the type of killer he was after. The same one his wife had met and escaped from. Marcus' gut instinct was he and his family was running out of time. Whatever was able to scare his wife, a strong, self-confident woman like Marie, was a serious threat indeed.

Dr. Harold Chapin was a fifty-five year old psychiatrist, he had been in practice for over eighteen years. At the request of the Carthon's family physician, he saw Marie on limited notice. His office was in a private office building shared by a dentist and a contracted surveyor. It was in a quiet and remote location—the type of environment psychiatrists prefer. For the first time since the accident Marie was wearing make up and had her hair in a tight bun. Her eyes were still blackened from the fractured nose she suffered during her ordeal. Marie's mother was in town helping out and insisted on making up her daughter before she went out of the house.

"Have a seat, or lay down on the couch, whichever you prefer. I want you to be as relaxed as possible," said Dr. Chapin. "This is a unique situation, you appear to be comprehensive, but you cannot communicate verbally." Dr. Chapin watched Marie for some sort of response. She chose to lie on the couch to avoid looking the Doctor in the eyes.

"I won't insult your intelligence," the Doctor continued, "I know what type of woman you are—Independent, compassionate, reassuring...and submissive."

Marie turned to look at Dr. Chapin, she by no means fell under the submissive category. It was a trick and she fell for it. "Ah," said the Doctor, "So you are fully aware of your surroundings, of course I did not mean submissive. You are a woman who is 'Pro-woman.' Anything to change the perception of the helpless, second class citizen, barefoot and pregnant image men have of women. You are dominant, a leader, and an activist—so now that I know there is nothing wrong with your mind it's time to figure out why you won't speak. You would like to speak again wouldn't you?"

Marie did nothing, she did not even blink, he tricked her once already. She tried to outthink his deceptive tactics.

"There is a communication problem between the both of us," said the Doctor. "I have an idea." Dr. Chapin grabbed a pencil and pad he had pre-positioned by his chair and slid it across the table toward Marie. Her eyes shifted toward the writing tablet and then back to the wall.

"There is nothing physically restricting you from writing, I would appreciate it if you would answer by writing out your responses. Is that okay?" Marie responded by turning her head away, toward the opposite wall. "Marie," he said, "I talked with your husband. He told me that you may have experienced something more severe than being hit by an automobile. He told me you may be hiding something. I would just like to say, these meetings with me are completely confidential. I only have your health and well being in mind. I don't answer to your husband or any one else for that matter. If you are hiding something you don't want your husband to know about, have no fear in confiding in me." Silence filled the room, Dr. Chapin gave

Marie a chance to think about his proposition, but she had already made up her mind and nothing was going to change that. She reached down and pushed the writing tablet back to the Doctor.

"I guess I will have to think of another way to communicate, huh. How about I just talk and all you have to do is listen. Yes, that would be acceptable. Then that's what I will do." Marie listened as the Doctor rambled on about any and everything that came to his mind. He rambled off unconventional thoughts and feelings as they came to him. This non-stop chatter was very annoying, Marie wanted to stop him. She figured it was just another one of his tricks to try to get her to communicate in one way or another.

She stumbled on his early tactic and this one was just as clever. If Marie chose to write on the pad, and communicate with the written word he would ask her questions about why she would not speak. If she wrote on the pad, everyone would ask her to communicate that way. And when she refused to answer why she cannot speak on paper it would be difficult to justify.

For Marie no communication was the best way, verbal or written. She was hoping the Doctor would tire of his senseless babble and stop, but it was no use. He was persistent, and she was stubborn. Marie's stubbornness was for the safety of her family, but none of them could understand that. They did not witness what she had, and they had no idea of the seriousness of his threat. Marie looked at her watch, only fifteen minutes had gone by—the next forty-five minutes felt like days.

With the doctor getting nowhere in his first session Marie returned to the seclusion of her home. With Marie temporarily disabled, her mother decided to stay at the household to help take care of the children and to keep an eye on things. Marie's mother spoke to her constantly, unlike the Doctor's droll babbling, Marie's mother read books to her and tried to comfort her by being supportive.

Marie acknowledged her mother's presence with her eyes and expression, but that is all she would do. She was careful not to communicate in any other way but a smile. Marie's mother was supportive and patient, Marie's husband was not. Marcus wanted answers and his frustration at the psychiatrist's session was not kept hidden. Marie tried to avoid her husband all night, leaving the room as he entered, just to thwart a confrontation, which she did not want.

Everyone was trying to figure out what was going on in Marie's fragile little mind, her mother, her husband, and psychiatrist all trying to solve the answer to the riddle. Except there was no riddle, Marie was perfectly fine as the psychiatrist deduced. There was a secret she was hiding, one that spared the life of her and her family—a whisper spoken to her as she was chased by her attacker.

At the top of the hill just before she fell to freedom, the blind stranger whispered something into her ear that she has not forgotten. He said, "You guessed wrong in deciding to run. For your punishment you will not speak another word to anyone. By breaking this rule, your penalty will be the death of you and your family. And don't think I won't find out." He then thrust her down the hill to the park below.

Five days have passed, five days of silence for Marie. The manner in which the blind stranger had pursued her gave her reason to believe he possessed some sort of unnatural power. The blind stranger moved like a phantom, he was quick and relentless. She saw with her own eyes and knew—no one could protect her. Now, silence is her greatest friend.

At night, was when Marie could relax—away from the pressure of others wanting her to speak. She would often go to the refrigerator to get a snack late at night when everyone else was asleep. Then she would sit at the dinner table and enjoy the solitude. But tonight she would not be alone, someone else had recognized her pattern and he wanted to have a word with her.

"You don't look so good. You are not taking good care of yourself as you did before." Marie was stricken with horror as she recognized the voice. The sound was coming from the living room. Where she was standing she could not see, it was pitch black and she dared not turn on a light. She was frozen once again, and trembling. "I haven't seen you in the park lately, I fear you were trying to avoid me. I know that can't be true, after what you and I have been through. I thought we were closer than that."

It was the voice of the blind stranger, Marie was smart to trust his threat. He was making his presence felt, ensuring his threat would not be taken lightly. Marie began to make a deep whining noise from the base of her throat—she was terrified.

"Don't make too much noise, I don't want you to wake anyone. Who knows what I will do then." Marie stopped the sound immediately. She strained to look into the blackness of the dark, hoping her night vision would adjust and she would see him. "Good, you are a good girl aren't you. I understand when the police questioned you—you did not say a word. And you haven't spoken to anyone since our talk."

It sounded like he stood up from the couch and was walking toward her. She figured when he got closer to the nightlight by the kitchen table she would see him, she wanted to be sure this was real. It sounded as if he was getting closer and still she saw nothing. Then out of the darkness a hand reached out and grabbed her drink. It was if it appeared out of the dark and went back again. She heard the sound as the blind stranger sipped the bottled drink.

"I was wrong about you, I initially figured your family would be dead by now. I have reconsidered your punishment, as a reward for being disciplined. You will be allowed to speak to one person, that is me. You can exercise your vocal cords when I talk to you and only then. Now, you may speak!"

Marie said nothing.

"You can trust me…If you don't speak I will become very angry."

She thought of what she would say, she wanted to choose her words carefully. With a dried, crackled voice Marie uttered, "Thank you, for sparing the life of my family and me."

"Don't waste your thanks on me, they are not out of harms way yet. And don't try to kiss my ass, I can tell that is beneath you. I will allow you a question, anything you want to know. But, be careful not to wake anyone, if they hear you speaking, and I am seen they will all be killed—understood?"

Marie knew exactly what she was going to ask. She wanted to know what she was up against. "Who are you?"

"I am Rameci."

"Do you have a last name?"

"I don't need a last name, there is only one Rameci. Not as confusing as what you people call yourselves."

It felt good to talk again, even if it was with the man she feared the most. She had almost forgotten what the sound of her own voice was like. Marie asked the third question very cautiously. "How can you do, the things you do? You move so fast."

"You people are fascinated by the smallest things. I may look like you, but you and I are as different as night and day. 'All flesh is not the same, there are heavenly bodies and there are earthly bodies—a natural body and a spiritual body.' That is what is written in Corinthians—they almost got it right. Do you follow religion closely?"

"I am a Baptist, I go to church when I can." A few tears began to flow down Marie's cheeks, it was a very emotional subject. The ordeal, her punishment, and now being able to talk—she had to find comfort in being able to talk only with her tormentor. And she fears he is taking the conversation into an area she does not want to go.

"Crying won't help you, there is no strength in that. You are going in the wrong direction. Did I hit a nerve? Oh I see, you prayed your God would help you. You probably have been praying since the day we met, and you saw your minister didn't you? Strength comes in many forms—I suppose that is one of them. When you kneel down to pray you are hoping a being like me will come down and guide you in the right direction. Maybe even take care of the problem for you. Well those days are gone, the time of intervention is no more. I am what was originally named 'a messenger.' I am one who fell from grace and is now spending my eternity among the wretched of this place. I am an angel…but not the type you pray would help you."

Marie did not believe him; she refused to. With all that was happening, her mind fought to grasp reality. These things do not occur in her reality, this all must be a prank. A sick joke played by a madman who wishes nothing but to torture her, and now he is attempting to confuse her further—to subjugate her by cooking up this theory of his higher power. With a shaken voice she spoke out against him—to call his bluff.

"I do not believe you, you are just trying to torture me so I will remain quiet—so I will be a part of your little game. What you did is nothing more than a magician's illusion. You can't be who you say you are. I refuse to believe it."

Rameci was amused, "Interesting, you just told me you prayed and now you are telling me you doubt the own conviction of your prayer. I hope you see how foolish you are."

"I don't doubt my prayers, I doubt you."

"If you doubt me then you doubt your own faith. Here I am, the proof of your beliefs and you do nothing but ridicule me—how pathetic. Humans pray to God, they pray to a higher power—all of his might and grace. Then the minute there is a power, a strength that they do not understand, they doubt it's from God. I am here telling you I am the proof you seek, and you refuse to acknowledge it. Should I doubt who you are—a scared woman, pushing out her chest, trying to be the pinnacle of her gender. Here to make a statement to all the critical males in the world—that you are their equal. So much that you failed to see what you really enjoy—is being feminine. You enjoyed when your mother put that make up on you this morning, she made you feel whole, and she made you complete. You play a good game to the fools that cannot see through your scared, fragile ego, but I can see the truth. You long to be a woman, you long to be all woman and everything that encompasses. But on the other hand you want to be respected at the same time—treated as equal, physically, intellectually…You cannot have it all Marie, if that was so I would be in heaven right now. Our sick creator has written the rules and we must *choose* our fate. Sacrifice is the key, one pleasure for another. You have been on earth all this time and still haven't figured that one out? Shame on you."

"Don't try to confuse me," said Marie, "you are just twisting everything around. We were not talking about me, we were talking about you."

"You need to mind your tone," Rameci said with a stern voice. "I will not be addressed in a contemptuous manner. What I give you for advice you should appreciate. You talk as if this were a game…With your life in the balance I am surprised you did not ask me one important question. Did I kill that woman? You just assumed I did, with no real evidence. Now you remain speechless, talking only to me—all on an assumption. Then when I tell you things about myself, you doubt them; you call me a liar and a deceiver. Are you interested in the truth or not? I can tell lies to you if you wish, if that is what you expect of me? But if you are not good company I will restrict our visits and you will have no one to talk to."

Marie shook her head, she realized she was overstepping her bounds, on her first opportunity to communicate she was endangering the limits of her new privilege.

"That's a wise decision," said Rameci.

"I would like to know if you killed that woman in the woods?" she said submissively.

"Now that's more like it." Rameci paused slightly before answering. "Yes, I killed that woman for a reason. I may tell you what that reason is some time in the future, if you ask nicely, but right now I do not wish to disclose that information. All you need to know is that I am very capable of extinguishing your life. You were wise to believe me, when I spoke to you in the woods. As you may have guessed when I told you how your mother pampered you earlier, I can see many things. You have no idea when I will show up and when I will be watching."

There was the sound of Rameci drinking the bottled beverage once again, by now Marie's eyes had adjusted to the darkness. She still could not see him; perhaps he did not want to be seen. Marie had a lot on her mind, everyday she thought of speaking. She played the scene over in her mind. Who she would tell—how would she save her family? In light of Rameci's visit her options were running thin.

"Is this a part of your game?" She asked, "Did you do this to that woman, visit her family, make her not speak to anyone? Then when you got tired of her, you strung her up and killed her? Is that what you do? Am I just playing into your hand? If so, I won't let you get the satisfaction."

Rameci began to chuckle, "If you could only hear yourself. You are entertaining to say the least. All of these fears, doubts, and reservations, and you fail to see the truth. You have within you 'the fear of loss.' It binds you in your decisions—it is the driving force that guides your actions. I can take many things away from you Marie—your house, your car, your children, and your entire family. Anything on this earth that you might covet I can take away. The things I threaten you with will fill your heart with sorrow and engulf your soul to the point of subjugation.

"This is the misery all humans seek to escape their entire lives. Physical pain and emotional pain, humans are driven to avoid these things, yet most of all they fear the loss of their own life. You were fearful of this when you leaned against the tree in the woods after coming to the conclusion that it was I who killed that girl. Do you know what happens to you after you perish? Have you ever thought about how it would feel for you to die? Of course you have, everyone thinks of these things. It is natural to fear the unknown, even if it gives you all the relief you seek. In death there is no pain, no sorrow, no hunger and no fear. All of the things you seek to escape in life, yet most people would endure all of that suffering just to avoid death. You fear the wrong things Marie, I keep you prisoner by playing your basic fears. With all the trials ahead of you from this day forward, death may hold the peace that you seek. I am not the one you should fear Marie, you should be afraid—of life."

Marie was looking straight ahead when Rameci appeared from the darkness. The size of his intimidating figure appeared to fill the room; he was wearing the same magnificent robes he wore before. His eyes were closed and he had the same walking stick, which he held in his right hand. He placed the near empty bottle back onto the kitchen table.

"Think of something interesting for our next talk, most of your questions were boring small talk. Now that you know what is available to you I don't want you to waste your valuable voice time. Until the next time…" Rameci appeared to be thinking, "I did not here your gratitude at getting a new privilege, besides the extension of your life."

Marie responded, except the sincerity was not there. "Thank you."

"Excellent!"

Rameci turned and began to walk toward the front door. His image faded to blackness just before reaching the entrance.

"Oh Marie…your silence resumes now!"

CHAPTER 15

The Pristine Case

The Pristine Murders, named after the town in which two of the eight victims were found, was the case in which agent Jack Ward was the primary investigator. Jack was a unique agent, known for seeing things often overlooked by other investigators. He followed both conventional and unconventional methods, whatever the situation demanded. Working for the FBI, there was a whole world of resources available that the common police officer did not have ready at their disposal. Serial murders are often turned over to the FBI, due to their complexity. The individuals who perform these acts of violence are often extremely intelligent and manipulative—they are very difficult to catch.

The first of the Pristine Murders occurred fourteen months ago, a young man in Louisiana was found in the woods near a residential area. Like the others, he was decapitated and hung upside down approximately forty feet in the air. By the time he was discovered there was little left to identify.

The similar theme of these murders is there are no witnesses, and no identification on the victims. Even more puzzling was the lack of physical evidence left behind. There were no hairs, no fibers, no skin, nothing other than that belonging to the victim.

The local papers carried the story for almost two months, but local investigators got nowhere. Without being able to identify the body, there were few options for investigators to begin. The killer knows this; and makes it extremely difficult for anyone trying to investigate the case. After the third victim was found, in three different states, with the same modus operandi, the case was turned over to the FBI.

In each case the head was removed. The principal means of identification is through facial features. Since the heads are never recovered, there is no way of using the first…or second most popular means of identification—dental records. All of the tips of the fingers are removed, and some bodies had several places along the surface where a thin layer of flesh was removed. Investigators believe this is where identifying marks like birthmarks or tattoos were present.

It was hard enough to catch a clever killer, but even more difficult if there is no clue as to whom the victim is. After death the body becomes distorted, they swell and decompose, trying to identify a torso is nearly impossible. The only thing left to go on is blood, and the only way to identify a victim through DNA is to get samples from the parents and compare them.

If authorities chose to do this, the only place investigators could begin in is through missing person's files. Thousands of people turn up missing everyday, all ages, all races of people—most of them do not want to be found. The process would entail taking hundreds of samples from parents whose offspring fit the general description and comparing them to the eight victims. Even in a small town, telling the parents of missing persons that they need blood from them to compare to a murder victim is outrageous.

Most of the parents hope their offspring, no matter what age, is alive and well, and will someday return. For the sake of curtailing mass panic, DNA can only be used to confirm the identity, not as a means of discovering the victim itself.

There has to be another way. That is the dilemma Jack Ward faces. He was desperate to try anything, and when he got the call from an elderly woman named Gertrude Revner, he was quick to try the unconventional and see what she had to offer. Gertrude, despite being hundreds of miles away, had somehow heard about the murders and claimed her missing granddaughter Cindy, was a victim. She also claimed the Reborn Kings Ministry was involved. But the blood from Cindy's parents turned up nothing. None of the female victims matched her profile.

Her parents believe she is still out there, and will soon return, but Grandmother Gertrude feels Cindy's life has met a grim end. As great of an investigator he is, Jack was beginning to believe the killer was getting the best of him.

That was until the last victim had a reluctant eyewitness named Marie Carthon. Marie's trauma was no accident, and Jack is convinced she is hiding the identity of this madman. Unfortunately for him Marie has bigger problems, she has not spoken a word since emerging from the woods with her life.

Despite the circumstances, this gives Jack hope. Eventually he knows she will come around, and help put and end to this fourteen-month killing spree. For now he must rely on more scientific methods for solving the case. He has traveled to the forensics lab in Virginia, where the latest body had been transported. Developing technology has catapulted the world of forensic science to new levels of effectiveness. Here, it is often the evidence that is barely visible to the naked eye that speaks volumes toward solving a case. Jack has come to the forensics lab for specific information, since his instincts tell him Marie Carthon has seen the murderer, he decided to concentrate on understanding exactly how the murders are performed. That way when Marie finally comes around to talking, he will have a face to go along with the profile.

The first obstacle the team wanted to address was the cutting instrument used for decapitation. Dr. Steven Nat, a twenty-year veteran in the world of forensics, was studying the neck wounds of the victims. He had accurate data on four of the eight victims that might prove useful. In the lab, photos were placed on a lighted board, there were twelve photos in all, each one taken at different angles. Jack walked into the dimly lit room and examined the photos along with the doctor, photos he was all too familiar with.

"I've stared at these same photos for hours on end," said Jack. "Hopefully, you will see something I missed previously, then I could finally make some progress on this damn case. Work your magic doc, what do you see?"

"This is amazing." The doctor walked over to the board to point out specific patterns of the wounds. "See here, the outer layers of flesh show no signs of being torn, the area does not show even the slightest signs of stress. Through the entire cut, it is incredibly smooth, the smoothest I've ever seen. It originates in one direction—lets say for example like a guillotine and it travels cleanly through the entire area. But a guillotine has a securing device that is placed around the neck, which would have left bruise marks along the base of the neck. Besides all evidence shows that the victims heads were severed while suspended in midair. Here is the amazing part of that."

Dr. Steven Nat led Jack down the corridor to another room, on the way, Jack stopped by the break room to grab a cup of coffee. He cannot go too long without a steady dose of caffeine. When he arrived at the room, there were three assistants setting up an experiment. Jack noticed a slab of beef hanging in the middle of the room, suspended about five feet from the floor. It was held by a large meat hook similar to the ones used in a butcher shop. There were also seven other slabs of beef lined up on a table next to the door. On the table adjacent to the meat were several cutting instruments, most of them were swords. The assistants were placing numbered tags on the swords for the experiment and placed another set of tags beside them. The matching number tags would be paired with the slabs of beef as they were cut.

"What I want to show you," said Dr. Nat, "is the different cutting patterns that may occur when simulating someone being decapitated while being suspended in midair. Let us start."

The doctor motioned for one of his assistants to begin; the assistant grabbed the first sword from the table. "I derived that the weapon used was a sword, the cut patterns suggest something that can be wielded at high speed," said the doctor. "Naturally, a sword came to mind." The assistant placed a pair of safety goggles on his face and positioned himself to take a swing at his target. Wearing a white lab coat and safety goggles, the assistant looked less than intimidating while holding the mighty weapon.

The sword was a short broad sword resembling the ones used by the ancient Romans—no longer than the modern machete. The assistant valiantly swung at the target and cut it almost three-quarters of the way through. His aim went askew slightly to the left. The slab of beef swung violently on the hook, it rattled and spun before settling down. After settling, the other two assistants removed the slab of beef from the hook, tagged it, and set up another slab. The team went though the various swords and slabs until there were no more.

With the practical stage of the experiment complete, the severed sets of beef were put on the table for examination. Dr. Nat went by and inspected slab, one at a time. "I wanted to show you the similarities of each case and compare them to our murder victims. Weapon six did the best at cutting the beef, the classic Japanese Samurai sword. The amazing part I want to show you is this—you see where the incision begins here, well somewhere through the cut it begins to change—see here?" Jack shook his head as if he followed the doctor, but his eyes were not as fine tuned to detect the differences pointed out. "This," the doctor continued, "is where the object began to move while the sword was going through giving you a change in the cutting angle."

"So, what does this prove?" Jack asked impatiently.

"Funny you should ask. Now I will show you the process in which I was best able to duplicate the decapitation performed on the victims."

The three assistants started moving again, this time they went to a table in the far corner of the lab and wheeled out a piece of test equipment. It was a large cylindrical tube design, approximately four feet long. There was a small keypad and complex looking computer attached to one end. The other end had a small opening, similar to a gun barrel. The piece of equipment was placed on a large stainless steel table, around six feet in length. At the other end of the table was a large receptacle. The assistants spent several minutes calibrating the angles on the two pieces of equipment. When they had the barrel end on one side of the table aligned with the receiver portion on the other end, they notified Dr. Nat.

"This is a LASER, Light Amplification by Stimulated Emitted Radiation. We will set up another sample and cut it using this. I just want to ensure the magnification is set correctly before we attempt it."

"Well, I'm going to need another cup of coffee before we start this one." Jack perceived the doldrums of all these tests cramping his fast paced style. He unenthusiastically left the lab and headed to the break room.

When Jack returned, he was given what looked like a darkened set of goggles to put over his eyes. These were safety goggles used whenever operating a LASER device. This device was a class IV LASER, one of the more powerful designs.

The light from this particular LASER was not in the visible spectrum, special precautions were made to ensure the unit was aligned before activating. An elaborate computer controlled the movement, it could be programmed to move within .0005" accuracy. Once the slab of beef was set into place, the assistants, Dr. Nat, and Jack went into the observation room. With a push of a button, the barrel end swung from left to right, and the lower one third of the beef slab dropped straight down onto the table. Dr. Nat elaborated on the latest experiment.

"All of the wounds on the bodies we were able to examine have the same angle cut throughout, as with the slab cut by the LASER the body did not move. If the bodies were held with one hand, it would take someone with incredible strength to wield a weapon fast enough to cut through cleanly. But that is not nearly the amazing part, my theory is whatever weapon was used to do this was extremely sharp. Sharper than any surgical instrument we use today. This is the only way I could duplicate the exact wound pattern on the victims."

"The weapon is that sharp, huh." Jack was not as impressed with the discovery as the doctor was.

"There are no known instruments in the world sharp enough to produce this type of cut pattern. If we could discover what it was made of, that might help us in narrowing down the weapons origin. I was hoping that an instrument this sharp would have a tip fine enough to produce metal shards as it passed through the bones of the spinal cord. I took the liberty of sampling the bones for traces of microscopic metal shards that might be left behind. I found particles of a strange substance, it ended up being unidentifiable—and it had some unique qualities. We haven't been able to decipher what it is yet but—."

"Okaaay," said Jack, cutting off the doctor. "I'm late for another…um…thing. Let me know what you find," said Jack, as he expeditiously walked out the lab.

"Scientists…"

All of this scientific excitement was boring Jack to tears. Good thing he set up another, avenue to pursue. Jack was going to see a criminal profiler; someone who analyzes the information presented and comes up with character and personality traits of the attacker. Jack had arranged the profiler to come to the lab in order to get a better feel of the evidence. By the time on his watch, he was fifteen minutes late.

Certain parts of the lab were no place for anyone of weak stomach, Jack was headed to the room where the autopsy was being performed. The latest victim was found within forty-eight hours of approximated time of death, so it was not in too bad of shape. The first victim was discovered after nearly three weeks and the humid Louisiana air did nothing to help in preserving the evidence. An outdoorsman witnessed chunks of maggot-covered flesh dropping from the trees, when he looked up and saw the fly infested-decomposing carcass of a human. These photos along with photos of the other victims were already being examined by Yeardly Catch, the criminal profiler. Jack interrupted her when he opened the door.

"Ms. Catch?" said Jack after entering the room. He was pleasantly surprised he had a female profiler. "Pleased to meet you I am agent Jack Ward."

"I am Agent Catch!" she said, emphasizing the word '*Agent.*'

"Pardon me, I was just putting my foot in my mouth—anyway I have a difficult case."

"The Pristine Murders, I was getting familiar with the case on the way down."

"Well, let me fill you in on what I know. This guy is tidy, comes in, and does the job. There is no evidence left on the victims, no strange hair, or clothing fibers, he strips away their identity and leaves them to bleed."

"That is the obvious, yes. My job is to point out what may not be so obvious."

She was way too business like for Jack's liking, he did, however, think she had a nice pair of legs. "Why don't you tell me *everything* you know so far." She demanded of Jack.

Agent Catch sat down on the sofa in the small lab, she had the photos of the victims tucked under her arm. As Jack was describing the details of the case she would occasionally pull out the corresponding photo to examine it further, then return it to the envelope. It took roughly half and hour to recap the pertinent facts of the case. When he was done Jack stepped out briefly to refill his cup of coffee. Afterward, he sat patiently while Agent Catch described the killer's personality.

"First let us state the obvious as we did once before. He is a strong man, intelligent, and clever. He attempts to hide what he has done, to a point. He does not intend to hide the bodies, nor does he want to hide the fact that they were murdered. If that were the case he would bury them or tie them down and throw them in a lake or something. Instead he hoists them upward which makes them hard to detect initially, but he knows they will eventually be found. This indicates he is not trying to hide the bodies permanently, just long enough—for what reason I cannot determine at the time.

Somehow he wants them to remain undisturbed for a few days. He is very cautious about identification and goes through great lengths to erase the victim's identity. They were nothing to him, ageless and faceless, they were just another body and he wants the world to see them the same way he does. The pattern of victims, spread out through five states, and the random order in which they were killed suggests he is searching for something. The victims held something he searched for, something he longed for. Unfortunately for the victims the thrill was not real, when fantasy and reality crossed the results were less than satisfying. That's when he becomes angry and kills them. We need to look for a common trait in the victims, strength, beauty, intelligence, or even self-confidence. An admirable trait that one might want to emulate. The killer is a man around thirty five to forty five years old—well educated, probably a teacher of some sort. We are looking for a clean person one who does not care for anything out of place. He is organized and precise, he keeps his appointments and is punctual. He also cares for nature; he is not an outdoorsman or a hunter except he is familiar with their tactics."

"You said…" replied Jack, after listening attentively. "The trait he is looking for is something admirable, but are you sure it is something of personal character he is after? I have absolutely nothing on the victims at this time. If I have to rely on personal information then I am back to square one."

"Precisely, it could be an object or other coveted prize he is after. Until we find out more about the victims, we won't be able to tell if his victims were merely random or cleverly calculated. He may be even playing a game with us, to confuse us. But my best guess is, from the pattern and timing of the murders, is that our culprit is searching for something. He is after something specific."

Jack cursed under his breath and thanked the Agent for her assistance. He was trying to make progress by avoiding the inevitable. He is now faced with what he has known for a long time. The victims must be identified; there is no other way. He must do what his heart tells him he must, no matter how hard it may be. The families of the victims have a right to know, before the month is over there will be eight—out of the thousands of missing persons cases—that will be closed. And the names of those eight, will be attached to the photos of the Pristine victims.

If Gertrude Revner is convinced her grandchild is involved somehow, he will pursue that avenue until it is exhausted, and he will take a serious look this time. But it is the latest victim that must be identified first. That is where the best chance for identification lies.

CHAPTER 16

Serena the Throne

After his informative interview with Mary Beth Reynolds, Dr. Prine was returning to the two-bedroom apartment he was renting in Ventura, California. He was only gone for six hours, but felt that was long enough. He was to leave his son with a woman he knew only though a colleague of his, but when that fell through he ended up leaving his son with a total stranger. Her name was Serena Capistrano, she looked harmless enough, and in the short time she was in Prine's presence she made him feel his son would be safe. How dumb, Prine thought, it must have been his eagerness to interview Mary Beth that influenced him into making a poor decision. Even the exquisite sites of Santa Barbara could not convince him to stay away one second longer.

Unknown to Dr. Prine, was Serena's involvement in the babysitting fiasco. Serena had arranged the whole thing, from the colleague's recommendation, to the original sitter devising an excuse to get out of it. All of the deception was so Serena could have Lexington to herself. She knew of Lexington from years ago and has followed his progress.

Lexington was a child prodigy; his intelligence was far beyond the level most adults would achieve, yet he was only nine years old. Serena was interested in the young boy's developing mind and what it could mean for the earth's future.

Dr. Prine had been using his cell phone for the past two hours trying to contact Serena at the apartment. He called once when the interview was over, leaving a message that he would be home in a couple of hours. The next call was midway through the trip, still he got only the answering machine. Then half an hour away he tried for the third time—now he was beginning to worry. This was someone he knew nothing about, other than where she planned on going to school, and she was with his only son. If something had happened he would have nowhere to turn on finding his son's whereabouts. Prine hurried to the apartment, it was shortly after ten o'clock. He opened the door and called out immediately for his son, there was no response. The answering machine was blinking, he knew three of the messages was his. Maybe there was a fourth message containing information on where they might be.

After playing the messages—there was only three, all left by Prine. He called down to the office, Serena said she stayed at one of the apartments there. Prine was hoping there would be information on who to contact in case of an emergency, they might be able to tell him what apartment Serena was staying. He had just picked up the receiver when Serena came through the door carrying Lexington, who was sound asleep.

"Hi, I didn't know you'd be back already," said Serena.

"Where were you? I have been calling for the past few hours."

"I left a message on your cell phone. Lexington wanted to see where I lived, so I took him over there. He fell asleep after a couple of hours and I didn't know if I could carry him up the stairs. I was waiting until you came over to get him—didn't you get the message on the cell phone?"

That let the wind out of Prine's sails. He was fully prepared to give her a piece of his mind. Now he was afraid to admit he failed to play the message left on his cell phone. He turned the phone off during the interview so he would not be disturbed.

Prine walked up to take Lexington from her arms, his limp body draped over the tall shapely Serena. Prine hoisted his son onto his body and carried him into his son's bedroom. He pulled the covers from Lexington's bed and placed his son down gently. Serena stood at the bedroom entrance and watched as Lexington was tucked away.

"That's a special little man you have," Serena commented.

"Did he behave?" Prine asked, almost ashamed at his previous behavior.

"He was absolutely perfect. He is a very bright young man."

"Lexington has won all sorts of awards, he is quite the young intellectual. I just don't want to deny him of his youth, so I really don't push him. I don't want him to feel pressured to perform; I want him to enjoy his life, every precious second of it. Coming from a teacher I bet that may sound odd to you. But even without my prodding, he has pushed the limits of his mind on his own—and it's *his* choice. He could probably help you out on some of your studies."

"He is that smart?" Serena tried to act surprised at the doctor's comments, but was afraid he would see through her deception. Afraid that Dr. Prine would discover she knew more about Lexington than she initially led on. She decided to cut her conversation with Dr. Prine short, if she were a good enough host he would probably ask her to watch Lexington again.

"Well, I thank you for trusting me with your son. I hope the miscommunication didn't damage your faith in me?" asked Serena.

"What faith? I'm sorry Serena, but I have no idea who you are. I hope you don't have anything planned for the next two hours. You and I are going to sit and talk until I feel comfortable in leaving you two alone. That is…if you are interested in watching him again?"

Serena was speechless, she had no interest in being social with Dr. Prine. Her curiosity with Lexington led her to information about his father, Dr. Walter Prine. Being a very competent psychologist in his field, she wondered how much of his craft would be applied in just a basic conversation. She did not feel comfortable at all in matching wits with Prine, and there was no way he would allow her to watch Lexington again if she refused. Backed into a corner, she did what she felt was her only option. "Sure, Dr. Prine. I wasn't busy at all."

Serena made herself comfortable on the living room couch, while Dr. Prine returned with refreshments. He grabbed the leftover pizza in the refrigerator—he had not eaten since midday. Prine sat on the sofa with Serena, placed her drink on the coffee table in front of her, along with sixty dollars, then leaned back and took a bite of his pizza.

"Serena," Prine said with a full mouth, "you must tell me how you got so tall?" Humor was always a good icebreaker.

"I just came out this way. Why, does it make you feel uneasy?"

"It doesn't matter—man or woman, who ever has more than four inches on me has my attention." Serena continued to laugh, "But I must add that you carry it gracefully."

"Thank you Dr. Prine." Prine recognized her stunning beauty, but chose not to comment on it. He preferred to keep the discussion strictly professional, however there was one thing he was willing to mention.

"You are wearing an exquisite fragrance, I never smelled anything like it."

Serena's first stumbling block, she was hoping he would ignore the scent, this was clearly something she wanted to avoid.

"I got it from Paris, at a small shop. I doubt if they sell it anywhere in the United States."

"That's okay. I wasn't interested in buying it for myself, it was just the first thing I noticed about you—well the second." After a moment of silence, Prine could sense Serena was uncomfortable with talking about herself. He decided to take the conversation down a more traditional path.

"Tell me about your parents, they are forking out a lot of money for your education. Letting you stay alone in an apartment off campus, they must be trusting and generous. What do they do for a living?"

Serena was interrupted by a knock on the door. "I have no idea who that could be," Prine commented. "I'll be right back." Prine went to answer the door. When he opened it there was a man, dressed impeccably, standing in the doorway.

"Is Serena here?" The man asked, "I received a message that she would be here." Prine turned toward Serena. "Apparently, you forgot someone was coming to visit you this evening," said Prine. The doctor opened the door wide enough for the man to enter; Serena recognized him as he came into view.

"Rapheal?"

Serena was unpleasantly surprised.

"I got the message and came to pick you up. I was worried. I have not seen you in a while and I didn't want to wait another day," said Raphael.

"You shouldn't have." Serena responded, trying to curtail her anger. "Dr. Prine, this is a friend of mine, Raphael."

"Pleased to meet you Raphael." Prine reached out to shake Raphael's hand and something happened. His mind was ensnared with thoughts of anger, he felt strange, as if they were natural enemies. Images of Prine's haunting dream came to mind, he felt as if a feeling of camaraderie had gone bad. His handshake was longer than normal, he would not let go of Raphael's hand. There was something familiar, he was at the brink of figuring it out, but the answer eluded him.

"I am ready to go," said Serena, stepping between the two men. Serena's distraction was enough that Prine finally let go of Raphael.

"Tomorrow at one o'clock I have an appointment. Do you think you will be able to watch Lexington for a few hours?" Prine was talking to Serena, while looking around her—his eyes fixated on Raphael. Serena moved over slightly completely blocking his view of the Raphael before answering.

"One o'clock is fine with me, I will be here."

Prine could not shake the strange feeling he got around Raphael. He closed the door after they had departed, and returned to his pizza.

"What are you doing here?" said Serena on her way to the apartment.

"I thought you would need my help. I noticed you were in there longer than you should. A professor of psychology is not a good person for someone like you to be chatting with." Raphael replied.

"I had things under control. By the way what are you doing...following me?"

"Maybe I would not have to if you kept me informed. I have not heard from you in a couple of days."

"I have nothing to tell you. There—that was easy! I don't appreciate you invading my space."

"You are here for a specific purpose yet you choose to pursue that young child. Leave him alone!" Raphael demanded, "He is none of your concern."

"The safety of *all* children are my concern Raphael."

"Well you are not doing a very good job at ensuring their future is secure. The angelic counsel wants a report on the latest disturbances regarding a certain fallen one. You have slacked off in your duties. Now what will I tell them? My chief throne has taken to babysitting? How absurd! You will do what you came to do."

At this point Serena figured it was fruitless to argue, once Raphael has made up his mind there would be no changing it. Raphael was like few others gracious enough to walk the earth, he was not of this world. He was an angel—even better—an archangel. Born of the

Heavens; crafted by God. Raphael: One of the seven most powerful beings in existence.

The angelic counsel, with help from the archangels, attend to Heaven's more delicate matters. They were left to govern the universe created by God. Earth is but one of their many responsibilities. There has been numerous events recorded in the past twenty-five years that have the angels of Heaven concerned. They know all cannot remain quiet for long. Eventually the fallen ones, the angels who have fallen from God's grace will reemerge in an attempt to dethrone the counsel.

This war, which originated shortly after the beginning of Heaven's existence, has it's moments of inactivity, but it is far from over. It is the job of archangels like Raphael, to ensure that Heaven receives no surprises.

"There is a lot of activity in this area Serena. We are all counting on you." Raphael opened the door to Serena's apartment, with her eyes toward the ground she walked inside like a child who has been scolded. "There is another thing before I go. Dr. Prine held onto my hand for a long time. Is there something about him you neglected to tell me?"

"There is, but I will not tell you at this time. I am not positive. When I confirm it then I will tell you."

"I doubt if it is very important. He seems insignificant."

"Goodnight Raphael." Serena closed the door. She could not lie to Heaven's soldiers, it was forbidden. She would risk being cast out of Heaven herself. Serena was also an angel. Nowhere near as powerful as Raphael, but she has been given a task of great importance. She is one of one hundred watchers that roam the universe, she is an angel under the title of Throne. Not much separate the fallen angels from the ones of Heaven, the difference is the Heavenly angels abide by all of Heaven's laws.

Lying for the sake of deception, to another of Heaven's angels, is forbidden. Her punishment would be to join the fallen ones as an outcast, never to be admitted into Heaven again. Serena was careful about what she said to Raphael. She did not agree to do as he instructed, nor did Serena hide the fact that she knew something regarding Dr. Prine origins. Serena was free to continue doing as she planned for the time being. But Serena knew she would not be able to get away with it for long. Raphael was no one to toy with, and playing games with the angelic counsel could cost her the price of eternal suffering. In her view that would never happen, she was on to something few angels had the insight to understand, and this eternal war may finally come to an end, through her angelic intuition.

CHAPTER 17

Dorothy's Secret

Wednesday—midweek though the upcoming historic seventh annual Miracle ceremony. This was typically the busiest week for Colleen Rigetti, assistant to Reverend Roland Stark. Her job was to clean up the odds and ends, and ensure all flowed smoothly—especially for this Sunday. She had been intercepting calls all week regarding the miracle selectee, and why a man has yet to be chosen to receive this great gift of power.

Mostly inquiring reporters and column writers have been flooding the office with messages, but there have been a few callers expressing their anger at being denied an opportunity. Jealousy begins to seep into the hearts of those who believe they are more deserving; that they have suffered more, or devoted their lives to God. Yet, they were passed by once again. It was a tough time for one woman trying to keep it all together.

Colleen's husband and children have learned, this is a week they will see very little of her. To make up for the gross inconvenience she will have all of the following week off, just to devote time to her family. Roland demanded it. He understands the importance of family and he appreciates what Colleen does for him.

Whenever times get rough for Colleen, she thinks about the upcoming reward for a job well done, and that usually gets her through the day. Her morning began promptly at seven o'clock. She called the private cell phone number of the guard she hired to look after Sheryl O'Connor. After getting a report of the previous day's and night's events, she grabbed a quick snack and headed to her office at the Hall of Kings facility.

Colleen's office is on the upper levels of the complex; a beautiful 1,400 square foot private space with hand crafted furniture and sliding glass door leading to the balcony. She had a marvelous view of the surrounding city, but she seldom had the time to appreciate its beauty.

Colleen had her ear to the phone, going through the arrangements for this upcoming Sunday. Ensuring all of the deliveries, the concessions people, and the camera crews were on schedule, and had access to where they needed to be. After three hours Colleen was starting to feel the stress of her tremendous responsibilities. She needed a break. She decided to take a walk to the soda machine located on the third floor. Off she went—a relaxing stroll will do her some good. In the stairwell, she met the first of the roaming guards.

"Afternoon Mrs. Rigetti," the guard said gleefully.

"Good Afternoon, Roy," she replied

Today was normally a day off for the workers at the Kings facility. That was for everyone except Colleen of course. The Hall was relatively empty. Even Roland Stark was at home relaxing—the calm before the storm. Colleen figured there would probably be a few others besides her crazy enough to come in today, but she did not ask the guards who they were. On her floor, the only occupied office was her's. When she arrived on the third floor lounge she nosed around the snack machines to see if there was anything worth eating. She did not spend too much time there before moving on to grab a soda.

"This sucks!"

The machine was out of Pepsi. She did not bother with diet soda—it was her favorite—or nothing. There was another lounge room on the first floor, after going all this way, she was not returning to her office without getting her drink. Off Colleen went to the stair-well once more. This time traveling down two more flights of stairs until she reached the first floor. There, she ran into a few more secu-rity guards. These were not so friendly as the first; they did not work her floor and did not know her personally. They did, however, recog-nize her as someone of importance in the organization and treated her accordingly.

"Good afternoon Ma'am," one of the guards said, after recogniz-ing her face.

"I won't be down here too long, just going to get a drink in the lounge."

Colleen had been here since the very beginning of the organiza-tion, from the time they struggled to keep one hundred members, until now. On this day, while simply going to get a soda, the growth of the organization finally hit her. "What is with all the security?" she asked herself.

Now, she was curious. There were parts of the establishment in which she never traveled. Areas of the arena, and personnel, that she has never seen. In that short period of time Colleen made up her mind to do some exploring. She was Roland's chief assistant for goodness sake. She had a right to know everyone who worked here. The first floor lounge room's beverage machine had the drink she was looking for. With her soda in hand, she began exploring the Hall of Kings.

Colleen stopped by each guard and introduced herself. She stopped by each office space, whether it was occupied or not. Colleen even took a grand tour of the arena seating area. More than two hours past as she explored every facet of the facility until finally she ended up on familiar ground. She was at the entrance way to the altar, this was were she ended up every week, watching the service from this spot. Colleen's expedition excursion was beneficial in uplifting her spirits. She had been feeling down because of the added pressure of the upcoming event. Now she felt relaxed enough to tackle the rest of the obstacles that lie before her.

Colleen walked to the elevator, although she explored mostly by walking, she was ready to take the quickest means possible back to her office. After entering the elevator she noticed two buttons leading to the lower basement levels. She figured…why not? Go down and check the place out. She had gone this far, why not go all the way. When the elevator door opened at level B2 she saw what resembled a huge storage space. Colleen stepped out to walk around a bit when she was abruptly greeted by two security guards.

"You are not authorized to be down here," one of them said. "You will have to return to the main floor."

"Sure, I'm authorized to be here. I am Colleen Rigetti; Roland's chief assistant. I just came to check out what's down here."

"I know who you are Mrs. Rigetti."

That left Colleen at a loss for words. The conviction in which the guard spoke convinced her that he was serious.

"I don't understand," she said, "you're telling me that the assistant to Roland Stark is not authorized to be down here?"

"This space is controlled by Jericho Black! If you want to gain entrance to the lower basement levels you have to go through him."

"Jericho Black, our sponsor?" said Colleen, befuddled by the guard's statement. "Well, what the hell down here is so important that it has to be secured by two guards?" Just as Colleen completed her question three more guards came from around one of the crates. They were carrying an object into the next room over.

"How many rooms are there, and how many guards are down here?" Colleen insisted.

"Please Mrs. Rigetti, the person you should be contacting is Jericho Black. I am not at liberty to discuss any of that with you. Now if you would please…"

The guard extended his arm showing Colleen the way back to the elevator. She stood there rebellious, refusing to leave. But then thought better of it and headed back to the elevator. Once she was inside she pressed the button to level B3 instead of the main floor. The elevator began to move upward, it took her all the way back to her office on the upper level of the facility.

"Bullshit!"

Just minutes before—her spirits were uplifted. Now she was furious. The security was turning into a military type atmosphere. This was a place of worship, not somewhere for secrets and confidentiality. She marched straight to her office, grabbed her belongings, and headed back out the door. She was going straight to Roland's place. Colleen doubted Roland was aware of all that was going on at the Hall of Kings. Especially, their sponsor, Jericho Black's, involvement.

At the front gate of Roland's estate—more security. Colleen's visit had to be called in before the gate was opened. That infuriated her even further. During the eighth of a mile drive to the front door of Roland's mansion, Colleen thought of all sorts of interesting phrases she could use to express her anger. Once she got to the front door, she had calmed down enough to use some restraint. This was a man of God. She needs to express her opinions to Roland without becoming overemotional. Roland, personally opened the door and invited Colleen inside.

"Pleasure to see you this evening Colleen. I was just watching television, seeing how badly the media is treating our young girl. Do you know they have already got her routine down? We may have to move her to some undisclosed location."

"Roland…" she paused before continuing, "there is something I want to tell you that you may not be aware of. It's about your ministry." She paused again.

"Well spit it out girl, this sounds important."

"I…Did you ever notice how many cameras there are around the arena?"

"You mean at the Hall of Kings? Yeah, well there are cameras placed in locations to catch all angles when I am on stage."

"No, Roland, there are cameras all over the place—On every floor, in every space. I took a tour today."

"You did? Good, I always wanted to do that. I was just much too busy to get to it."

"Stop jabbering and listen. There were less than twenty people at work there today, yet there are over fifty security guards there right now. Not only that, but there are more cameras watching your every move, than there is in all of Hollywood. I went into the lower areas today. You know level B2? There is an area down there that looks like a storage area, and when I asked one of the guards for a tour, he refused. He said he wasn't at liberty to discuss what went on down there. Is that crazy or what?"

"Was it a big guy? I think he just doesn't like you or something." Roland began to chuckle in amusement. "You sound like there is some kind of conspiracy or something going on down there. That is where they store equipment and supplies, things like that. They are not hiding anything from you."

"Then why wasn't I allowed to see it. I am your chief assistant."

"Gee, I don't know. They were probably busy. I wouldn't make much of it."

"No, that's not it Roland. When I asked what was down there they did not answer. They didn't even tell me that they worked for you. They said to see Jericho Black. So what does Jericho have down there that we are not supposed to know about?"

"Okay Colleen listen. I think you are overreacting on this one, but just to settle things I will talk to Jericho in the morning."

"I want to be there!" she insisted.

"The way you are right now, I don't think so. You need to cool off. The stress is getting to you. Look, I will talk to Jericho tomorrow, ask him about the spaces in the lower levels, and come back with an answer for you—how's that?"

It was a substandard response as far as Colleen was concerned, but for now, it would have to do.

❧   ❧   ❧

FBI agent Jack Ward was getting dizzy from all of his trips across the country. He had just flown back into California. The visit with the forensics lab was a bust. Although he received all the interesting scientific data he could handle—and then some, the end result was something he knew all along. He must try and identify the victims in the Pristine murders or else he will not get any further than he is right now.

All Jack has now is a bunch of bodies. How this all ties in to what Gertrude Revner claims—he has no idea. A little more than a week ago he asked a psychologist, Dr. Walter Prine to investigate the Miracle phenomena. It seemed a far cry from the case he was working on now. The only thread of evidence linking the two was carpet fibers found on one of the victims. The fibers were proven to come from a lot of carpets installed on a particular brand of vehicle. That vehicle was the same one Cindy Revner's driver license was found in, and the history of rentals traces that car to being rented by the Reborn Kings around the time of the third victim's death.

In the grand scheme of investigations the evidence was all merely circumstantial. So why was Jack, a skilled and heralded investigator taking advice from an old woman in a nursing home? Because he really had nothing else to go on. Walter Prine was scheduled to meet Jack for the second time. Prine had just completed his interview with the first miracle member, Mary Beth Reynolds. From his phone conversation, Prine had a different avenue he believed had not been explored to the fullest. He asked for Jack to bring the FBI's copy of the church shooting. Prine said the tape revealed some interesting facts. This was promising news, maybe with this new information, Jack could revisit the Kings ministry, and maybe discover who was driving the car in which Cindy's license was found.

There was no restaurant meeting this time. The two were to meet in the lobby of the hotel where Jack was staying. Of course he was not there, he had not checked in yet. Jack was too busy being on the road, but he did not forget. Soon after Prine entered the lobby Jack arrived, and he brought the tape just as Dr. Prine suggested. Jack was a smooth character, he walked into the lobby like he owned the place. Prine noticed his presence right away.

"Oh, please. Give me a break." Prine mumbled to himself.

"There's my man." Jack walked over to Prine, constantly distracted by every skirt that walked by. "I love California doctor. How about you, have you blended in with your surroundings yet?"

"Like a chameleon."

"You need to ditch that preppy look Doctor. That look went out in the eighty's."

"You are just jealous, women prefer the intellectual type."

"Boy you sure know where to hit a guy where it hurts. Give me a minute to check in, then we'll head up to my suite."

Prine and Jack joked around as if they were old friends. In their fields it was rare to find someone which they enjoyed being around. After reaching the suite, Prine made himself comfortable on the couch. Jack joined him shortly after trading his shoes for a nice pair of house slippers.

"You talked to Mary Beth?" Jack started off, "What interesting things did she have to say?"

"She started out with the same old story, but I was able to distract her enough to have her retell it using different words. She mentioned how she got to the church and why she sat where she did. Her friend picked the seats, she claimed they were the best seats in the house."

"Were they?"

"When I looked at a copy of her tape it appears that way. In fact everything she said, down to the finest details, were contained on that tape."

"So what is your latest discovery? You didn't get me all excited unless you have a latest discovery."

"The friend of hers named Dorothy. Mary Beth described everything that was going on until she got shot. Then her account of what went on was blurry. While the camera crews were focused on her I wanted to know what her friend was doing. Nothing special at first—I just thought, if I were in her shoes I would feel terrible. If I had tried for weeks to convince my friend to attend church and she accidentally got shot there I would feel incredibly depressed. I wouldn't want to leave her side. I would probably be begging her forgiveness with every breath. All people react different to similar situations—Dorothy's actions were just plain strange."

"I wanna see what you're talking about. Give me a minute." Jack retrieved the tape from his bag and inserted it into the VCR. "How far do I have to take it."

"Fast forward it to after the shooting," said Prine. "…Here, play the tape. Concentrate on this woman in the far right corner. Her behavior is normal for this situation; she's panicking and confused. Now she runs to the back room, to the rear of the church. Here she is again a minute later, she has someone else with her."

"That's Jericho Black! I thought that slick money grubber got involved with the church after the miracle. He's a big time entrepreneur that can smell success. He's got a lot of projects going on at once, all worth mega-bucks. He *is* good. He must have seen Roland's talent and knew he would be somebody one day. Those rich bastards always get the breaks. Anyway, he is the reason we can't get close to the ministry, his money and political influence keeps even the FBI at bay."

"They walk in and out of the camera for a while, I can't really see what they are doing. Now, they come back in—do you see her?"

"She's still talking to him."

"No, she's pleading with him. She's begging him. Now watch—what ever she says just then convinces him to help. Now she repeats it again, just to make sure she heard it right the first time. He makes his way through the crowd, and talks to Roland. Then he reaches through and touches Mary Beth—right by the gunshot wound. She grimaces, then he runs off. He is out of view for several minutes you can't see him but you can see Dorothy rather clearly. She looks over to the side, then she clasps both hands together in front of her face. Pause the tape."

Jack hit the pause button, a hand came into the picture, passing another man the challis in which the water that made history was contained."

"Dorothy looks like she was praying, but I think she was relieved."

"So you are saying this is a scam of some kind. What do you think is happening?"

"I don't know exactly, I am simply going off of Dorothy's behavior. But, I believe there is some sort drug involved."

"I got you. Possibly an experimental drug that has yet to be approved. Jericho has his hands on many different projects. Maybe, he came across a miracle drug during one of his many business ventures. He is probably trying to fund it. It would make him filthy rich if he could prove it works. Let's say hypothetically that was true, how would that girl Dorothy know about it?"

"Dorothy worked with Mary Beth as an insurance adjuster. Do you suppose new drug companies insure their experiments, especially ones they perceive as highly profitable?"

"I have no idea Dr. Prine. That's one I will have to check out. So you think this girl Dorothy let her friend become a human guinea pig."

"What did she have to lose? The wound was fatal, except I think the drug worked better than any of them expected. What I can't figure out is why Jericho did not decide to sell the rights to the drug. Seven years of development, surely it would be ready for the open market by now."

"I think I can answer that one for you Prine. Think of what happens when a new drug hits the market. Have you heard of reverse engineering? The other pharmaceutical companies will dissect the drug to see how it works. They get a basic idea of the major components, then change it slightly without decreasing its effectiveness and…Viola! They escape patent laws, stick a generic label on it, and have a drug 'just as good' as the original while selling it for less. But this accident was probably the best thing that could happen. They don't have to go through the millions of dollars spent in research and development, they don't have to get FDA approval, and they virtually have no competition. Religion is big business, but best of all its tax-free…You derived all of that from the reaction of one woman. Prine you really are the man!"

"It's just a theory. First you have to prove that there is a drug. Without that, it's all theory. The person handing the challis over is Jericho Black, we can't see him, but that's his hand. There is one thing I need from you. Before I interview Dorothy I need to know what she says to Jericho. The video does not have good sound quality, however there is a clear shot of her speaking. I was hoping you could take it to someone who is good at reading lips. Maybe they can determine what Dorothy is saying."

"Look no further, I am an expert at it. One of those special hobbies of mine. After staring at people through binoculars year after year you develop certain skills."

Jack rewound the tape to the exact spot he needed. After several attempts, he failed to decipher what was being said. The video quality was far too poor for something like lip reading.

"Prine, let's go. I am going to take this tape to a television studio. They will have the enhancement equipment I need to view this properly."

Prine and Jack drove to the local television studio. Jack walked in and flexed the muscle of his FBI badge; soon he was set up in a studio with his own studio engineer. His name was Brian Wooldridge.

Brian was a skinny kid with glasses and a whiny-pitched nasal voice. Jack preferred to have someone else, but was told by the station manager that Brian was the best. So he went against his instinct and decided to give the kid a shot. *He really had no say in the matter.*

"Brian," said Jack, "there is an image I want you to focus in on. It's awful blurry and I am hoping you can clear that up for us."

Brian responded, "That depends on a lot of factors—first we need to know what quality the tape was recorded on. The quality of the camera, the film that was used, and how long ago was it recorded. It also depends if this is a duplicate or the original. Then we need to know what size image are you trying to focus in on, and how fine the detail are you expecting to pick out. If you want to read the year on a quarter or something like that you can forget it. Most recorders don't clarify things in that fine of a pixel range unless it was recorded digitally. And then…"

"Shut up, for a minute," said Jack. "I don't want to hear a bunch of technical crap. In the past twenty-four hours I have enough scientific jargon to write a journal with. I simply want to read a woman's lips on this tape—that's all!"

Brian took exception to Jack's rudeness. "I don't have to work under these conditions Mr. FBI man. I was just patriotic enough to take pride in doing something for my country. But I would appreciate some professional decency when I am doing my job."

Prine watched as Jack's eyes widened. He thought this would be a good time to intervene before it got ugly.

"Look Brian," said Prine. "My partner hasn't had much sleep lately. What we need is very simple. There is a woman, who is not the main point of focus for the camera. She passes some important information on to an informant. Now national security is at stake here. You are dedicated to your country and we appreciate it. See what you can do."

"Oh...my..." said Jack. "I heard all the crap I can take for one day. I will be roaming around the studio, call me when you get the info—will ya."

Jack left, and Brian was glad to see him go.

"Your friend is high strung."

"Comes with the job, let's get going."

Brian worked, as Prine pointed out exactly what he needed. They located Dorothy on the tape, zoomed in on her image, and started the enhancement process. The tape was duplicated several times which made it very difficult to get a clear image. After one hour of digital imaging they were able to achieve a desirable result. Prine called Jack into the studio to analyze the video. He played the newly enhanced portion over several times until Jack came up with these words—"She is the one working the case."

"Are you sure that's what she is saying?" asked Prine.

"Pretty sure. It doesn't quite play into what we theorized, but it is something to work with."

"'She is the one working the case.' What case that could be?" Prine wondered.

"I don't think going back to Mary Beth to ask her is wise. The best route is through her old place of employment. Obtain a record of everything she had been working on at that time and see if anything has Jericho Black's paw prints on it. The rest is up to you Prine. You need to interview Dorothy. Do your thing once again. Maybe you can draw the information from her."

"Mary Beth said that Dorothy had lost her faith, she no longer attended church or did anything of that sort. She must know something. The greatest miracle to modern man proven scientifically, caught on video and you being right in the middle of it, turning your back on religion a couple of years later? I don't buy it. She knows something about this whole miracle situation."

"Great job, Prine. Give me a call when you set up the meeting with Dorothy."

CHAPTER 18

The Shooter

Jericho Black is the wealthy entrepreneur responsible for bringing Roland Stark and the Reborn Kings Ministry out from mediocrity and into the limelight. With the seventh annual Miracle Ceremony only a few days away, Jericho was making some last minute inquiries to ensure everything was on schedule. He took his job seriously, primarily because he loved money. Most of the people working for Jericho say his love of money is second only to his cold personality. He rarely has more than a few words to say to anyone, unless they have an interest in fattening his bank account. He is a fierce investor with a nose for profits.

That day, Roland Stark came by the office unannounced. Roland was concerned about Colleen's claim of some secretive operations occurring on the lower levels of the Hall of Kings facility. After being announced in by his assistant, Jericho Black openly welcomed Roland into his office.

"What brings you here today, Roland? Is something wrong?"

Roland ensured he was seated comfortably before answering.

"We rarely see each other anymore Jericho. How have you been doing?"

Jericho's facial expression showed he was in no mood to socialize.

"I am rather busy Roland with last minute arrangements preparing for Sunday's ceremony. I hope you did not come here just to visit."

"No, I didn't. There are things I guess I have not paid much attention to lately. I guess I've been too busy myself to notice. I just came from the Hall of Kings and noticed the security there…Don't you think it is a bit excessive?"

"Not at all."

It was blunt and to the point.

"Are there any other issues you wish to discuss, Roland?"

From Jericho's viewpoint *that* subject was closed.

"Wait a minute Jericho, I want to discuss this further. My people feel threatened by all the guards roaming around down there."

"It's simple Roland. If your people are where they are supposed to be, and they stay out of security's way, they will be fine. There haven't been any reported cases of the guards grabbing one of your people. So where's the complaint coming from?"

"Colleen was in at work yesterday and one of the guards gave her a hard time."

"Which one, I will get to the bottom of this immediately." Jericho picked the phone up from the receiver.

"It was on level B2," said Roland.

Jericho placed the phone back down on the table.

"What was she doing on level B2? There is nothing on level B2 that has anything to do with her."

"What is on level B2?" Roland asked curiously.

"My personal business papers! I do have an interest in the facility. That is where I store my secure documents!"

"You don't have to get loud with me Jericho, I was just asking. Those guys would not even answer her questions. It just shook her up a bit that's all."

"My guards take their jobs seriously, as they should. That is what I pay them for."

Roland was not done with the questioning. He was just getting started.

"I happened to notice the number of camera's around the arena when I visited this morning. What are they for?"

"It helps the guards watch your ass—what do you think Roland."

"You don't have to be rude all the time. I was just saying that when I visited the security room it did not look like they had access to all the cameras. I was thinking most of them were probably for show and wasn't hooked up to anything at all."

Jericho tried to calm himself; the questions were getting under his skin. The majority of the cameras were connected to monitors on level B3. This was where Roland personally monitored the activity of the entire arena and controlled his security guards from. Whether Jericho had a fetish or it was simply paranoia, he was determined not to be taken by surprise.

"Okay, Roland here is the scoop. I am going to say this slowly so that I don't have to repeat myself ever again. The security in the place is for your protection, Colleen's protection, and the stinking protection of everyone in the place. It is something that cannot be taken for granted, nor can it be overlooked. With the amount of people that frequent the place every week we need to ensure that they will be safe. Psycho's come in all forms—you know that. I am trying to ensure a safe environment for good people who come to worship together."

Roland was satisfied. He felt bad for overreacting to the situation with Colleen.

"Sorry, Jericho. I just had to investigate it. It just seemed odd that's all."

"I hope I put your concerns to rest Roland. You're a great man and a great leader. I want to make sure you remain with us for as long as possible."

"That decision is purely in God's hands."

"Sure Roland."

Roland Stark rose from his seat in Jericho's office and began to leave. He stopped just short of the door and turned around. He remembered something else.

"There has been a report that one of our employees has turned up missing. He works on the lighting, his name is…"

"Orlando James," Jericho interrupted, "I have received the news also. He does work for me after all. I have his time card; he just hasn't showed up. I was just about to give the order to terminate him. I can't have people taking time off whenever they wish."

"Jericho, the family has asked me to pray for him—this is not like him. I just wanted to know if he actually showed up at work last Sunday."

"Yes, he was here. I have his time card. It shows he came—punched in and punched out at the normal time."

"Alright, just do me a favor. Could you hold off another couple of days before firing him."

Jericho nodded in agreement. It was only a matter of time before Jericho would make the termination final. Orlando James stumbled onto something he should not have while adjusting the lighting last Sunday. Jericho was positive he was not coming back—ever!

After Roland had left, Jericho Black picked up the phone and called the head security guard on level B2 of the Kings facility.

"I just heard Colleen Rigetti was down on that level a few days ago…You did not think something like that was important enough to report immediately…I won't expect another mistake like that from you…Did you dispose of the ball and its contents? You better have…And make sure you get a blood sample from Sheryl O'Connor…How? The same way we always get it. She is scheduled for an examination today! Go to the hospital lab and acquire a sample…And it better be her blood or you will be seeing yours!"

❧   ❧   ❧

Prine has faced many challenges before, mostly from one-time phenomena which are very difficult to prove of disprove. In the world of psychology, one-time events can hardly be used to draw any conclusions on. But here is a situation with the Miracle ceremonies—there are six total, and each one has scientific proof of its validity. The evidence is relatively flawless from a researcher's standpoint. As a victim of his own private torment known only to Gertrude Revner and himself, the source of this power could probably shed some light on Prine's own unique situation. The answer might bring closure to the nightmares.

For more than ninety years, Prine has not aged and he has not been ill. For some that would be considered a blessing, but the fear of not knowing how you got that way, made his situation most unnerving. Who was his mother? Who was his father? These are some of the things he wanted to know. He carries dreams of previous lives inside his head; they revisit him each nigh as he sleeps, reminding him of his torment. Cursed, is the only thing Prine can figure happened to him, and his dreams serve as clues to uncovering the secrets of his past.

It is time to put a closure to his life, he knows this, there is nowhere left for him to hide. An old person, like Gertrude, from his past could identify him. If anyone of importance took the claim seriously, Prine feared he would end up in a lab somewhere being poked and prodded. His unique situation was something mankind would want to benefit from.

He has no family, no lineage, no proof of origin; his fear of someone exposing him is only the beginning. He would be a project, and time would be on the scientist's side. Why not? They had an eternity to figure out his secret. Generations of scientists could hand down the project to their siblings until they got the answers they sought.

Existing as an experiment was not the way Prine wished to live out eternity.

His curse was so chilling that he felt there was a method of torture connected with it. He could not die, but whenever anyone around him did, he could sense it. He could feel their essence traveling to another plane. The death of a person nearby was like a drug—a feeling of nirvana. So enticing that he sought out the passing of a human life. It was a soothing feeling of relief, which he could not explain. A mild sort of comfort for a tormented soul.

Everything in Prine's life he considered sporadic and incomplete, but this miracle, whether it was authentic or not, was monumental. Whoever was behind it could possibly solve his mystery.

This would be another day of travelling along the California coast. Prine was going to visit Dorothy Grablford, once known as Dorothy Clark. She was the old friend of Mary Beth Reynolds, and was responsible for introducing Mary Beth to the ministry. Dorothy was not as privileged as Mary Beth and lived by modest means in comparison. Unlike Prine's previous meetings, this one was not arranged in advance.

Dorothy's actions made it highly unlikely that she would agree to be interviewed. So Prine decided the object of surprise was the best option. Dorothy was a happily married woman and a mother of three young children; she lived in a three-bedroom home not too far from Ohai, California. Jack Ward pulled the strings and provided Prine the information he needed to get to the front door. Hopefully Prine could pull off the rest.

"Good afternoon, I was wondering if I could speak to Dorothy."

Dorothy's husband stood at the door momentarily. He then suspiciously went to retrieve his wife. Dorothy came to the door a few seconds later.

"Can I help you?" she asked.

"I am Dr. Walter Prine. I am doing research on the Miracle phenomena. I recently visited Mary Beth Reynolds and…"

"Stop right there Mr. Prine, that is very old news. It is a subject I do not wish to discuss—goodbye."

"Wait," Prine insisted, "let me be totally honest with you."

Prine thought the conversation might go this way and came up with a back up plan.

"I am working with the FBI, I am an analyst and psychologist. When I examined the tape I noticed your behavior. It stood out as being strange. I believe you have held a tremendous secret for seven years—I am not positive…I just have my suspicions. The man we believe you are protecting is Jericho Black."

Dorothy thought she would never hear that name again.

"If you want Jericho Black, I am afraid I cannot help you. I don't know much about him."

"Sure you do."

Prine was now recalling information sent to him straight from FBI investigators about Jericho Black during the time of the Mary Beth was shot.

"I know that the company you worked for, was dealing with Black Inc. I know that you personally worked on insuring rare items for Jericho. Artifacts uncovered by his team of archeologists. Both you and Mary Beth were working on something for Jericho during the time of Mary Beth's shooting. Funny thing, is that Jericho was there also. On the tape, I saw the both of you talking."

"What is your point?"

It did not seem like she was going to be easily persuaded to cooperate. Prine felt it was time to get nasty.

"When we arraign Jericho Black for attempted murder, we will bring you in as well…Now is the time to straighten out your story."

Dorothy was defiantly amused by Prine's threat.

"You can't scare me that easily. If I even think about speaking against Jericho he will know. I am aware of what Jericho can do. Compared to him, your threat was nowhere near as effective. I'll take my chances with the FBI—Goodbye!"

Dorothy closed the door on Dr. Prine and the meeting was over.

❖   ❖   ❖

After five solid days on the road, sleeping in the car, and dining in rest stops, Thad, William, and July arrive in Nevada. The three have plans to capture Sheryl O'Connor, the woman chosen for this Sunday's historic Miracle ceremony. Driven by William's intense desire to get back at the Reborn Kings Ministry, he figured this was the best way to hit them where it hurts. The trio was tired and wanted to find a quiet place to relax. A place that would not attract too much attention, while they formulated their next plan.

From the intense publicity they were able to identify the town Sheryl lived in, they then found room at a motel in that same town. They each took turns freshening up, washing away the foul smell from five days of being cooped up in a small car. It was Thad's turn in the shower. William and July did not like each other. They were constantly at each other's throats. The robbery they pulled off in Rockaway eased the tension slightly. William felt she had to prove herself before he considered her part of the group.

In his opinion she earned that trust and more. July had to shoot one of the cocky security members of the neighborhood gambling establishment to show him she meant business. They never discussed the shooting incident during the entire trip down. July felt that if the others did not mention it, she would not bring it up either. With Thad in the shower William thought it was the perfect time to discuss it, without intrusion from Thad.

After several minutes William broke the ice. "So...what did it feel like?" July remained silent.

"You know what I am talking about girl. Did you smoke him or just grazed him?"

Without even raising her head, she responded. "He went down, that's all you need to know."

"That's what I'm talkin' about. So how did it feel? You felt that rush of adrenaline? It felt good didn't it. Some people just don't understand how a person could kill somebody. I know—it is a feeling of power. Can't everybody do it. You see some people hold a gun, point it at someone, and just shake like they got a vibrator stuck in their ass. Scared to death if they had to pull the trigger. If you're gonna play the game, you better play it all the way through. That's what my daddy taught me. If you're not prepared to shoot don't even pick it up. I'm proud of you girl. There are grown men, men in prison even, that wish they could do what you did."

July just listened. She did not agree, but she did not want to fight about it. She wanted to forget it; she wanted to erase the whole thing from her mind. That young, cocky jerk did not deserve to get shot. She felt it was her fault for not being intimidating enough. She did not take control as Thad had showed her. For that, a young man was possibly dead. It was something that did not make the headlines where they were, so July had know idea what happened to the young man. July looked for it in the newspaper everyday, while following the exploits of Sheryl O'Connor. In contrast, Sheryl's story was all over the papers.

July began to get impatient, Thad her boyfriend, was taking a long time in the shower. Thad was the buffer between her and William. She loathed William. July felt he was a phony the minute she saw him. She just waited for the opportunity to prove it.

"I didn't take too long did I?" said Thad after exiting the bathroom.

"Hell yea baby bro," William answered. "We need to plan our next move."

Thad got dressed and joined the others by the coffee table at the rear of the motel room. He listened to William's plan for capturing Sheryl O'Connor; it was plain and simple. Storm the house, grab the girl, and hold her until 11:00 p.m. Sunday. William was proud of himself and his plan. He left the motel room to track down a street map. Before he returned to the room he stopped at a local bar. William cleverly struck a conversation with someone who knew about Sheryl and where she lived. However, back at the motel, Thad and July thought the plan was disastrous. The two confided in private about the plan and William's obsession.

"This is a far cry from the first plan," said July. "I was beginning to think he was hiding a brain in under that mat of hair."

"The heist was good! The best he has ever come up with. We are going to get nowhere this time. We have to think of something else."

"Why does he want Roland Stark so bad, Thad?"

"He just does not like him. Roland reminds him of another preacher…One of William's old buddies, his best friend from when they were kids, started listening to a certain preacher. He used to be a terror, even worse than William was. William told me how cold his friend used to be—he didn't take shit from no one. He got caught one day, snatching purses from women on the street, and they sent him away to Juvenile.

Now for this guy it was nothing new, he had been to 'Juvie' before. But when he came out this time he was different. He started going to school, improved on his grades, he turned his attitude completely around. He didn't shun William away; he invited him into his new life. His friend introduced William to a counselor, an up and coming preacher. This guy was good with words and talked to William on several occasions. William said he almost fell for it.

Then it happened—William's best friend was coming home from the movies. He was confronted by some of his old enemies, they heard he had gone soft. William's friend stood there, he refused to be sucked back into that old game, and they killed him.

Eyewitnesses say that the boy acted like nothing they did could hurt him. He did not run—he began to pray. They stabbed him in the heart with a thud—'boom' and made sure he was dead. The articles in the papers told his whole story. How the bad kid had gone good and how they were expecting him to make something of his life. It was a story William never forgot.

When William saw Roland for the first time, with his slick talk and energy. It reminded him of that counselor from years ago. He said if people like that would have left his friend alone, he would still be alive today. He was so convinced that he set out to put a bullet in Roland Stark, but he missed. You know the Miracle shooter…that was him, William. I don't know what happened, but he missed badly and shot that woman instead. Now Roland is bigger than ever, he has more followers than ever, and that just pisses William off to no end. Ironic isn't it. Well, he is dead set on getting him this time, for making him a fool the first."

July shook her head, befuddled at the whole thing.

"You gotta be shittin' me! I never expected this. We came all this way because Roland Stark reminds him of someone else? Why doesn't he just go and kill that other guy?"

"I don't know what goes on in that twisted head of his. As far as I know he probably did kill that guy already. After you get to know William you will see that some things are better left alone. The more you know how he thinks, the scarier the world becomes…knowing guys like him are walking around freely. But so long as he is on my side, there is one less I have to worry about."

July was dismayed. She expected something more serious, than a vendetta. This was a child hood delusion. Getting involved was a mistake from the beginning and she could not let Thad be involved anymore. Little did she know Thad felt the same way about her involvement. So now they would devise an alternate plan, one that would hopefully put the two of them as far from harms way as possible.

"I can't believe I came here," said July. Thad felt the same way. He finally said what was on his mind the whole time.

"I didn't want you to come at all!"

CHAPTER 19

Invitation to Disaster

Nightfall, it was easy to locate Sheryl O'Connor's home. There wasn't a person in the town who did not have an idea of where it was located. On the Friday evening before Miracle Sunday, William would attempt to capture and kidnap Sheryl O'Connor. Neither July nor Thad could understand the relevance to this act. This only made sense in the mind of William Richardson.

This career criminal was worse than being out of control; he was in full control. He calculated and schemed his way through many atrocities. Some of which his good friend Thad knew nothing about. William is the great deceiver—sometimes he is magnificent, with lavishness and brilliance, and other times he is a simpleton. The truth is that he is always calculating.

Even his apparent failures are well planned. If the parole board ever knew the limits to his manipulation, he would never walk outside prison walls again. But they did not know, they were victims just like everyone else around William. As the years went by Thad began to recognize this. Thad was no fool either. He had an idea of William's methods and began to develop a plan of his own. A day in which he would separate his tether from William—without William taking it the wrong way.

After entering the housing community, they drove slowly through the streets looking for the small yellow rambler occupied by Sheryl O'Connor. The time was 2:18 a.m. early Saturday morning. As they drove through the neighborhood, Thad was careful not to drive down the street the house was on, that would be too obvious. The road they were looking for was Salty drive.

While retrieving a map for the job, William made sure he stopped off at a bar near the community Sheryl lived in. Information came easy once a person has a few beers in them. Especially if the seeker of information is gracious enough to buy a round. After an hour the details surrounding Sheryl's life began pouring out of the local's mouths. The great thing about asking questions in a bar is that no one gets suspicious. For conversation's sake, a drunken person is willing to tell an open ear anything and everything.

William started talking to a middle-aged woman sitting at the bar. Whether she really knew Sheryl was not clear, but her jealousy was obvious. She constantly referred to Sheryl as "that bitch." William fed on her drunken hatred until he had all the details he needed. She said she knew someone who lived on the street behind Sheryl's—Salty drive.

The home they were looking for now, was a white house with black trim, and in the yard was a Dalmatian lawn ornament. Midway into Salty drive Thad saw the house. Thad pulled up behind another car and parked directly behind it. No masks were worn; they wanted it to look natural, like they were there to visit an old friend.

Casually, all three of them walked up the driveway of the home. They continued on between that home and the house beside it. Immediately, the dog next door began barking. William was prepared. The woman said that dog was known to keep people in the neighborhood up all night. The neighbors would be used to his outburst and would not be looking for anything peculiar. Just to be safe, they brought along a steak, lightly coated with a barbiturate. Thad hauled it over the privacy fence and in no time, the dog settled down.

The plan was working flawlessly, and they maneuvered their way into the back yard with ease. The other bit of information, William obtained, was that the person who's yard they were in, was handicapped. He did not move around that well, so the probability of him looking out the rear window was slim.

All that was left was climbing over the fence and into Sheryl's yard. She did not have a dog so they did not have to worry about that being an obstacle. But William *was* briefed on there being talk of a security guard hired to look after her. He sat in the front of the house in a parked car. He was best known for chasing off reporters. So long as they did not make a sound climbing over the fence William felt they would be in no danger of being discovered.

All they had to do was make it to the rear sliding door. From there they would be hidden from watchful eyes and they could enter the home easily. William was the first to run toward the rear sliding door and was hit with a bright spotlight. There was a motion sensor spotlight, which lit the backyard when it detected movement. The bright light caught the attention of the security guard out front assigned to watch after her. He installed the system in case some reporter tried to sneak in from the rear. July was on top of the fence when the light came on; she froze. Thad and William were in Sheryl's yard.

They heard the footsteps as the guard came charging through the yard.

"Someone's coming!"

"Hop the fence, hop the fence!"

July got down from the top. Thad and William hurled themselves over the fence from which they came. If the guard coming was dumb enough to follow them into the next yard they would take him down there. The three of them lay on their backs, parallel to the fence, looking upward. If a head peered over that fence William would put a bullet in it.

The clever guard who looked after Sheryl all week ran into the backyard. He checked the rear sliding door to make sure it was locked, and searched the area with his flashlight to see if someone was still hiding close by. He walked by the fence where the Trio was just on the other side. He stood there several seconds, and then he turned and walked away.

"I am about to call the police and report an intruder!" he said aloud before clearing the backyard. "You reporters have to learn to respect a person's privacy. In about five seconds I am going to make the call!"

What William did not realize was that reporters have been sneaking around in the back of the home all week. This was nothing new to the guard. It occurred so often the guard suggested Sheryl be moved to a hotel room a few days ago. The guard remained by her home as a decoy. The house was empty.

After the previous years, the Reborn Kings Ministry was becoming proficient at keeping the selectee for the Miracle ceremony hassle free for a few days. Colleen had a room reserved for Sheryl back in California, and early Saturday morning, at 2:25 a.m., Sheryl was a whole State away. She was sleeping quietly in that room.

After a few minutes, William, Thad and July made their way back to the car and drove off. William was dejected; the plan had failed. On the trip back to the motel room not a word was said. They parked the car outside the room—that was where William let his emotions show.

"What the fuck, the three of us running like scattering cockroaches? Why didn't we blow his ass away and take what we came for? Jump the fence—who suggested that?"

It was July, and William stared at her as he asked that question.

"I was stuck. We did not want to wake up the whole neighborhood with gunshots."

"I wanted that bitch!" William insisted, screaming at the top of his lungs. "Time to pack it up. We are going to California. It's not over yet."

    ✤   ✤   ✤

"Is there a God?"

Prine thought this question came out of nowhere. It was asked by his son, Lexington. It was Saturday morning, throughout the week Prine was preoccupied with the case. While in the apartment, he was constantly planning strategies, that he would use to gain information, from people he was going to interview. And when out on the interviews he would be gone for several hours. His work, however, was coming to a close. With Dorothy Grablford unwilling to cooperate his case was dead in the water. Jack Ward was running around using his contacts. Debating on whether to start mass DNA testing or not. Through the arduous task of gathering evidence, the team of Jack Ward and Dr. Walter Prine came up with nothing more than a handful of unanswered questions. Dr. Prine promised he would not be so consumed in his work that he neglected his son. So today, he decided to go to Ventura and charter a boat. The plan was to go fishing. This would give him the quiet time they both needed to catch up.

The water was unseasonably calm, for the pacific coast. Prine had no problem with that. He was not known for his sea legs. Fishing was Lexington's idea, it was something he always wanted to try. After several hours on the water Lexington began to open up to his father. Prine supposed it was due to the Miracle ceremony. Being so close to the activities they were surrounded by talk of it everywhere. When the question about God arose, Prine hesitated. He knew the discussion would have to come up some day.

With all that was going on in the world, this would be a good time to discuss it.

"I try not to think about God too much son," Prine responded. "I have my suspicions. I suppose there must be."

"I heard the other kids during the last semester, discussing whether, it was appropriate or not to bring God into school. There was a big debate over it and there was some interesting arguments."

"Do you want to hear my opinions?"

"Sure, it would be fun."

"I believe the idea of God got distorted son. People are wishful, they wish the world would be something it is not. People inherently desire happiness. If they cannot get it here, maybe there is another world in which they can find their happiness. I have studied thousands of religions in search of an answer. There are many differences, but each one has one thing in common as its final objective—happiness. They put all their hopes in a Supreme being that will one day save them. A destroyer of misery and injustice, who will someday bring order to the world."

"You don't think a being like this exists?"

Prine thought hard before answering. He thought about the images in his head, the suffering he caused and the pain he endured. He thought of the Pristine Murders, Cindy Revner, and everyday life.

"No, Lex. God has had plenty of opportunity to institute justice. If he does exist, I am positive he is not what most people expect."

"What about the Miracle Sunday ceremony? It's just a day away. You don't believe that either?"

"I am a firm believer in the supernatural. It goes against my core beliefs, but for a reason I am not ready to reveal to you yet, I do believe in a higher power. And I am sure, *even that* has some sort of explanation to its power. I study things for a living—life and human behavior. I rely solely on action and reaction to determine what *is*. In this world nothing happens without some sort of action, work, or reaction. Things do not just appear and life does not just happen.

"The farther we go the more we realize there is an explanation for everything. How various life forms are developed—the human

DNA—life in all forms is like a giant puzzle. In this world we learn how to take the puzzle apart in order to understand its pieces. Then we put them back together again. We are not geniuses for doing that. The puzzle was there long before we got here. Someone or something created the pieces and made them all fit.

"Look at the clothes on your back. I can probably explain the whole process of how they were manufactured. To a child who does not understand, the subject of something, as simple as clothes, is a mystery. But they did not just appear. You and I understand that someone did the work. Water, air, the earth, and all its inhabitants did not just appear. Someone did the work. We can duplicate life in a lab, in which case scientists do the work. But scientists are merely recreating what someone has already done—mimicking the act of another. I am explaining all of this because this is what I can see. This much is evident and obvious. The world did not just appear from nothing.

"Now, let me explain the other side. When people think of God they are not looking for that being. They are looking for the being, who if powerful enough to create, must surely be powerful enough to make them happy. They are looking for the being who rights the wrongs, in their life, and in the lives of others. They seek the ultimate hand of justice and the deliverer of eternal happiness. I searched the world son, more than you will ever know. That being, *that God*, has not shown any evidence of his existence."

"You don't sound like an atheist, Dad. I thought you were, you never thought do discuss the matter before."

"Because I do not want to influence your beliefs with my beliefs. I am just someone who lost hope."

"Well, I believe you are wrong. I don't have any great argument as to why. I just know you are wrong."

Although he was only nine years old, Lexington Prine was a prodigy. He was an intellectual and mathematical genius. His father refuses to push him past his childhood years in an attempt to develop his intelligence to its limit. So he takes classes for the gifted with his age group. This special group still poses no real challenge to Lexington's intelligence. Its only purpose is to keep his teachers happy. Scholars usually do not take an interest in faith, so it was surprising the subject was brought up at all. Prine was about to find out why.

"Look at the water dad. It's soothing, isn't it?" Sparks of shimmering light reflected off the tiny ripples of the ocean surface. The hypnotic effect had a calm warmth to it. Prine was more relaxed than he had ever felt since arriving in California.

"I sometimes think your words have hidden subliminal messages in it, Lexington."

"No, I'm just good." Lexington replied.

Lexington and Prine shared a good laugh. It was a relief getting back to the simple pleasures of the world—companionship and good company, between a father and his son. Lexington had to grow up fast after his mother died from an automobile accident, when he was four years old. Although he loves his father dearly, a young man needs a motherly influence. He never admitted it openly, but Lexington wished there was a motherly presence in his life. His time with Serena, over the past week, made Lexington realize what he was missing.

"After fishing…can we have Serena over for dinner. I want her to taste some of the fish I caught," asked Lexington.

"I believe Serena is busy. I don't want to impose on her. She is a grown woman and she has a life of her own. It wouldn't be right if we did not to respect that Lexington."

"Dad, the other night when you were out, I thought about you. I got this strange feeling that you were in trouble. It lasted only a few seconds. Does that sound strange?"

"Strange? No, I am just flattered you were concerned for my safety."

"So, what happened?" There was no denying it. This sort of thing happened before. Prine knows his son can sense certain things about his life. He was better off just explaining the situation.

"I believe it was when you went over to Serena's apartment. I though you guys would be home. I called and there was no answer. That was when I started to worry."

"I knew it. Hey dad, do you think when we get back to the college we can do a test between you and I for clairvoyance. I think we can prove that phenomena."

"It has been tried many times before Lexington. I just don't think we can make the tests valid. I am sorry I just don't share your enthusiasm."

"You are just trying to discourage me. I know the difference, it is not working either."

Lexington was not buying his fathers downplay of the phenomena clairvoyance. The ability for two minds to link together to form a second sight—a mind capable of unnatural intuition. Lexington was positive of this sense, since he discovered it at the tragic loss of his mother's life. He was just a four-year-old boy, but he remembers every feeling and emotion his mother went through in her fatal accident, even though she was five miles away.

No one knew she was off the side of the road. The car was hidden in the trees. Hours before the call came, before his father burst through the bedroom door, with tears in his eyes. Long before anyone saw the broken glass on the road and decided to investigate, Lexington knew his mother had died. Dr. Prine had often attributed the lack of emotion from his son being due to the fact that he was too young to fully understand. But that was not true.

Young Lexington was with his mother when she died, mentally he was right there. He made his peace hours before anyone else knew. Lexington hid this ability from his father because his father did not want to believe it. Now it was time to let it all out.

"Since mom died I have been hearing things," said Lexington.

"Hearing things? You know I am a psychologist right? You know what that means when someone tells me they are hearing things?" Prine began to laugh.

"That is why I have been keeping it a secret."

Prine saw that his son was serious. "Go ahead, tell me what they said."

"It basically tells me things like 'the world is good' and how one day people would come to see the light."

"Interesting."

❧   ❧   ❧

Saturday afternoon William, Thad, and July arrive in California. They find another motel, away from the city. A place that would be far enough from the religious crowd coming to witness the Miracle Ceremony. Thad and July kept to themselves. William was still frustrated at the botched attempt to capture Sheryl the night before. Roland Stark would win out again, the thought of it made William's blood boil. This time he planned to do it right. He was going to analyze the Kings facility, expose its weaknesses and come up with a plan to cripple the organization and Roland in particular.

William did not care how long it took. Roland's time on top would soon come to an end. After settling into the motel room William grabbed the car and left. The other two did not ask where he was going and neither of them cared. This was the first real time the couple had to themselves in a week. They were going to use this time wisely.

After freshening up, Thad and July had important business of their own to discuss. Mainly getting rid of William, which meant getting him out of their lives for good. The only way to do that, was to make William not want to be around them. That was the real test.

"July, it is not your problem," Insisted Thad. "The situation is out of control, all you have to do is leave. He doesn't like you anyway, so you are out. You need to take advantage of that and leave."

"I can't leave you here with him. *You* will be the one that ends up getting killed. I feel it in my heart. That sleazy bastard would end up walking away without a scratch."

"Nothing I could think of would work!" said Thad frustratingly.

"There is one thing I thought of a few days ago," said July. "It is despicable, but I am willing to take the risk if you are." July paused to light up a cigarette. "We set him up to take the fall. The plan has to be set to where we split up, then we tip the cops off and they pick him up."

"And then they pick us up for being his accomplices! It's not going to work."

"You haven't done anything except violate parole. If we let the cops know he is armed and dangerous, they will probably shoot him while trying to make an arrest. You know how violent he is. I don't see him going down without a gunfight. He will be killed and we will have nothing more to worry about. You and I can go on to live a normal life. We can get jobs like you wanted and get a place of our own. So long as he is alive he will intrude on our lives—I know you don't want that."

Thad did not know what to feel. Who was worse—William or July? "Listen honey, he is not going to die by my hand. That's all I have to say. If anything, we tell him our intentions to start a normal life and then we leave."

"You think he is going to go for that?"

"If there isn't a better plan than killing him, then I will just tell him we are leaving."

July was uncomfortable with William—partly because of his motives, and partly because of her beliefs. "Listen, Thad, I know you don't believe in these things, but I do. William's reasoning for wanting to see this Roland guy dead is completely off the wall. I know you were raised different than I was—so you don't understand. Whatever gives this guy the power to heal people also protects him. That power probably protected him in the church that day and prevented him from getting shot. That power is real, and if we don't have a just reason in seeing him destroyed, that power will turn and destroy us! I know this is all hocus-pocus to you Thad, but I believe in it. This guy Roland has got forces looking after him, and if we take those forces lightly we will be the ones that end up dead. Don't you notice how everything we do to get this guy goes bad? That's our warning to stop before it's too late. If we don't listen, we are going to burn in Hell. I'm sorry honey, but I am getting spooked. Let William continue his accursed quest on his own. We do not have to burn along with him."

In a stern voice, Thad insisted, "God, or no God, I will not turn on William!"

July heard what Thad had said; her plea fell on deaf ears. She knew Thad's firm stance would not allow them to live in peace. She would work hard to come up with an alternative. In the end, she just hoped it would be good enough.

❀   ❀   ❀

Later that afternoon, Prine and Lexington returned to the apartment. They each caught a few fish, nothing really to boast about. They had the fish cleaned and filleted, at the pier. All that remained was to season and cook the fish. Lexington still thought of Serena and wanted to call her to invite her over, but remembered what his father had told him earlier. Serena was a woman who needed some time to herself, Lexington had to learn to respect that.

Serena was doing as she always did when she had some quiet time. She was sunbathing down at the pool. She was never alone. Serena always attracted some sort of attention. This time it was one of the other tenants, a young man eager to know the female angel a little better. She let him down easily, as she does with most men. Her interest lied elsewhere. The young prodigy Lexington was taking well to her and she knew it. Against the wishes of the archangel Raphael, she continued to spend as much time as she could with the boy.

Eventually the time invested would pay off. But she had to make Raphael happy also.

During the time away from Lexington she began looking into relocating the angel known as Nukial. Nukial was a fallen angel with many secrets, he knew things that Raphael feared would endanger the years of peace heaven has enjoyed for so long. Serena had done her part—she could report to Raphael and inform him of Nukial's whereabouts at any time. But she will hold on to that information until it is absolutely necessary to tell Raphael. For now she will continue on as she planned, enjoying the rich sunlight.

The smell of baked fish was in the air, Prine and Lexington was about to eat when there was a knock at the door. It was Serena, and Lexington was beaming with delight upon seeing her. Prine thought the visit was rather unexpected; he had no idea Serena had the interests of Lexington on her mind. She was wearing a white robe over her bathing suit—she did not bother to change once discovering the two had returned from their time fishing. Prine welcomed the leggy angel inside, as his son would have been most disappointed if he did not. The three of them sat down, like a family, and enjoyed the fish fillet dinner.

"Serena," Lexington asked, "do you believe in clairvoyance?" Prine looked at Lexington, as he did not believe he was bringing another party into their earlier discussion.

"Sure I do Lexington, it is one of those mysteries of the world. Parents sometimes know when their children are in trouble and so on, even though they are miles away."

Lexington gave his father a smile; he had someone else on his side.

"What about you Dr. Prine?" Prine almost choked on his food laughing. Serena did not see the humor in the question. Prine answered, "I have a strange feeling that I am being set up by you two."

Before Serena could respond the phone rang, Prine left the table to go answer it. When he returned he had another question to ask Serena.

"Could you watch Lexington tomorrow?"

"Sure," she answered, "for how long?"

"For most of the day. That was agent Jack Ward. He said he has something in mind for tomorrow…more work. He has two tickets to the Miracle Sunday Ceremony courtesy of the FBI."

Serena could not resist the question. "What do you think of the Miracle? From a psychologist's viewpoint."

Prine did not hesitate, and answered Serena's question.

"It's a trick."

CHAPTER 20

Miracle Sunday

Since 9:00 a.m. Sunday morning William Richardson sat in the parking lot of the Hall of Kings facility. The persistent felon obsessed with destroying the Reborn Kings leader, Roland Stark, was there to do his homework. He watched everything he could possibly see from where he was parked. The deliveries, the workers, the parishioners—anyone coming in or going out of the facility. He sat there studying every facet of the construction. He studied the design and architecture. William observed the guards by the entrances and studied their patterns. If he could come up with a way to enter the building, and be able to roam freely, apart from the congregation, on this day where the security was at its highest, then next week, he would surely succeed in getting Roland Stark once and for all.

From one of the northern service entrances he saw a man, dressed for success step outside. He had two bodyguards with him. William picked up his binoculars to get a closer look. He had hoped it was Roland Stark, but he would not be that lucky. It was however the next best thing, it was Jericho Black. Jericho stood outside impatiently, pacing from side to side, mumbling something—exactly what—William had no idea. But his actions looked suspicious enough for William to take interest.

About two minutes later a black sedan pulled up. Jericho was obviously waiting for whoever was inside. The person attempted to get out, but Jericho ran over to the driver's door and shut it. He was pointing his finger and looking around the parking lot. There were cars parked all around the lot, but it was not even close to being full. It was still too early for that. The ceremony would not start for at least another seven hours. Jericho looked as if he was concerned about being seen, but more concerned about the person in the car being seen.

Jericho was quite animated as he disciplined the driver of the black sedan then he threw an envelope in the car. Jericho scanned the lot again for anyone who might have seen anything. He tapped on the top of the car and stepped back. The car began to head toward the exit. The driver had to head toward William's position in order to exit the facility. As Jericho and his guards headed back inside William started the car. This may be the break he was looking for. When the car passed William, he pulled out behind it.

Sheryl O'Connor had a busy week. She had been poked, prodded, and examined by every means necessary. The Reborn Kings welcomed science to check out the Miracle participant thoroughly, just to show their faith to the media. Everything from a basic examination, to a CAT scan, was performed to determine if there were any abnormalities with Sheryl to begin with. She was given a clean bill of health. Tomorrow, there would be new tests taken, and the results would be compared to the first. As in the previous participants, Roland Stark expected nothing different.

Sheryl was already inside the facility, waiting for her moment at the altar. She was extremely restless, although apprehensive about receiving the miracle water. She could not wait for the whole thing to be finally over with. The hours passed by slowly, and more and more people began to arrive at the Hall of Kings. Eager parishioners and the media could not wait for the service to begin. Sheryl was in a private room on the upper levels of the arena. Colleen and Roland entered around 1:00 p.m. They wanted to go over the basics of the Ceremony one last time, before they went down to the lower levels of the facility. Sheryl paid attention to Roland as he told her when to come out, where to stand and so on. When Roland was satisfied, he comforted Sheryl one last time, and then headed off to prepare himself for his sermon. The big moment was just a few hours away.

Dr. Walter Prine and agent Jack Ward arrived at the Hall of Kings Facility two hours before the service was supposed to begin. Jack had a plan—get close enough for Prine to use his interviewing skills to talk to a specific person within the organization.

That person was Colleen Rigetti. Jack made several phone calls trying to see if someone would talk to him. The timing was perfect—Colleen was still frazzled over the security incident a few days ago, when she was forbidden to go into the lower levels of the facility.

So with Jack calling at the opportunistic time, Colleen sent him two tickets and agreed to talk to the agent. Jack took advantage of the lead assistant's hospitality. He manipulated his way past security by showing his badge. Both he and Prine insisted they had an appointment to meet Colleen at her office on the upper levels. Jack even got one of the guards to unlock the office so they could wait inside. After a few minutes of waiting in the office, Jack left. He said he was going to check out what was taking her so long. Prine sat patiently, waiting for Colleen Rigetti. That is when the word got out that she had visitors.

Colleen was still in the room with Sheryl when one of the guards knocked on the door. "Excuse me, there is agent Jack Ward here to see you. He is waiting up in your office." Colleen was puzzled. "Who let him in my office?" she asked.

"I did, he said he had an appointment to meet you in your office. He showed his badge…" The guard knew he had made a mistake. It was not entirely his fault, he was manipulated by two of the best.

Immediately, the guard got on the radio and called for the nearest guard to head to Colleen's office. Colleen instantly had him cancel the order. That would attract too much attention. It was too late now, she had to face the agents in privacy whether she liked it or not. If the guards stormed in it would look very suspicious and Colleen was not convinced of any wrong doings within the organization just yet.

"Call Brenda and have her take Sheryl downstairs," Colleen told the guard. "She knows what to do. Be strong Sheryl, everything is going to be fine."

Colleen headed toward her office. For the sake of minimizing attention—it was too late, the initial call to head to Colleen's office was intercepted by Jericho Black. He wore a transceiver, a miniature, hands-free, style that fit comfortably over his ear. It was tuned to the guard's radio frequencies. Jericho turned to two of his most trusted guards and gave them instructions.

"Go, check it out."

Jack Ward was still roaming the halls in the upper levels of the facility. He was looking for any unlocked offices, people walking around, or just anything out of the ordinary. He saw two large gentlemen walking toward him, his instincts told him to head back to Colleen's office. The guards that Jericho had sent caught him before he could turn down the last corridor to Colleen's office. "Can we help you sir?" one of them asked Jack.

"I am here to see Colleen Rigetti." Jack displayed his Federal Shield.

"That doesn't do you much good up here. You still need permission or a warrant. Do you have either?"

"I had an appointment," said Jack rather snidely. The larger of the guards called on his miniature transceiver. The earpiece prevented Jack from hearing what the person on the other end replied. The guard shook his head, confirming the order. "Okay, sir. I managed to contact Mrs. Rigetti. I will take you to her—come with us." The guards escorted Jack Ward toward the elevator and down to the ground floor. They took him to an office located on the East Side of the facility. The guards opened the door and escorted him inside. There waiting in the room was Jericho Black.

"Agent Jack Ward...what a pleasure to see you again." Jericho smiled a devilish grin.

Colleen made it to her office undetected and opened the door. Dr. Prine was sitting on the large sofa adjacent from her desk, patiently waiting. "Who are you?" she asked. Prine introduced himself. "I don't know who you agents are," said Colleen, "but I did not agree to a private meeting. I was just being cordial, as a gesture to show that we have nothing to hide."

Prine started right away. "You seem uptight for some reason. You don't want anyone to know you were talking to the Feds in private do you? Does Roland know you invited us here?" She now knew she had made a gross error in judgement. Giving the agents those tickets was a mistake. They had already sensed her suspicions that something in the organization was not right, and Prine was feeding off of it.

"Do you know," said Prine, "I examined the tape of the original Miracle where Mary Beth Reynolds was shot. It was quite amazing. I did not see you in the tape though."

"I wasn't here then. I was hired afterward."

"I am going to stop beating around the bush, Colleen. The truth is that we are investigating a missing person case, which we believe, is related to the ministry. The leads come back to someone in this organization. Do you know of anything suspicious?" Colleen fought with her better judgement whether or not to tell him about the security on the B2 and B3 levels.

"No," she said, "there is nothing out of the ordinary."

Jack Ward and Jericho Black was left alone to discuss the real reason Jack was there. The two had met on several occasions before. Specifically regarding the disappearance of Cindy Revner. Legally,

Jericho was clean. There was nothing but a driver's license belonging to Cindy, which was left in a car the Ministry rented around the time of her disappearance. Other than that, the agency had nothing on him and Jericho knew it.

"Is it the game of cat and mouse that excites you Jack? Is that why you return so often? Or maybe it is because you enjoy being frustrated," asked Jericho.

"I know the driver's license belonging to that girl has some relevance to the case. I can feel it in my bones—and you are hiding something."

"Why is the FBI so concerned with the case of a missing girl. Is there some political ties with her family I don't know about? Who would have thought Cindy Revner would cause so much attention."

"You remembered her name?" Jack asked suspiciously.

"Of course," answered Jericho after hesitating slightly, "you mentioned it so many times before how *could* I forget it." Jericho and Jack became engaged in a mild stare-down, neither one was giving in.

"I want you to understand why this is so important to me," said Jack. "I know I should not tell you this, but the case has remained a secret for long enough. I am hunting a murderer, a serial killer. He has killed eight people so far, and I better not find out it is you."

"Is that all?" said Jericho nonchalantly. "I thought it was something serious." Jack became angered.

"I take my job very seriously," said Jack. "This asshole beheads his victims and hangs them by their feet for me to find."

Jericho looked as if he had seen a ghost. "*He does what?*"

"Brutal isn't it." Jack continued, "The carpet fibers found on one of the victims match the carpet in the car that Cindy's license was found in. It's a long shot, but that is all I had to go on in almost nine months. I want to know who was driving in that car! You guys rented it! Go back through your records, I don't care how you do it. I want a name!"

Jack was quite loud as he made his demands to Jericho, but Jericho was off in his own world. He barely heard a word Jack had spoken. Ever since Jack described the murderer's technique, Jericho's mind was elsewhere. "*It couldn't be!*" Jericho whispered to himself.

The roar of the crowd brought Jericho back into reality, the ceremony had started. In fact it was well on its way. "Did you hear me Jericho?" Jack asked.

"I must be going now," he answered. "I will do whatever I can to help you, agent. Good day." Jericho stormed out of the office and down the hall. The water was about to be given to Sheryl at any minute—he did not want to miss it. Jericho arrived at level B1, behind the altar entrance. He looked around for Colleen, but saw her assistant Brenda in her place. Roland and Sheryl were already on the altar together. She was dressed in a beautiful white gown that went down to the floor. Her hair was wrapped in a tight bun, she looked wonderful. Roland was standing in front of her, he was talking specifically to Sheryl; the microphone was off.

Roland offered his hand and Sheryl instinctively placed her hand inside his. Roland reached for the switch and turned the microphone back on. His speech was broadcast through the facility.

"During this week I got to know Sheryl, we talked about different things. We talked about where she was spiritually and where she wanted to be. We talked about what she expected out of life and we talked about her frustrations. She, like many of you, has traveled from great distances. That is honorable, because there is no distance you should not be willing to travel to know God. Sheryl are you ready? Do you know why you are here?"

The scattered cry of 'Amen' was heard throughout the arena.

"I believe the lord has been crying out to you Sheryl, but you have not been listening."

'Amen"

"He has been Crryyyyinnnggg OUT—but you haven't heard a thing.

'Amen'

"Today, you are going to hear. Today you will be listening because his cry is going to be soooo loud that it is all that you will hear. He will fill your eardrums with the Hoooly Spirit-a, and you will have to answer him Sheryl."

'Amen'

"You will answer him today, he has chosen you as his witness!"

Sheryl could see the sweat forming on Roland's brow. She felt the sweat in his palms as he held her hand. Two men from the arena security maneuvered their way behind her. One of the guards she recognized as the man who escorted her to the altar last week. Roland released her hand and went to retrieve the challis. Roland returned with the challis and as he walked, he treated it as if it were the most revered item on the planet.

"On this earth there is nothing more precious than water. It gives life, it sustains life. The body is primarily composed of water. For you my dear Sheryl, this water, God has blessed. God has led you here for a reason. It is time to drink and be reborn."

Sheryl looked into the challis. The fine crafted platinum challis contained what appeared to be ordinary water. She made a point to look at it before she drank. The challis was cool to the touch. Condensation water droplets were already forming on the outside. She grabbed the challis and slowly raised it to her lips. As she drank there was silence—all eyes were on her.

She looked past the cup into the congregation as she drank. Faces that were a blur because of the distance suddenly came into view. She could see clearer than she ever had before. She handed the cup to Roland in astonishment and removed her glasses. She did not need them anymore. She felt an overwhelming sensation to giggle like a schoolgirl, but she caught herself and smiled instead. It was a good feeling, extremely good. Roland returned the cup to the altar, she watched him walk back toward her. Suddenly, thousands of images began flashing before her, it was accounts of her life.

She stared wide-eyed into the crowd. She could instantly recall any event in which she thought of, crystal clear images, things she believed she had long forgotten. When she broke her leg riding a bike at age seven, riding the school bus at age five, even images of her mother singing to her when she was no more than a year old. But not only could she see the images, she could hear, smell, and feel them as well. All of her senses, she could actually relive the event.

"Are you ready Sheryl?"

The sound of Roland's voice brought her back to the present time. Roland pulled out a small surgical knife from his jacket pocket. The two security guards stood closer to Sheryl and grabbed her arms. They held her firmly and outstretched her arms to the sides of her body.

"Remember what we discussed earlier. This is the visual proof of the power that has entered you through the Holy Spirit. Do not be afraid. THEY CANNOT HOLD YOU SHERYL." Roland screamed out.

"I know these are big strong men Sheryl, but you are powered by the Holy Spirit, a strength that no man can equal. I ask you not to hurt them my dear."

Sheryl watched as the men used leverage in an attempt to hold her arms steady. Before she could decipher what Roland meant she moved her left arm and moved the security guard with it. He had done this before, he moved the entire weight of his 250-pound frame to stop her outstretched arm from moving and he could not. Sheryl did the same with her right arm. To no avail, the guard could not restrain her. She watched the straining muscles of the man on the right and stopped when she was convinced his effort was genuine.

She thought about her command over her body, she needed only to think of what she wanted to do and her body would find the strength. Neither man could stop her from swinging both arms together and crushing Roland between them. With the knowledge of this power she allowed Roland to continue to the next test. Roland held the surgical knife in his right hand and walked to Sheryl's left. He made a six-inch incision in her left palm. There was a simultaneous moan of thirty thousand people as they sympathetically felt the pain of her gash.

"Now witness why no one can harm you, when God is on your side."

As quickly as the gash was made it began to heal. In seconds the wound closed shut and sealed itself. A drop of blood, which ran down her palm, was all that escaped before the wound completely healed. Roland took a cloth from his pocket and wiped the palm of her hand, revealing the healed palm to all in the arena. Sheryl moved once again, against the weight of the men restraining her, this time they released their grip. She pulled her hands in front of her to examine them closely. She saw a fine hair like scar on her left palm.

With her fingertips she gently massaged the scar to feel if it was real. The overwhelming event caused Sheryl to drop to her knees. She doubted all of it, every second until now. Tears of joy flowed from her eyes, and the crowd began rejoicing. The noise level reached new heights as Roland began dancing around the altar once more, and Sheryl cried, as she never had before.

❦   ❦   ❦

Six hours had passed since Sheryl drank from the challis. Slowly since, her senses had all returned back to normal. Even her eyesight returned to normal, and she had to put her glasses back on to see clearly. She was now seated in the upper deck of the David section, in the seat she was sitting when selected one week ago. She sat alone thinking of what it all meant, until joined by Roland Stark. He had once again showered and applied plenty of baby powder to help absorb the moisture from his overactive glands. He sat down next to Sheryl to help her sort out the obvious changes to her new life.

"They told me you would be up here. I thought you might need someone to talk to—a person to confide in. I know talking to a man of God can be scary when you are not ready for God. Sometimes we can be boisterous—we shake our finger and tell you that you need to straighten up your act. But I am not going to do that Sheryl. That is not what you need. I come to you not as a preacher, but as a person you can talk to before you head out into this crazy world."

Roland said all the right things, he had a knack for knowing just what buttons to push. Sheryl was not a die-hard Christian, she gave religion very little thought in her life. But what she experienced was such a life-changing event; she felt ashamed to admit that she avoided God for so many years. A preacher might be over critical, a friend would simply listen.

"Words cannot describe what I felt today. So many emotions…so many sensations flowing through my body and mind. After this I have no idea what to do with my life. This is a feeling I will never forget."

"People who have been lucky enough to receive this gift have all experienced what you have, and they were at a crossroads. They felt as if they should now dedicate their lives to a different cause. My advice is not as a career change, but an attitude change. Let others see 'the new you' and be curious. Soon they are going to want to know what you have. They are going to want that same good feeling that you display everyday and when they ask, just tell them. It's that simple. Your attitude will be enough to spark their curiosity."

"Thank you—friend," said Sheryl.

Roland was satisfied, he reached out to someone else in need and hopefully his words would make an impact. But before he could get out of his chair, Sheryl had another subject to discuss.

"Reverend, has anyone ever experienced any strange messages during one of these blessings?"

"Second sight? I guess some have experienced unexplained occurrences."

"I felt someone was communicating with me and it was not God. It was someone who had passed on recently. He kept insisting about my seat, he was repeating C117. It was not clear. I had difficulty concentrating with everything else that was going on. I did however figure out that he was warning me. Warning me of what? I could not understand, he kept repeating 'land of games.'"

"Land of games—are you sure it isn't something from your past?" Roland asked.

"Not like anything I had experienced before."

"The lord works in mysterious ways, this is probably another one of those circumstances. Take care of yourself my child and keep in touch."

❦   ❦   ❦

The pressure was exhausting, but it was finally over. Jericho Black made it through another Miracle Ceremony. The entrepreneur's reward for coordinating the grand efforts between the ministry and television was a fat check for his efforts.

Jericho was back in his executive office at his corporate building. Black Inc. and its investors would reap the benefits of Jericho's massive drive and vision once more. He thought to relax and take it easy for a while, but there was nothing of the sort planned for tonight. There was an urgent call made to his office earlier, one which he had to respond to immediately. He picked up the phone and dialed the number.

"Why are you calling my office?" Jericho was not big on 'hello.' He was returning the call of Regina James, wife of the missing worker. She was looking for her husband Orlando. Last week Orlando stumbled across something he should not have. He saw several tickets that accidentally fell off the stage. The tickets from the ball used to draw the person selected for the ceremony. Jericho listened to Orlando's wife intently, but could not believe what he was hearing.

"What do you mean he is really missing? Are you sure you trust your husband, Regina? Maybe he ran off and left you?" He listened closely to what she had to say. His level of anger went through the roof.

"Regina, I am telling you I will check this out! I will put some men on it right away! I promise you we will find your husband!" Jericho placed the phone down in disgust.

"Shit!"

Everything came crashing down at once. Jack Ward's description of the murdered people still haunted him. For those murders he was innocent. For Cindy's case he knew a little more than he was letting on. He had his suspicions on who was driving the rental car that her license was found in, but kept that information to himself. Those instances were not nearly the end of his troubles. During the ceremony he became aware of another nuisance.

Dorothy Grablford informed him that someone was looking to tarnish his image. The person's name was Dr. Walter Prine. Then Prine made his presence known by snooping around behind the scenes and questioning Colleen Rigetti. One of the floor guards informed him he saw Colleen and Dr. Prine talking for several hours, while the ceremony was going on downstairs. He did not know Dr. Prine was with Jack Ward, but that would not have made a difference anyway. Dr. Prine was a civilian, not a Federal Agent.

Jericho was not known to be forgiving, and Prine just made it on Jericho's most hated list. What brashness, what arrogance, Prine was asking to be taught a lesson. No one comes into Jericho's place and gets away with taunting the millionaire. But how was he going to do it. Jericho noted Prine's appearance, since he was a doctor he probably would not respond well to physical violence. Maybe, Jericho thought, the best thing to do is to send a few guards, to *his* place.

CHAPTER 21

Parable of the Wicked

The mystery surrounding Marie Carthon was becoming an increasingly popular topic of conversation around the water cooler. Neighbors were interested in her health; Doctors were concerned about her progress. In both cases Marie's well being was in question. Was she able to cope with the accident, and why did a traffic accident produce such a traumatic affect? On the outside, the Carthon home was filled with despair, but inside there was a woman learning to cope with her new life.

A few days have past since Marie's second meeting with the menacing being known as Rameci. Rameci is a fallen angel; at least that is what *he* claims to be. Marie has no idea what to think of him. He comes in the night and is said to be watching Marie at all times. She cannot speak, it is forbidden. That was the small price she paid in exchange for the lives of her family. If she breaks the rule, her family will be slain, and there is little anyone can do to help her.

The police, FBI, and her loving husband are powerless against the wrath of Rameci. The hardest thing for Marie is that she has to face this trial alone. Rameci has affected her like no other being she has ever met. From what Marie has seen of him so far, she will do little to test the credibility of his claim.

Since the fateful day in the park outside her home, Marie struggled with her sanity. The fear factor, at a level she had never experienced before, caused her to make rationalizations, in order to keep her mind in check. *It couldn't be real,* she thought. Marie repeated this in her mind day after day. At times she almost convinced herself it was just an illusion. She would see her husband Marcus and the words would be at the tip of her tongue, but she did not speak. The pain from her injuries were all too real, and a constant reminder of her torment. But it was the mental pain that was excruciating in comparison. It was a risk her conscious would not be able to handle if Rameci was real.

Then Marie received another visit from Rameci. This visit helped sort the pieces of her broken thoughts. She has now accepted what has happened to her. Marie is reuniting with her inner strength. But most of all she is preparing for the next visit from Rameci. The fallen angel said he will grant her the privilege of speaking with him and him alone, and she was gathering her topics of conversation. Marie cannot write anything down, that was her decision—not Rameci's.

Marie knows if she is seen writing, then her husband will use it as a way of communication with her. She knows what he will ask; she got a hint from the psychiatrist she visited earlier in the week. Marie's husband wants to know what happened in the park, and if she had witnessed a murder. This was a question she did not want to answer. It was better for her to remain totally unwilling to communicate. At least this way the safety of her family would be ensured.

Every night Marie continued her new routine of awakening in the middle of the night to have a midnight snack. Looking out and wondering, if the fallen angel would emerge from the shadows. Early Monday morning, around 1:45 am, Marie had taken out carrot sticks and ranch dip from the refrigerator. She sat quietly, trying not to disturb anyone sleeping in the house, and she waited. She remembered

Rameci enjoyed the fruit drink she had several nights ago. Marie made sure there was another one just like it on the table tonight. She was frightened, as she was every night. Trying to escape the bondage of silence was her goal, but keeping her family safe was paramount. How could she play this devil's game and come out on top? She weighed these questions over and over again.

The infinite variables of different outcomes, played like a video in her mind's eye. Some played out to grim conclusions. The bottom line was that her family would never be safe unless she buys some type of pardon. If Rameci was willing to play games and pass a judgement of silence, he may be willing to make a different bargain. It was a shot Marie felt was worthy of taking. All she had to know now was what she was up against.

After forty minutes of sitting at the kitchen table, Marie saw a hand emerge from the darkness and grab the drink from off the table. Her heart jumped from the initial fright, and the pace quickened from the anxiety. She heard the gulping sounds of Rameci drinking the cool beverage. Like the obedient pupil she was, she waited patiently for Rameci to lift the blanket of silence placed over her. The half-empty bottle was placed back onto the table. Then the soothing voice of the fallen angel began to speak.

"It seems like you were waiting for me. Is your husband and children sleeping? Is your mother sleeping as well?"

Marie nodded her head.

"Good—I did not plan on returning so soon. Since you had nothing much to say the last time I thought I might give you another chance. You should use this time wisely. If you begin to bore me, I will silence you and leave. Is that understood?"

Again Marie nodded.

"Then your silence is lifted."

"Why did you kill those people?" Marie asked with her first breath. Rameci was surprised she started off immediately with a question.

"Those people? So you know there is more than one. How clever of you."

"I overheard my husband speaking with the FBI. They are on to you. They have more clues than you think."

She heard a smug grunt come from Rameci before he answered. "They have nothing. They believe they have you, a material witness. But *I* have you! What *they* have are scattered clues that they will never be able to piece together."

Marie stopped to listen, she thought she heard something in the next room. Hopefully, it was just her husband turning over in bed and nothing more. Rameci continued to elaborate on her misconception.

"You are so eager to share this information about the police with me. Do you believe that would possibly scare me? I can still eliminate their primary witness at any time I feel, and you have already admitted who the primary witness is."

Marie felt the cold harshness of his words.

"I know they cannot help me. Only you can save me," she said.

Marie made an attempt to search for any sign of compassion from her oppressor. He just laughed in return.

"You are wrong. Only *you* can save you. However, your family does belong to me."

That uneasiness in the pit of her stomach was returning. Marie desperately fought to keep it under control.

"What do you mean?" she pleaded, "I did everything you ask. I showed my loyalty to you in many ways. Why is the life of my family still in jeopardy?"

"You show me no loyalty whatsoever. You have obeyed me only out of fear of loss. Get it straight, the loyalty you show is to your family. It is that loyalty in which I use to control you."

Marie's plan was backfiring. Sensing that her feeble attempt at psychoanalyzing has only angered him, Marie quickly and humbly apologizes.

"I am sorr-."

Marie's throat was dry and crackling. Anxiety and the lack of exercising her vocal cords made it difficult to speak. She reached for the half-empty bottle of juice Rameci placed on the table.

"I would not drink from that if I were you," said Rameci. "It will be extremely disagreeable for you. You would surely die from drinking after me."

Marie promptly put the bottle down and went to the refrigerator for a different drink. Her curiosity got the best of her. She made a mental note to find out why.

The cool liquid passing through her esophagus was most soothing; the painful lump in her throat, from lack of speaking, and anxiety, had subsided. She listened again for signs of anyone awakening and eavesdropping on her conversation. When it was safe, she continued.

"The woman in the woods: You never told me who she was or why you killed her. Why did you kill any of them?"

Marie figured if she knew the reason he killed, she would have a better chance to protect her family."

"Who they are is not important," he said. "They are nameless and faceless bodies."

"Then just tell me why you killed them. Why did you kill the girl that I saw hanging there?"

"No fault of her own; she was tainted. Her body had been violated—infested with a vileness I have been pursuing for thousands of years."

"She had some type of disease?"

"No, you need to learn to listen without using your ears. I hunt a creature that took something from me. A precious item in which few in Heaven know anything about. So you see, the lives of a few humans means nothing in comparison. Their suffering, as well as yours, will never be anything compared to mine."

Marie was severely distraught by his last statement.

"I have no idea who or what you really are," she said, hysterically. "Only that you have some gift of popping in and out of nowhere and an appetite for violence. Even if you are who you claim to be I want you to understand that my suffering means something. Fuck why you killed those other people—what do you want with me!"

Rameci came out from hiding so that he may be seen. Out of thin air he appeared before her. His flawless white robes shimmering in the darkness.

"So you are not a true believer. Well it doesn't matter. Your miserable kind could never figure out what it is all about anyway. Your life, the life of your family—do you think that really matters in the grand scheme of things? It is like a gnat on an elephant's ass—insignificant! What I have planned for you is mere entertainment. Your shaken hands and quivering lips are for my amusement. Nothing more than a reminder as to how pitiful your species is. You have the power to end your trials and you don't even realize it. You're so weak it's disgusting.

Know your enemy! Is that what you had planned. Well you better fucking listen to what I am telling you. I am Rameci, an ex-angel of Heaven here to make your life a living hell! You stumbled onto my pursuit of Heaven 's greatest prize and you are too goddamn stupid to realize it. If more beings knew what I was onto, the angels of Heaven would pour from the sky like water. I am here to answer any question you ever wanted to know and you are only interested in the lives of a few. You don't even admit I am who I say I am."

❧   ❧   ❧

Prine knew he was making enemies with the type of questions he was asking about Roland Stark, leader of the Reborn Kings Ministry. He saw the leader as a typical spiritual leader claiming to have insight into the supernatural. Either they gained power and popularity through healing the sick or they were simply out to get your money. In light of recent incidents Prine believed Roland qualified as both—maybe even worse—a swindler and possibly a murderer. Although he could prove nothing, the deeper he dove the more ominous it became.

Prine's job was initially to gather information in which Jack Ward could use to ask questions and get closer to the ministry's people. He had no idea how the ministry could possibly be related to a missing person case, but they were most definitely hiding something. After a four-hour long talk with Colleen Rigetti, discussing the Ministry, Roland, and Jericho Black, Prine felt her dismay about the whole thing falling apart.

It never became more evident than when Prine noticed two gentlemen following him from the apartment parking lot. It was around 2:19 a.m., he had just left Jack Ward—comparing notes after his talk with Colleen, and he was on the way to his room. The two men were not hard to spot, each one looked like professional wrestlers. The shortest was around six foot three and close to 300 pounds. Prine quickly figured it was some of the security guards from the Hall of Kings. If it was the two he was thinking about, they surely had the look of bar room brawl veterans. *This was not going to be pretty.*

Dr. Prine was no pushover, he looked preppy but his physic carried a stout 210 pounds of mass. Along with his mysterious origins, the ability to live without aging was minor compared to the speed and strength that came along with it. Prine was ready for the confrontation and was about to show these guys they had no idea who they were messing with.

"Excuse me," Prine announced, "now that you know where I live I would appreciate it if you would tell your boss what a bang up job you did. All I want to know is…who your boss is? Is it Roland or Jericho?"

Prine turned around, he was standing in the dark underpass between the parking lot and the apartments. He thought this would be the perfect spot to hide from inquiring eyes. The two gentlemen following him stopped within a few feet.

"You ask too many questions slick," said one of them. Prine recognized the deep Brooklyn accent. "You needz to watch yourselves around heea. Youz might get hurt an all. I-don' want that to happen. Y'seem like a good guy."

The two gentlemen looked at each other smirking, especially when they noticed they had Prine cornered. It was an isolated part of the complex, they figured Prine was extremely stupid to stop there. For that time of the evening there was a good chance that no one would come wandering by. The two men took a step closer hoping to intimidate the smaller Prine. They were towering over him and dwarfed Prine's figure. Prine raised his eyebrows in contempt.

"I know, there are all kinds of dangers right where you're standing," said Prine. "...like slip hazards."

Before the two could figure out a witty comeback, Prine swept the larger one off of his feet in one fluid motion. The other, sensing the fight had already begun, reached out and instinctively tried to grab Prine. Prine side stepped the grasp, locked one arm under his, grabbed a firm handful of hair from the back, and used the assailant's momentum to thrust him face first over his buddy. With Prine still holding his arm behind him, he could do little to brace his fall and his face slammed violently onto the pavement.

The first man down quickly rose to his feet and charged like a furious rhino. In a flash Prine stepped forward and the two men collided chest first like sumo wrestlers. Normally the lighter man would have fallen, but Prine's strength was extraordinary and it was the larger man who was caught off balance. Prine thrust his left hand under the chin of the larger assailant and stood him straight up. The look in the assailant's eyes said it all. Never has a smaller man manhandled him in such a fashion.

The incredible thrill of combat was now coursing through Prine's veins, like his reoccurring dream this was something he truly enjoyed. As the man tried to regain his balance, he grabbed Prine's shoulder to keep from falling backwards. Prine used his other hand to grab the man's index and middle finger and snapped it back sharply, releasing the man's grip from his shoulder and breaking both the index and middle fingers of the attacker.

But he was not done yet, when the man began to scream in pain, Prine grabbed a handful of the attacker's right cheek and hurled him to the ground once again. This time he was not so quick to get up—he stayed down. Prine gathered himself and adjusted his glasses, he stepped over the battered guards and continued on to his apartment.

Prine sat in the living room of his apartment, the rush of adrenaline subsiding. He remembers how long it has been since he faced a good fight. The dream that haunted him was puzzling because he could not figure out its meaning. But the part where he begins to fight was invigorating. He paused slightly wondering if his attackers would follow him up to his apartment. That was absurd. He saw in their eyes, the eagerness to fight had escaped them. Prine quickly beat it out of their system.

A thought began to prick at Prine's mind. The feeling he got before he threw the larger man down for the second time, it was not a look of surprise, it was a look of concede. You would expect two guys of physical stature as they were, and obvious veterans of the bouncer business, to be more persistent. You might even say they should have fought to the very end. "How could they live with themselves knowing someone of my stature beat the both of them?"

Prine pondered quietly. Men like them have a reputation to uphold, if word got out that one man they were sent to ruff up beat them up instead, they would be finished.

Reputation and intimidation is a major part of being a bare knuckled bruiser. Prine was right…they gave up too easily. Not because they were being overpowered, but because they knew it was fruitless. Their initial look of shock turned to understanding, then they conceded. It was if they—*understood who they were messing with*!

❦   ❦   ❦

After the long discussion with the angel Rameci, Marie was beginning to believe him. Maybe this *was* above her ordinary means of comprehension. What else would make sense? His actions are unquestionably strange and his abilities are beyond understanding. She must let her mind consider the possibility if she is going to get anywhere with him, or does another person have to die before she believes. There was no need to go to extremes to make a point. Marie was ready to accept Rameci as a fallen angel.

"I would like to change the conversation." She stated gingerly, "I believe you Rameci, the fallen one. But you must realize I am confused. You don't appear to be an apparition, and apparitions cannot drink fluids. If you expect me to believe you, you must understand your image goes against everything I have been taught."

"So it is knowledge you seek. Okay, ask away."

"Earlier when I reached for the drink, you said I would die. Why, can't I drink after you? If your body is of spirit then it would be purified," said Marie.

"You misunderstood what was said at my last visit. This body of mine is definitely of physical mass, just like yours. Except, it is highly evolved. Its regenerative properties far surpass the human body and it is capable of functioning indefinitely. But the foul diet I choose to eat is not so agreeable to humans. My saliva is compatible to that of the Komodo dragon. It has no poison, but the bacterium in the mouth of this beast is worse than any poison known to man. Because of what I choose to eat, the bacterium in my mouth is just as volatile. In each case it is fatal."

Marie stared at the bottle Rameci drank from and made a mental note to dispose of its contents.

"Your body is a physical body?" she asked. "I always believed angels were spiritual, then how do you appear and disappear?"

"No, I do that another way. I do not disappear; it is more like an illusion. I would explain it, but you wouldn't understand anyway."

"Give me a try, I am smarter than you think."

She heard another smug laugh emerge from Rameci, "That's what you want to believe, but you are predictable. When you first started the questions you directed what was being said. You were searching for some sort of weakness and you still are. But I quickly turned the tables on you, now you are asking the questions I want you to ask.

Next you will probably ask me something about God."

Marie realized the fallen one was right, she was playing into his hands. *What is his game?*

"Shall I continue and tell you about God?"

Rameci was excited, although she could not see him, she could sense it by the tone in his voice. Rameci had slipped back into the camouflage of nothingness some time ago. From thin air his hand appeared and grabbed the bottle in which he drank from earlier. Then Rameci continued.

"What do you want to know about your *God*? Do you follow the texts of the world, all claiming to be the word of God? Do you feel the restrictions in each passage? The word of God is filled with things you cannot do. On earth is the same as in Heaven. We, the fallen angels, exercised our rights. We have taken our spiritual bodies and traded them for physical ones. We live life as it was meant to be lived—on our own terms. But you are not interested in the angel's tale are you. You are only interested in what concerns you, is that right?"

Marie nodded in agreement.

"You want to know the truth. But, in the physical form as you are in, truth does not exist. Take a traffic accident for example. There may be fifteen witnesses, and each one with a different account of what took place. If you ask each one of them if what they saw was true, they would respond with a yes. Each person would swear to it. But there can be only one truth, which one is it? The answer is all fifteen accounts are true in a sense. To the human mind there can be no absolute truth, the human mind is only capable of understanding 'perspectives.' Whatever perspective you can formulate through the five senses is accepted as 'the truth.' It is the truth to the mind that computed it and to that mind alone. The absolute truth, as I prefer to call it, can only be understood through the spiritual body. I will not tell you what has been properly deciphered in the holy texts and what has not."

Twenty minutes have passed. To Marie, the time that elapsed felt no more than a minute. There were many things she still wanted to ask, but settled on what came to mind next. The question of the fallen ones sight.

"Are you blind?"

"Yes."

"You sometimes act as if you are blind, then you act as if you are not. Were you created that way or did you lose your sight."

"It was taken from me. I lost my sight some time ago."

"With a body as superior as you claim it to be, how can you lose your sight?"

"It is superior not invincible. It can be destroyed."

"What happens then?"

"My soul returns to the only place it is accepted—Hell. There I will remain imprisoned until the final days when I get a chance to fight for my freedom. I promise you, that fight will be won by our side."

"How do you function as if you can see clearly? You even knew about my mother applying makeup and how I felt around her. These are things that you must see to be able to know."

"You are wrong. It is not as extraordinary as it appears. There have been humans, who after losing their sight, have been known to develop the same abilities—to a minor degree of course. With my angelic body, the enhanced senses overcompensate for my lost one. So much that I now feel vision is a weakness. The first form of deception comes through the illusion of sight. Magician's trickery works off sight alone; the illusion is sometimes strong enough to render the mind helpless. Look at you, you are afraid of what your mind cannot place into a safe reality. The image of the woman hanging caused you to be frightened. Would you by as afraid if you just heard a woman was hanging from the tree? You might have been concerned but not frozen with fear. The loss of sight can be advantageous…in my case it is a blessing."

Marie thought of what she would say very carefully, she remembered that Rameci said if he were bored he would end the visit. She sensed the end was near.

"To lose your sight there must have been something or someone strong enough to do it."

"How perceptive of you, you are right again. It is the angel responsible for my loss of sight, which I seek. I killed those people, the pitiful humans, because they carry the stench of his being on them. I hunt by smell; I fight by sensing vibrations in the air. I killed those people and hung them so that their blood would drain from their carcasses.

That is the only way to get rid of the false scent they emit from their pores. I believe he is doing this to throw my senses off track. He knows I am on to him and when I finally catch him the game will be over, and I will send his soul where it belongs."

"Then you will be leaving soon?" Marie asked, "To hunt the angel who harmed you?"

"Not until I can pick up his scent. Until then I will stay here. I can pick up the smallest trace of his scent from nearly 1000 miles away, but I have a feeling I am much closer than that. Patience is my greatest weapon and when I catch him I will enjoy every precious second of his destruction."

"How long have you been hunting him?"

"Over the last three hundred years."

If this was true, Marie knew her chances of freeing herself was very slim.

"Speaking of time, your time is done, Marie. I enjoyed it, you showed a little more signs of fighting back. That's good, possibly you will get used to your new life."

From the darkness the near empty bottle of juice was placed back on the table. Then Rameci said once more—

"Your silence begins now!"

CHAPTER 22

The Angels Come to Play

Two large figures move in the shadows down the long corridor on the sublevels of the Hall of Kings. Security guards Rin and Jacob—defeated by Prine—were traveling deep into the private spaces of Jericho Black. Both were bruised and slightly broken. Rin sustained a fractured nose and Jacob now had a splint supporting the broken fingers he sustained during the encounter. As they rounded the corner they were met with resistance by Jericho's personal body-guard.

"What are you two doing here?" he asked.

"We gotta talk," said Rin.

"Well spit it out."

"Not with you, we gotta talk to Jericho."

"You fella's look like you got hit by a Mack truck. Let me take a good look at you."

Jericho's personal bodyguard stepped closer and examined their bruises. Clearly agitated by the uncomfortable situation, Rin asked again. "We need to speak to Jericho!"

"Anything you have to say can be said to my bodyguard," said Jericho from behind the shadows. "This is my most personal bodyguard, we have been together for some time."

Jericho emerged from the shadows of the next room, dressed casually with a cigar hanging from his mouth. "I mean whatever you tell me I will share with him anyway."

Jericho stepped closer and put a hand on the shoulder of his bodyguard. "That will be all for now." The bodyguard left Jericho in the company of the other two.

"What is it that demands my full attention at this hour?" Jericho asked.

"The professor who was inquiring about our activity was paid a visit," said Rin.

"And it appears he beat you up instead is that it?" Jericho responded. "What is the problem? Take more men and return."

"It's not that simple," said Jacob. "He was fast and strong. We suspect…"

"Suspect what?" said Jericho, annoyed at Jacob's incompetence. "This better be damn good!"

Rin chose his words carefully.

"We suspect—he is *similar* to you sir."

"Who?" Jericho demanded.

"Dr. Walter Prine, sir."

Jericho reached out to examine the hand of Jacob, he carefully looked over his broken fingers bound in a splint. Jericho put his face within a few inches of Jacob's, staring him directly in the eyes. He then began to squeeze Jacob's injured fingers in his intense grip.

"Who the hell do you think you are talking to?" Jericho said, directing his question at Rin as he squeezed Jacob's hand. Jacob winced in pain through gritted teeth. His face trembled under the intense pain. Saliva began to escape from his lips, but he dared not scream while Jericho's face was so close to his.

Rin spoke quickly. "His speed, his power, we saw it before sir. We could tell."

"And you think by concocting this story, that I will not think less of you for getting your asses kicked by some lousy professor?"

With a swift motion Jericho grabbed the ring finger of Jacob and jerked it back violently. The deformed finger stood straight up and the loud crack of another finger being broken echoed through the corridor. Jacob grunted and cringed, he fought to stand straight as the pain was too much to bear.

"Well, Mr. Rin, you should thank Jacob here for saving your life. If he had cried out I would have killed the both of you for being weak. But you are not off the hook yet. We will all go to visit this Dr. Prine and if he is anything less than an ordinary man...I will kill you! Not for losing to him, but for thinking that making him *seem* above human would save your asses."

✤   ✤   ✤

The bond between father and son is sacred indeed. Fathers rarely have the time during their busy schedules to spend with their children in today's ever-demanding world. Prine takes this responsibility seriously, this was all he ever wanted—a true family.

Something he could claim as his own. He had that dream for five years, before the death of his latest wife Kione. This young Japanese woman left him with a legacy none had ever left him before. She bore him his only known son, Lexington. For that her memory will forever be revered in his mind.

Since coming to California he had the opportunity to bond with Lexington even more. Prine's work was coming to a close. There was little left that he could do for agent Jack Ward. He reported the little scuffle he and the guards had the night before, to Jack. Except when he explained it, he said the guards were just there to *scare* him.

Going to the movies was his favorite thing to do. Prine had not forgot his incident of a few days ago with the Reborn Kings guards, he just did not think they would be returning so soon. Upon opening the door to the apartment Prine was in for a rude awakening. As he flipped the light switch he could see that he and Lexington were not alone. A survey of the room revealed both of his previous attackers were already there, standing at forty-five degree angles around the front door. A third figure was further back, merely observing for now.

"Lexington, get behind me son."

The man in the background Prine noticed as Jericho Black, the figure in the video. He was now getting personal visits from the entrepreneur—this was getting interesting.

"I have no intention of changing my opinion about the ministry," said Prine. "Even if you brought Roland Stark along with you." Prine turned to the two security guards, Rin and Jacob, then back to Jericho. "Were you the one who sent these two altar boys a few days ago?"

Avoiding Prine's direct question, Jericho spoke. "You are not what I would call Reborn King's material anyway, Dr. Prine. I came to investigate a claim these two have with you. It is simple...then we will be on our way."

"What is it, what do you want?"

Jericho began to speak. "Achodn miahj-behoneg."

"What?"

Rin and Jacob began to laugh, they were amused by Prine's look of confusion.

"Wait!" In his dream, Prine heard of the language before. He recognized its style. The dream that plagued his peaceful sleep was beginning to come to light. This man was trying to communicate in that same language. The old woman was right. She told Prine if he did as she asked he would find out about his origins. Standing just a few feet away was Jericho Black, the one that could answer all of his questions.

"You boys have wasted my time, he's nothing," said Jericho. "If you kick his ass now I might reconsider my threat."

Prine looked over at the guards, still bruised from the last encounter. "So you guys are ready for round two? Personally I learned my lesson the last time," said Prine.

"Very funny you prick," Rin yelled aloud.

"Care to dance again big man?"

"Oh, I got something for you this time preppy boy!" Yelled Rin.

"Yes," said Jericho from the background, clearly amused by the exchange of words, "show Dr. Prine what you have for him!"

Rin could only look on with raised eyebrows and a blank stare. He wondered if Jericho would leave them out to dry if Prine overpowered them as he did before. He turned to look at Jericho once more. Jericho laughed heartily.

"Oh, sorry. It was me, which you brought along to take care of Dr. Prine. How silly of me."

Now this man would surely pose a challenge, Prine thought. He reached behind him for the door, opened it and thrust Lexington outside. Before Lexington could turn back around the door was slammed shut. Lexington stood outside the door, he wondered if he should run for help or pound the door until his father opened it. Instead he just stood there and waited.

"Is everything alright Lex?" The sound of a female voice to his left—It was Serena. She was coming up the stairs. "SERENA!"

"I thought I heard someone slamming doors. Are you okay?" she asked.

The tears in his eyes said it all.

"My father—I think we should call 911. There are men inside and my father…" Lexington wiped a tear from his cheek and started breathing heavily.

"I am going to call the police okay," Serena said. "Come over here, away from the door."

"No, I'm going to stay right here until he opens the door."

Serena ran down the stairs to her apartment, grabbed her cell phone and ran back up to where Lexington was standing. Lexington heard the tone as three digits were pressed and the sound of a voice on the other side. Serena began relaying the relevant information to what was going on, while Lexington tried to listen to what was going on inside the apartment. He had his ear tightly pressed against the door.

"The police will be here any minute sweetie. Come away from the door," said Serena.

"You did not call the police, you dialed information. The tone for the 'nine' button sounds different. You dialed a "four." Why won't you help my father?"

❧   ❧   ❧

"I was going to have them attempt to beat you up again," said Jericho. "But you are too cocky for your own good. I am going to take this one."

"The great entrepreneur is going to get his hands dirty? I thought I seen it all," Prine responded.

Like professional warriors the two began to prepare for battle. Jericho rolled up his sleeves and Prine thought for this battle, he'd better remove his glasses. A numbing-tingling feeling began at Prine's fingertips and coursed through his entire body. This was exciting. The taller, slender, Jericho Black casually approached his target.

It began—Jericho started throwing punches wildly, Prine managed to sideswipe, duck, and dodge all of them. Then it was Prine's turn. He went of the offensive, and nailed Jericho with a straight punch, right between the eyes. It barely knocked Jericho off balance.

"Is this what you boys were afraid of?" said Jericho jokingly.

Prine could not believe Jericho took one of his best punches and joked about it.

"I am going to have to hurt you before you take me serious. What are you, a Principality?"

The next brutal exchange of blows did not go Prine's way either. This time he was hit. For the first time in a long time—he felt pain!

"What the fuck!" But, this was it, Prine's mysterious origins was about to come to an end. This man would finally explain all that Prine could not recall about his past and how he got to be this way.

Jericho's speed, reflexes, and strength was superior to his. But, Prine was no slouch when it came to fighting. In the early 1940's in Canada, Prine fought in illegal rings along the countryside to earn money. Going against the toughest, raw fighters of that time, and beating them all easily.

The reality of Prine's new situation was reinforced with another smashing blow to the cheek, this one hurting more than the last.

"You are not so cocky anymore are you? Plain old Angels have wings. Where are yours?"

"What?"

A crushing blow to the stomach sent Prine to his knees. *"What did he call me?"*

He was so stunned by the turn of events that Prine did not hear what was being said to him. Jericho began taunting him, then the torture stopped. Jericho became distracted. He heard something that angered him to no end. It momentarily saved Prine and doomed another. From Jacob came a phrase that quieted everyone in the room. "Tierch inage," it meant, "Send him to Hell!" Rin could not believe his buddy just said that…neither could Jericho.

For years Prine contemplated death—he welcomed it. Whatever caused him to live as an immortal was becoming tiresome. That was before his son was born, now he wanted nothing more than to live. He wanted to see his son mature as a man, and have his own family. Death was no longer an option, especially knowing his son was right outside the door.

He was not sure of all that was happening, he was still trying to recover. Prine only knew that Jericho was now on the other side of the room. Prine focused in on where Jericho was standing. But there was another person who caught his eye, his nine year old son. Lexington was now standing inside the door. Lexington's eyes were fixated down at the now lifeless body of the security guard, Jacob. Jacob's eyes were wide open, his head was twisted completely around toward his back. The body lay no more than five feet from where Lexington was standing. No one noticed when Lexington slipped back inside.

He was there long enough to see Jacob's neck broken for his insolence. Jericho Black performed the grim and powerful act. Jericho was now headed back toward Prine, Lexington knew the same fate awaited his father and he began to cry. This caught the attention of Jericho Black.

He once walked the earth as a demi-god, hoisted above all men. Soon power turned to boredom—from boredom to suffering, and then to insanity. But all was changed with the birth of a little boy. The missing pieces of his soul were replaced when Lexington entered his life. He had never looked forward to a period of time in his long complicated existence until now. He was not about to let it slip away just yet.

"Who is that boy?" Jericho insisted as he stood over Prine's beaten body.

"He is my son, so don't you dare to even look at him for another minute."

"I know you call him your son, but who is he really?"

"I said he is my son!" Prine raged.

"You insist on this charade. You are incapable of bearing a…"

Just then the size ten boot of Prine connected, dead solid perfect, with Jericho's chest. The delay was just what Prine needed as his wounds began to heal at an astounding pace. His body was not about to let its host die that easily. Prine decided to try a few close combat-grappling moves. His newfound power matched Jericho's—no he exceeded it. The blood was now surging through Prine's veins. In no time he had Jericho pinned against the wall.

"Anyone who thinks of messing with my son will pay," said Prine. His left fist was pressed against Jericho's neck. He used the leverage of his body to apply pressure. Jericho attempted to break free, but could not. The strength of Prine overwhelmed him and Jericho was in shock because of it. Jericho desperately tried to figure how the tables turned so quickly.

Although Prine would not openly admit it, the confrontation was pleasing, especially from a worthy opponent. He began to experience extreme euphoria and, he was getting stronger. Jericho gasped, and tried to free himself again, but to no avail. Then Prine began to notice an incredible burning sensation coming from his left hand. It was the wound on his fist, it began to open. Jericho noticed Prine's attention shifted to his fist. Jericho looked down, the pulsating wound looked like a small mouth opening and closing. Puckering…it was gasping for something. What Jericho saw put fear in his heart. He struggled, with Prine's fist on his throat to say the word, "Morningstar!"

Suddenly Prine was not feeling so good, sweat began to trickle from every pore of his body. A cold and clammy feeling developed on his skin. He dared not let go of Jericho, no matter how bad he felt. With a strained voice Jericho made a last plea for his life. "Rin—get the kid. Grab the boy!"

"I don't think so!" it was the sound of a female voice Prine was familiar with. It was Serena. She had a small caliber handgun pointed at Rin, daring the giant to move.

"The boy is off limits," she continued.

"That is not going to save him, or you," said Rin, as he simultaneously pulled out a larger semi automatic weapon from his coat pocket. "This time I came prepared. I am going to let you in on something," Rin continued, "your weapon is useless in here. There is a good chance you won't get hurt if you just lower your weapon."

Rin was sure his point was getting across to the tall beauty. One, because she looked like a model, and two, because she looked as if she had no intention of pulling the trigger. Rin looked behind him at the superpowers locked in combat against the rear wall.

"I will not hurt you sweetheart. I will allow you to open the door and leave just as quietly as you entered."

Serena lowered her weapon and pulled young Lexington close to her body.

"How dare you?" she said in a most disdainful tone. "Aside from the boy, *you* are the only mortal in this room."

A surge of power was felt within the room, her long blonde hair began to dance from the incredible energy. Jericho, who was still trapped against Prine's intense grip, thinks to himself. *What the hell is going on? Divine energy?*

Another surge of power was felt as Serena's bright green eyes turned white. This was all Rin could take. Those damn angels were taking over. First his friend was savagely killed, and now this. Panic set in, his only solution was to point and shoot. As he raised the weapon Serena reacted instantly. She grabbed Lexington with her right hand, positioning him away from the gun. She accelerated so fast, carrying him in her arm, that she ran across the wall to escape harms way. Her speed was such that gravity could not overtake her. She scaled the length of the apartment, around twenty five feet, running down the side of the wall, and exited the through the rear sliding glass door in an explosion of broken glass. It happened so fast, Rin barely got off one round.

Prine screamed, "Lexington!" and he released Jericho to run to the shattered sliding door. It was too late. Serena and Lexington had disappeared in a cascade of broken glass. Prine leaped from the second floor balcony and began running frantically through the grounds.

He desperately searched for the only thing he valued, his son. Prine thought of the series of events that led to this point. It was all too difficult for him to comprehend. But he found comfort in knowing there were others in the world just like him. Maybe they could help him fully understand himself. That is…if he does not kill them first for harming his son.

Around a quarter of a mile away, east of the apartments, Prine could make out a small figure standing under a tree. It was Lexington. He stood peacefully waiting and quickly acknowledged his father running toward him.

"Dad."

Prine fell to his knees and hugged his only son.

"I am sorry, you got involved in all of this son. I almost got you killed."

"I am alright Dad."

"No, tomorrow I will send you back, somewhere where it is safe."

"I saw you fighting Dad. The safest place I know is right here."

He was flattered at his son's comment. Prine stared down at his fist, besides being sore it was now back to normal. Just a huge gaping wound.

"Serena," said Prine, "where is she?"

"She went off in that direction." Lexington pointed toward the slightly wooded area north of the highway.

"What a rush. Did you see how she moved? I thought my stomach was in my feet," said Lexington. "Tomorrow when she comes to look after me we can…"

"Whoa, wait a minute. She is not coming near you ever again."

"She saved my life."

"Saved it? You guys went plowing through a sliding glass door and over a balcony."

Upon hearing his own words he realized Lexington did not have a scratch on him.

"Well, anyway son, I need a minute to figure out exactly what happened, then we can go back. There is a dead guy in our living room, and busted glass all over the place. The police are probably combing the area now."

Life ever since his mother died had toughened the nine-year-old quite a bit, his intelligence surpassed many adults and his maturity was well beyond his years. But he is however, still just a nine-year-old boy. Being exposed to what just transpired may have been too much for him. Prine thought about this and wondered what his son was thinking.

"Dad…did you see the way that tall guy moved? It was like a blur. His hands looked like it just flicked that guy's head and boom—he hit the ground. One minute he was facing the other way and the next minute he was looking at me. Then he fell to the ground. I was so scared I was afraid to move."

One thing was troubling Prine about the whole situation, his son's reaction.

"You seem to be taking all of this in stride son. Isn't all of this a little hard to believe?"

"I've been warned about this kind of stuff."

"Warned—really!"

"Yes, by Serena. She said, she was a Throne sent by the archangel Raphael. She said to keep it a secret—just between us two."

"What?"

"She said she knows you might not be human, and that you might be leaving. She also said she was here to protect me."

"She is an angel, a Throne, and she was there to…to…baby-sit you." It sounded ridiculous after hearing it from his father's mouth.

"Yup, I thought it was just a fable, but then I thought—*what if?*"

"And you believed her?"

"Remember when I told you that sometimes I hear things—that voices would tell me how the world was good and about God? Well, tonight I realized that the voice I heard and Serena was one and the same. When I was inside the apartment, she told me she was on her way in, and not to worry, she was an angel. She spoke to me through my mind. She's pretty and she smells nice. Why wouldn't I believe she is an angel? She told me all kinds of stories about Heaven and the angels whenever she watched me, but…"

"Stop there son, not another word. This Serena is in big trouble now. We are going back."

CHAPTER 23

Gathering Thoughts

As heavenly beings were created they carried titles. Some opinions differ as to why, but they each have different skills and talents. Some differed physically and others mentally and spiritually. The familiar titles are Seraphim, Cherubim, Throne, Angels and Archangel. But there were more. Many of them are not as familiar, because the majority of these others fell from God's grace and were cast from Heaven. Among them are the Virtues, Principalities, Dominations, Powers, Authorities, and Morningstars.

The Domination, or Dominion angel known as Nukial, was one of these who fell from God's grace. He is now living out his existence on earth. At the present time he is not known as Nukial, but as Jericho Black. Jericho had instructed Rin, the security guard from the Hall of Kings, to remove his deceased comrade and dispose of the body. He did not want the Police or any outside influence to get involved. Jericho promptly contacted Dr. Prine's landlord and made arrangements for all damage to be charged to Black Inc.

He saw something, which he never saw in all the years since leaving Heaven, and he was determined to get to the bottom of it. Nukial is a hoarder of special gifts; the wealth he accumulated on earth was due to his talents of persuasion. It is rumor throughout the angelic community that he has many rare and priceless artifacts. Things of value to not only this world, but to Heaven as well. He saw this as another opportunity to improve his standings in preparation for the final battle.

Jericho, just might be the first angelic being to figure out what was happening, except it would mean nothing if he could not survive. As far as his ability to keep the police out of his little confrontation at Dr. Prine's place, it was too late. The sound of gunshots were already reported by one of Prine's neighbors. Jericho and Rin just barely got Jacob's lifeless body out in time. Jacob died, not because of his arrogance…his crime went much deeper.

A walk through the park after hours could prove to be dangerous for some people. However, this was a good place for Jericho to gather his thoughts. The darkness and solitude the night air provides has a medicinal quality to it. Even for a treacherous soul like his. Peace can be disturbed by the slightest of intrusions; Jericho's came in the form of a Throne named Serena Capistrano.

"You love walking in the park, do you Nukial? I bet you like killing young girls as well."

Jericho was startled—more like ashamed—that he let an oversized Throne like Serena sneak up on him.

"You have the stench of divine presence all over you," said Jericho.

Angels traditionally have a sweet, pleasing smell about them. It is also known as *divine presence*. Angels who are no longer welcomed in Heaven loose their divine presence. Angels can quickly distinguish what side others are on by the presence, or lack, of this unique smell. Once Heaven is closed off to an angel they loose the amorous scent. To fallen angels the smell of divine presence wreaks with what they consider vile puke. A stench that is most displeasing—it reminds them of what was lost.

Apart from his invasion of solitude, Jericho realized he does not have to *figure out* what was happening. He has all the answers right in front of him. These two knew of each other, by reputation only, from the Great War of Heaven. They had never met until today.

"Tell me," said Jericho, "you track me down to ask me if I murder young girls? That doesn't make any sense to me. Thousands of people are murdered everyday, but I bet you don't even stop to remember their names. Why is Heaven so concerned with this one?"

"Heaven is not interested, only me."

"What is a lovely Throne doing messing with the big boys?"

"Big boys? You think too much of yourself Nukial. You are no more than a small time punk."

"So it has come to this. I am tired of smelling your stink anyway," said Jericho. Natural enemies—the heavenly angels and the fallen ones are almost expected to battle whenever they meet on the field. "I am going to free you of your physical constraints Serena, and send you back to Heaven for good. You smelly beings foul the air down here for us decent powers."

A flash of power was felt once again as Serena's surge of energy prepared her for battle.

"Time to end your life here on earth Nukial. This is going to be sweet."

The sexy Throne was no stranger to combat. She may not have looked like a threat, but that body of hers carried more than just attitude.

"That flash of power doesn't impress me at all," said Nukial. "It's what you do with it that counts, and I doubt you have the skills. If I take care of you now that is just one less heavenly being I have to deal with later."

Serena's volatile attitude began to show. "You think you can take me? Bring it on! I'm not ascared of you!"

"That is only because you are a fool."

Jericho was not afraid of her power, but there was one thing that kept him from attacking. The thought of a fallen Morningstar and a Throne together was something the angelic world did not see often.

This was too difficult for him to fathom. Any of the heavenly angels know the Morningstars are their most natural and despised enemy. Morningstars are responsible for leading the fight against God to begin with.

"She did save the boy," Jericho said under his breath. "Maybe it had nothing to do with the Morningstar."

"What did you say?" Serena replied. "Speak up."

"Never mind, I wish you no harm Serena."

Serena was angered, she was ready to fight, but powered down just the same. Heaven's army did not allow aggressive violence. It was against the rules. There has been a truce between the two sides for some time now. Only if the angels of Heaven are attacked can they fight to defend themselves. Breaking this rule of Heaven would cause Serena to be cast from Heaven—then *she* would be a fallen one. Jericho understood these rules well. Like the most criminals, they understand the laws better than the ones enforcing it. Jericho did not want her dead just yet. There were questions to be answered.

Jericho asked, "who was the boy you had toting in your arms today?"

"Someone I felt needed protection, especially when I saw you in the room."

"No…the human was going to kill the boy. I was occupied elsewhere. But it was funny you did not say he needed protection from the Morningstar."

Jericho waited for a reaction; Serena struggled to find the right words. Jericho's specialty was information, he bought and sold precious knowledge during the Great War of Heaven. He was clearly on the side against God.

"Let me make this simple," Jericho continued. "The Morningstar is raising this kid as his own. If I were looking down from Heaven I would suspect some sort of foul play."

"You keep calling him a Morningstar," said Serena, "but he is not one. I don't know what he is."

"I am telling you he is a Morningstar. I saw the scar up close, where his spike was removed."

"You lie!" Serena screamed.

"If you were not such a devout heavenly angel I would think that it was you who were lying to me. You can check it out if you want, I am sure he will show you."

Serena was flustered, Jericho picked up on this immediately.

"Is there something I am missing my dear Serena?"

"Shut up!"

Serena gave Jericho one last glare, her beautiful bright green eyes piercing his under the moonlit sky. Then just as quietly as she appeared, she disappeared under the darkness of the shadowy trees.

"Until the next time, lovely Throne."

Heaven has its many rewards besides eternal life, and satisfactions are abundant. All of the feelings human beings crave their whole lives—security, love, happiness, and a multitude of desires are all fulfilled. Any and every need is quenched. All negative feelings are expunged. But free will remains—the greatest gift known to all creatures, which coincidentally is the greatest problem Heaven ever faced. The Great War of Heaven was all about free will.

If free will truly existed in Heaven God's laws would not be held against the defiant. Lucifer the brilliant, powerful, and intelligent Morningstar, led the rebellion against Heaven's laws. His defiance made him ugly and evil—those that followed him, lost their place in paradise.

Heaven is paradise. However the mind can fathom it, Heaven becomes their wish. The war of Heaven was all about the angels. They were the ones who occupied Heaven during the disagreement. Long before intelligent life was created on earth. God's most precious gift, free will, came to disrupt the paradise of Heaven and later on earth. The decision to exercise free will at all costs, or being loyal to the creator, caused a tear between the heavenly bond of paradise, and sides were formed.

Close friends in Heaven became divided and they remain that way even now. The option was simple, conform to God's laws or be punished. But that was not good enough. Some demanded another world be created where they were free to live life without God's constricting demands. In a strange twist of fate that world was granted. An angelic prison called Hell. But there was another alternative each angel had.

They could take their physical bodies and live out life in that form, residing among the millions of worlds created in the universe. There the angels resided until God decided to create intelligent life. Now the angels were no longer welcomed in those worlds, they had to vacate them or be destroyed. The angels refused and bloodshed was the only option.

Once their angelic bodies were destroyed their souls would return to the only place they were welcomed. For the fallen ones that place was Hell. But in order for them to be destroyed the angels of Heaven had to take *their* physical bodies. That left the angels of Heaven vulnerable to being destroyed themselves, in which they would return to Heaven.

Each angel was given one body and one only—but what a body it was. It is the kind men and women dream of—physically perfect in every way. Constantly regenerating, this makes the body last seemingly forever. The cells maintain this process at an astounding rate, which keeps the body from aging. The physical strength within each body is capable of plowing mountains. Their skin is as tough as steel and practically impenetrable. Bodies, which can withstand extreme heat and cold, radiation, speed and 'G' forces that, would tear the common man to pieces.

Yes, they would be considered Gods by man's meager standards. That is why they had to go. By all accounts what infuriates our creator the most is the thought of someone worshiping another God. The angels loyal to God respect his kingdom and roam among men in his service. They do not attract attention to themselves.

Heaven is great and being in God's service has added rewards, but there is one thing the Throne Serena admits she wants to experience. Something Heaven cannot grant, that is the gift of creation through another life. Love, expressed through her own flesh and blood. She watched Prine and Lexington from a distance for many years. She knows his emotion and affection is real. As incredible as the angelic bodies are they have no reproductive system. Prine's son is obviously not of his own flesh, but he treats him as if he was. Serena wanted that experience for herself.

After talking with Jericho Black, Serena sought the counsel of Heaven. She was there only twenty minutes and she did not want to stay in Heaven one second longer. The counsel's decision was upsetting her. She began the exhausting journey of her soul returning to its temple on earth: her physical body. This was how angels traveled from Heaven to earth.

The angelic body, once born, remains on earth. Only the spirit can return freely. Serena's body sat in a prone position as if she was meditating. Whenever an angel does this, their bodies are easily susceptible to being destroyed. For this two guardians transport themselves from Heaven to stand watch. They do not intervene, but they are there to warn the owner if anyone wishes the body harm. The journey takes less than a second to complete. Serena could soon feel things she only feels in the physical form.

Her senses detected gravity, breathing, and the smell of horrible cooking from next door. Yes, she knew she had returned to earth, she then opened her eyes. Serena focused in on something that was not there when she left. Dr. Prine was sitting in a prone position also, directly in front of her. His eyes did not waver from hers. She had no idea what he was going to do.

"Do you have something to tell me?" asked Prine.

"I did not invite you into my apartment."

"I did not invite you into my son's life, yet you are more involved than I would ever imagine. But that is small potatoes. I want to know about me."

"What about you?"

"Don't mess with me. I'm not in the mood."

Serena was not used to being talked to in that manner and it showed.

"*YOU*? Let me tell you what you are. You are a devil, a demon—a fallen angel whose place is in Hell! That's who you are."

Prine was in disbelief. Never in his wildest imagination did he believe that was possible. He sat back on the floor and leaned against the back of a sofa, staring blankly across the room.

"I want Lexington," Serena demanded, "no need for him to fall to the same fate as you."

"Forget it, he is my son. What happened in the past remains there. His place is with me."

"Didn't you hear what I said?"

"I heard you," said Prine, "but I don't believe it."

"Because you have no recollection, right?" Serena's aggressive posture toward the fallen angel subsided. The hammer of curiosity smashed her iron defenses. Even more so—she was in awe of Prine, and his innocence through his accomplishment was fascinating. Her harsh tone softened. She asked of Prine: "How did you do it?"

"What have I done?" he said.

"You overcame a punishment—you're so naïve, you have no idea of the curse handed down by God. That scar on your left hand."

"There is a dream," Prine explained, "where something is cut from my hand. I feel the pain each time it is dreamt."

"You are a Morningstar. There was a spike, which protruded from the back of your hand. It distinguished you from other angels. You were the first heavenly beings created after God created himself. Morningstars were blessed with extreme intelligence, second only to God. They were the brightest spots of Heaven, truly magnificent beings. Your gift became a nightmare for Heaven. Morningstars led the rebellion against God and persuaded others to do the same, prompting the Great War of Heaven. In the physical form, that spike, was an incredible weapon. It was capable of easily penetrating the tough skin of the angelic body, but that was not the worst of it. When angelic blood touched the porous surface of the spike, it was sucked in and absorbed in the Morningstar's body.

The Morningstar was then able to transform, for seven seconds, into the most awesome force of destruction. We called it seven seconds of hell for any heavenly being unlucky enough to be caught in the wrath of the Morningstar. The Morningstars called it 'Elizal's Rage' after the first Morningstar to ever use it.

But the Almighty God intervened and instructed us to remove the spike from the Morningstars. The rest of us figured that would keep them from slaughtering us, but their intelligence in battle would still be superior—except that was not the case. God insisted we trust him, and we did. There was a chemical effect that occurred in the body of the Morningstar once the spike was removed, causing them to go insane. It had the familiar effect of the modern day lobotomy—rendering the Morningstar harmless. It was said to be a punishment handed down, for the crimes against God and Heaven. Whenever a Morningstar's spike was removed and left on the battlefield, the other fallen Morningstars would perform a mercy killing. They could not bear to see one of their own reduced to a vegetable. In the history of Heaven, there has never been a Morningstar that recovered from being 'despiked'—*until you.*"

Prine listened carefully to what Serena had said. It placed certain aspects of his dream in perspective. Prine considered the possibility of what Serena said as being true. In a somber expression of recognition…

"And you think because of my past, I will corrupt my son as well?" asked Prine.

"You still call him your son? Lexington is the son of your deceased wife. You are just his step father."

The discussion began to heat up once more.

"You are lucky I no longer have spike. I sure know who I would use it on."

"Don't be upset with me because of your shortcomings. If you have not been paying attention I just told you that you are an angel, and angels cannot reproduce."

"Bullshit! What do you call this."

Prine pointed down at his genitals.

"They are only for show buddy. Haven't you figured that out yet."

Serena made a gesture with her hand pointed downward swinging it back and forth. Prine became infuriated.

"You think so huh?! If you were a REAL woman, I would show you how well it works."

"Stop dreaming!"

"Fuck you! He is my son. Stay the hell away from him, physically and mentally."

Prine got up and left Serena's apartment, furious and confused. He believed every word Serena spoke, even though he did not want to. All except the part about him not being able to perform sexually. Out of all the other explanations, hers was the only one that made sense to him. He thought back to when he fought Jericho, his hand, the scar—it opened and a strange feeling came over him. It was longing for something, and that something was blood.

The spike craves angelic blood for strength, a high, and an extreme rush of adrenaline. When he fought Jericho, Prine felt it. The wound opened hoping for a drop of precious blood to flow down its receptors and give him the strength of 'Elizal's Rage.' Prine suspected it was all true even though he could not remember any of it. The only thing that he was not ready to face, was the comment about his son belonging to someone else.

❧   ❧   ❧

Silence in a car between two people can be an extremely awkward feeling. They both had a lot on their minds, Prine and Lexington. Questions about themselves and each other, the biggest being, who were they? For Lexington, he wanted to know what it meant to be the son of an angel. For Dr. Prine, the question was how does he regain his memory. But this time it was not a life as a human, he was looking for his story in Heaven.

What part did he play leading up to being cast out of Heaven? Prine started out being an investigator, interviewing people to help out Jack Ward in his pursuit of the solving the case of Cindy Revner. Now, the desire to see the case through to the end was the furthest thing on his mind. The time had come to meet with Jack one last time, and inform Jack of his intention to return to the College. It would not be easy; Prine was getting personally attached to the case, the victim—even the suspects. But at this time his emotions were askew. Trying to cope with his knew life had just moved to the top of his priority list.

"Did I do something wrong, Dad?" asked Lexington. Prine had been daydreaming for the past two minutes. The last few miles on the road was a blur, he does not even recall how he navigated through traffic without getting in an accident. Lexington's question finally brought him to his senses.

"I've been talking to you for over three minutes now. You haven't said a word."

"Sorry, Lexington, I was just preoccupied with something else."

"You mean about last night?"

"You know I care about you, all we have is each other. Since your mother died I felt we grew closer. Maybe we had no other choice. I just want you to know, although you are only nine years old I realize there is no fooling you. I can't explain away what you saw, or what you heard, and try to convince you it was all some dream."

"It felt like a dream Dad, it really did."

"Lexington, I want what is between us to be strong. I want you to know there is nothing I would not do for you. I won't play games with you. You are the only one I can count on and I would not jeopardize that bond. I am here for you now as I have always been, nothing has changed."

Lexington stared out of the passenger window as they drove down the freeway. "So, now what Dad?" He may have been a boy genius and extremely perceptive, but he was still a boy. "You won't go to Heaven, or go off to be someone else's guardian, will you?" Prine knew what it was like to be alone in this world. His son, for as long as he existed, would never have to experience that kind of emptiness.

"I will never leave you my son."

Prine remembered all that Serena had told him, but that still did not define who he was. His thoughts and beliefs, the reason he sided with the fallen ones against Heaven, were no longer a part of his conscious mind. Until he could remember all of it, he would not attempt to explain it to his son. Lexington was the person in the world that looked up to him the most. He owed it to his son to get it right.

CHAPTER 24

Falling Apart

Jericho returned to privacy of his office in the Black Inc. building. His clothes slightly torn; he opens the armoire located by the balcony, to pick out some fresh attire. Jericho was a businessman, not a fighter; that is what he said during the Great War of Heaven. He was known more for his skills at gathering and selling information, than inflicting physical damage. If he had suspected Dr. Prine was a Morningstar, he would have stayed right where he was, and would have told Rin and Jacob to do the same.

But eventually, he would have been a sitting duck. Jacob, his trusted guard, was far too observant, and an obvious thief. He knew things he should not have. When Jacob spoke in the angelic tongue there was a chill that ran down Jericho's spine. Jericho wrote certain things on pieces of paper—certain angelic phrases. He thought he put them in a safe place, but not safe enough. The phrase was not the part that cost Jacob his life; it was the items placed along with the written phrases. These were priceless items that were collected over thousands of years, the very rarest of possessions. The value to humans might be overlooked, if they did not know what they were for.

The angelic phrase 'send him to hell' was placed with a particular item—but had Jacob discovered its earthly value? That was what Jericho needed to find out. From Jack Ward's description of the murdered victims, there was a good chance that Jacob *had* discovered its earthly value. Jacob's life was taken the instant Jericho realized what his devoted guard had done. Because of Jacob's thievery, Jericho's life was now in danger.

As with the life of all the fallen angels, Jericho knew this day would come. When it rains, it pours, and Jericho was about to discover his problems on earth was just beginning. Jericho thought it best to take a nap, it was late and the battle with Prine had fatigued the deceptive Dominion. He rested for four hours, that was all his troubled mind would allow.

His office was complete with a bathroom and shower. He arose to prepare himself for a cool shower. Perhaps that would settle his nerves. Jericho softly closed his eyes and let the showerhead's pulsating jets, directed right at his face, massage his facial muscles and relax his whole body. He dried off and covered himself in a plush, velvet soft, terry cloth robe he bought while in Paris. Jericho made his way over to his armoire to pick out another set of clothes when the phone rang.

That phone was on a direct line in, a call that could not be intercepted by his assistant. Not too many people have the number to his direct office line. He answered the call. It was a woman on the phone, she was crying, and she was hysterical.

"You bastard, you told me everything was okay. You said you would find him."

Regina James was the wife of the missing worker, Orlando. Orlando was a lighting technician that worked at the Hall of Kings. He discovered the fixed selection of the Sheryl O'Connor when he stumbled across the multiple tickets, with her seat number on it, drawn for the Miracle Ceremony. Less than seventy-two hours ago, Jericho assured Regina that he would do all he could to locate her husband. He did not even lift a finger toward fulfilling that promise. She was calling to inform Jericho that her husband had been found. They pulled his body from a raw sewage plant after a worker discovered a blockage in one of their lines. Regina had been talking with police all night after identifying her husband's body.

The vengeful wife was now informing Jericho that the police were on their way to get him.

"You bitch, I did not kill your husband!"

"Save it for the police. I will enjoy seeing a rich boy like you being hauled away."

"Why would I kill him? I gave him seventy million dollars to keep his mouth shut. I bought him a new identity—all the things I promised the both of you. Why would I turn around and kill him?"

Jericho was speaking the truth. He did not choose to kill Orlando James, he thought to buy his silence instead—to the tune of seventy million dollars. A new life and new identity awaited Orlando, but apparently he did not make it. Jericho, like Prine, knew what it was like to change identities. With increasing technology, where Prine saw the ability to assume a new identity becoming increasingly difficult, Jericho's vast wealth could still buy him one easily. This time Jericho had nothing to do with the death of a human. It would be hard to buy himself out of this one. Either way, it was now Jericho's current identity that was on its last days.

"What did you tell them?" Jericho insisted. Regina began screaming invectives at Jericho. Jericho ignored her and began repeatedly slamming the receiver on the desk. Jericho was furious. His time was up, going through a murder trial for a man of his wealth would mean big news. He could afford all the high priced lawyers he needed for a trial, but if Regina told the police Jericho tried to buy their silence after discovering the Miracle selection was fixed, his image would be frozen in the minds of people everywhere. There would be no where on earth he could hide without being recognized. His reign as an entrepreneur has come to an end, it was time for *him* to assume a new identity. Unknown to Jericho, was another person who knew something of the murder, that person was calling Roland Stark that very moment.

Roland was at his home when he received the call. On the other line was Sheryl O'Connor. She had awakened to the news that a worker at the Hall of Kings was murdered. When she heard the name of the man, Orlando James, she had to warn Roland and explain the meaning of her vision. "Reverend Stark," Sheryl said, "remember I told you of a vision I had at the time I drank of the water?"

"Yes, Sheryl. I remember."

"I told you it was something like 'land of games.' When I turned on the news this morning they mentioned a name of someone killed—that works at the Hall of Kings. His name is Orlando James—it wasn't 'land of games' I heard in the vision—it was Orlando James! He was trying to warn me. That is why I was up in my seat. During the vision he mentioned something about my seat number."

Roland Stark was finding this all hard to believe. "I heard of this Sheryl, the police spoke to me too. He had been missing since last week. I gave them all the information about him not showing up since the previous Sunday."

"No reverend, he was killed the morning of the service! He mentioned about the Miracle being a fake; that a partner of yours was behind it. He also made it a point to tell me your life was in danger."

"Do you believe it to be a fake?" Roland asked. "Is your experience, even the vision you received fake? If you believe the Miracle to be a fake, then your vision is fake as well."

Roland could hear the frustration in her voice as she tried to explain. "I don't know reverend, but in my heart I believe your life is in danger!"

Roland's faith in his God did not allow for him to be troubled by Sheryl's vision. He put the faith in the hands of his God to deliver the truth. He was however, troubled about his partners involvement.

This was the second time in as many weeks that someone has warned him about Jericho. Before Colleen left for vacation she eventually told him about the FBI inquiring about Jericho Black. She also told Roland she talked with the agent for several hours. Roland was going to make a trip to the Hall of Kings to see if he could find Jericho. Roland's instincts were right on the money.

On the morning of Miracle Sunday, a man in a black sedan had pulled up outside a service entrance at the Hall of Kings. That man was Orlando James. Jericho, threw to Orlando, the means of obtaining the new identity and of accessing the money. Jericho set up an elaborate network of contacts to help Orlando on his way, all the information was contained in that envelope. Orlando was set, all he needed to do was to pick up his wife and head to the airport.

The problem Orlando ran into on the way home, was the career criminal, William Richardson. William was in search of information on how to enter the Hall of Kings. He wanted to know how to move around freely, without much interference from security. Orlando exchanged his life for that information, he thought William would keep his end of the bargain. He did not.

William got more than he bargained for. Not only did he gain the information he needed, he received a new identity and access to seventy million dollars. And Orlando received two bullets in the chest at close range.

Marie Carthon was feeling much more at home than she has felt in the past couple of weeks. She had converted herself into a homemaker, quite a far cry than what she used to be. The Carthon's was sitting at the dinner table ready to eat. Marcus had returned from work, his mind was still on his wife and her condition. She still had not spoken a word to anyone other than Rameci in over two weeks, true to her word, guaranteeing the safety of her family. But frustration began to hit the Carthon home, and it was reaching its boiling point. She could not expect things to stay in control forever.

This was a situation that had to be addressed. A family cannot function in this fashion without some questions being answered. Marcus, Marie's husband, has had enough. The volatile situation was destined for a head to head confrontation. It was inevitable. Marcus sat at the dinner table for five minutes, the entire time, not a word was spoken—by anyone. Marcus was about to change that.

"How was your day Marie?" said Marcus

"It was fine," Marie's mother responded.

"Sorry, Mom, but I was talking to Marie." The tension began to build in the room.

Marcus was at his breaking point. He could not handle Marie's silence anymore. "Mom, I would like you to take Steven and Carl into the next room."

"But Marcus," Marie's mother pleaded. Marcus's voice only became louder.

"Take my children into the bedroom and close the door!"

Mother was confused, and worried. She looked at Marie, who stared into her plate, and then back to Marcus. Marcus wanted a few words with his wife, and he would not be denied. Reluctantly, Mom got up from the table and escorted young Steven and Carl into the bedroom. The door shut behind them and Mark began.

"You will talk to me Marie," he said. Marie put on a big smile, but did not show any teeth. Her lips were pressed together, it was a nervous, compliant type of smile. Mark's voice became increasingly louder.

"What does that mean Marie! I don't understand that, open your mouth and speak!" The phony smile was erased from Marie's face; she remained silent. Marcus slammed an open hand down on the dinner table; a startled Marie, jumped upon hearing the loud sound.

"There is nothing wrong with you Marie, I played this game long enough. I spoke to the Doctor, he told me there was nothing wrong with you. You can speak if you want to, as your husband I demand you talk to me!"

Tears began to stream down Marie's cheeks. She tasted the warm, salty solution as it seeped between her closed lips and into her mouth. He did not understand. Her silence was securing their lives, the lives of their sons, and Marcus's life also. She clasped both hands in front of her, making a pleading gesture, for him not to push the issue. If she spoke Rameci might find out and inflict his punishment.

"I have spoken to the FBI," Marcus continued. "Do you know who Jack Ward is? He is an agent investigating the murder of a woman in the woods. The same woods you went running in every morning, and he says you saw something. I want you to talk to him. I want you to help them catch this madman. Do you know he killed others, that they have been hunting this guy for months? Marie, talk to me, talk to the FBI—goddamit say something!" Mark stood from his seat and kicked the chair back, he ran to where his wife was sitting and got inches from her face. With his index finger pointed inches from her nose he screamed.

"DO YOU WANT SOME MADMAN TO WALK IN HERE AND KILL US? DO YOU WANT HIM TO LOP OUR FRIGGIN' HEADS OFF MARIE? IS THAT WHAT YOU WANT FOR YOUR FAMILY, IS THAT WHAT YOU THINK OF US? THE FBI IS WAITING FOR YOU TO HELP THEM OUT. YOU WILL TALK!"

With tears still streaming down her cheeks, Marie shook her head no, the entire time her husband was talking. How could she tell him without endangering the very lives she struggled to protect? All was fine so long as she kept her lips shut; her family would be safe except she could not tell him that. All she could hope for is that her husband would give up, that he would become so frustrated and not bring up the subject again. She shook her head frantically hoping he would sense the fear in her heart and back off.

Marcus grabbed a pencil and a writing tablet, he slammed it on the table in front of her. "Write it down—whatever it is write it down!" he insisted. He grabbed her hand put the pencil in it and began writing "*I need help*" while guiding her hand. When Marcus released his grip, Marie threw the pencil across the room and knocked the tablet onto the floor. This time Marie was pointing the finger at her husband. She was no longer crying. With closed lips she was warning him, she shook her finger for him to never do that again. The strong person she was before the incident had suddenly reemerged.

Reluctantly, Marcus backed off and walked to the phone. He pulled out the business card that was handed to him by Jack Ward. He was calling the psychologist the agent had recommended, Dr. Walter Prine. He spoke on the phone for five minutes, Marie did not care to listen to her husband's conversation. When the call was done, Marcus was more frustrated than ever. In light of the recent revelation, Dr. Prine was unwilling to help him out. Prine was heading back to his home in Northern Virginia.

❧   ❧   ❧

Roland Stark eagerly awaited the arrival of Jericho Black. He was waiting on the B2 level of the Hall of Kings facility, knowing this was where Jericho spent most of his time. The police was looking for Jericho, they wanted to question him on the murder of Orlando James. They were asking questions all day on his whereabouts. Roland did not tell them, but eventually he knew, Jericho would show up down here. Roland gave the entire security squad on that level the day off—he threatened them that Jericho was now a fugitive and if they did not want to get mixed up in a scandal, they should do as he instructed.

At midnight Jericho Black came marching down the corridor of the B2 level. He walked into one of several rooms, near the back left corner of he floor. Jericho opened the door and saw Roland dozing off in one of the chairs. It looked like everything was falling apart—he might as well do it all the way.

"Good evening partner," said Jericho, alerting Roland of his arrival. Jericho went over to the computer and put the hard drive he was carrying next to it. "What are they saying about me now?"

"The police and FBI are saying a lot of things. For you—they want to question you about a murder. For the ministry—they are looking into charges of *fraud*. Why do they want to charge me with fraud Jericho? They tell me the wife of the Orlando James says you were paying him off because he discovered the Miracle drawing was fixed. She claims that we hand picked the participants. Of course it is all just a claim—I was waiting for you. I need you to go down to the precinct and tell them the truth."

Roland was sincere, the entire time he spoke.

"No can do!" Jericho replied. Roland's disappointment was expressed throughout every muscle of his body. His posture and facial expression turned from hope to despair. He was now looking toward the ground as he spoke.

"I will pray that you will do the right thing Jericho."

"You are wasting your time. I am not going to the police nor will I be caught. I am going to disappear, but not after I clean up some unfinished business. You have to fend for yourself, you can lie or you can tell the truth, but I am leaving."

"I am a man of God, I always tell the truth, or I say nothing at all." Roland explained.

"Of course you do, but I have not explained our situation yet. Once I do I think you will choose to say nothing." Jericho moved closer to Roland, he wanted to make sure Roland understood every word. "Roland, do not ever attempt to try another Miracle—you will be severely disappointed. God did not heal those people…I did."

Roland shook his head in disbelief. "Nonsense, utter nonsense," he insisted. "It was the hand of God!"

"Wrong, Roland, it was the hand of a fallen angel. A Dominion, or *demon*, as you humans prefer to call it. You have an incredible gift Roland, a gift of preaching the word and I took advantage of you. I have deceived many an angel to get what I want, so don't take it too personal."

"If you have deceived me in some way that is one thing—don't call yourself a demon. You can always be forgiven. I will pray for you," said Roland.

"Prayer is not necessary Roland. As I said you have an incredible gift, but I can tell you need proof for this one."

Jericho pulled a knife from his pocket. He pressed the sharp end against his wrist and attempted to slash it by pulling down sharply. The blade did not even mark the skin. He handed the knife to Roland so he could verify its sharpness. Jericho held out his wrist.

"You can try to slash it if you like. Most of your weapons won't even scratch the angelic skin." Roland closed the pocket knife and put it onto the table. "I could also show you great feats of speed and strength, but you don't seem like someone who would be impressed by that sort of thing. But you can look into my eyes Roland, and you can see for yourself. You will be able to see if what I say is the truth or not."

Roland was afraid to look, he did not want to know. The combination of an honest preacher and a fallen angel, teaming up to deceive the world, was a thought he did not want to face. All of the things he has worked so hard to attain, was now in jeopardy. It was not the physical possessions he has worked hard for, it was the leadership. The spiritual leadership of millions of souls, guiding them toward the lord, and showing them the awesome power of God. Now, it turns out to be the power of a demon, and *he* was that demon's pawn.

Roland preached the words, "beware of the false prophet," many times, not knowing he was referring to himself. The eyes of the demon lay right before him; all he needed to do was stare into them.

But Roland did not need to look at them, in his heart he knew Jericho had spoken the truth. There was a feeling he got, over the years, whenever he dealt with Jericho—but this was the absolute worst he could imagine.

"You are on Holy ground!" Roland declared. "You will remove yourself immediately."

"This is the house that I helped build. I will leave when I am good and ready."

"You have tainted this house long enough. God has renounced your welcome here! Satan and all of his kind will not…"

"Shut up!"

"You will not…" Roland's preaching was cut short.

"YOU, will not—don't you dare think you can preach to me! I have roamed the earth for thousands of years. I have seen people like you come and go. For me, your existence here is but a blink of an eye. I have lived in Heaven, I have seen God, spoken to God—touched God. I know the word of God straight from his lips. In your meager existence don't you *ever* think that you can preach the word of God to ME!" Jericho had stood during his entire tirade with his finger pointed down at Roland's face. He remained in that position for several seconds, putting the exclamation point on his statement. When he was satisfied he moved his hand and began to gather his things.

"There are certain *things* I need to investigate before I disappear completely. Until then the B3 level is completely off limits, even to the police. They are not even to know about it—understood. If anyone but me, heads down there—I will kill them personally. Do you understand Roland?"

Jericho, true to his word, had some investigating to do. He had to evaluate the extent of the damage caused by one of his most trusted guards, Jacob. Over the next two weeks, with each move he made, Jack Ward and the FBI, were right on his heels. Each time, Jericho Black was able to elude them. Jericho led the agents through Denton,

Texas, then through Illinois. He took them through New Jersey and Maryland.

They continued to chase him through Atlanta, Georgia and over to Utah, as well as six other locations throughout the United States. At each state he stayed at a specific location, it was tracked and plotted by the FBI. The Federal Agents interviewed anyone that may have come in contact with him as to where he was headed next. Whenever they would close in on his location, he would be on the run again. Jericho remained one step ahead of the agents at all times. Then Jericho simply dropped out of sight. All of the agent's leads went cold. They simply lost track of him. After two weeks of leads, Jack Ward came up empty once more.

For Roland Stark, life was not much easier. The media was broadcasting the claims of Regina James, stating the Miracle ceremony selection was fixed. That is all she knew of the situation. They also broadcast her claim that Jericho Black murdered her husband, and the recent disappearance of Jericho. They gave play by play accounts, on the evening news, as to where he was last spotted, and that Jericho continued to elude agents time and time again. The Hall of Kings was not filled to capacity for the first time since it was completed. Roland was also true to his word, he did not lie; he was a man of God. Instead, he chose not to say anything about the subject—at all.

CHAPTER 25

The Angelic Council decides

Heaven: the ultimate reward of existence. Its inhabitants are among the most pure of morals according to God's code. A council is beginning to form, to discuss the latest developments on earth. The most revered angels in Heaven are expected to speak.

But God does not. He began to withdraw from the angel's affairs and left Heaven's responsibilities in the hands of the council until the final days. Some say that it is a test to see if the angels can manage on their own, others believe the Great War of Heaven was too much for God. They believe the war hurt him in a way others could never imagine. But that is just hearsay. Although he is not directly involved, he presents an ever-watchful eye.

He has left the decision making in the trusted hands of the senior Seraphim's and archangels. Gabriel, the chief speaker of God has arranged this latest meeting. In a magnificent garden of Heaven, highlighting all of its brilliance and splendor, they gathered. Beneath the huge Oak tree, that stood hundreds of feet high, the heavenly leaders began to assemble. Gabriel, also known as the voice of God, along with chief angels, Michael and Raphael, Samuel, Sachiel, Anael, and Cassiel made up the Angelic Council. At the meeting were two other archangels, Raguel and Jeremiel. They were not a part of the council, but they were respected enough to sit in on the meeting. Besides, Heaven holds no secrets…that is what they would like to believe.

After embracing one another; Heaven's customary form of greeting, the chief angel Samuel started off the meeting. "Why are we meeting again so soon, Gabriel?"

"Earth," said Gabriel, "You know of Earth don't you? Of the millions of galaxies under God's creation, the planet called Earth was the one the Morningstar's claimed as their own." All of the chief angels were familiar with the statement.

"The Morningstar's are no longer a threat," Michael interjected. "Why has it now become an issue? We know of their weaknesses, we know how to fight them. There are only a handful of Morningstar's left in the universe, the rest are in Hell."

Anael, the female chief angel, spoke for the first time. "Don't claim victory so soon Michael. Let's not forget Lucifer is one of those few still out there. You of all angels should know better than to underestimate their power." Her words caught the immediate attention of the others. They did not forget the Morningstar's ability, or their projected potential.

"Lucifer is thousands of galaxies away," said Sachiel, "he has been quiet for more than a millennia. His followers are scattered across the universe. Why are we still talking about the Morningstars? There are far more powerful fallen ones we must contend with. The Morningstars are a dying breed."

"Not quite," echoed Gabriel. His strong voice was complimentary, and worthy of being the voice of God. "Brother Raphael has something to share with the council." The chief angels turned toward Raphael, eagerly awaiting his word.

"The Throne, Serena, reported to me a boy which she detected strong sensory power and intelligence. He could detect life-force and energy to a certain degree, so Serena decided to communicate with him—spiritually. The boy responded!" A moan was heard from several of the chief angels, they were flabbergasted. "Serena," Raphael continued, "was attempting to persuade the boy to use his gifts to help mankind, he is only nine years old."

Cassiel, the cautious one, began to speak. "For a human to detect life-force is something rare, this incident should be treated with concern. Did the boy detect a vision or something?"

"No," Raphael continued, "nothing as insignificant as that. But his skill is the best that she has ever recorded."

Sachiel asked specifically, "Is it the best that she has recorded, or is it the best ever recorded?"

To the chagrin of the other members, Raphael stated, "By far, it is the best *ever* recorded. Fifteen times greater than Solomon—*after* God enhanced his mind." All of the chief angels were now as concerned as Cassiel.

"He could see directly into Heaven!" Samuel shouted.

"That is not all," Raphael added, "for now the boy believes what he has seen is all a dream. Serena has been able to allow him to think that is all it is. Where the real trouble lies is that the boy is being raised on earth...by a *Morningstar*."

"That is absurd," Michael shouted. "Your Throne must be mistaken!"

"No, she has since taken her physical body to check it out thoroughly. She has met the fallen one face to face. He has the scar where his spike was removed, he is a Morningstar."

Gabriel immediately tried to quiet the group. They had erupted in tiny groups conversing among themselves. Once order was restored, through Gabriel's commanding voice, Raphael was urged to continue. "We do not know his angelic name, but we are trying to find out now."

"You say he is raising the boy—is that correct?" asked Samuel, "What condition is he in to do that? If he is without the spike, he is fit to do no more than drool and mumble incessantly. His mental faculties…"

"His mental faculties," Raphael interrupted, "has been restored, and his intelligence is returning."

Order was disrupted again as the chiefs conversed among themselves for a second time. Michael was in deep thought. The council quieted when he shouted, "So, there is one more Morningstar. Nothing we cannot handle."

The rest of the council did not share his confidence.

"You are showing the Morningstars the same contemptuous, disrespect you have shown them in the past," said Anael. "I expected you to learn your lesson from your last battle with them Michael."

"Here, here," said Samuel, "Something must be done to rectify the situation, now!"

"We cannot initiate a fight with the fallen ones."

"Then we will get them to fight us. A Morningstar would clearly initiate the battle if given the opportunity."

"He did not kill the Throne when he met with her. What has he done to make us think he will be fooled easily?"

"We cannot just sit and wait for his true power to be reawakened!"

"THAT IS ENOUGH!" The commanding voice of Gabriel brought the bickering to a halt. It was time for Gabriel to take control. "I agree with all of your concerns. Who knows if this Morningstar will ever reach his full power of intellect and persuasion? Without the spike his physical and mental power is limited. We will do no more than wait. Raphael, have Serena continue to communicate with the boy. Have her teach him all she can about our cause, instruct him on the ways of God and righteousness. That will be the way to handle this. With the Almighty's influence, the boy should hopefully choose the right side. That is all."

Gabriel was done and the meeting was over. The chief angels embraced each other again and headed on their separate ways along

Heaven's many paths. All the more wiser that a serious threat to their existence is present on the planet earth.

Raphael did as Gabriel had instructed. He met with Serena to tell her the council's decision. Raphael did not bring up Serena's alternative. He thought it was silly and it was best not to mention it to the council. Serena wanted to take the boy and raise him on earth. That way, the security of Heaven would be ensured. But Raphael paid her no attention.

Serena asked Raphael, "Have you given any consideration to what I talked about earlier?"

"The boy is like any child his age, he has the energy and zest of innocence."

"Innocence? He is being raised by a Morningstar! One who has overcome his physical restrictions. A Morningstar who has undone God's punishment."

"What?"

Raphael was extremely angered. "Don't you ever assume a fallen angel can undo what was done by our creator. He merely overcame a physical and mental handicap, that is all."

"Well, he is the *only* Morningstar to ever do it since *our creator* pointed out a way of crippling them."

"It would be nice if Heaven were not sacrificed for a New World. Who knows what the Almighty has planned? Until he voices his commands I and the council have full command over Heaven's matters."

"Listen Raphael, all I want to do is educate the boy of our ways, he will choose like everyone else," Serena pleaded.

"You insist on defying me on this. I stand firm. If you continue I will inform the council of your aversion to perform Heaven's duties."

Serena reluctantly agreed to drop the argument.

"Good, then as I discussed—the first sign of aggression from the boy you shall take him as a serious threat. Kill him if you have to."

Raphael was out of line. The council is unclear on what to do. For some time now the affairs of Heaven has been left in the hands of the angelic council. The Almighty God who created Heaven and Earth, left the angelic council in charge for an indefinite period of time. Since that time God has not uttered a word, only his presence is felt. Some angels speculate the Great War of Heaven was too much for him. The division, which tore Heaven apart, tore him apart as well. He is now contemplating creation…all creation, to see if it is worthy of continuing. But he has been silent for too long and the angels are beginning to worry. There are far too many things in the universe they do not understand, and when God stopped communicating with them, things were never the same. The angels are the instruments of his will, they are there to do his bidding. They are not used to deciphering things on their own. Serena knew Heaven's situation was not good, although she had all the confidence it would turn out all right. It was the journey, which she was concerned about. The bumps along the way might be too painful to endure. Serena looked toward the Heavens, and shouted.

"Jehovah, we need you!"

❀   ❀   ❀

Jack Ward's frustration toward the case was reaching an all time high. He was dealing with a highly efficient killer, one with patience and intelligence who left investigators absolutely nothing to go by. Without an eyewitness he had to rely on microscopic, physical evidence. Out of eight murders there was only one victim which carried any type of physical evidence to go by—carpet fibers. In the present world of forensic science, the odds of collecting so little evidence out of all those murders was astounding. The Pristine murderer would be free to kill again, if he so chooses, without investigators having a clue as to where or when.

Even the pattern to the murders was sporadic. He struck at different times and locations. The victims were both male and female of various body types. Short, tall, blonde, brunettes, heavy set, and slim, with various nationalities. He chose his victims at random without any type of physical preference.

Over the last two weeks Jack has chased Jericho Black across the United States. Jericho was wanted for questioning regarding the death of one of his workers. Jericho was not actually considered a legitimate suspect in that case. There was not enough physical evidence to charge him. There was only the word of the worker's wife, Regina James. Besides all of her claims there was not one solid shred of evidence. It was Jericho's behavior toward being brought in for questioning that made him a suspect. Jericho refused to meet with police and then went on the run. But Jack did not lose sight of his original case: The Pristine murders.

After getting the latest criminal profile, the FBI agent decided to go back to the only lead he had, which was a hunch from an old woman with a missing granddaughter. That woman was Gertrude Revner. Her feeling about the disappearance of her granddaughter, Cindy, being related to the Pristine Murders was never fully investigated. He only knew that Gertrude somehow found out about the murders and called the FBI drawing conclusions to Cindy. Call it a long shot, that a woman in Connecticut somehow got a hold of a local paper in a small town in Alabama, and linked the murder to her own granddaughter's tragedy.

It was an aspect Jack ignored, but he thought, just to make it official, he would go to ask Gertrude how she could connect the two incidents. He would pay particular attention to anything he may have missed the first time. An observation technique he picked up from Dr. Prine. In short, he would listen to her without the preconceived notion that she was a domineering old woman strung out on massive doses of medication.

Jack made the exhausting trip to the Wiltshire Nursing home in Connecticut, after briefly stopping by the office in Washington D.C. This had been his third trip back to the East Coast in four days. Jack thought it was best he rest awhile before visiting Gertrude. He picked a hotel directly across from the Nursing home, the accommodations were adequate and cost was of no concern when the government was paying for it—so long as it was below the predetermined rate. The hotel often catered to families traveling long distances to visit their loved ones across the street.

The prestigious Wiltshire Nursing facility attracted people from all over the Northeast. Jack checked into his room and settled down for a good day's rest. The only room available was a first floor special, which was substandard compared to what he was used to. Rest, was the only thing on his mind. He has not had much of an opportunity to do so lately.

After only one hour of lying in bed he was awakened by verbal commotion outside the hotel. He could hear a woman screaming at someone. He arose from bed to close the window when he saw Gertrude outside the Nursing home. A man was helping her to a car. Gertrude was walking with a cane, hunched over, laboring with each step. The man to her right was assisting her.

"This is getting interesting!" Jack declared.

Gertrude was not the type to be outside the home. She was supposed to be recovering from a broken hip, and that did not look like a family member that was with her. Jack was positive the family forbade it due to her physical condition. It was 5:00 p.m., and Jack was not prepared to confront the withered old woman, but this was something out of the ordinary. He quickly got dressed and headed out to his car. Gertrude got into a dark blue LeSabre. By the time she was seated and strapped in, Jack was in his car and had pulled around to the parking lot facing the Nursing home. The dark blue sedan pulled out of the lot and headed west, Jack pulled out behind them.

Cautiously he tailed them, to the highway and through the city. The car came to a stop near a brown brick townhouse. This was a classy part of town; the kind of neighborhood Gertrude was known to frequent. The man driving got out of the car and opened the door for Gertrude. He assisted her to her feet and along the sidewalk to the stairwell leading up to the townhouse. Jack parked a good distance away, he used his binoculars to watch them walk to the door. Gertrude inserted a key into the door and opened it. The driver handed Gertrude a plastic bag filled with items, the kind you get at a grocery store. She said something to the driver and walked inside. The driver headed back to the car and sat patiently.

"Alright," said Jack, it was time to see what was going on.

Jack left the car and walked down the parked cars toward the LeSabre. With badge in hand, he stopped by the driver's window, displayed the badge, and had the driver roll down the window.

"Yes Officer?"

"I'm Agent Jack Ward. I am with the FBI. What are you doing here chief?"

"I-I'm waiting for my mother, she is visiting an old friend."

"Your mother? What's your name?"

"Paul Milan."

"Milan?" Jack knew he was lying. "Who is your mother visiting, and why aren't you inside with her?"

"Some old friend named Doris. I get bored with two old women talking. I like staying out here. Is there a problem?"

The driver was getting suspicious with the agents questioning. He had done nothing wrong, except lie about who was inside.

"Listen chief, obviously you don't know I am a friend of the family. I happen to know that Gertrude Revner is up there, not your mother. I followed you from the Nursing home."

The driver did not take the news well.

"I don't understand. Why were you following us?" the driver asked.

"Why did you lie about who was inside?"

"Because she told me not to let anyone know where she was going. I do whatever she says, she can be a royal biddy."

Jack knew exactly what he was talking about.

"From now on there will be no more lying to me or I will take you in. Got it?"

The driver nodded in agreement.

"Good," Jack continued, "I want to know how long you have been coming here and who lives here?"

"I take Gertrude here twice a week. I have been doing it for the past six or seven months."

"And who lives here?" asked Jack.

"I have no idea."

Jack was not accepting that as an answer.

"You better come up with a name quick. And I mean it better be on the tip of your tongue."

The driver was exceptionally calm for being threatened by a federal agent, maybe because he had nothing to hide.

"Like I said before, Gertrude does not want me to know who she is visiting and that's that. She says, she pays me to take her here and that's all she pays me for. She doesn't want any conversation or companionship. She gives me a shopping list, I grab the groceries, head to pick her up, drive her here, wait in the car for five hours, and drive her back to the home."

"She's here for five hours?" Jack asked.

"Four or five hours, yea."

Jack tried to calculate all that the driver was telling him. She probably had a gentleman friend she came to visit. A friend she did not want the rest of her family to know about. The problem with Jack was that he was not known for being subtle. Jack thanked the driver for the information and headed toward the front door of the townhouse. He was going to use that knowledge against Gertrude, possibly to find out just how she got her hands on that Alabama newspaper. Jack walked to the top of the stairs and rang the bell. He pushed it several times with no response. He then tried the door, it was open. He stuck his head inside and yelled.

"Hello, Gertrude?"

There was no answer.

"Hey, this is Jack Ward from the FBI. I know about your secret sweetheart. Come on over and introduce me."

Still there was no response. Jack tried to peek around the half open door looking for any type of movement.

"If no one comes to greet me I will consider it an emergency and enter the premises. You people are old, you might both be passed out or something…In need of medical attention…I could not get that off my conscience…I'm coming in…Alright!"

Jack took several steps inside the house and paused. The hallway leading to the living room had solid oak hardwood floors. Jack stopped to admire the shine it held. The art decorations on the walls were also to Jack's liking. He could see the living room area ahead and called out again for Gertrude. *Now this was becoming strange.* Did she think she could hide until he decided to leave? That was not going to happen.

"I am going to plop my behind right here on the couch until somebody comes out to see me," Jack insisted. Jack walked into the living room and did as he said. There was a bright white sofa near a glass coffee table. Jack made himself comfortable right there. He began to look toward the kitchen for any evidence of his favorite addiction.

"Do you guys have any coffee brewing? I sure could use a cup."

Still nothing—Jack got up and walked into the kitchen. There was a coffeepot but it looked like it had not seen coffee in years.

"You guys don't use this thing enough, it still looks clear."

It looked uncommonly clean; the whole place was spotless. Not one item was out of place. Jack opened a drawer. There was silverware inside that also looked brand new. He opened a few of the cupboards; there was very little food inside any of them. He then went to check the refrigerator; there was a few items inside, but not much.

The townhouse was classy, an upper class dwelling filled with art and decorative items. But it felt empty. The only thing that did not belong was a wooden crate, about three feet high, near the fireplace. It was probably used to store wood for the wintertime. He noticed a foul stench when he approached the crate. Jack walked closer to look inside and made a frightening discovery. There was a body inside the crate, on its side in a fetal position.

"What the freak?"

It was an adult woman, rather young, her body barely fit into the crate. Jack made sure what he saw was real. She was alive! She was breathing, short shallow breaths. Her skin was pale, with small red spots all over her exposed skin. Jack saw her wince as a fly landed on her skin. Apparently the red spots were from the biting flies. She was malnourished from what he could see. There was a blanket that covered most of her body; she appeared to be nude underneath.

"Are you alright miss?"

Her shallow brown eyes shifted to look up at Jack. It was the eeriest feeling Jack ever experienced. Jack reached into his pocket for his cell phone and he pushed auto dial.

"Listen, this is Jack Ward. I need a black and white, and an ambulance, over on 55 West…"

"NO, NO, NO, GET AWAY FROM HER!"

Gertrude's cane struck Jack across the shoulders from behind. The impact knocked the phone out Jack's hand. The battery pack was dislodged from the phone after it hit the ground, cutting off Jack's call with the local precinct. She continued swinging the cane frantically; Jack put his arms up in defense. He did not want to hurt the 80-year-old woman, but he would if he had to. Jack knew of her deteriorating mental state and tried to reason with her instead—the only way he knew how—rather loudly.

"If you don't put that damn cane down I am going to knock you on your ass!"

Gertrude continued to swing while Jack backed up, until Jack was no longer standing in front of the crate.

"You frigid jerk! You get away from her now!" she said.

Jack lost his cool and let her have it.

"What the fuck is that? What is that woman doing in the box?"

The feeble old woman jumped on top of the open crate with the woman inside as if she was protecting it.

"Get the hell out of here, no one invited you in! Just keep walking and don't let the door hit you on the ass on the way out!"

"Get off of that crate," Jack insisted.

"Shut up!"

"Are you alright in there miss? You look like you need medical attention. Do you need a doctor?"

"Shut up!"

"Do you need help?"

"SHUT UP, SHUT UP, SHUT UP!!!"

Gertrude yelled hysterically, Jack countered by raising his voice. Gertrude broke down in tears, desperately trying to protect her precious cargo. Jack could not believe what he was about to ask. His instincts as an investigator told him there was a strong possibility his thoughts were true.

"Is that Cindy? Is that your missing granddaughter?" asked Jack.

Gertrude erupted, "Yes, you stupid jerk! Now get the fuck out of here!"

"I am putting you under arrest, Mrs. Revner. Get up!"

Gertrude responded in a stern voice. "I'm not moving!"

Jack grabbed Gertrude by the arm and attempted to pull her off. The old woman had plenty of fight left in her. She was kicking, and screaming at the top of her lungs. She even tried to bite Jack's hand, but her dentures came loose and fell into the crate. Jack let go after that, he never thought he would have to draw his weapon on an 80-year-old woman, but after her latest move he gave it some serious consideration.

"Fine, we can do this the hard way."

Jack walked over to get his phone. He reinstalled the battery pack. Gertrude began crying once again.

"Since when does our government know what the heck they are doing? You wasn't supposed to find her you idiot."

"I have no idea what kind of scam you are pulling, but it looks like something *sick* to me."

"I need Dr. Prine," Gertrude insisted.

Jack took a step in Gertrude's direction. Jack was not going near her, but she thought he was.

"Step back you jerk! The only way I will get off the crate is if Dr. Prine is here. He's a psychologist. I want to see him now, and no one else. Don't you call the ambulance, police, or FBI until he gets here."

"I will follow protocol you old hag. Don't you dare tell me what to do."

Gertrude was quiet, and then she began speaking to Cindy, the girl in the crate.

"Okay sweet heart, he's coming. He'll be here soon, don't worry," she told her granddaughter. Gertrude redirected her attention to Jack.

"This girl suffers from a severe mental state. She needs a professional, and the one I choose is Dr. Prine."

This was a challenging situation for Jack. He was unsure of what to do. Part of him wanted to sling the woman off the crate and haul her to the nearest cell. The other part of him realized the girl made no attempt to get out. She was frightened. Gertrude, as obnoxious as she was, surely was not capable of frightening her granddaughter into a box. Cindy seemed healthy enough to speak, but she remained quiet during the whole ordeal. Maybe Cindy was drugged, or mentally unstable. For this kind of evaluation he did need an expert. From what he saw of Dr. Prine, Jack was impressed. Therefor, indulging Gertrude might be the best thing to do. Jack pulled out a business card, on the back had Dr. Prine's phone number at his residence in Northern Virginia. He dialed the number.

"We all stay here until he arrives," said Gertrude. "No one else."

The phone was answered on the other end.

"…This is agent Jack Ward…I have a situation. You will have to see this with your own eyes doctor."

CHAPTER 26

What Rameci Has Done

Bravery comes in many forms, for some it can be subtle, for others it is more obvious. Marie Carthon the once strong, self-assured, woman was starting to show glimpses of her true self. Her fighting spirit was striped away from her one morning while running though the woods outside her home. There she witnessed a body, hanging upside down, decapitated, and suspended thirty feet in the air. An angelic being named Rameci then laid claim to the body, and in the process Marie's fighting flame was extinguished. That day her heart was taken from her, and fear engulfed her entire body.

Her husband, Marcus, was tired of Marie's insoluble situation. He wanted her to return to normal. The showdown between the two of them a few weeks ago caused the couple to tear farther apart. Marcus began staying away from the house; he would not come home for hours. The silence at home was too much for him to face. Therapy was doing nothing at all, because Marie did not want to be helped.

Marie's concern lied with her family. She thought she was keeping them safe. Marie did everything she was asked to do, but it was destroying her life in the process. It was just a matter of time before her husband's support would breakdown completely. Marie's choice was whether saving their lives, was worth the loss, of their love and companionship.

When Marie woke up that morning, she had already decided enough is enough. She was going to share her pain with someone, a person she could trust. The choice was a hard one, but she chose her mother. Her mother had taken time away from her life to care for Marie in her time of need. She was compassionate and worthy of Marie's trust.

Marie was folding clothes in the washroom; her mother was talking as usual. She had been doing so from the time she arrived. She spoke as if nothing was wrong. Marie's mother read to her, and was the source of her support. Without her she would not have made it this far. Marie's mother was talking about her father, how she used to take care of him before he died. She told Marie about his mannerisms, and paranoia. Marie thought of how special her mom truly was.

In all of her life she took this woman who bore her for granted. Today she would show her appreciation, and entrust her with her nightmarish secret. Marie grabbed her mother in a tight embrace, her mother was caught by surprise, but quickly locked her arms around her daughter and returned the hug. Now was the time, and Marie would have to face the consequences of her actions. She was ready to take the risk.

Marie put her lips to her mother's ear and whispered. "I love you, Mom."

Her mother was overwhelmed with joy, she tried to pull away to look Marie in the eyes, but Marie clasped her tight against her body.

"I knew you would pull out of it," her mother said. "I told Marcus to be patient, and you will come around."

"He must not know a word of this Mom. This is for your ears only!"

Marie began to describe what had happened in the woods that day. She explained the body, the chase, and most of all she explained about her tormentor. She told her mother all about the being called Rameci. She told her mother how he comes to visit her, and what he claims to do if she speaks to anyone. Marie's mother went cold, as her emotions plummeted, from joy to utter terror.

The two women remained embraced in each other's arms, locked in support of each other. Marie's mother was a religious woman who believed in these things. She did not need any other proof than the word of her daughter to gain her trust—and respect. As their bodies were locked in support of one another, the reigning thought they shared between them was...*what now?*

Jack Ward made the call to Dr. Walter Prine; his friend and associate. He explained all that had transpired between Gertrude and her granddaughter. Prine agreed to meet them. He needed to talk to Gertrude for other reasons, like obtaining her father's journal. But this seemed far more interesting. Jack made other phone calls setting up a seat on the quickest flight to get him there. He also made arrangements for Prine to be picked up from the airport and driven directly to the home.

Eight hours later, Dr. Prine arrived at the Connecticut townhouse. The neighborhood was alive with flashing red lights dancing across the dark night. There was at least five police cars parked outside, all in a row, ready to storm in on the agent's word. Prine was allowed to walk up to the front of the barricade, he was escorted by an officer. Prine and the officer continued up the stairs and to the front door. The officer asked Prine if he knew what the situation was. Apparently Jack left the officers out of the information circle. Prine told the officer that he was left in the dark as well. Then the front door was opened by Jack Ward.

"That will be all officer," said Jack. "Dr. Prine, come on in."

Prine entered the home and began to walk down the hall. Halfway down, Jack stopped him. "I have to warn you doctor. This is a strange situation. I'm sure in your line of work this may be something you've dealt with before. That's mainly why I agreed to this. But as soon as you say it's okay I am going to yank that old woman off the crate and arrest her for creating this whole missing person sham, and wasting the department's precious time."

Silently, Prine agreed, and the two of them continued on. When Prine entered the living room he saw Gertrude, dressed in a light blue gown with floral patterns, draped across the wooden crate. Inside he could see the head of a young woman, apparently in her early twenties. She had short brown hair and was whispering something to Gertrude. Even for the field of psychology, this was something he did not witness often.

A frightened young woman, quivering inside an open wooden crate. Afraid to move and too terrified to speak. Then there is the question of her grandmother. However Cindy got into this state, it appears her grandmother was encouraging her irrational actions. Gertrude turned her head when she realized Prine was in the room.

"There she is," said Jack. "She had a chance to calm down. I would like to hear what she has to say about this. We are all ears Mrs. Revner."

With her voice crackling, Gertrude said to Jack, "I don't want you in this house!"

Jack became infuriated once more. "You sent me on a wild goose chase! You convinced me the Pristine murders were connected to this woman's disappearance. You had me go half way across the country chasing my own tail! I am staying! Not only that but I will be pressing charges against you! How long did you think you could play me? You think my time is a joke?"

"IT *IS* ALL CONNECTED!" Gertrude screamed, "And you did not waste your time. There is one exception…*You* were not supposed to find her…he was…Eximus."

Gertrude pointed at Dr. Prine. Prine was quiet throughout the whole exchange. In light of his recent discovery through the angel,

Serena, in California, Prine was still trying to cope with what he was. When Gertrude pointed at Prine, he knew that Gertrude knew as well. She did not insist on him coming here for his skills as a psychologist. She was looking for a higher power.

After being on the crate for a third of the day, Gertrude's muscles had stiffened severely. She attempted to lift herself off of the crate, but could not. Prine stepped in to assist her. He felt as if her tiny bones would snap under his enormous grasp. He lifted her as delicately as he could. When Gertrude was off the crate, Prine could see Cindy clearly.

"How long has she been confined to the box?" asked Prine.

"Close to eight months. For as long as she has been missing. I come here to take care of her. I give her food, and empty her bedpans; I wash her and talk to her. She is becoming bedridden. The whole left side of her body is filled with sores from lying on the wooden crate for this long, and her right side is covered with insect bites. Her skin is turning to mush. She will have to go through months of physical therapy just to be able to walk again."

Gertrude's tough exterior was broken. The harsh language had ceased. She was now pleading; begging for help. There was a look of concern in her eyes, concern for the life of someone she truly loved.

"I will talk to her," said Prine.

"She doesn't need a psychologist," Gertrude responded.

Gertrude stepped closer to Prine, her glassy, brown eyes staring into his, looking for some sign that he knew what she was talking about. Jack Ward on the other hand, felt as if the old woman had deceived him again.

"You had me contact him because the girl needed her psychologist, now you say she doesn't need one. That's it!" said Jack. "Step back Dr. Prine, she's coming with me."

"Eximus, she needs you Eximus!" said Gertrude clinging to Prine.

"Eximus?" Prine responded.

"Yes, that is your name—your *real* name." Gertrude whispered it, so Jack could not hear. Prine stopped Jack from coming closer.

"Give me fifteen minutes, then you can do whatever you want with her," Prine told Jack. The agent bit his tongue and agreed to step back. Gertrude was now on her knees, she had her arms around Prine's legs in a tight embrace. Feeling uncomfortable, Prine helped the woman to her feet and over to a nearby chair. Gertrude collapsed into the chair, she was physically and mentally exhausted.

The journal deciphered by Gertrude's father must have contained the story of Prine's angelic origins. Gertrude cooked up this whole elusive scheme to get Prine into the investigation. Obviously, she is not as crazy as it first appeared. But no one knows this except Prine. The doctor wondered if she attempted to tell Jack about him. But that would not be a problem, right now Jack thinks she is mad. Prine can use this to his advantage. He walked over and set his hands on the crate. Until now, no one was able touch it, Gertrude saw to that.

With a sympathetic voice, Prine attempted to reach out. "Hello, Cindy…"

"She will not speak to you. She is only allowed to talk to me. She has seen the killer, the one they are after. The one that beheads his victims and hangs them up to bleed. That is why she is in the box, and she will not come out until he allows her. No portion of her body is allowed to be outside the boundaries of that box. This was the punishment, and her obedience allows her to keep her life. She was allowed to have one person care after her and she can talk to that one person alone. She chose me."

Jack's ears perked up upon hearing there was a witness—he realized there was someone who could help him track down this killer. Then he remembered Marie Carthon. Marie is the athletic mother of two, who he believes is also an eyewitness. The split second of excitement he had after hearing Cindy could identify the killer, was quickly replaced with befuddlement. Marie has also not spoken. *What the hell is going on here?*

Jack could remain silent no more. "She is so afraid that she will not come out of that box? Afraid that the killer will get her? Hellooo! Does no one trust the Judicial System anymore? I can protect her. The agency can protect her. There is another person you know, someone else who I believe has seen the murderer. Her name is Marie Carthon, she lives in California. Both of them have no faith in the police? What kind of bullshit is this? The Government can protect you Cindy, you just need to put your trust in us. That's what we are here for."

"NO YOU CAN'T," screamed Gertrude. "You will be lucky to protect yourself once he finds out you know about him. Dr. Prine, for the safety of my granddaughter, my family, and even the safety of that short fool over there, he must not hear another word of what I have to say."

"The hell with that! I am not moving!" Jack plopped back down into the sofa where he was seated earlier and folded his arms in contempt.

"BOOM, BOOM, BOOM!"

Cindy began to pound on the inside walls of the crate trying to get her grandmother's attention. Gertrude struggled to her feet and over to where she was. Prine stepped aside as Gertrude knelt to hear what Cindy had to say.

Gertrude turned and said to Prine, "We don't have much time. He will return soon."

Jack almost came out of his seat.

"He will come back? You mean he actually comes here?" Jack could not get his cell phone out fast enough. "This is Jack, get the team ready. I need a warrant to do surveillance on…"

Prine reached out and turned off the power on the phone. Then, he leaned over to whisper in Jack's ear.

"Let's hear all what she has to say first. You might be wasting your time. The whole thing might be made up. I believe they both have to be evaluated mentally. But these things take time. We have to observe them in their environment and see how they respond. The first step though, is listening. Based on the results, we can decide what actions to take later. From a professional standpoint, this is the best option."

Prine used his trump card as a psychologist to keep Jack from causing any further distractions. This way, the more ridiculous Gertrude's story sounds to Jack, the more he is apt to determine she needs mental help instead. And whatever she says about Prine would not be given any validity.

"We need to hurry then," said Prine. "Tell me all you know, Gertrude."

Gertrude straightened up as best she could, and began to tell her story.

"Nearly eight months ago Cindy met a boy. This young man had gotten in an automobile accident when he was younger and there was a huge settlement awaiting him when he turned of legal age. He was twenty years old when she met him. He was spending his money wildly, partying in Santa Barbara every weekend. That is where she met him.

"Cindy went back to his place, he let her in on a secret that he knew. He told her the Miracle was a phony. That it was done with a radical new drug that somehow sent the bodies healing and adrenaline levels into overdrive. He said that someone within the organization had gotten hold of it and was looking for financiers. They could revolutionize medicine and make a fortune. So he showed it to her. He did the drug right there. In order for it to work he had to add some of his blood to the serum. He took the liquid filled capsule and emptied it into a tablespoon. Then he picked up a knife and pricked his finger. He put two drops of his blood into the tablespoon and then licked the spoon clean.

"Shortly afterward he was energized, Cindy said he used the knife to slash his chest and the wound quickly healed. He was running and jumping around, like she had never seen anyone do before. He hoisted her over his head with one hand displaying his impressive strength. He then decided to test his strength with a real challenge. He went to the exercise room of his house and loaded up over 400 pounds. He bench-pressed the weight with ease. Then suddenly they were not alone anymore. The boy stood up and began to walk toward Cindy when a tall man dressed in white robes suddenly appeared behind the boy. Cindy said he…"

Gertrude knelt down while Cindy whispered into her ear.

"She said, he walked out from thin air directly behind the boy, grabbed him, and pulled him back into the nothingness. They were both gone in a matter of seconds. She thought it was all a prank, some kind of magician's theatrics. Then she did the worst thing she could possibly do. She reached forward, where the boy was standing, and everything went black.

"When she regained consciousness, she found herself in the woodlands of Alabama, and not too long after she saw the body of the young boy hanging by his feet from a nearby tree. He was still alive. He was reaching upward, trying to free himself from the bondage. She says, 'what came next was unclear.' His body suddenly went limp, and his head was missing. The blood poured out onto the land, and Cindy ran and did not look back. After discovering where she was she called me and explained everything. She knew the only person that would believe her was me. I knew she was still in danger, that's when I bought this place and secretly decided to move her in. But she was hunted down, and the stranger told her if she so wanted to hide, he would find her a suitable hiding place. It became this crate. The stranger, from what I understand, takes this very seriously. He calls himself Rameci."

"Beep, Beep, Beep." Jack Ward's beeper activated. He turned on the phone and dialed the number. He needed to take a break from the psychobabble coming from Gertrude anyway. Jack was now convinced both of the women were crazy.

"This is Jack…What?"

Jack listened while the other person spoke for nearly five minutes.

"Listen, doctor, I will leave you to your patients. We have evidence of who the real killer is. *A person, that we can actually lay our hands on.* We put out a warrant for Jericho Black. I've been wasting my time with these loony's long enough and missed out on the real detective work. Thanks a lot Gertrude."

The FBI agent hurried out the door. Within minutes the flashing lights outside the townhouse also ceased. The neighborhood was quiet, and Gertrude went into the kitchen to get something to eat. Prine and Gertrude were free to talk candidly. Prine started off.

"Where is the journal?"

"The original deal is that you help my granddaughter and I give you the journal," said Gertrude.

"The deal was that I find your granddaughter," Prine answered.

"Well now I am changing it. You misinterpreted what I was saying, Eximus. I want you to be prepared for what I am about to tell you. You are an angel, the answers you seek about your past lies in that knowledge."

Gertrude paused, waiting for some sort of reaction to what she had just said.

"Did you hear me?"

"I heard you. I found out about two weeks ago, it is no longer as shocking as it was then. Other angels found me. For ninety years, nothing, now all of a sudden I am up to my ass in angels. All ready to tell me who and what I am. I have one who wants to take my son away from me and one that tried to beat me to a pulp. Everyone is suddenly eager for my knowledge and skill—well let me tell you—I am sick of this. Gertrude, my son has a right to know who his father is. I want you to hand me that journal."

"I will not give it to you until you save my granddaughter," Gertrude insisted.

"And I will not risk my life for your granddaughter. I have someone else I have to think about. All this time I thought I was immortal, well I am not. When I fought that other angel I suddenly realized

I could easily be destroyed. That does not bother me, leaving Lexington alone does. I will not risk that for your grandchild, I don't even know her, and I barely know you."

"But, you would do it for my father, wouldn't you?" asked Gertrude. "The one who cared for you, the one who restored your mind. My father, the one who deciphered your scrambled thoughts and language. You would do it for him wouldn't you? Look—take a look into Cindy's eyes. She has his eyes. She has the eyes of compassion. Take a look Eximus, see for yourself."

Prine walked over to the crate once again. Cindy's eyes had a yellow glaze to them; she looked as if she could not last much longer under those conditions. His eyes glanced over her pale and fragile body. Gertrude removed the blanket that covered her to reveal her naked frame.

"Look," said Gertrude, "she used to be a beautiful woman. Fabulously attractive to any man, now her skin is as decrepit as mine. Take a good look Eximus—see what she has become; all for the entertainment of a madman. Her muscles are like Jell-O; she can barely raise her arms. Sores cover the entire left side of her body. She is so weak she can't even control her bowel movements. Soon, she will need a respirator to assist her breathing and an old woman like me cannot keep this up much longer. I have done all I could. All this, simply because she was in the wrong place, at the wrong time. My grandchild does not deserve to live like this. Eximus, I beg you, help us."

Prine grabbed the cover from Gertrude's hand and covered Cindy with it. He paced around the floor, and thought heavily on his actions.

"You are asking me to kill another angel!" Prine responded.

"It is nothing new, you have done it before."

"Whatever reason I killed before was for my benefit. I am going to have to have more time to think about it."

"Well, Eximus," said Gertrude. "I am afraid she does not have much time left. You now know your angelic name. You help my granddaughter and you will know everything else. This...*Rameci*...is an angel also. He cannot be allowed to terrorize innocent people any longer."

It *was* a hard decision. Prine had no idea what he was up against. He had no idea of Rameci's power. Prine did not know how he could kill another angel without the spike. Without the knowledge of his previous life his ability to make a rational evaluation would be impaired. Gertrude was not relinquishing her father's documents until her granddaughter was safe.

Prine wondered if she had any documents at all. Gertrude might simply be reciting all that she could remember what her father said about him. The risk was too great to weigh his son's future against. As heart rendering as it was, Dr. Walter Prine's final answer was, "No!"

CHAPTER 27

Jack's Revelation

In just three days, Jack Ward has missed out on a wealth of information collected by the rest of his team. The investigation had taken tremendous leaps forward. While Jack was chasing Jericho Black and
later Gertrude, the team of investigators pursued the evidence without him. What his team collected was the most encouraging news
Jack had heard in months. The investigation lead to the sublevels of
the Hall of Kings, one of the investigators questioned Colleen Rigetti.
She led them to the B2 level. In one of the offices the team recovered
a computer hard drive.

The computer belonged to Jacob Barbarelli, one of the security
guards who worked directly for Jericho. After tapping into the hard
drive and accessing his email information, investigators discovered
something interesting. The drive contained contacts of twelve different people, all of considerable wealth. They were identified as potential investors. The email sent to these people explained that the
Miracle performed by the Reverend Roland Stark, was actually
achieved through use of a serum-like substance.

It was just as Dr. Prine had deducted, due to Jericho's reaction,
when Prine saw the original Miracle captured on tape. Jack Ward

had followed that lead and came up with nothing. That was because Jack was looking into Jericho's company, Black Inc, for any activity with established drug development companies. Jack would never think to look for an outside group of investors to handle the deal.

Jacob Barbarelli sought investors for research and development, through independent individuals with considerable wealth, who were looking for diversification. The first email with the proposed plan for investment was sent over one year ago. Over the next twelve months the prospects were contacted one at time. Jacob outlined how the drug was administered; he assured them that the drug was completely organic and totally safe. He sent each potential investor a small sample as proof.

Once all the addresses were gathered, the other agents on Jack's team immediately attempted to contact the twelve people involved. Within a day, they were able to contact four out of twelve potential clients. The four investors remembered receiving the packages, but they did not think it was a wise investment. They also did not believe the drug they were sent in the mail was safe, so they promptly discarded the contents. The other eight prospects they could not locate, they were all classified as *missing*. The latest prospect was reported being missing just three weeks ago, a woman by the name of Victoria Parkins.

Victoria was a fashion designer from New Jersey. Friends say she was interested in investing in another field, and was excited about getting in on the ground floor of something new. On a hunch, investigators took a blood sample from the body of the last Pristine Murder victim. They questioned Victoria's parents about their blood type. The probability of the Victoria's parent's offspring having the same blood type as the victim tested was ninety eight percent. The next step was DNA testing. Since the forensics team did not have a way of obtaining a known blood sample from Victoria they used the next best thing—body hair.

The missing woman's home was where samples of hair was recovered, from hairbrushes and combs used by Victoria. When DNA testing was done on the hairs collected from Victoria's home and compared to the DNA of last victim, they found a perfect match. She was the first victim to be identified. The team had been working feverishly since then, trying to identify the other victims, so far five of the eight have been identified—all from the list of names contained on the hard drive.

It looks like the investigators hit the jackpot. The team was looking into the whereabouts of Jacob Barbarelli, but they have been unable to track him down. Little did they know that Jacob was no longer among the living. But that was of little consequence, Jericho was the primary suspect. Investigators believe Jacob is just the pawn, there are several emails that implicate Jericho Black to the case. Investigators have come to the conclusion that it was Jericho who was the mastermind behind this, and that he had attempted to cover his tracks by traveling across the country to where the victims lived.

When investigators were chasing Jericho around the United States, they found that each city he hid in, turned up being the towns in which each of the murder victims resided. The team figured Jericho was tampering with evidence, but with Jack Ward on his tail he quickly fled to the next city. They now had enough evidence to indict Jericho; Jack gave the word to press forward. He obtained the authorization to freeze all of Jericho's assets. Jericho would definitely be in need of serious cash. They figured they could hamper his efforts by cutting him off financially, making it difficult for him to flee the country.

The team also seized all of Jericho's computers for access information in order to find anything he may be able to use as collateral for fast cash. The team successfully locked any and all funds associated with Black Inc, the hunt was on, Jericho Black was now on the FBI's most wanted list.

For days the trail had been cold, they could not locate Jericho anywhere. For the moment it appears he may have already fled the country, but Jericho had some unfinished business to attend to. He was not about to assume a new life just yet.

Jericho was closer than he had ever been to claiming his greatest victory. For the life of a fallen angel on earth, it was a story of assumed identities. Jericho Black always knew the time would come where he would have to leave this life behind and move on to the next. Nukial, Jericho's angelic name, had been assuming new lives for centuries. He had all the assets and connections to make a successful transition, even with the modern day hindrance of improved identification techniques. But Jericho was caught off guard by the recent turn of events. He was not properly prepared this time. Before he realized the time to escape had arrived, he was public enemy number one.

The network in which he set up for just an occasion was useless without money. But all of his plans to flee have been put on hold for now, somehow, someway he knew he would gain access to enough money to make the transition. Right now, he was in the middle of another important mission. While the FBI was chasing him, Jericho was chasing Dr. Walter Prine. Prine's every move had been monitored by Jericho and when Prine got the call to head to Connecticut, it had been intercepted and monitored by Jericho.

He copied the directions and made his way to the address given. By the time he arrived at the Connecticut townhouse owned by Gertrude Revner, Prine had already left to go back home. That did not stop Jericho from finding out just what was going on. The police had all left, they did not expect the man they were hunting would be visiting Gertrude Revner's home. Gertrude bought the place for her granddaughter Cindy, but Cindy did not get the chance to benefit from her grandmother's generous gift.

It was late, too late for Gertrude to head back to the nursing home. She notified the driver to come back in the morning. Then,

Gertrude got comfortable for a night's rest, but she could not sleep. The two women, Gertrude and Cindy, were distraught; Gertrude's plan to save her granddaughter from the inhumane treatment of Rameci was failing. Gertrude invented an elaborate scheme to get an angel named Eximus to defend her loving grandchild. She always had knowledge that her father had assisted an angel regain his sanity in the early nineteen hundreds. She had no idea if her father's claims were true, until her grandchild revealed her frightening story of Rameci and his constant torment.

When that happened she was willing to believe anything, and she gambled on the tale her father confided in her many years ago. But Dr. Walter Prine, whose angelic name is Eximus, refused to help her. All of her plans were for nothing. Gertrude knew she did not have much time left on this earth, but to watch her grandchild wither and die before her was too much to bear. Gertrude stayed by her granddaughter's side, she dozed off occasionally, but did not sleep for long.

It seemed like just an instant, but when she opened her eyes, after a quick nap, she saw a man standing by the crate. He was looking down, and simply observing for now. Gertrude was startled, she thought it was Rameci. She had never seen Rameci, she had only known of him through Cindy's descriptions of him. But it was not Rameci, the person that stood before the crate was Jericho Black. He had broken his way into the townhouse and was assessing the situation. Gertrude was afraid to move, she was afraid to speak. Then Jericho noticed she was awake.

"How long has she been in here?" Jericho asked.

Gertrude quickly figured out it was not Rameci and asked who he was.

"I am a friend of Dr. Prine," Jericho responded. "Well, not really a friend, more like an acquaintance."

"What are you doing in here?" asked Gertrude.

"I was looking for my acquaintance," he answered. "Do you happen to know where he went?"

"Dr. Prine has returned to his home. *That bastard!*"

Jericho was amused at Gertrude's attitude and harsh language. "Yes, he is a bastard isn't he?" Jericho put one hand on the crate and tapped his finger on its wooded surface. "I assume the woman is staying in the box of her own free will. Of course, that is the only way she is still alive."

Gertrude's ears perked up. "You know about this?" she asked.

"Yes, unfortunately I have seen this before. Many years ago, before *even* you were born. He is a devilish one that Rameci—a sadistic genius."

Gertrude rose to her weary feet, she was overcome with joy. "You are one of the other angels Prine spoke about?" she asked.

"Prine, spoke about me? I don't believe it—what did he say?"

"Nothing, he just mentioned that others had found him."

"Good, I did not want there to be any confusion on what I am about to do. I assume you asked for Prine's help. What did he say?"

"He refused to help, Sir."

"He refused? Why…he is a bastard!"

"So, will you help us? Will you take on Rameci?" Gertrude asked, almost begging.

"Me? NO, I am not in any condition to do such things," Jericho answered disdainfully.

"But with the grace of God you can…"

Gertrude was interrupted.

"God? Oh my! *You misunderstood what kind of angel I am.*"

Gertrude felt her heart plummet into the pit of her stomach as Jericho began caressing Cindy's face with the backside of his hand.

"But," Jericho continued, "you are in luck. I will get Prine to help you. See—we are not all bad. Some of us just have different things that motivate us. Fortunately for you I know what motivates Dr. Prine."

❦   ❦   ❦

William Richardson has caused his fare share of problems in the last few weeks, and no one has any idea of who he is, or what he has done. William, the ex-convict bent of destroying the Reborn Kings Ministry, abducted and killed Orlando James. In doing so, the act set off a chain reaction, and in the wake of that murder, the Ministry is suffering in ways William could never imagine. He could never have calculated such a destructive act would result from the death of a Ministry worker. But Orlando James held the key to the mystique behind the miracle.

He discovered the participants were hand picked by the ministry, not God. Roland Stark had always claimed the women who were picked were done so because of God's will, but he was deceived, along with his followers. Jericho Black personally picked all of the participants, but why? Because Jericho, not God, provided the Miracle healing the following week. The fallen angel known as Nukial, was responsible for more than his share of deceit. He has since severed ties with the ministry and is on the run. But what has he left behind?

Roland Stark was struggling, with his emotions and with his faith. If there ever was a test provided by God, this would be it. Angels were always known as winged beings, with a cascade of light surrounding them. The clouds would part, shining beams of white light would shine from the Heavens, and the angel would ride that light all the way to earth. With its wings, extended in all its power and beauty, the angel would glide down to deliver God's message. Then there was the other type. The bat winged-hoof toed-horned-tailed creatures, causing pain and destruction wherever he went. In this day and age how could Roland Stark blame the ministry's recent troubles on a demon? How could he admit that all of the supposed "God's work" was performed by a demon? The greatest, most prominent religious figure, next to the pope, was in cahoots with *a demon.*

In Roland's mind he could only think, "what does that make me?" Was his leadership a sham? How much manipulation did Jericho have over his following, his allure, and even his sermon? Roland imagined himself being a puppet on a string, and the master at his controls was Jericho Black.

Instead of addressing the recent issues Roland chose to avoid them. His followers began to wander, they were constantly listening to the reports in the media. The media had gotten a hold of Regina James, she spoke about Jericho, and how the whole ceremony was fixed. The doctors and scientists who claimed they could find no foul play in how the Miracle was performed after examining the participants, suddenly began developing destructive theories on illusion and mass hypnosis. They began saying that the ministry were masters at controlling minds through hypnosis and no one can believe anything they saw. With Roland refusing to answer the claims, his followers began to flee.

With the entire ministry self-destructing, William Richardson still was not satisfied. William returned to the hotel, where Thad and July were waiting. He had been gone for several days. William had taken a lot of time away from the others, which left Thad and July plenty of time to plan their separation from him. Through all of their elaborate schemes, all they could come up with in the end was the direct approach. They would tell William that the time had come for them to go their separate ways, then they planned on just walking away. It seemed simple enough, but Thad was taking no chances.

He instructed July to leave, to go back to New York and wait for him at her grandmother's apartment. After days of pleading, July reluctantly agreed and she left. This was the way Thad wanted it from the beginning, just between the two men. When William arrived back at the motel room, this time, it was just his old friend waiting for him. William entered the room and placed the car keys on the table. "Where's July?" he asked.

"She left me. She said she did not plan to live this kind of life," Thad answered.

"She's not some spoiled kid? What does she mean by this 'kind' of life?"

Thad shrugged his shoulders as if he did not know.

"It doesn't matter," said William, "one less person in my way. Let's go baby bro. It's time for us to finish this thing." William raised his thirty-eight revolver, the same one he used to attempt to kill Roland with the first time. "I kept it all this time. We are going to get it right, I want you by my side, just like it was before. Then we take down this clown."

Thad took a deep breath. "You don't have to kill him anymore, he's through."

William was visibly aggravated by his partner's comment and he stretched his neck to the left, then right, to ease the obvious tension. "What do you mean baby bro?" Thad took another breath before speaking.

"I mean the ministry is crumbling. Haven't you paid attention to the news? It's all over, the guy is a fake, and now he is exposed. You brought him down, just like you said you would."

"But the world doesn't know it was me."

That was the statement Thad was not prepared to hear. "It was all an accident," William continued, "a fluke. I just don't feel the satisfaction baby bro. And I have come too far *not* to get my satisfaction."

Thad became angered. "It's useless!" he insisted. "Roland has fallen, that is what you wanted. You were here to expose him for the phony he was. You succeeded, take that for your satisfaction and let's get the hell out of here."

William shook his head in contempt.

"No," said William, "you are wrong again. Roland is planning a midnight vigil tonight. All of his followers are welcomed to attend. He is finally going to answer his critics in a live forum, in the parking lot of the Hall of Kings. There have already been reports of thousands of people flocking to the facility. All with their candles and prayers, he is going to pray for that guy killed, and address the future of the church. So, it's not over yet. That fat bastard with his fancy talk and spiritual crap is going to fool those people again. And like idiots they will be following him."

Thad was bewildered. "Listen Will, no one can recover from what he went through. He is giving his final farewell. He is a phony, like you said all along. Take my word for it. We go there and hear what he has to say. If he plans on saying he is giving up preaching, then we leave. If he plans to rebuild then I will do whatever you want. Does that seem fair enough?"

"Well baby bro, let's head out and see what crap the minister is trying to shovel this time."

❦   ❦   ❦

Jack Ward could hardly contain his excitement on the way back to his office in Washington D.C. One of the young agents assigned on his team named Peter Atkins began filling Jack in on all the minor details of the evidence gathered. Jack's pride was slightly marred. He was the agent in charge, yet when the bulk of the evidence in the Pristine case was being gathered and investigated, he was wasting his time running down Gertrude Revner. A woman who he now considered to be a mental risk.

Pete broke down the evidence inch by inch, the biggest being the DNA evidence used to identify five of the eight victims. Jack thought it was ingenious, his team was developing hunches and using their instincts, just as he has done. While Peter explained the details, Jack's wounded pride quickly healed, he felt like a proud papa. Pete even had a fresh pot of coffee brewing for him when he arrived. But there remained large holes in parts of the investigation. The biggest being, Jericho Black. The agency thought to do a profile on the entrepreneur, if they had an accurate account of his life up to that point they might better be able to predict his next move. As of twelve years ago, they really had no record of Jericho Black ever existing. His whole identity turned up being an alias. His birth records, parents' history, and every lead to his childhood were all fabricated. To investigators, Jericho Black was becoming more of a mystery with each passing moment.

"Pete," said Jack, "any leads on Jericho?"

"The man has the uncanny ability to disappear. We have nothing. We locked up all of his accounts and assets accept his credit cards. If he uses one of those, we got him. The computer is set nationwide; a black and white would head directly to where he decides to use it. ATM, Hotel, airport, or just to pay for dinner. But he hasn't used one yet."

Jack nodded his head in approval.

"Good job, Pete." Jack had other questions on his mind. If the case would go to trial, he knows how important obtaining the murder weapon could be. "Has anyone had any clues about the murder weapon?" asked Jack.

Pete sighed in frustration. "I spoke to the scientists in forensics, they have some kind of sample from one of the victims…" Jack remembered the doctor mentioning it when he was there several weeks ago. "Yes," said Jack drolly, "go ahead and continue."

"Well, they seem to think it is some sort of natural metal, but nothing that they can identify. They are way out there, in outer space somewhere, on where the substance could have come from. I don't know, they were going off into space/ time continuum crap. I just got out of there as quickly as possible." Jack could sympathize with the young agent on that one.

"There is one thing Jack that is extremely puzzling, I was hoping when you arrived that you could figure this one out."

"Sure, what is it?" Jack felt honored again.

"First let me explain our thinking. We were puzzled at how we had such a hard time identifying the victims so we set out to estimate the times of death for each. We started with the most recent victim, which was not too hard because she was found rather quickly. They estimate her time of death being June 30, at approximately 10:00 a.m. Well, we have more than one witness who contends that Victoria Parkins was in a board meeting that same morning and did not leave until 9:00 a.m. Her assistant told me she was scheduled for another meeting at 10:30 a.m. That was when they first discovered that she was not where she was supposed to be. So as far as forensics' estimate on the time of death, we have no reason to believe they made a mistake."

"What's the problem?" Jack asked, "she left the office, Jericho intercepted her between meetings, took her to the woods and did her. Was the issue time? Let's say the forensics people were off in their estimate of time of death, maybe by two or three hours. Jericho had maybe three hours to take her to the murder location in Maryland and kill her."

Peter had to make a clarification. "Jack, the fourth victim was found in Maryland. You found the last victim, Victoria, the one in California." Jack was so eager to close the case that he was not thinking clearly.

"Are you sure," asked Jack, "that she did not have an emergency? Where she booked a flight and headed to the coast?"

"We checked all flights Jack. She did not fly out. We even checked all of the private flights leaving the area for any hope of a chartered flight taking her to the west coast. We could find nothing at all. All of the murder victims were found thousands of miles from their homes. The third victim lived in Denton, Texas and ended up in West Virginia. The sixth victim lived in Utah and he also ended up in West Virginia. The second victim, the male we found the carpet fibers on, lived in California and ended up in Alabama."

Jack felt the cold reality of Gertrude's words coming to haunt him. He was afraid to ask but he knew he must. "Repeat that last one again please," Jack asked of his young assistant.

"The second victim lived in Santa Barbara, California and ended up in Alabama. It's the boy who we found our only bit of physical evidence on. The carpet fibers from the rental car." *The same car Cindy Revner's license was found in.*

Reality is a sensitive thing, when testing the obscure limits of what our minds consider 'the real world' our first reaction is complete denial. But when we face the possibility of that obscure theory actually being a tangible part of reality, the sudden sensation of absolute terror engraves a mark in our soul that we carry forever.

Jack Ward had just been marked, he listened to Gertrude's story of Cindy's terrifying ordeal less than twenty four hours ago. The story of a being coming out of thin air to capture and kill a young man Cindy was interested in. And when she stepped forward, she was suddenly propelled to the woods of Alabama. The question of the murders, and the victims, being thousands of miles away from where they were abducted, in a cryptic way, had just been answered. Jack could not begin to describe what was in his heart. He thought about Cindy cooped up in that tiny prison of a wooden crate. He thought about a woman named Marie Carthon, feverishly running through the streets, being hit by cars, all to escape the grasp of this murderer. The possibilities in the real world were suddenly getting a lot larger for Jack. The scope of reality was expanding past his normal boundaries. It was here, in this realm of possibilities, that Jack would find the strength to return to Connecticut, and find out from Gertrude, *what the hell was really going on.*

CHAPTER 28

A Life Changing Decision

Reverend Roland Stark of the Reborn Kings Ministry consulted in his strength, the Bible. There he found the answers he sought. The time for hiding has passed, the arduous task of facing his trials had begun. The Ministry was under a lot of pressure; the public wanted answers. Hopefully all of their concerns would be answered tonight. The sweat was beginning to form on Roland's brow, his clothes were becoming damp from the perspiration. He pulled out a small terry cloth towel from his jacket pocket and wiped his face with it. Pacing along the corridors of the Hall of Kings facility, he examined its grandiose architecture and its unique decor. It was a marvel for the senses—tall corridors, marble columns, statues, both large and small, of the saints, and of course—the angels. On each of the walls was a story, a testament of faith. They contained the stories of the seven miracle participants.

Each story was written to tell the individual experiences of each of these women. Every one was unique in their own way. Roland walked the great hall to find the showcase displaying Mary Beth Reynolds's story, the first of the miracle participants. It was a story of joy, where tragedy turned to triumph. He read how the doctors were baffled, upon discovering that a bullet was still lodged in her body. And how the press and the media begged that if the miracle water came from Roland Stark that it be done again.

The media claimed how no authentic religious experiences could ever be shared with the world because of its personalized nature. All of the previous physical evidence regarding a religious phenomena has always carried such ambiguity surrounding the facts, that it could never be taken seriously, except for those who personally experienced it, or those with blind faith.

The faith healers who touch a person on the forehead and declare, *You're healed*, and those who touch religious artifacts and suddenly claim to have their diseases cured, are part of the 'questionable' phenomena. Situations in which people are pushed into church in a wheel chair, and run down the aisle after being healed by the Holy Spirit, were often shrouded in doubt.

No one has ever gone to their doctors to find out if they were really terminally ill, if they really were confined to a wheel chair, or if they were really cured at all. These were often people the congregation had never seen before and would never see again. And people rarely cared, there were very few investigations done on religious figures and their healing claims. It was something that was always left alone, for the integrity of the church and their faith.

Roland broke the boundaries of that unwritten rule—actually he shattered it. He invited doctors and scientists to test God's power. Because he had the ultimate conviction about his work. Mary Beth Reynolds was where it all started, her showcase in the Hall of Kings included the bullet that was pulled from her body. It was encased behind a glass display, with spotlights shining upon it. The bullet was a dark copper color, it was bent, curled, and deformed. The small thirty-eight caliber slug was the staple of the church and the Miracle itself.

Roland had the key to the showcase lock in his pants pocket, he had been thinking about this for some time. Roland inserted the small gold key into the lock, and released the mechanism. He opened the display case and removed the slug from its holder. He held it up to the light so he could get a good look, his pale fingers, explored its rough edges and numerous grooves. The Miracle would have been written off as another religious claim if it were not for this bullet.

He thought hard about what it meant to him—the significance of this tiny bullet. Roland dropped the bullet in his pants pocket, it was his now. Roland was interrupted by the sound of footsteps headed in his direction, he closed the showcase but did not bother to lock it. Around the corner came one of the security guards, one of Jericho's ex-guards. Most of the security had been let go, there were now only a handful of guards who remained to watch the entire complex. This one used to be one of Jericho's most trusted, now he was Roland's most trusted. The guard was Rin. "They are just about ready for you Reverend," said Rin. Roland approached the guard and put his hand on Rin's shoulder. "Let's go!" he said. And the two men headed down the corridor toward the main entrance.

The stage was set, outside the Hall of Kings facility, in the parking lot. It was almost midnight, Roland stood at the entrance door and looked out into the night. Outside the arena were thousands of his most loyal followers, the lot was nearly full. The parking lot lights shined down upon their eager faces, they were ready to pay their respects to one of Roland's workers and to hear him face his accusers. The latest estimate had the crowd's number at around fifteen thousand. A podium was set up and spotlights were directed upon it. One at a time, as it neared midnight, the people began lighting their candles. The parking lot lights were turned out, the moon above provided a light blue illumination on the zealous crowd.

The timing was perfect, all the candles were lit, it was midnight, and Roland Stark stood at the podium. Roland reached into his pocket, and removed the tiny bullet, he placed it on the podium. He had nothing written, or rehearsed, today he was speaking from the heart. About the horrible death of a worker, praying for his soul, and whatever else comes to mind.

"Hello, I am pleased to see so many faces. I would like to acknowledge all of you who took time from your schedules to make it here today. A tragedy has befallen one of our endeared members of the church. A worker named Orlando James, he was taken from us, and he left behind, a loving wife and a child. The media is also here today, unlike the times in the past, I will not cater to them. I used to rearrange my schedule, and have make up come and try to make me look pretty—I understand how hard that must have been to the poor girl." There were scattered chuckles from the crowd. "I know I did not like it, I spoke against it. But I did not speak against it loud enough. I tolerated it, for the sake of all of you here today. But, I realized something, as I look back, at the preparations week by week, at the scheduling and demands—I realized I was not really doing it for you. I realized I had been fooling myself—I was actually doing it for me. Tonight, the media may as well not even be here. I will not pose for the cameras, or walk over to the left so that when they switch images I will be in the right spot for a close up. No—today when I say I am here for you, I really mean, I am here for all of you."

Thad and William stood out among the thousands of people, they were one of the few who did not have a candle lit. William was listening to what Roland had to say, and so was Thad. Thad was hoping Roland would fail, that the crowd would hear what he had to say and loose interest. He was hoping that not only a few people showed up, but that those people would quickly leave. Right now Thad's chances of that happening were slim to none. Not only was the turn out hundreds of times what he expected but people were steadily pouring into the parking lot. If things continued at this pace he knew William would pursue his quest to destroy Roland Stark—through death. For William that was the only way to put his own personal demons to rest. Thad had and important decision ahead of him, in his heart was the overwhelming desire for the madness to come to an end.

"What do you think William? This guy is through, come on—let's go," said Thad. It was a long shot attempt at persuasion, one that William was not about to buy into.

"I KNOW you are not seeing the same thing I am, or else you would not be saying that shit. Look at all these people Thad, he ain't about to run out on all these people, they already bought into his crap. They're brainwashed already. They already proved he's a phony and look—like ignorant sheep here they are back for more. These preachers always talk about sheep, that's because sheep are one of the dumbest animals on the planet. Sheep can't think for themselves Thad."

"So, what! Who cares about these people? Let em go off and be his dumb sheep. That has nothing to do with us. This is about getting ridiculous Will!" Thad had finally come to the point of defiance. The day was inevitable and the time was now. When he stared out the window of the Queen's apartment several weeks ago, it was in preparation for this day. The day when he would finally sever ties with his troublesome comrade and seek independence. And maybe even pursue a life as an honest citizen. William sensed something was wrong, his old friend was not himself.

"What's going on Thad?" William asked. Thad was as blunt as possible.

"Me and July, want to…" That's as far as Thad got.

"I knew it! So, a woman got in between us, is that right baby bro? She didn't leave, or if she did, she left because of me—is that right? And you're gonna go back to that whore and leave me out. Ain't that some shi…You were just a little punk, thug when I met you."

William cut his speech short. He was angered, but most of all he felt betrayed. He remained calm enough to make one last request. "Just help me do this one thing."

"If it means killin' that preacher, I say no," said Thad.

"She talked you out of doing that too?"

"No, that was my decision. I have nothing against him."

William snapped, his anger over the timing of Thad's declaration was more than he could stand.

"I don't give a damn if you tongue kiss that sweaty fat boy!" said William. "You are gonna help me! I did not come all this way to be standing among his followers and then go home with nothing. I killed that jerk that they come to pray for—ORLANDO. I got a layout of the place, and stole his uniform. Does that sound like someone who is just gonna walk away after that? Hell no! We got one more job baby bro, me and you. That's the way it's gonna be—period. I want you by my side when I do this…end of discussion! After that you can return to that slut, and have little slutty babies for all I care."

Thad remained quiet, he would not attempt to say another word. He was hoping it would not come to this, but his instincts always told him to expect the worst with this man. William was so furious he did not even realize Roland was speaking, and Thad was too consumed in thought to listen either.

"I…am not going to stand before you today and attempt to defend myself," Roland continued. "You are too smart for that, and I am not going to insult your intelligence. The truth is what I am sworn, by oath—to my creator, to uphold. So how can I stand before you and say, that I had been deceived. I cannot do that. How can I say, that a member of my organization, had done things against my knowledge? How could I explain that demons invaded the house of God and had their way? They were not the ones you hear the word from or worshiped with…I was. They were not the ones you bestowed your trust in…I was. With that said, the major question lingering in all of your minds is…was the Miracle real?"

Roland paused to gather himself and take a sip of water. He then realized what he had just done and held the water up so that everyone could see. "Water: the giver of life, the quencher of thirst, and the sustainer of life…how could something so simple be the source of such mystery? There is a famous expression among preachers, and it has been for generations, 'the lord works in mysterious ways.' I know if you have ever been involved in religion, you have heard that expression many times. It has become of late, that I realized, the phrase has a deceptive purpose. It is a means of explaining what we, the religious leadership of the world, do not understand. If a religious experience occurred in a way we never expected to happen, we simply say, 'the lord works in mysterious ways' and no other questions are asked about it. I said that during the first Miracle, when Mary Beth Reynolds had this lodged in her body."

Roland held up the tiny bullet he tucked away in his pocket earlier. "And I said it again, just a few weeks ago, to Sheryl O'Connor, when she had a vision of the trials I would be facing today. I am here to tell you that the lord *does not* work in mysterious ways. God is steadfast and straightforward, honest and truthful. It is people—that are the mysterious ones. The way we respond to situations. How we act and react. The way we think, feel, and love is ALL a mystery. We beg, we dare, and we demand to be mystified. There is nothing that captures the attention of our minds more than some unexplained phenomena. The mystery of the unknown, where our minds cannot explain what the eyes just processed. We oohhh, and aahhhh, and we are impressed by its majesty. We come to witness the spectacle, and we revel in bewilderment. Like magician's trickery, its very purpose is to deceive. While everybody is looking up here, he is shifting something around down there. And we miss the real magic, which is right here, among all of you in this congregation.

GOD DOES NOT NEED TO PROVE TO YOU HE IS POWERFUL!

He is not here to entertain you with his might! I—as a vessel of his power—proclaim that I have abused that power. I thought that healing people was the way to bring you closer to God. The healing was real, but while that was happening, God knew half the people that came to my sermons were not there to hear about HIM—they were there to witness the spectacle. They were more privileged in knowing they were part of the 'Reborn Kings,' and Roland Stark, the one who has God in his hip pocket.

Those of you here today, want to know the truth. The small number of you here today, want to know, if I stand for what God stands for. The tragedy of one, Orlando James, has taught me I still need to learn what God stands for. I would like to show you, if you would allow me to be your humble preacher. The power of God lies in the WORD, not in the miracle. Yes, I misled you—I led you all to believe that healing of the body...was more important...than healing of the spirit."

Roland had the attention of all, his words captivated the thousands of followers eagerly awaiting to hear what he had to say about the scandal surrounding his ministry. Like a crafty politician, Roland avoided the direct question, but his message was understood just the same. The Miracle was no longer proven to be real or exposed as a fake. It was where it belonged, in the shadows of the unexplained. Where only those directly involved can attest to its validity. Although thousands of other followers had not shown their loyalty, those that attended were thankful.

Roland continued to speak and he urged the crowd not to blame Jericho Black or God. Those who chose not to return to the ministry were implored to find other places to worship. If they were truly interested in knowing God, they would pursue that journey with their last breath. Roland closed with the vigil honoring the memory of Orlando James and praying for his soul. While his words echoed in the minds of most, there was one who could not wait until he was done. After two hours, William Richardson, nudged his old friend Thad, and informed him the moment had come.

It was nearly 5:00 a.m., Thad and William had entered the facility through the front door. William was wearing the workers uniform he stole from Orlando James. Outside, there were still a relatively large number of people, they were scattered about the parking lot, discussing the events of the night. Inside the Hall was quiet; the lights were dim. William and Thad swiftly made their way over to the service area on the north side of the facility. There they would find the elevator that led to the upper levels of the Hall of Kings. This was where William hoped to find Roland Stark.

Before he entered the building, he made sure Roland was still inside. William monitored the entrance Roland used to leave the building. With all the people and press still outside, there was a very good chance that Roland had not left. William and Thad faced practically no obstacles on their way to the elevator. The tone of security had been drastically reduced. Once they reached the elevator William and Thad would act as if they belonged. William would be the worker, and Thad would be the cousin he brought to meet Roland. Once inside William would draw his gun on Roland and end his life.

William and Thad reached the elevator without incident. The outline that Orlando provided before he was killed was flawless. Everything was as he said it would be. William pressed the button for the service entrance and they both entered the elevator. They headed for the top floor. In William's right pants pocket was the thirty-eight-caliber revolver he would use to kill Roland. The same one he used when he attempted to kill him many years ago.

Their pulses quickened as the door to the elevator opened. Their breathing became swift and shallow. For William, it was excitement, but for Thad it was something else. William put on a phony smile and began walking briskly through the corridors, peeking through the glass office windows on that floor. He acted innocently, but he knew exactly where he was going. The office to Roland Stark was on the side opposite of the service elevators. William walked as if there was not a care in the world, Thad followed behind humbly.

The door to Roland Stark's office was just ahead. Thad had hoped Roland was not inside. William tapped lightly on the door, then turned the doorknob. It was unlocked, he pushed the door open slightly and peered inside. William reached into his pocket, but did not pull the weapon out. He pushed the door open a little further and scanned the room in detail. It was empty. The grand office space of Roland Stark had a fabulous view overlooking the hills. The midnight sky was just showing signs of early morning light. William stood under the threshold with the door wide open, Thad was still outside in the corridor. His back was against the wall and he was facing away from the office space. He was simply listening for when the gunshots would ring out, he did not want to see any of it.

After the period of silence, he turned to look into the office. He was relieved to see the office was empty. "Let's go." Thad whispered. Just then—a door to another room open up and Roland emerged.

"Good morning gentlemen. Can I help you?" asked Roland.

"Hello," said William, "this is my cousin. I told him I could get you to meet him. I thought you wouldn't mind—come on in here cousin!" William motioned for Thad to enter and stand beside him. Thad took a couple of steps inside the office, the unnerving emotion wore on his conscious. Part of him wanted William to just pull the trigger and end it, the other part wanted William to end his sickening quest of destruction. Thad sensed this was just one of many. William would not stop with Roland, someone else would emerge and he would be dragged to do another dirty deed. Thad precipitously made his stand.

"Reverend," said William, "earlier you held up a bullet, that came from that girl that got shot. Did you ever stop to think that that bullet was meant for you?" Roland displayed a perplexed look on his face. His daze quickly turned to horror as William drew his concealed weapon and pointed it at Roland's head. Instantaneously, Thad stepped in front of the weapon and pulled the barrel toward the floor.

"What is your problem baby bro?" William asked.

"You are the problem."

"Are you going to prevent me from shooting him like the last time?"

Thad was reminded what happened in the church many years ago. He stood beside William as he prepared to shoot Roland Stark. Something inside of him protested, and he grabbed William's arm as he attempted to shoot. The bullet ended up striking a woman a few rows ahead of them. The woman was Mary Beth. Thad had saved Roland's life once before, it seems he would do it again. Who knows why he stood up for the Reverend's life, he was not a man of religious beliefs. For some reason, William's thinking was so twisted, not even Thad could stomach the senseless act.

"You know," said William, "every night I sat in my cell, I remembered what you did. That just burned me. Then I figured it. You are caught up in this fool's ramblings just like my man Freddie."

Freddie was the boy William knew as a youth that was killed in his prime. William blamed his death on a slick-talking counselor, who began to steer Freddie toward the straight and narrow. William believes he was killed because he went soft, and now he believes Thad has fallen under the same spell.

"Yea, Thad, I said when I get out I would give you another chance. That's why I insisted you come here, so you can make it right. Didn't I tell you that from the beginning? Make it right! You're tainted goods boy, there's no hope for you."

William raised the pistol and pulled the trigger before Thad could grab his arm again. Thad was shot in the midsection. The force of the blow felt like a hammer hitting Thad at the point of entry. Thad curled over in pain, but still managed to grab hold of the smoking barrel. William yanked the gun away from Thad's grasp and pointed it at Roland. William had now drifted into the corridor. Before he could squeeze off another round he was blindsided from the right. His hand was smashed against the doorframe and the gun was knocked loose. Jericho's ex-bodyguard, Rin, had heard the commotion and quickly came to Roland's aid. Rin recovered the weapon at the doorway; William desperately scampered away.

Rin went in pursuit but was stopped, by Roland. "Call an ambulance," Roland pleaded, "this man needs our help!"

With each pulse from Thad's heart, blood was forced from the open wound. The office carpet beneath Thad's body was stained red. Thad was partially seated upright at a forty-five degree angle, his head was resting against the back of Roland's desk. Thad stared wildly, his eyes danced around, observing the small group of workers assembling at the office entrance. Roland stayed by his side and waited for the ambulance. Colleen and several others were in the office, praying for the man fighting for his life just a few feet away. Roland looked around into the faces of his followers. He could not help but think that he caused all of this. Death surrounded him, and constantly tested his resolve. After his great speech on rebuilding, here someone comes to throw another dagger to cut him down.

Unknown to Roland, one of Colleen's assistants traveled to the lower levels of the facility. She went to the altar, and had retrieved the precious challis of life. She hurried back to the upper levels, hoping desperately that she was not too late. Four minutes later she arrived at the top floor. She ran into the bathroom and poured water into the challis. She stepped quickly, trying not to spill any of the water on the ground. She knew Roland used ordinary tap water and through the power of God converted it into the life healing waters. She arrived, and worked her way through the crowd. Members of the staff rejoiced, they were pleased to see that someone had gotten the challis of life.

Colleen ran forward and took hold of the challis. There were several people along the floor, trying to apply pressure to the wound. She could not make her way around them. Roland was on the other side of those assisting, she could not hand it to him directly. Rin stepped forward and offered his assistance. He held out his hand. Colleen handed Rin the challis. Once the challis was secured in his hands, he turned away from the others and poured the water onto the ground. He then placed the empty challis on top of Roland's desk. The small group of people who witnessed his act was left aghast.

"What are you doing?" Colleen's assistant yelled loudly. Roland did not realize what was going on, until the distraction. He then noticed the water on the ground, and the challis on the desk behind him. Rin stood by the challis, looked Roland in the eyes, and gave him a nod. Rin's display left the door wide open; the rebuilding process of the church could now resume.

"He's right." Roland declared, "that is not the way God teaches us to save people. This is the only way I have been taught!" Roland put his warm palm on Thad's forehead. "I want everyone in this room to bow their heads and grab your neighbors hand," he instructed. "Young man, I want you to know that it's not too late for you to learn about your God. God, the creator of life loves you and is ready to forgive you of your transgressions. But first you must want to be forgiven. You must believe in him and you must do it on faith..."

Roland continued to pray for Thad, until the ambulance arrived. He told Thad everything he needed to know, in order to save his most precious possession—his eternal soul. Thad died shortly afterward, tears were shed for him.

In the parking lot the majority of tears came from July. She did not go to New York as she was expected to. She decided to wait at the Hall of Kings for Thad to emerge with his new life. She watched as Thad and William entered the building a couple of hours ago. Then saw only William leave on his own two feet. She hoped Thad would not be too far behind, but her worst fears were realized when the ambulance arrived to retrieve Thad's body. Guilt began to consume her thoughts. If she did not force Thad to change his ways he might still be alive. But Thad was not there to tell her it was *his* decision to change his ways. Even if he could tell her, those words would not provide much comfort to a soul in mourning.

CHAPTER 29

Save the Children

After visiting with Gertrude Revner for a second time, Dr. Walter Prine, had discovered another small piece of his previous life—his angelic name. She called him Eximus and she pleaded with him to save the life of her grandchild. Cindy Revner, who was once thought of as a missing person, was being tormented by a fallen angel. She was confined to a wooden box for a prison; her crime was being in the wrong place at the wrong time. Dr. Prine's decision not to help Cindy was not easy. He felt her pain, but the risk of leaving his son an orphan was too heavy a price.

For the past few days he thought about what his decision meant to the family. He remembered Elise Revner; he also remembered the look on Felix's face as he peered through the small window on Gertrude's door. And how could he forget Gertrude, and the way she flung her body over the crate protecting her grandchild. There was the love of the whole family right before him.

Those were all reasons for him to help, but that was also the main reason he did not. Prine wanted that for himself, the love of a family. One-day Lexington's children, and their children, would show the same type of love in an encouraging environment. In the optimistic future of his mind's eye, this is what Prine desperately wanted for himself.

Prine tried to put the images he had experienced, in the past few weeks, out of his mind. It was time for life to return to normal—as normal as it can get for a fallen angel. Except, others knew who he was now. Angels on both sides of the angelic war was learning of the Morningstar. He would soon learn that it would be difficult to remain as Dr. Walter Prine. Hiding his secret from humans is one thing, hiding from other angels would prove to be a challenge.

Prine had just met with the Dean of the college. He was discussing the details his sudden departure and his schedule for the fall. Now that he was home, his regular Childcare provider, Nola Franklin, had resumed duties looking after Lexington whenever Prine was away. Nola was a single mother, she worked hard to get her license and this was a means of making ends meet. Nola watched several other children; a total of five. Her three-bedroom home was converted into daycare palace during the day. Everything was safe and approved by the state. Since it was still the middle of summer, most of the kids stayed with her for the majority of the day. Lexington, however, was just supposed to be there for a few hours. He was one of the older kids, so he helped out with the others by keeping them entertained.

Nola's Daycare was just a few blocks away from Prine's home. Prine had stopped by the grocery store to pick up a few items before returning home. He planned on cooking a big dinner and treating Lexington to fresh baked cookies after dinner. When he pulled into the community, which he lived, he noticed several flashing lights. Police vehicles were scattered about the complex, at least twelve vehicles. There were a few cars patrolling, and one officer was asking a young couple on the sidewalk questions, but the majority of the cars were concentrated around a particular house. It was near the home of Nola Franklin. Prine's car was stopped a block away, he tried to see if it was actually Nola's house or the home next to her's. From that distance he could not be sure.

The officer walked up to the driver window.

"Do you live in this neighborhood sir?" the officer asked.

"Yes, just down the block—what's going on?"

"I suggest you head straight home. Do not be wandering around after you get home."

"Wait, I have to pick up my son from daycare."

The ominous feeling leaped into Prine's heart after witnessing the officer's momentary, blank expression. "You need to pick up a child from Nola's Daycare?" the officer asked.

Prine hesitated. "Yes."

"I'll need to see some identification please."

Prine handed the officer his driver's license and watched him as he examined it. With Prine's license still in hand, the officer stormed over to the barricade where the police had blocked off the street entrance. He yelled at another officer to move the police car, he then motioned for Prine to enter. Prine slowed down as he drove past the officer, slow enough to retrieve his license without coming to a stop. He tried to read the officers expression as he drove past; he sensed nothing.

Prine got closer to the house, he saw that the police cars were centered around Nola's place. The door was open, a woman ran outside. It was Mrs. Baker, a woman who Prine has met previously while picking up his son. She was clutching her two-year-old daughter in her arms. She ran from the house to the center of the walkway with tears streaming down her face. A man, Mr. Baker, ran up from the sidewalk to meet her. He hugged both his wife and his daughter in a strong embrace. Mrs. Baker began repeatedly kissing her child on the forehead.

He could not hear what they were saying, Prine only knew they were overjoyed and relieved. Something had taken place inside the daycare, something big enough to scare every parent who ever left his or her child in the care of another. Prine promptly stopped the car right where he was, and exited the vehicle. He was walking quickly toward the front door of the daycare. Officers stormed across to intercept him halfway to the front door.

"What is your name sir?" an officer asked.

"What is going on here? LEXINGTON!" Prine screamed frantically though the open door. More officers came over. The two officers that stood in front of Prine could not stop him.

"LEXINGTON!" Prine screamed again.

Prine dragged a few more officers as he pushed his way to the front door. "Let him go!" one of the inspectors yelled out. They did, and Prine hurried though the front door. He looked around the room, there were officers, both plain clothed and uniformed, everywhere. In the corner he saw Nola amidst a team of investigators. When she saw Prine, she broke down in tears. From across the room, she begged for forgiveness.

"Oh Lord, Dr. Prine forgive me! I'm sorry…I'm sorry…" A police officer grabbed Nola and helped her back into her seat. She tried to stand, but instantly collapsed from all the anxiety. An investigator who was questioning Nola whispered in the ear of one of the uniformed officers. He then began to walk toward Dr. Prine.

Prine was numb; he was not concentrating on what the investigator was saying. He was hoping it was all a mistake. He felt the feeling of despair in the air. Another woman, Bernadette Carson, was on the couch with her five-year-old boy in her lap. An investigator was taking her statement. She tried to show Prine a look of empathy when she noticed him watching her. Prine turned his head in denial, hoping Lexington was in the next room. He was not.

"Dr. Prine," the investigator said, "I regret to inform you, that as of 4:12 p.m., someone forced their way into the daycare, and abducted your son."

"I'm sorry Dr. Prine, I'm sorry…" the continuing hysterical pleas of Nola, the daycare provider, echoed across the room. Her crying was so forceful her face entire face was a shiny, beet red. "Don't hate me Dr. Prine…Don't hate me…" she bellowed.

The investigator tried to grab Prine's arm and escort him outside. The investigator wanted to get way from Nola. Her reaction was only making the situation worse. But Prine wasn't about to leave.

"Who was it!" Prine screamed toward Nola.

"He was tall, he broke the door down…" a sobbing Nola responded.

"Look, Doctor," the investigator pleaded, "it is better if we talk outside right now.

The investigator walked outside, and Prine followed behind him. The investigator was a husky gentleman, wearing a brown jacket with a cheap brown tie. The knot on the tie was poorly made, he was obviously not a person of style. The investigator tried to button his jacket, after he notice Prine was looking at how his cheap tie was made, too short and barely reached his belly button. He then decided to offer Prine some gum instead.

"No thanks," said Prine. "Where's my son?"

"This is what happened Doctor, around 4:05 p.m. Nola received a knock on the door. She looked through the peephole and did not recognize the guy. She put the chain lock on the door and opened it just enough to ask the guy what he wanted. The kidnapper then kicked the door down, ran into the house, grabbed Lexington and another little girl then he left. Nola was knocked unconscious. Another little boy dialed 911 and tried to explain what happened. By the time we got here Nola was conscious and the little girl was left on the front lawn, before the sidewalk."

Prine figured the girl left on the sidewalk was the Baker's child. The way the parents were clutching her outside, it had to have been her.

"So Doctor, my biggest question to you is—do you have any enemies?"

"Enemies?" It was something Prine had not thought of before. After California there could be an assortment of suspects. There was Gertrude, she might be furious after he refused to help her. Maybe

Jericho Black, or Rin, both of whom Prine left battered and bruised. Last there was Serena, who let it be known, that she was interested in Lexington.

"First," the investigator continued, "we have to go to your home. The kidnappers may attempt to contact you there. They may have left a note or some demands."

Prine began to walk towards his car. He stopped and turned toward the investigator.

"Don't follow me!" Prine demanded, "you might not like what you see."

Prine got into his car and hurried home. After Prine turned the corner the investigator looked at one of the uniformed officer and said, "Follow him!"

Prine arrived at his home and checked the mailbox right away, he sorted through the bills and tossed them to the floor. Next, Prine flung the door to his home open. He picked up the phone and called his message service, there were three new messages. He sped through the first as if it were of no great importance. Then he started the second message.

> "Hello Dr. Prine, this is Jericho Black. No need to be alarmed, the boy is with me. There will be no police, no FBI—nothing! This is angelic business."

Jericho left specific instruction on what Prine should do. When the message was finished Prine erased it. Dr. Prine marched back outside and toward his car. A police car had blocked him in. The officer was still sitting in the car, he radioed in to the chief investigator as for what to do. Prine stood by his car door and waited. The officer set the radio transmitter down, and put the car in reverse. Prine got into his car and left—the officer followed behind.

Prine picked up the phone and tried to contact Agent Jack Ward. He was afraid the police would try to detain him for questioning, he could not let that happen. If the authorities tried, Prine was prepared to get ugly. After twenty minutes the officer radioed in to the chief once more. "Looks like he is headed for the airport, Chief."

The Chief put out the order.

"Stop him!!"

The officer in pursuit turned on the lights and sirens, Prine continued to drive. Prine had left a message on Jack Ward's cell phone, he desperately needed Jack to return the call. Jack, however, was hundreds of miles away. He had just gotten off the plane in Connecticut, his phone was turned off due to airline restrictions. He was going back to see Gertrude Revner. The information about the Pristine murder victims and the locations in which they were found had Jack disconcerted. His thoughts were on the case and he had forgotten to turn his phone back on.

Prine took the exit to Reagan International Airport, the officer was behind him with lights blazing. Prine yielded for traffic, a man walked out into the street. Prine looked in the rear view mirror and saw the man stop between his car and the police car.

This was his chance, Prine floored the accelerator and sped out into traffic. The man was dressed impeccably in a maroon colored business suit.

"Get the hell out of the way!" the officer demanded.

The man laid both hands on the hood of the car. *WHOOSH*, the whole car rocked under the surge of energy. The engine stalled. He walked over to the officer and put his hand where the officer could see it. A flash of light from his palm dazed the officer. The officer's head began to wobble; he looked around blindly. The curly haired man leaned forward and began whispering in the officer's ear. The officer picked up the radio transmitter. Simultaneously as the curly haired man whispered the words in the officer's ear, the officer repeated them over the radio.

"Chief, I was wrong. He was not headed toward the airport. He just turned around and is headed north on the outer loop."

"Well stay with him. I am calling for backup," said the chief.

This would buy Prine some time. A few minutes later Jack Ward would get the message and inform the officers that Dr. Prine was working for the bureau. They would take it from here. The chief called off the pursuit. Jack Ward turned around immediately. Gertrude would have to wait again, he was going to assist Dr. Prine.

As for the officer, he recovered and gained his senses with no harm done, except a slight headache. The curly haired man turned out to be the archangel Raphael. Raphael calmly lit a cigar and was seen headed east.

❉   ❉   ❉

Marie Carthon had not received a visit from Rameci in several weeks. Marie considered that a blessing. The menacing Rameci was driving her and her family to the breaking point with his sadistic treatment. Silence was a unique form of torment. Anyone, who was ever unfortunate enough to go through torturous treatment, would say the worst form of torture, was mental torture.

For the common prisoner, solitary confinement is an extreme means of punishment. The prisoner is locked in a confined cell with no one to see or talk to. Prisoners were known to invent imaginary visitors to occupy the cell with them. Those that did not invent some sort of constructive distraction were known to go insane. Prisoners of war will also attest, that true torture begins, once your captures have your mind. Silence is also used by parents to punish disrespectful children. A parent can refuse to speak to a child until the child makes amends. But silence on an adult level it is devestating, especially when the ability to explain what is happening is taken away.

This was nothing new for the fallen angel Rameci, months before, another young girl stumbled across his murderous scene. She was punished also and confined to a crate box. The woman was Cindy Revner. Marie and Cindy do not know each other, but they share a common bond. Rameci enjoyed what he did to these women, it actually pleased him more than murder.

Marie was still fighting to keep her family together. Her children, Steven and Carl, were more tolerable than the adults. Marie's mother was the most supportive. But her husband Marcus, was loosing patience. Primarily because he knew there was nothing wrong with her. Marie simply refused to talk to him. Marcus was hurt and upset. He wanted to help, he considered himself the source of support for the family. Now he feels Marie has turned her back on him, and the family.

Marcus was going to see a counselor—alone. He sought the answers to saving his marriage. The counselor told him all the same things, be patient, your wife needs time, you need to be there for her in her time of need. But they did not live in that environment, nor did they ever face a patient with a situation similar to his in the past. The counselors were just speaking textbook trash as far as Marcus was concerned. They had no idea what it was like to live under those conditions. In the end Marcus continued to drift farther and farther away. He found his comfort in a bottle and that was where he spent most of his time.

At home Marie had done a terrible thing, she risked all when she secretly confided in her mother. One day while doing the laundry she whispered in her mother's ear and explained her whole ordeal. Her mother insisted that she not do it again. It provided Marie with minor comfort knowing that her secret was shared with another. But how long would she be able to continue the charade?

Marie was at home. Since her attack there was not much reason she sought to leave the house. It was 5:00 p.m. in the afternoon. She was looking for her children, so that she could take their dirty school clothes. Carl was in his room, but Steven, the oldest, was nowhere to be found. They both came home from the school bus, and they both were heard playing around a few minutes ago. Marie went from room to room searching for her son; she could not find him.

Marie ran to the door, looking outside, wondering if he possibly slipped out of the house. Still there was no trace of Steven. Marie ran into the guest bedroom, where her mother was napping. She awakened her mother. Marie had a picture in her hand of Steven, then she motioned, alerting her mother that her son was missing. Marie's mother arose from bed and assisted in the search for Steven. Marie's mother yelled throughout the house, hoping that Steven was hiding from her.

When she got no answer she turned to Carl. Carl was sitting on the bottom, rack of the bunk bed. He and Steven shared the room, they were only one year apart. The scene was chaotic; Marie's mother pleaded with her grandchild. If he knew anything about Steven's whereabouts he should tell her immediately. Carl simply put his index finger to his lips, signaling them to be quiet. Then he pointed toward the doorway. There stood Rameci, his robes glistening under the bedroom lights. Steven was standing close to Rameci's body. Rameci's right hand was over Steven's mouth, preventing him from saying a word. Rameci held Steven firmly against his body as they faced the others.

"Were you looking for him?" Rameci asked. "What a handsome young man this is."

"What do you want?" asked Marie's mother. "Let him go!"

"I am afraid I cannot let him go. He now belongs to me. Don't play dumb with me grandmother, I am sure you know all about *who I am.*"

Marie shook her head furiously. Trying to indicate that she did not break his trust.

Rameci raised his voice; he was extremely annoyed.

"DON'T PLAY IGNORANT WITH ME!" he screamed. "You know what I am talking about."

Carl covered his ears and hid under the bed. He had seen the magic Rameci was capable of when he snatched Steven from thin air. Little Carl also stared into the black nothingness of Rameci's eyes. Steven and Carl were both fascinated with Horror movies. Now Carl did not wish to see another one for the rest of his life. For Carl, the boogieman manifested himself, and he stood in the doorway holding his brother. Rameci's massive frame filled the doorway. Steven's tiny chest rose up and down as he breathed. Steven tried to stay as still as possible. Marie's mother tried to reason with Rameci.

"If you want one of us, why not take me? I wish to exchange places with my grandchild."

"SILENCE, woman! Another word from you and I will snap his neck!"

Steven closed his eyes tightly after hearing what Rameci would do to him. Carl, who was hiding under the bed, tried to squeeze his hands against his ears as hard as he could. He did not want to hear another word, especially the sound of his brother's neck as it was broken. Marie's mother obeyed Rameci, and did not utter another word.

"The person I want to hear from is Marie," Rameci insisted.

Marie said nothing.

"Oh—why so quiet? Are you waiting for me to lift your silence before you spoke? Why obey me now? You did not think to obey me when you whispered our secret into your mother's ear." Marie dropped to her knees and covered her face with her hands, she was ashamed.

"I told you," said Rameci, "I would be listening!"

Rameci's technique was devilishly ingenious. He knew the instant Marie had broken his trust. But he waited, he made her think she had gotten away with one. The more time that passed the more secure she was about her action. More than a week later here he was ready to inflict his punishment. He caught Marie and her grandmother totally off guard and defenseless.

"Your silence is lifted woman!" Rameci instructed. "ANSWER ME!"

Marie did not know what to say. She felt like she let her family down. She looked at her mother, her son hiding under the bed, and her other son, who was in the grasp of the demon. How could she tell

Steven she was sorry? How could her words possible provide any comfort? Marie had to put all of that out of her mind. Rameci grew impatient. Marie had to find the strength, to get through this. She thought of what she would do to escape the situation. The game had been played long enough. It was time to make a stand. The final question was—would they survive? Marie played her hand.

"Rameci, take your hand off of my son right now!" Marie insisted. She stood to her feet and faced him. "I should have faced you in the woods, if I died then, my family would be safe. Your problem is with me—not them. Let go of him!"

A devilish grin developed on Rameci's face. Rameci took the thumb on his right hand and maneuvered it over Steven's nose. He applied pressure sealing off the tiny air passages of Steven's nostrils. Steven tried not to think about it at first, but he was previously breathing so heavily there was not much air in his lungs to begin with. His mind soon gave the signal for Steven to breathe, but he could not. The mind signaled his body again, making it unbelievably uncomfortable for him not to. Marie saw the muscles in Steven's chest contracting, trying to gather air. Steven was suffocating.

"Let him go!" Marie demanded.

Steven could no longer remain calm, he reached up and tried to remove Rameci's hand but could not. His arms began flailing wildly. He kicked and punched and scratched but nothing would break Rameci's grip. A muffled cry was heard coming from Steven's tiny body.

"GET THE FUCK OFF OF HIM—DEVIL! I AM READY TO FACE YOU NOW!" Marie screamed.

Rameci removed his hand.

"You now understand what I was talking about—don't you. It is better to die in fear, than to live in it. Once you die the fear dies with you."

Rameci had his hand on Steven's shoulder. Steven, the brave son of Marie, frantically fought to gain his breath. He did not try to leave Rameci's side.

"You were brave young man," said Rameci. He then reached down and patted the boy on his butt, scooting him toward his mother. Steven ran into his mother's arms, she gave him a huge hug and apologized for her act.

"It's time Marie, time to end this," said Rameci.

"What is he talking about Mom?" asked Steven.

"It's time for me to go with him son."

Carl, no matter how hard he tried to cover his ears, heard every word. He came from under the bed and pleaded with his mother. The three of them shared one last embrace. The youngsters held on to their mother tightly, as it was the last time they would get to do so. Marie pried herself from her children's grip and stood. She turned toward her mother and said her good-byes.

"Listen, Rameci, my mother does not fall under the same punishment. She and all of my family are to be left alone—got it!"

"Understood! Grandmother, I have no quarrel with you."

Marie paused to look around the boy's room one last time. "Tell Marcus, I am sorry! And that I still love him." Marie's mother shook her head and covered her eyes as Marie stepped toward Rameci.

"Come Marie," said Rameci. "Come and take your place among the dead." Rameci's arms were outstretched at his sides, awaiting her to walk toward him willingly. Marie stepped forward, while her mother and children held each other in tears. Marie's mother could not bear to watch, and she held the children's heads so that they would not see. Marie got within five feet of the fallen one when he suddenly put his arms down. Rameci began to sniff the air around him.

"Yes!" he said. He began sniffing again. "This one is strong!! Yes!" Rameci proclaimed, "After all of these years, I FINALLY HAVE YOU!!!"

Rameci stepped back into the hallway. "I will be back for you another time Marie." Rameci stepped into the nothingness behind him and was gone. Stillness, as the threat to their happiness was gone. Around the Carthon home there was a temporary sigh of relief.

The vanishing act was enough to sober up the inquiring eyes of Marcus Carthon. Marie's husband had entered the house unnoticed and stood in the hallway long enough to see Rameci depart.

CHAPTER 30

Secret of the Rhine

In less than six hours after receiving the message from his son's captor, Dr. Walter Prine was in California. He was able to buy his way onto a flight; he offered $400.00 to anyone willing to sell him their seat, plus tickets to later flight. A young man returning home from a business meeting gladly took him up on his offer.

Prine played the specific instructions left on his voice mail over in his head again and again. Jericho Black told him to go to the Hall of Kings facility. On the sublevels of the facility was where he would find Lexington. He also said the only reason Lexington was taken was to get Prine out of Northern Virginia. The last fight between Prine and Jericho was prematurely interrupted. If Jericho was eager enough to entice Prine into another fight, he sure picked the proper motivation.

Prine was ready to hurt anyone who got in his way. He hurried through the airport, heading toward the rental car booth. Willing to take any vehicle they had available, he stopped just short of the booth, when he noticed Serena standing near an airport exit. She tried to give Prine an encouraging smile, but it had no affect on him.

"Hello, Doctor," said Serena, "I am here to give you a ride."

Prine gave Serena a most suspicious look. "You better not be mixed up in all of this." The last time they met, Prine and Serena did not leave on the best of terms either. He wished to avoid Serena for the rest of his days, unfortunately, he could not escape her for long. Serena drove Prine to the Hall of Kings facility. The door to the northern entrance was unlocked, as Jericho had stated. They walked into the arena and toward the service elevator. Prine pushed the button to level B2. As the elevator door opened on level B2, Prine asked Serena a very important question.

"Are you here to help me get my son back?"

"I am here to do what I can," she answered. Her response did not provide much comfort.

Jericho had a built in system, which kept those who did not have *a need to know*, from entering the B3 level of the facility. Whenever someone presses the B3 button, without pressing the emergency stop at the same time, the elevator would carry them to the upper levels of the facility. Prine simultaneously pressed the B3 and the emergency stop buttons, the elevator doors closed and the elevator headed down one more level.

The two angels, Prine and Serena, left the elevator and headed toward the room in the middle of the floor. Prine turned the knob and cautiously entered the room. There, sitting quietly, was Lexington, he was watching television.

"Dad, Serena!" said Lexington. He ran to greet his father. After Prine checked to see if his son was okay, he turned his attention to Lexington's captor.

"Where is Jericho?" asked Prine in a commanding voice.

"He's in the back," said Lexington, as he pointed to a door at the far-left corner. "He already knows you are here." Lexington motioned to the far wall, with all the monitors. It was the room Jericho used to monitor the operations of the entire Hall of Kings.

"Take my son out of the room Serena, I don't want him to see this."

Prine headed toward the door, it opened before he got there.

"Your son is not out of danger yet, Eximus!" Jericho proclaimed, as he emerged from the back room.

Prine was frozen, like a child who had stuck his tongue on the metal ice tray—he could not move, nor could he barely speak…"What?"

Jericho continued, "you look surprised. Shouldn't I know your angelic name? Is it some great secret or something? Oh—yes I forgot. No one else knows it, except for Gertrude Revner."

Prine did not know what to do, Jericho's statement seemed to take the wind out of Prine's sails. What did Jericho have to do with Gertrude? Prine had no idea the two had met. He decided to let Jericho talk. He needed to know more about the situation.

"Sit down Prine, you need to hear all of this. You think that old hag double-crossed you? You searched for Cindy, while she was stuck in a wooden crate and Gertrude knew everything! Well, you don't know the half of it."

Serena and Lexington had yet to leave the room. In light of Jericho's new information, Prine signaled for them to stay. The three of them sat and listened to Jericho.

"I love my money Prine, that is the thing that drives me. With it I can buy the nice things my personality demands. During this whole Orlando James incident, the FBI has frozen my accounts. That biddy Gertrude has money, and she agreed to pay me, to help her."

Prine was still confused, Jericho was talking in circles. "What does that have to do with me?"

"You were the one chasing the secrets to the Miracle. Shall I tell you how it is done? It is quite interesting." Jericho paused to sit on the video console before continuing.

"The blood of an angel is a powerful tool for humans. Within it lies the key to curing most of their diseases. Some angelic blood is more powerful than others. One angel in particular is named Baccius. Baccius is an angel of Heaven, with extraordinary healing power, even by Heaven's standards. One drop of Baccius's blood instantaneously heals humans and gives them a taste of angelic strength. It is a virtual nirvana for any human lucky enough to experience its pleasures. I was able to obtain a small sample of Baccius's blood during a battle, and from it I was able to develop a serum. Because of the potency of Baccius's blood, the serum was diluted. Less than a drop of his pure blood was enough to sustain the same healing effect in humans for several hours. I kept it, as it should be, a secret of the angels. I used the serum to make Roland more powerful than he could possibly imagine. But like all things there was a catch.

"A rogue angel named Rameci had blamed Baccius for his loss of sight. Rameci vowed to hunt Baccius to the ends of the earth, and beyond. About a year ago, one of my trusted security guards discovered the secret of the serum and sought to make money of his own. He tried to gather investors and become rich off of legalizing it—what a fool! Anyone that uses that serum in excess is doomed. The divine presence that all of Heaven's angels carry: *the fragrance of Heaven*, is still in Baccius's blood. Those that took the serum in the capsules Jacob provided, took a strong enough dose to where their bodies emitted the scent. This is the same scent Rameci uses to track Baccius. Rameci finds the origin of the scent, and when he realizes that they are not Baccius, he did not just simply walk away. He kills them to destroys the scent. Rameci's methods are sever and destroy. The headless bodies, hung upside down to rot, are trademarks of his methods."

Straight from the mouth of the man behind the Miracles—Prine suspected it was some sort of substance administered to the participants, he just did not know how it was done.

"So how did you avoid getting the Miracle members killed?" Serena asked.

"I hand picked the members. Women typically require less serum to be effective. Then it takes less serum for women of a particular blood type—type 'O'. I have an ability to detect human blood types just by looking at them. The one thing the scientists never explored, was why the Miracle participants always had the same blood type. With the low level of serum I administer, Rameci was unable to detect it."

"What about others using the serum," Prine asked, "wasn't you afraid of someone else drinking from the challis before the ceremony was about to begin?"

"In order for it to work, the serum must first be mixed with a small amount of the person's blood. If my blood is added to the serum, and you drink it, it won't work. The person drinking it has to have their blood added, or else it is just plain tap water."

"Sounds like you had it all planned out," said Prine. "So far, it sounds like all your problem, not mine. What does that have to do with you and Gertrude?"

"Like I said before, it is all about the money. She needed you to help her, and I needed the money. So we came up with a plan. Don't be upset with me Prine. You are here with your son, and now I am giving you this gift."

Jericho reaches behind the console and pulls out a black case.

"Did I miss something?" Prine said befuddled. "What does that have to do with you taking my son?"

Jericho was not known for his subtlety.

"Haven't you smelled him yet? He reeks with the smell of angelic presence. *The scent of Baccius is all over that boy, Prine!*"

Lexington looked down at the bandage around his wounded finger. Earlier Jericho accidentally pricked him with a letter opener. Lexington removed the bandage from his index finger, there was not a trace of the injury. Lexington also remembers feeling different, after drinking the water Jericho provided with his meal. But he thought nothing more about it.

"Rameci will be here shortly and have him swinging among the trees!" said Jericho.

Enraged, Prine toppled his chair trying to charge toward Jericho. Jericho opened the black case, positioned on the console, and pulled out a sword. When Serena saw the sword she grabbed Prine by the back of his pants and yanked Prine backwards. Jericho swung downward; the sword grazed Prine's cheek as he was pulled from harms way.

"Let go of me," said Prine.

"Not so fast, Doctor. Where did you get that sword?" Serena asked of Jericho.

Jericho, in his usual obnoxious tone, "Please explain to Eximus what this is. I know he lost his mind and all but in the angelic world his ignorance will send him to Hell."

"Look at your face Doctor," said Serena. "You will see something you probably haven't seen in a long time."

Prine wiped his hand across his cheek—on his hand was blood. Prine has never seen the sight of his own blood for as long as he could recall. The angelic skin is tougher than kevlar. It is not known to be broken so easily, especially by a sword.

Serena explained what Jericho had in his hands.

"When angels fight, it is a long drawn out battle. Our bodies are so tough and our regenerative properties are so advanced it is hard to destroy. Our fights were always hand to hand combat, and some would last for months. We basically have to pound each other to death. But certain angels had advantages, like the Morningstar, who were equipped with a built in weapon capable of easily penetrating the tough angelic hide. To make the battle for Heaven easier, God crafted five heavenly swords of destruction.

"They were given to the archangels to use in battle. Soon the swords became coveted items, and were sought after by the fallen ones. Most of the swords still belong to Heaven; some of them, fell into the hands of the fallen ones. From the look of that one, it was given to the archangel Michael. Michael was responsible for the destruction of Morningstars. The name of the sword is Kiernol—its nickname is the Great Equalizer."

Jericho held the sword for Prine to see. Its color was bright silver, the blade was four and three-sixty fourths inches wide, the guard was eight and twenty nine-sixty fourths inches across, and its hilt extended down another ten and one-eighth inches. The sword's weight was thirty-nine pounds. The metal was not of this earth, and its blade was honed to perfection. There was not a surface, or substance on this earth, that the sword could not easily penetrate. The grip was wrapped in black leather and the center of the blade was layered in carvings. The angelic writing in the center of the blade told of its origin and the name of whom it was first given to—Michael.

"That sword is Heaven's property," said Serena, "give it to me now."

Jericho pointed the tip of the sword toward the ground and dropped it. The massive blade cut through the concrete floor with ease. The blade slowly glided down as the earth swallowed it, until it came to rest at the hilt.

"If you are foolish enough to try and take it I will give it to you," said Jericho. "Otherwise, its new master is Eximus. I will give this to you to defend your son with. I trust you will take good care of it. It is a matter of irony—this very sword was probably used to cut the spike from your hand Eximus. Now you get to be reunited with it. Except this time you will be the one that gets to wield it."

Prine stepped forward to draw the sword from the ground, but Jericho snatched it out first. The blade had not even been scratched. Jericho extended the blade forward putting the tip of the blade into Prine's chest. The burning pain of the Great Equalizer tore into Prine's sternum. Prine did not utter a sound, even through the intense pain.

"Do you think I am crazy? You get the sword *after* I leave here."

It was Prine's first thought, to grab the sword and strike down Jericho. Prine would worry about saving his son after Jericho had been split in two. But Jericho would not make it that easy to kill him.

Jericho continued his demands. "First I want to see if you know how to handle this thing. This is a most precious item as you can tell, I don't want to know that Rameci killed you and took the sword easily."

Jericho removed the tip of the sword from Prine's chest. Again, the wound was not deep, but it easily broke the skin. Why was this happening to him, Prine thought. It seems as if both Jericho and Gertrude had teamed up to conspire against him. They wanted Prine to take on Rameci and they did not care how it was accomplished. Gertrude wanted to save the life of her grandchild Cindy. Jericho wanted enough money to start a new life. Their malice was at the expense of a little boy name Lexington.

For Eximus / Prine the safety of that boy was paramount. Lexington was his flesh and blood, and the only thing that brought joy to his existence. Just as Jericho stated to Gertrude, he knew how to properly motivate Prine. But Prine had a dark side; he was no stranger to taking a life. As he examined his small chest wound he vowed, if he survived this ordeal, there would be a few more souls joining Rameci in Hell.

"I need a moment with Serena," Prine said to Jericho. Prine took Serena's hand and led her out of the room. There he discussed Serena's involvement.

"Lexington's life is at stake," he continued, "will you help me?"

The beautiful Serena delivered a blank stare; Prine still did not understand what was happening. "I cannot—his life is not mine to defend. The angels of Heaven do not work that way. We do not interfere with the confrontations of others. Unless Rameci wants to attack me, I cannot engage in battle."

"I don't believe I am hearing this from you," said Prine. "You are an angel of Heaven, aren't you supposed to protect all creatures from harm?"

"We influence and guide, we serve God's will. If God does not command of me to fight for the boy, then I cannot."

"I thought you loved him?" said Prine bluntly. "But you would simply let him die."

"That's ridiculous, if his body—his temple is destroyed, you will still be able to see him. He will be…" Serena stopped her sentence when she realized whom she was talking to.

The Morningstar would not get the same privilege of visiting Heaven. Prine caught on also.

"I see! *You* will be able to see him—not I." Prine was beginning to understand the difference between the two sides—Heaven and Hell. "Get out of my sight, you disgust me."

Serena wanted to say goodbye to Lexington, but thought better of it. She reluctantly turned and walked down the hall toward the elevators. She left Lexington in the care of the fallen angels—a Morningstar and a Domination. She entered the elevator and turned around to see Prine still standing in the middle of the corridor. He had called Lexington into the hallway and was now hugging him. Prine was looking down the long corridor toward the elevator. As the doors closed, Serena absorbed all of Prine's scornful glare.

Prine was on his own.

"Don't worry Dad, she won't be too far away. I can read her thoughts. I can read your thought too, even the thoughts of Jericho." Lexington revealed to his father.

"How strong did the serum make you?" Prine asked.

Lexington took his father's hand and squeezed.

"That's impressive," Prine commented. "But what about your ability to read thoughts?"

"I can read them instantaneously. I can tell you what a person is about to say, even before they say it."

Prine knew that knowledge would come in handy. What Prine did not know was that Jericho was taking no chances. In an effort to quickly lure Rameci, Lexington was given the largest dose of Baccius's serum ever administered to a human being. Over eight ounces of non-diluted serum. Jericho wanted to be sure that Rameci would show. Jericho was desperate to get rid of the troublesome angel, for more reasons than one. The overdose would not harm Lexington, it just prolonged his newly acquired skills. The normal dose would last for several hours, Lexington's would keep him wired for almost a year.

Jericho, Prine, and Lexington traveled up to the B1 level. There they took the stairs that lie behind the altar to the main floor of the arena. The main floor in he Hall of Kings was seventy-five yards in diameter. The marble altar and four columns that surrounded it were positioned near the center. The altar would not pose as too much of an obstacle, there was still plenty of room for an angelic battle.

Jericho had the black case with the Great Equalizer clutched under his arm as he walked. In his other hand he carried two weighted poles. He placed the case down on one of the stairs leading to the elevated altar. Jericho got in position and threw one of the poles over to Prine.

"Humans fight with these weapons—swords—all the time," said Jericho. "We angels do not have the luxury of using such weapons to destroy our enemies. The five heavenly swords are the exception."

"I studied the Japanese art of Kendo," said Prine, "I know how to handle a sword in battle."

"We will practice with these weighted poles," said Jericho. "That should be sufficient enough to get you ready. But first I must warn you of what you are up against. The angel named Rameci possesses one of the heavenly swords also. His sword is named Rhine Splitter. Angels are unique beings, but some are more extraordinary than others.

"There are some angels who have the ability to manipulate time. Out of all the angels with special skills, these are the most troublesome. Many of the time altering angels were cast from Heaven. During the angelic war, they were responsible for destroying many of Heaven's army. To counter time manipulation, the sword Rhine Splitter was given certain properties.

"A 'rhine' is what angels refer to as a travel stream. Like magnetic lines of anomaly they are all around us. But unlike magnetism, humans have yet to discover its scientific relevance. There have been theories in space; humans call them worm holes—'rhines' fall under the same principle except they are right here on earth. A 'rhine stream' can transport you to another location within seconds, even from thousands of miles away.

"There are an infinite number of streams on this planet, but unless you know where the other end lies you can get lost easily. It takes a special skill to access the 'rhine wave' but it is a convenient means of attack or escape. You can transport yourself behind your enemy in a Pico-second. The 'rhine' ability became the primary means of escaping from a time manipulating angel. Rameci has mastered the principles of the 'rhine stream.' He can seemingly pop in and out of nowhere. The power lies in his sword, this is the enemy you must face."

Fucking great…It gets worse by the second.

Serena waited by the northern entrance. Although she did not show it, her heart was with Lexington. She was bound by loyalty not to interfere. But there was something she *could* do. It was a couple of hours before agent Jack Ward arrived at the Hall of Kings. He went through the same entrance that Prine had instructed, and he was greeted immediately by Serena. This was the first time Jack had laid eyes on Serena and Jack was easily distracted.

"Hi, Dr. Prine sent me here to meet you," Serena said.

Jack fought the urge to stare; he tried to remain focused on helping the Doctor find his son. "Where is he? And who are you?" he asked.

"My name is Serena, Dr. Prine is on the arena floor. But my job is to keep you away from there."

Jack began to chuckle. "You can try, but I am afraid this is official business. Kidnapping is a serious offense and I am a federal agent."

"Lexington is with Prine, they are safe for now. But you will be in danger if you follow them."

Jack became annoyed and began to head toward the elevators. "Don't you want to know about the killer who decapitates his victims?" asked Serena. "I can tell you all about the killer—even how he gets his victims from one point to the next."

Jack stopped and turned around. "What do you know about it?"

"I know everything. Come, there is something I must show you."

Serena led Jack to the security room nearby. Jack was brought to the room before, when he questioned Jericho the day of the Miracle ceremony. Serena opened the door and had Jack enter first. Once Jack entered, she closed the door locking him inside.

"Are you a religious man Agent Ward?" Serena asked through the door.

"Very funny, now open the door!"

"Look at the screens, there you will find the one that monitors the arena floor. You can see Lexington, Dr. Prine, and Jericho all safely moving about. They will be joined by another—that is your killer. I am afraid you will never be able to capture him, you can only see him. Once you see what he can do, you will know why you are locked in here."

Jack thought it was all a joke. He tried to exit the room, but could not budge the door. Jack got on his cell phone; he was not able to get any reception. The phones that were normally in the room were all removed. Serena did not want any distractions.

"Please, Jack, you must trust me and you must trust Dr. Prine. If you are willing to sit quietly, for an hour, I promise you will have your answers. All I ask is that you keep an open mind."

This was against all that Jack was taught. His gun was drawn, yet he did not feel threatened. He trusted the gentle voice of the Throne angel. Jack put his pistol back into its holder. He walked over to the few monitors in the room. This was the regular security surveillance room; not nearly as elaborate as the one Jericho used. Jack wondered where the normal security guards were. There were only three on duty today and they were all handcuffed in one of the stairwells. Jericho came by earlier and made sure the guards would not be in the way.

Jack walked to the boards and turned on the monitors. With all of his training in saving people he was forced to be a spectator. Jack located the monitor with Jericho and Prine, he could see Lexington standing on the stairs leading to the altar. Jericho and Prine were dueling with large steel poles and Jack could not believe his eyes.

They were moving at unbelievable speeds. From what he could tell, Jericho was no match for Prine. Jack smiled, "And here I thought the Doctor was just a college bred, preppy boy."

On the floor of the arena, Prine was getting the best of Jericho. Although this was a warm up for the up coming battle, Prine made it a point to make Jericho pay. Each blow inflicted was just the beginning of pay back, for involving his son. Soon, Jericho was too bruised to continue.

"That was pretty good," said Jericho, clutching his side. "*You son of a bitch!*" Jericho was breathing heavily; Prine barely broke a sweat.

"I am going to get some rest," said Jericho. "I will be back to help you kill that monster. He should be here in a couple of hours. The sword is on the steps, it is yours!"

Jericho descended down the stairs behind the altar. Prine knew the Domination angel would not be returning. Nor did he intend on helping Prine fight. His statement was a ploy to get Prine to concentrate on obtaining the sword—instead of seeking revenge on him. Vengeance would have to wait; right now his main focus was survival. Prine walked the stairs to the altar and opened the black case. The Great Equalizer and all its magnificence was inside. Prine's admiration for the weapon was soon interrupted.

"Father," said Lexington, "someone else is here with us!"

The time had come; Rameci was in the building.

CHAPTER 31

Prine vs. Rameci

Prine and his son stood on the main floor of the altar of Hall of Kings, the same floor the service was performed every Sunday. Prine had just finished a sparring session with Jericho Black. Jericho did not pose much of a challenge; he appeared to be much weaker than Prine had anticipated—*weaker than in their first battle.* The two angels practiced with weighted bars, the ones used for weight training. These bars were around six feet in length and weighed about forty-five pounds each. It was the only thing Jericho could come up with to simulate the weight of one of Heaven's five swords; the Great Equalizer. Jericho Black revealed his coveted weapon and then gave it to Prine, to defend his son against the murderous wrath of Rameci.

Halfway into Prine's rigorous training session, there stood Rameci, at the foot of the entrance to the stage floor. Jericho knew Rameci would be arriving at any moment to claim Lexington. And Jericho was sure to be nowhere in sight when Rameci arrived. Rameci stood in his traditional, shimmering, white robe and waited at the entrance with his walking stick. It did not take long before he was noticed. Prine was warned, the blind angel used his handicap to catch others off balance, so he was prepared. The life of his son was his to defend; Prine was ready to do business.

"I was here admiring your form," said Rameci, "you must be an expert." Rameci used the walking stick out in front of him to guide himself up the remaining stairs.

"I am confused," said Prine, "you watched me? You have your eyes closed and you move with the aid of a walking stick."

Rameci smiled, "Some say I developed a sixth sense. It helps me throughout the day. But I have no time to chat. I was invited here."

"Invited?" asked Prine.

"Yes, I am interested in the other person that is with you, the small one. I was wondering if that person could step closer to me."

Prine noticed Lexington taking several steps backwards.

"The person you are referring to is my son. He has no business with you."

Rameci took several steps forward and Lexington took steps in retreat.

"Of course, he is why I am here," said Rameci, tapping his stick in front as he walked. "I am looking for someone in particular. I just need to talk to him for a while. Come to me little one."

Prine was about eight feet from Lexington, he motioned for Lexington to stop moving. He did not want his son to wander too far away. Rameci gave Lexington the creeps. Before Rameci arrived Lexington thought to read his mind in order to gain the advantage. But now that Rameci was standing before him, he was afraid to.

"What is your business blind man?" asked Prine. "We have more important things to take care of than speaking to you." Prine was rude to the stranger, he had an idea of who the man was, but he was not sure. Jericho neglected to tell him what Rameci looked like.

"This is a huge arena," said Rameci. "What is this place?"

"This is the house of God."

"No, I've been to God's house. It is much smaller," said Rameci. No one else saw any humor in it.

"Listen blind man, playtime is just about over. I want you to turn around and leave!"

Rameci did not argue, or object. The two turned their separate ways and began to walk away from each other. Rameci turned around and took several steps toward the stairs. Prine turned to walk toward Lexington. Out of the corner of his eye, Prine saw Rameci vanish. As he faced his son he could see Rameci reappear fifteen feet behind Lexington.

Prine grabbed the Great Equalizer from the altar and ran toward his son. Lexington closed his eyes tightly and tensed his body. Rameci ran in the direction of the unsuspecting boy. His hands were outstretched, ready to claim his prize. Prine and Rameci arrived at the same time and Prine thrust the Great Equalizer into Rameci's side. In an instant, Rameci slipped out of his robe to avoid the sword. It happened so fast, the blade went through the robe and was now draped over Prine's sword. The sleeves of the robe were resting comfortably on Lexington's shoulders. Lexington could feel the wind on the nape of his neck as Rameci sucked his arms through his sleeves, and out of his robe, to dodge the blade. Rameci was now standing twenty feet away, bare chest, examining a small wound on right side of his body.

"Your speed is impressive," said Rameci.

"As is yours!" Prine was looking down at the robe as it covered his sword. He had never seen anyone move fast enough to leave their clothes behind.

"Your weapon was able to penetrate my skin," said Rameci, examining his small wound. "May I ask where you got it."

"I heard all about you Rameci. Let's not pretend to play silly with each other."

"Then you should know—the boy must die like everyone else. Since you are a fallen one and you know my name, what shall I call you?"

"That is a small matter, nothing for you to be concerned about."

"How rude? You disregard the most honored of angelic customs; the pride of ones name. Well, I will just call you—*angel with no name*."

Rameci spit gummy, saliva from his mouth into his palm. He applied it to the wound on his torso. The milky, pliable substance sealed the wound and stopped the bleeding.

"So, tell me, angel with no name—why is a fallen angel protecting a human?"

"This human happens to be my son!"

This got Rameci's attention. "You *are* crazy," said Rameci. "Then I will not feel as guilty, when I send you to Hell and take your sword…*Crazy angel with no name*." Prine did not appreciate being mocked.

"I was tricked into this fight demon. But it won't be that easy. The sword belonged to the archangel Michael. And now it is mine."

"The Great Equalizer?" He knew of the sword well. "One of the five heavenly swords of destruction. That sword was said to be lost many moons ago. Neither Heaven nor Hell claimed to have had it. Nice work, angel with no name, but I possess one of the swords also."

Rameci put one hand up above his head and reached behind him. The displacement of airwaves created a visual ripple, as he moved his hand forward. Out of the nothingness, came a magnificent sword. It was a massive double-edged sword, similar to the Great Equalizer. Its carvings and guard was different, but it was a work of skill worthy of being crafted from the hand of God.

"Unlike the Great Equalizer," Rameci stated, "this sword has several advantageous properties. Its name is the Rhine Splitter."

Rameci pointed the blade tip toward the ground and dropped it. The blade glided through the arena floor and came to a stop at the hilt. Prine did the same with the Great Equalizer. The swords made a searing whine as it cut through the concrete and came to rest at the guard. Only the hilts remained extended above the ground. Rameci began stretching; he had not been in an angelic battle in a long time and wanted to prepare properly. Prine on the other hand did not want to take any chances with Rameci and his disappearing act. He did not trust Rameci one bit.

Prine took Rameci's shimmering robe and began to make a harness from it. One in which he could strap Lexington to his back. If Jericho were right about Rameci's motives, it would not matter anyway. Once Prine died there was no place Lexington could hide. The safest place, for now, was strapped to Prine's back. Prine just hoped the added weight would not slow him down too much.

When the harness was prepared Lexington climbed inside. He straddled his father piggyback style and positioned his head where he could still see the action. Prine made sure he tied Lexington tightly to his back, like if he was a second skin. Lexington complained of having his circulation cut off, but it was the only way. Then, Prine waited until Rameci was ready.

Rameci pulled his sword from the ground in front of him; Prine did the same. The two angels were ready. The battle was significant in a way; the swords were created to quickly defeat fallen angels. They were never meant for sword fighting. Two angelic swords have never clashed before.

Rameci made the first move, a head on attack. Prine countered to block it and the swords clashed. The high pitched reverberating sound echoed through the arena. Bright blue sparks from the intense heat were generated each time the swords hit, fine dust particles from the impacting of heavenly metal ignited and dropped to the ground. Like before, Prine felt a surge of adrenaline rage through his body. He started to become stronger with each strike. The swords clashed so strongly it knocked Rameci off balance.

Prine went in for the kill and came up with thin air. Rameci was safely across the room and Prine's weapon was imbedded in the concrete floor.

Prine pulled the Great Equalizer from the ground, this was becoming a problem. Rameci had a special power, a means of escaping danger. Unless Prine could figure out a way to counter it, he might end up on the wrong end of the Rhine Splitter.

It was as if Rameci had sensed Prine's concern.

"You had your fun, angel with no name. But this is why the other angels left you to return to Hell alone."

Rameci ran to the right, then quickly disappeared. Images of Rameci appeared all across the arena floor. From the left side to the right. With each appearance he steadily inched closer to Prine. Prine tried to keep up the best he could. When the images got close enough Prine gambled and lunged with his weapon to the right. He was a split second too late. Rameci reappeared to his left and stuck the Rhine splitter three inches deep into his left shoulder. Prine swung wildly trying to counter and was jabbed with another blow to the appendix. Prine was jabbed with the Rhine Splitter three more times and each time he was just a split second too late. The injuries started to mount and Prine's entire torso was sore.

"Ha, Ha, I could do this all day!"

Rameci became impudent and was toying with Prine.

Lexington was watching the amazing feats of Rameci along with his father. His father needed help, Lexington was observant. He noticed a pattern to Rameci's attack. Whenever he would disappear over to the left, he would end up forward and to the right. And vise versa when he disappeared to the right. Rameci was still gloating about his dominance when Lexington whispered his observation into his father's ear. Prine thoughts registered another idea—a counter attack.

He remembered when Gertrude was describing how Cindy was sucked into the hole that was created when Rameci fled. There must be a certain time frame in which a person can follow him. Prine figured if he was engaged in battle when Rameci shifts, he would be sucked into the 'rhine wave' right along with him. It was the only chance he had.

"Why don't you fight like a man instead of all this elusive trickery," said Prine. Prine thought he would entice Rameci into using his gifts one more time.

"Why should I fight like a man when I can fight like an angel," said Rameci.

He then went into his elaborate attack. His image appeared to the left and to the right. And in each case his body appeared, as Lexington had pointed out, forward and opposite of his last position. When Rameci got close enough within striking distance,

Prine faked a strike, then turned around immediately to his next projected position. The two swords clashed, and Rameci was startled. He tried to flee, but Prine stepped into the 'rhine wave' right along with him.

Once inside the wave, Prine's sword flew with a fury as Rameci jumped from one position to the next. As Rameci shifted, the hole was open just long enough for Prine to shift right behind him. Prine did not focus on what was going on around him; he concentrated on Rameci and was sticking close to the fallen angel. Prine was swinging his sword as mightily as he could. Rameci barely got his sword in position for defense, he could not keep this up much longer without getting hit.

Prine's next blow was so vicious, it broke Rameci's concentration and he flew past the next 'rhine wave' and across the arena floor. He just barely managed to get his sword up to deflect the blow. Rameci and Prine were both breathing heavily after that exchange.

Rameci laid on his back and he began to suspect what Prine already knew. The longer the battle went on, the stronger Prine was becoming. It was time for Rameci to end it. Rameci got to his feet and raised the sword named Rhine Splitter over his head. He prepared for an overhand strike, but that was only a distraction. As Prine concentrated on blocking the blow from above Rameci spit a milky residue from his mouth directly into Prine's eyes. Instinctively

Prine jumped back and managed to escape Rameci's blade, but the damage was done.

"I thought I would even the odds a bit," said Rameci.

Prine's eyes stung severely. The vile bacterium from Rameci's mouth began to work on Prine's vision immediately. Within seconds his eyes were useless.

"Dad, are you okay?" asked Lexington, still strapped tightly to his father's back. He saw his father laboring to keep his eyes focused. "Dad, here he comes!"

"I cannot see son."

"*IT IS TIME TO SEE HELL, ANGEL WITH NO NAME!*" Rameci screamed from across the arena.

Rameci moved in for the kill, his display of theatrics was impressive. He flashed from one spot to the next. Circling in for the final blow.

"Forgive me son," Prine asked of his child, as he knew the battle would be soon be over. But Lexington did not respond.

Rameci inched closer with each appearance. There was a bright flash as the Rhine Splitter reflected off the lights from above. Prine closed his eyes and stood with his sword pointed forward, no need in trying to clear his vision. He attempted to use his other senses to help him find Rameci, but they were not acute enough to do much good.

Prine concentrated anyway despite his fruitless senses. Rameci appeared directly in front of the tip of the Great Equalizer and stood. Prine had his eyes closed, pointing the sword in front. Lexington was draped over his father's back his head was over Prine's right shoulder; his eyes were intently focused on Rameci. Rameci slowly raised his sword above his head. "HRRRAAAAAAAHHH!!!" Rameci screamed his battle cry as his sword came barreling down towards Prine's skull. Then Rameci vanished; he appeared to the left of Prine, then to the right. The tactic was meant to confuse Prine, as he would obviously depend on his hearing to counter. Prine lunged forward, leaving himself vulnerable, then abruptly spun to his left, two hundred and seventy degrees.

"CLANG!"

Sparks flew as the sound of colliding swords echoed through the arena. Prine blocked the attack.

"Surprised?" Prine said, with the most devilish of grins.

"It can't be! Impossible!" Rameci was bewildered. "You cannot have equaled my senses in this short of time."

Prine did not have to—it was Lexington. The serum gave Lexington the ability to not only read minds, but to see what the other person was seeing. What if he used his talents to transmit thoughts instead of receive it, he asked himself? Perhaps the same would be possible with images? Indeed, that is exactly what he had done. Lexington used his incredible gift, with the aid of the serum, to transmit visual information to Prine's Occipital lobe, in the back part of the cerebrum. The part of the brain responsible for interpreting objects that are seen. Lexington was providing a crystal clear image to his father. In essence, Prine was now looking through his son's eyes.

But something more extraordinary was beginning to happen. Rameci's sword the Rhine Splitter, was designed to fight angels with the ability to manipulate time. By traveling through the rhine the master of the sword could counter the attack. But angels who manipulated time were extremely difficult to kill. If an extreme case of danger were present the sword would transport its master to safety—many miles away. The Rhine Splitter sensed Prine had the advantage and was pulling away, in an attempt to flee.

Rameci fought the wishes of the sword with all of his might. "NOOO!" he screamed. I cannot lose to him! I will kill him!!! I will KILL HIM!!!"

Rameci's pride was now at stake. He was proud to be among the ranks of the 'Angels of Principality.' He could not fall to this creature—whoever he was. "Angel with no name you will soon be in

Hell!" he proclaimed. Then he backed into the rhine wave for an attack. Again, Prine stepped into the wave right behind him. The sound from the furious clashing of swords reached an unbearable decibel level inside the enclosed arena.

Both angels swung their weapons mightily. At speeds that were a blur to the normal human eye. Agent Jack Ward was watching the action on the monitor from the surveillance room. His mind could not process the visual information fast enough to keep up with them. But Lexington carried the blood of Baccius through his veins and it allowed him to see the movements of the enormous angelic powers.

Prine slipped through the 'rhine' along with Rameci ensuring he stayed close, images sped past Prine's peripheral vision. Lexington kept his eyes focused on Rameci. Electrical pulses of neuron information flashed across the complex synapse network of Lexington's elaborate mind at an astounding rate. And instantaneously transmitted the information to his father's brain.

Prine was able to knock Rameci off balance once again. This time used a head butt to the bottom of Rameci's chin to send him streaming across the floor. With Lexington on his back, Prine leaped into the air. Rameci managed to get to one knee. The Rhine Splitter shook violently, pleading with its master to escape. Rameci ignored the warning—his pride got in the way. He managed to get the sword in a position to block Prine's strike—but it did not matter. As Prine came down with his weapon, the Great Equalizer hit the Rhine Splitter and shattered it. It then continued on through Rameci, tearing diagonally through his torso. Pieces of the Rhine Splitter shot across the arena and Rameci screamed in agony.

Rameci let the remaining half of the sword slip from his fingers. Rameci eased his hand over to measure the depth of his wound; he attempted to muster enough spit to seal it, but knew his attempt was futile.

Prine stood over Rameci, and watched his blood pour out onto the concrete floor.

"My son has nothing to do with the angel called Baccius," said Prine. "Neither did all those others. You hunted in a treacherous manner, I will not mourn in your trip to Hell, brother."

Blood was now present in Rameci's mouth as he labored to speak. "Baccius? Who ever told you I was after him. Baccius has already been destroyed."

Prine felt a sharp pain from his own body, the subsiding adrenaline made him aware of his own injuries. He cut Lexington loose and rested on the ground not too far from Rameci.

"I smell the abhorring smell of angelic presence all around me," said Rameci.

Lexington looked around the ground floor of the arena; fifty winged angels surrounded them. The heavenly angels observed the last few minutes of the angelic battle. In the middle was Serena.

"Hello, Lex," Serena said happily.

Lexington ran over and gave Serena a hug. Prine collapsed to the floor, dropping the Great Equalizer by his side. The battle was physically exhausting, and the wounds from the Rhine Splitter did not heal as quickly as Prine expected.

"What is your name stinky one," Rameci yelled from the floor.

"I am the Throne called Serena."

"And I am the Principality called Rameci. It is nice to see—that someone still honors the proper battle etiquette." A black oily substance seeped from Rameci's eyes—tears. His pain was intense, but he fought to speak.

Serena looked over toward Prine. "He does not recall the tradition. He is a de-spiked Morningstar," she said to Rameci. "The first to ever recover from God's curse."

Rameci coughed a few more splatters of blood.

"Now I don't feel so bad," he admitted.

"But I did not live this life to be sent to Hell at the hands of another fallen one. Do you know what I mean Throne?"

Rameci, despite the intense pain of his injury, got to his feet. Lexington concentrated so that his father could see the image of Rameci moving. "Don't worry Lexington," Serena assured him. "This is now between Rameci and me."

Serena prepared herself, she was about to be attacked. Even in death Rameci had his pride. He fought in the Great War of Heaven and believed in his cause. Serena's hair danced behind her and her eyes turned white. Rameci painfully picked up the broken sword and lazily charged. He almost fell forward trying to attack. For Serena it was the easiest battle she would ever have. This was a mercy killing. Rameci wanted to be sent to Hell by a warrior of Heaven—it was a sense of honor.

Serena grabbed Rameci's arm with one hand and put the palm of the other hand on Rameci's wounded chest. A surge of energy shot from her hand and through his chest wound like a wave, severing Rameci in two. The fallen warrior fell in two halves, Serena had finished the cut the Great Equalizer had started, and Rameci was finally on his way to Hell.

Serena stepped away, and the fifty angels surrounding the arena moved in. They scoured the grounds like busy bees, looking for the shattered pieces of the Rhine Splitter sword. Gathering all evidence, including Rameci's body. They worked like a cleanup crew, diligently searching and collecting items. Their job was to leave no evidence behind. Even blood and skin tissue left behind by Rameci could be analyzed and used to benefit mankind. That was not allowed, the angelic body and all of Heaven's items were not meant for the advancement of mankind. The fifty winged angels made sure there was nothing left. One of the angels got close to Prine, it appeared they were after the Great Equalizer.

"You touch it—you taste it, as I split you in two!" said Prine. His sight had returned, the milky substance was clear from his eyes. The angel promptly backed off. "Now Serena, it is your turn to back off as well. You refused to help me save my son. You and your stupid rules of engagement. Now that he is safe, here you are by his side again. I suggest you leave now, before I recover."

"You will never recover," Serena informed him. "You have been contaminated by Rameci's saliva, it slowly deteriorates the body. It may take close to a hundred years for you to fully deteriorate, but you will eventually die."

"A hundred years is good enough for me," said Prine.

"No, Dad," Lexington interrupted. "She was there during the battle. When you were blinded she spoke to my mind, and told me what to do. She showed me how to act as your eyes, how to put the images where you could see. Let her help us Dad."

Prine did not need it; his own regenerative properties began to heal his wounds. Prine was able to stand on his own, without pain. He took Lexington's hand, and in the other, he carried the Great Equalizer. The battered Morningstar headed toward the altar's exit, but he had one last thing to say. "In time I may forgive you, Serena—if what my son said was true—Thanks."

The fifty winged angels collected all their heavenly evidence. They ascended above the arena and began to disappear in a cloud of brilliant light. Serena walked up the stairs of the arena seating. She had not forgotten about Jack Ward. She was heading to the surveillance room to free him. Jack Ward was glued to the monitor. His eyes captured all he was able to see—his mind tried to make sense of what it could. Jack watched as his good friend, Dr. Prine walked down the back of the altar exit, with his son safely by his side.

Jack heard the door unlock; he was in the room a little more than an hour. He opened the door and looked out into the large empty arena. In all of his life he had never felt so alone. He did not have the urge to use his cell phone; he had no idea who he would tell his story to—*who would believe him?* This story wasn't meant for anyone, except him. He was allowed to see what he had for one reason, he could finally close the case of the Pristine Murders. There would be no more victims. The file would undoubtedly end up in the piles of the unsolved. He suddenly became consumed with nervous energy...he knew what that meant.

For Jack, the only thing he had on his mind at the moment, was the overwhelming desire to escape—with a nice cup of coffee.

CHAPTER 32

Dr. Bonney's Journal

It took less than a week to track down his fleeing adversary. Prine finally caught up with Jericho Black, as he hid in a dreary Motel room in San Antonio, Texas. The Domination angel would have to pay for his transgressions against Prine's only son, Lexington. Jericho gave Lexington a large dose of Baccius' serum, maliciously putting the boy in harms way of the vindictive angel called Rameci. Prine was left to dispose of the beguiling Rameci on his own. After being successful, it was now Prine's turn for vengeance.

10:30 am, a knock on the door came from the cleaning lady. She wanted to know if it was okay to enter, change the sheets, and prepare the room for other potential customers. Jericho was set to check out, but he was extremely sluggish that morning. The woman stuck the key into the door lock and opened it.

"Hello, we are here to clean the room!" she announced before entering. She became startled as a man approached her from behind.

"That's okay," said the man, "come back in an hour. There will be plenty to clean up then." It was Dr. Prine. He pushed his way past the woman and entered the room. "Sir," she said, "I can't let you…"

Prine closed the door on the woman before she could finish her sentence. He then attached the security lock from inside, so there would be no interruptions.

Jericho was not lying in bed, and was not in the bathroom. He sat in the dark corner with the blinds closed. He was in one of the chairs at the rear of the Motel room, with a box cutter and a small tube of clear liquid on the table next to him. Jericho did not look as if he was in the best of health. Jericho was hunched over in poor posture, and he was shaking as if he had Parkinson's Disease. Jericho was not alarmed by Prine's presence.

"You sure did a number on me with that pole, Eximus," said Jericho. "Look's like I am not going to make it."

Prine saw a clear tube of liquid on the table. Jericho panicked, after he realized he had left it out in the open. He tried to grab it, but Prine wrestled it from Jericho's hand.

"You must take me for a fool Jericho," said Prine, examining the liquid contents.

"Stand up!"

Jericho struggled to his feet, and stood as erect as he could. "What were you doing with that box cutter?" Prine asked. "It doesn't work does it? You must be one desperate angel if you would continue to try and cut yourself with such a primitive weapon." Prine broke out in laughter.

"What is so funny?" Jericho demanded.

"Through your whole elaborate plan," said Prine, "you forgot one minor detail. You forgot to store a vial of your own blood while you still possessed the sword. In our battle, Rameci said something that struck me as odd. While he was dying, he told me that the angel Baccius was dead! So how could Rameci be causing all of this strife, misery, and death by hunting for Baccius through his scent, when he knew Baccius had been destroyed?"

Jericho did not answer.

"Just as I thought," Prine revealed. "Rameci was not after Baccius—*he was after you!* Your body is rotting apart. Serena had told me, that's a tell tale sign of Rameci's infection." Due to Jericho's reaction, Prine knew that he had gotten it right.

While Prine lied on the floor, recovering from the injuries sustained during his battle with Rameci, he began to make sense of it all. Rameci must have expelled the same putrid substance from his mouth and infected Jericho. But Jericho somehow managed to escape. Rameci must have known that Jericho had the serum, and he studied the unique scent it emitted whenever someone would take it. Every time Rameci detected the scent of Baccius in the air, he thought it was Jericho, taking the serum to cure himself.

Rameci's perplexed look at the mention of Baccius being alive had triggered Prine's elaborate thought process. That was why Jericho made sure he was no where near the battle when Rameci arrived.

"How much time do you think you have?" said Prine, tightly securing the serum in his left hand.

"I think that beating you gave me, cut a few years off my time."

Like Serena had told Prine, the bacterium stays in the body, slowly deteriorating the incredible angelic defenses until it destroys the host. It takes approximately one hundred years. Jericho had been infected nearly ninety-seven years ago and felt his life was slipping fast. The two beatings Prine had inflicted on Jericho's body had accelerated the deterioration. Jericho was still suffering from internal bleeding, caused by the blows made with the weighted pole. His body could no longer recover as quickly as it could in the past and he was dying.

"How long did you have the serum, Jericho?"

"I developed it over two thousand years ago. Rameci and I knew each other previously. We were never what you would call *friends*. We were more like business associates, we were often seen together. After many battles with the heavenly angels, Rameci would often come back badly injured. He would trade items for the serum. It was a good partnership. But less than a century ago he claimed that I stole a heavenly item from him, which was worth more than any amount of serum I could produce. He said he traded it without realizing its true value, and now he wanted me to return it—I refused. I then discovered what millenniums of eating foul, disgusting, maggot-infested carcasses, mixed with the acidic secretions from a Principality angel can do to the body."

Since becoming infected, Jericho had estimated it would take about three ounces of serum for him to recover completely. But Jericho did not last this long, through the Great War, without possessing a reasonable amount of intelligence. He dared not take the serum until he could figure a way of killing Rameci first. He would take the serum to cure himself, and lure Rameci in for the kill at the same time. Although, there were still gaps in the story, Prine asked about why he decided to save Mary Beth Reynolds.

"Why did you risk the safety of your own life on a human being?" asked Prine. "Did making money become so important that you would gamble on Rameci finding you?"

Jericho answered bluntly. "I would not give two cents for the life of a human. But I found my means of killing Rameci, and I would let nothing interfere with my plans."

That is where Mary Beth Reynolds came in. A private company in the United Kingdom had discovered a rare and precious metal item buried beneath the earth in an undisclosed location in Africa. Instead of reporting the find to the African government, certain businessmen within the company, managed to smuggle the item into the United States. When they thought it was safe, they formed an independent business group and tried to assess its value.

They also sought a means of insuring the item. Jericho got word of the priceless artifact, and its description, from his own personal insurance agent, Dorothy Grablford. When Mary Beth was shot in the church, no one but Mary Beth knew of where the company had stored the item. Jericho had no choice but to save her, or else he would not have gained the only means of ridding himself of the fiend known as Rameci. With Mary Beth healthy, Jericho eventually recovered his prize—the Great Equalizer.

"You had the Great Equalizer for years," said Prine. "What were you waiting for? Were you that afraid that you might lose?"

"Hell, is a large price to pay for being ignorant, Prine. I had no idea how to fight with a sword. Rameci had the Rhine Splitter for over a millennium. Besides, I could not figure out what the Great Equalizer's *special power* was. Obviously, you *had* figured it out Eximus, or you would be in Hell right now."

Prine did not feel anything *special* when he used the sword. But he put that information in the back of his mind for later.

After Jericho had a means of fighting Rameci, he had to get familiar with using the weapon. He studied several forms of sword fighting, but by the time he had recovered the Great Equalizer, his strength had deteriorated to the point that it did not do him much good. Jericho's manipulation was legendary. Jericho managed to ensnare one of the most revered of the fallen angels, a Morningstar, and obligate him to act as his champion.

"Then along came a Morningstar by the name of Eximus / Prine," said Jericho. And Jericho used Lexington as bait to lure Prine into destroying Rameci for him. It just so happened that Gertrude had a common enemy, and needed the same thing. Now, Jericho was in hiding, waiting for his angelic body to deteriorate to the point where the box cutter's razor could penetrate his skin. Without a sample of his own blood, mixed in with the serum, it would be useless.

"This is the serum of Baccius," said Prine, as he held the tube in his hand. "You need this to cure yourself."

In Jericho's most childish, voice he mocked Prine, "You Morningstar's think you are so smart! But I got you to kill him for me, and you did not even know it!"

"Well, listen to this. Before I killed Rameci, I got hit with his vile, diseased mouth as well, and I don't have to wait for my body to deteriorate."

Prine reached behind his shoulder. The air ripples behind him began to expand outward and Prine pulled the Great Equalizer from the center of the airwaves.

"I have learned all kinds of tricks since then," said Prine.

When Prine shattered the Rhine Splitter, a small piece of the sword became imbedded in his forearm. When the angels came close to Prine, as he laid on the floor, it was the piece imbedded in his arm that they were after. Prine took the shattered remains, and tied it into the leather surrounding the hilt, of the Great Equalizer. The small shard was just strong enough to access a rhine wave that would hide his precious weapon. Prine was able to walk around inconspicuous, while having quick access to the sword whenever he needed it.

Jericho was astounded, he leaned forward. Prine stuck the tip of his sword in Jericho's sternum and pushed him back. "I don't know what you are so excited for?" Prine opened the end of the container.

"We can share it," Jericho pleaded. "There should be enough for both of us in there."

Prine curled his lip skeptically. "I think there is only enough for one of us, and I don't intend on living past the next hundred years anyway."

Prine poured the serum out on the dingy matted carpeted floor of the motel room. Jericho screamed as the contents seeped into the foam padding below. "NNNOOOOOO!!!!" he screamed again. The tip of the sword pressed against his chest was not nearly as painful as Prine's malevolent act. Jericho's screams was followed by silence and a blank stare. He did not blink, his eyes did not wander, he simply looked at the Great Equalizer. "Kill me then," Jericho said in a low voice. "End my misery. I deserve to die—by your hand!"

"From what my son said, that was the last of the serum. And your reaction confirmed it." Prine pulled the sword tip out of Jericho's chest and hid the sword back into the rhine, its safe hiding place. But there was one more thing Prine needed to know.

"So what is the object Rameci was after?"

Jericho smirked, "That is something I will take to my grave, Morningstar. If I cannot have it no one will!"

It must be something of immense value. Prine thought to test Jericho.

"I will trade you the Great Equalizer for it. And while the blood of Baccius flows through my son's veins, his blood will be able to cure you. All of this I will exchange for the object."

"Ha!" said Jericho. "The Great Equalizer is a child's toy compared to this. I will take my prize to Hell, Eximus."

Prine was now convinced of its value, if Jericho was not willing to bargain, it must be valuable. Prine had the answers he sought.

"I want you to go to Hell suffering Jericho, there is nothing else I can think of that would please me more. May you body rot, here and in Hell, and may Rameci smile upon your arrival."

Jericho fell onto the smelly carpet floor, he began to whimper on its dingy surface. Prine left the room, satisfied that vengeance was his. After a minute, Jericho's cries turned to laughter.

"Prine you are a fool!"

Jericho still had one more vial of the serum left. And the puncture wound to the chest, inflicted by the Great Equalizer, provided all the blood he needed to cure himself.

"Nukial, is not done yet…Eximus!"

Jack Ward spent the last few days filing reports. In his mind, the Pristine Case had unofficially been closed. Considering previous FBI records, the amount of serial murder cases that went unsolved were far too many. And it left a sour taste in the mouths of most agents. Many serial murders would simply stop occurring, without anyone being charged…with no real explanation as to why. It had often been speculated that the killer must have been incarcerated for some other offense or had died. For the Pristine case, Jack Ward had no physical evidence to present, regarding the murderer's death. Jack, with the help of a gorgeous blond, witnessed the fight in the Hall of Kings. He knew there would be no more bodies suspended in mid-air. The file would remain open, but Jack would sleep in peace, knowing that the case of the Pristine Murders was closed.

One of his major issues was putting the unknown victims to rest. The other members of Jack's investigation team continued on without him. And with the information they acquired from Jacob's computer, they were able to identify all eight victims.

Baron Meyer

Stephanie Walters

Carol Delgado

Lois Caldwell

Victoria Parkins

Christopher Ball

Charles Stohler

Florence Carlen

The families had been notified and they could finally begin to move on with their lives. For some of the grieving family, the search for the murderer was foremost on their minds. Now that they knew what happened to their loved ones, they now sought justice.

How could Jack comfort them? Justice had been served, but how could he convey that to the families? People with supernatural powers dueling for the safety of mankind was not an explanation that they would willingly accept. As painful as it was, Jack realized it was something they had to deal with—*on their own.*

Jack could not even explain the truth to the rest of his team. How the murderer actually transported the bodies those great distances, in that short of a period, would remain a mystery. Disappearing and reappearing somewhere else, was not the type of criminal explanation he was ready to put in writing. Jack tried not to focus on the case any longer than he had to. There were still some issues that he was not ready to face at the time. But there was one thing he was compelled to do before he closed the file completely.

Jack stood at a familiar door, he came here once before seeking help. This time he was here to put a closure to personal feelings and to help him understand what really transpired during this long investigation. He rang the doorbell, it appeared no one was home. Then someone came to the door and opened it, just wide enough to speak through. It was Marcus Carthon.

"Agent Jack Ward," Marcus did not seem thrilled to see the agent. "Forgive me if I do not invite you in. This has been a rough time for the family and…" Marcus searched for the right words, "we prefer to spend our time with each other." Marcus's voice began to break down as he spoke. There was a tremendous burden on his shoulders, and sorrow in his heart.

Marcus was in the hallway just long enough to see Rameci before he slipped through the rhine wave and out of sight. The conversation that followed was intense, as Marie spoke to her husband for the first time in over a month, and explained everything. Marcus was down on himself for acting so poorly during the ordeal. Now, he faced the chore of possibly raising two boys on his own.

The days went by, and the family waited for Rameci to return to take their loved one. Marcus wanted to fight, he wanted to run, he wanted to *save* his family. And lovely Marie, convinced him that this was the best way. She would hand herself over willingly and sacrifice herself for the safety of the family.

Somehow, Jack was able to see the family's strife in Marcus' eyes. He had to get in there and convince them that everything was okay. "Marcus, how is your wife doing?"

"She is just fine," Marcus answered.

"I need to talk to her…about the case."

"There is nothing she can do for you, agent. Now if you don't mind, I need to get back to my family."

"Is everyone there? What I have to say, does not have to be said in private. But I must speak to her."

Marcus became agitated. "You cannot help us! Just leave," he insisted. Marcus tried to close the door. He stopped when he felt a hand touch his shoulder. Marie had come to the door, she was looking much better than she had been previously. This was the first time Jack had ever seen Marie. She opened the door and let Jack come inside. Jack walked into the living room and saw the rest of the family.

Marie's mother, and her sons, Steven and Carl, were sitting and waiting for Marie to join them. Marie and Marcus sat together on the loveseat and invited Jack to sit in the chair opposite them. Jack refused he preferred to stand, he placed his briefcase beside him as he prepared to address the family.

"Thank you, for inviting me into your home. This is not a business visit, this is actually a social call. Everything I say here is off the record. The FBI will not be held liable for anything I have to say today. I want to talk about a case I have been working on—the Pristine Murders." Jack paused, he was searching for the right things to say.

"I want to talk about how insensitive I was. I overlooked certain things because I was driven to find the killer…When I saw that Marie had possibly witnessed the murder, I was overwhelmed with excitement. I wanted nothing more than for her to work with the police artists for a sketch. I wanted her to look at mug shots. I wanted her to tell us everything she could possibly remember.

"And never once, did I consider her personal safety. I work for the federal government. We protect people all the time. We may not always be successful, but we have means of protecting people. And sometimes we are so bent on catching the perpetrator, that we are willing to risk the life of the witness, just to put the perpetrator behind bars." Jack stopped again and looked down at his briefcase.

"In all the years as a law enforcement agent, I have never seen any-thing like this…A little more than two weeks ago, I saw a woman. She was curled up, in a wooden crate and she was too afraid to come out. Her grandmother said, the girl had seen something. The girl witnessed a murder…now her new home, was a wooden cage. There was no top to it, it was not fully enclosed. But it might as well have been, because the girl did not leave. She was afraid to move. She was told to stay inside the box and she did!" Jack sighed and rubbed the sweat from his brow.

"All I know…is that I seen this thing." Marie and Marcus had looked at each other. Jack could not possibly be talking about the same being, could he?

Jack continued, "this thing was like a man, but he moved…he moved like the devil." Marie was now at the edge of her seat, and so was her mother. Jack continued again, "all I know, is that if this thing is what you were afraid of—then fear no more, because it is dead."

Marie did not know what to think; the idea was far fetched. If he *is* talking about the same being that plagued her in the night it, would take more than words from an FBI agent to convince her.

Marcus asked Jack, "are you saying that you killed him?"

"Me? No…what I saw…you might think I am crazy," said Jack.

"Try us!" said Marie's mother from across the room. She had the look of a woman who wanted to believe, but needed more. They all had the look, even the children.

Jack knelt down and laid his briefcase flat. He then lifted the lid and stood back up. "There is no body or no pictures of the body. But when I went back, there was this." Jack reached down and pulled the white shimmering robe worn by Rameci, out of the briefcase. It was still glistening. Jack put his hand through the hole Prine made with the Great Equalizer. The robe was not made of heavenly material. It was not evidence that was worthy of the angels of Heaven, so they left it there, on the arena floor.

406 The Blind and the Caged

Marie snatched the garment from Jack's hand and carefully examined it. Jack explained, "it was confusing...there was a battle, he hit the ground. I saw him split in two—then the angels came down from above and..."

Marie slowly rubbed her hand over the silky material, she even explored the damaged areas of the garment. She put it to her nose and took a deep breath, smelling it for some trace of Rameci's scent. Marie suddenly dropped it and put her hands to her mouth; she was trembling. She let it build up inside her until finally, she could not hold it in any longer.

Marie screamed at the top of her lungs. "AAAAHHHHHH, I'm free! Ha, Ha, Ha!!"

Marie was overwhelmed with excitement, as her children ran and jumped on their mother. "Are you gonna stay with us Mom? Are you gonna stay?"

"Yes," said Marie, "that bastard is dead. I am here to stay!" The joyful hugs from two ecstatic children almost brought the rugged agent to tears.

"This is for real isn't it? Oh my God! Our prayers have been answered," said Marie's mother. "Thank you so much agent. Thank you!"

The family went back to their celebration, and Jack quietly slipped out the door. Jack was not the one to thank. The man who he went to for help, Dr. Walter Prine, was the one they should be thanking. But Jack could not bring himself to go see Dr. Prine or deliver the message. Prine was not a man, and Jack did not fully understand. Jack's common life could not readily accept anything supernatural as being part of his reality.

He could not explain the things Prine was capable of, and deep within his soul he was deftly afraid of Prine...his new friend. It was a shame when he thought about it, Jack really enjoyed the doctor's company. And he especially regrets, that he could not personally thank Prine, for what Prine had done...for him also.

❦   ❦   ❦

Detective John Cassleby of the New York City Police Department experienced some bazaar things in his career, this was just another one of those instances. Behind the two-way mirror he watched the suspect. He was joined by two other detectives, Ronald Beaker, and Jeff Donaldson. John was the detective that was set to do the questioning, the other two were merely there to observe. The woman sat, in the empty room, waiting. She was dying to have a cigarette. It was customary to let the suspect wait, that way they could observe their habits before beginning the interrogation.

When the time was right, Detective Cassleby walked out the door of the observation room, and emerged inside the room with the suspect seconds later. The woman did not even acknowledge the detective entering the room. She sat fidgeting with her fingers until he asked her the first question.

"State your full name and your address please," said the detective.

"July Matlow, 7426 One Hundred Seventy Fifth Street, Queens, New York," the woman responded.

"You're in a whole lot of trouble Miss. Do you realize that?"

July shrugged her shoulders as if she did not care. She was calm and cool. July asked for a cigarette. Detective Cassleby pulled out a pack of cigarettes and gave her one. He then lit it for her and pushed the ashtray in her direction.

"Why did you stay there July? Did you not realize what had happened? Or do you just get off on that kind of stuff?"

July took a drag of her cigarette before answering. "I enjoyed it…Yea, it was good," she said smiling.

Cassleby looked back toward the two way mirror, the other detectives were watching.

"Okay Miss Matlow, let's start from the beginning. Around 2:00 a.m. you were sound asleep in your apartment…"

"That's right," said July, "I thought I heard something, but I wasn't sure. I tried to go back to sleep, but I couldn't. I was real jumpy—I haven't been able to sleep through the night in weeks. So I laid there with my eyes closed. I tried to convince myself I was just hearing things. Sometimes you get so paranoid your mind plays tricks on you. But this was no trick, I heard it again. I grabbed the little bat I had at the side of my bed and brought it up to my chest. It was dark, but I could see. My eyes were adjusted to the dark. I looked around my room, I saw nothing. About an hour or so went by, and I did not hear anything else. I began to get settle down, and it seemed like I closed my eyes for only a moment. When I opened my eyes again, he was standing over me."

July took another drag of her cigarette. You could tell the retelling of the story had affected her—at least this part of it. "That ugly son of a bitch was staring at me. He must have been watching me for a long time, cause he knew I had that bat under the covers with me. He put his hand on the bat, holding it down, and with the other hand he smashed me across the face with his gun. I was seeing stars, that's all I knew."

"And you knew him?" asked the detective.

"Oh yeah, his name is William Richardson."

July took her last drag from the cigarette and extinguished it. "William started screaming all kinds of stuff," she continued. "Like how I took his best friend and turned him against him, as he continued to pound on my face. Then that sick bastard got another idea, he was gonna jump on me. He started pulling down my pants. I kicked and screamed, and fought him with all I had, until he latched on to my throat. He got a hold of it good, and he would not let go."

July stopped to rub the wounds around her throat. There were purple bruises all around the front portion of the throat area. The bruises outlined William's hand as it was pressed against her delicate skin. She also had huge purple and blue scars that covered the entire left side of her face. A bandage covered her left eyebrow, where it took ten stitches to close the open wound. Afterward, she took a deep breath and continued. "I thought I was gonna die. Blood had run into my eyes, and it was blurry. I didn't see too good, but the next thing I know William was snatched off of me, and he started screamin'. Then I heard the gunshots. Boom, boom, boom, boom, they seemed to last forever."

The police recovered the Beretta 92F, semi automatic handgun from the scene. All fifteen shots were fired. They found rounds embedded throughout the apartment. It was difficult to predict its trajectory. Bullets were scattered in every direction, which struck investigators as odd. No one was hit, there was no traces of anyone's blood, besides July and William's.

"So, who was the mystery hero?" asked the detective.

"Never saw him before," July answered quickly.

Detective Cassleby looked back at the mirror once more. She answered that question too quickly to be telling the truth.

"Okay," said the detective, "what happened next? You got up from the bed to see what happened…"

"I got up, and stumbled with the first step. I was woozy. The whole left side of my face was pounding. I took the case off of one of the pillows and held it over my eye to stop the bleeding. Slowly, I walked into the kitchen, I was hoping to find William dead. But he was still alive. He was sitting in a chair, his arms were tied behind the back of the chair and his feet were tied to the legs. The man was beating the crap out of William, he was asking about some envelope."

"What did he say was in the envelope?" asked the detective.

"He didn't say," July replied. "But it belonged to him, and William had it…William had these five needle things sticking out of his body. The man put one in the side of his neck, one around his ribs, one on his foot and one on each thigh. Whenever William didn't give him the right answer he touched one of those needles and William screamed like a banshee. I bet it hurt somethin' awful!"

"Weren't you scared?" asked Cassleby.

"No, I was enjoying it. He said I could watch," said July smiling.

Cassleby shook his head in disbelief. "Then what?"

"Then William told him where the stuff was. It was in his car. The man went down to the car and came back about five minutes later. He opened the envelope in front of William, to make sure everything was there. He was satisfied. He then turned to me and said, 'He's all yours!'"

"And then you killed William Richardson," said the detective.

"No, I did not lay a hand on him."

"The mysterious man just decided to kill him, is that right?" Cassleby asked.

"Only after I told him that William was the one who shot Mary Beth Reynolds, and that he had it in for Roland Stark for years."

Cassleby was dumbfounded. "The preacher?" The detective looked back at the mirror for a third time. "What does Roland Stark have to do with what was going on in your apartment?"

July almost slipped up. "I don't know," she replied quickly. "It just sounded like something that would piss him off...and it did!"

Cassleby was totally confused now. "So, your statement got him so mad, that he decided to kill William Richardson."

"Well, it was ugly," said July. "You saw the apartment and what was left of him."

The detective became frustrated and began raising his voice. "And you are telling me that you just sat there, while William Richardson was being tortured to death. His intestines were being rolled onto a rotisserie wheel like hot dogs, and you just turned on the TV, and sat and watched television."

As nonchalantly as she could, July Matlow answered, "Yep!"

With the aid of the serum, Jericho Black had made a miraculous recovery. July knew exactly who he was. Every law enforcement agent in the continental United States was looking for Jericho Black. Nothing would be sweeter than to bust a big time entrepreneur. Thad had confided in July as to who the shooter of the original Miracle was, and it was about time Jericho knew who the thorn in his side really was. William was responsible for Jericho having to risk using the serum to cure Mary Beth for the Great Equalizer. He tried on several occasions to kill Roland Stark, a man who Jericho considered an investment. Then he killed Orlando James and caused the whole investigation into the miracle phenomena. William messed with Jericho's life and Jericho's money. It was time William got acquainted with the other side of Jericho, the fallen angel known as Nukial. July was happy to let the entrepreneur know just how troublesome William Richardson had been to his company.

Detective Cassleby calmed himself after the outburst. "After being in the room all that time, you don't remember what he looked like? How tall he was? If he had bad breath? Anything? He saved your life damnit!"

"Nope," July answered, "I can't remember a thing. Except, he did say one thing...He had me repeat something over and over again while he was killing William."

"What was it?" asked the detective.

"He had me repeat the words, 'Tierch Inage,'" said July.

...*Send him to Hell!*

❖ ❖ ❖

The Wiltshire Nursing home was Prine's last stop before returning to Northern Virginia. Prine's actions while he was at the nursing home, would determine if he would take to the road and assume a new identity, or live out his days as a College professor. He thought long and hard about what Jericho and Gertrude had conspired against his son. But before he passed final judgement he would give Gertrude one last opportunity to clear her name.

Dr. Walter Prine had come a long way since his first visit to the home. And all that Gertrude promised had come through; he knew what he was. He even got a glimpse of the power he was capable of. All that remained was the object he sought to begin with—the journal. Dr. Clifford Bonney's Journal, the deciphered text of Prine's once scrambled angelic mind. All that he was, his memories of God, and of Heaven. The reason he followed Lucifer, and the battles he fought in the Great War of Heaven, was all in that journal. At least he hoped it was.

The nursing home looked like it did on most weekdays, practically very few visitors. Prine took the elevator to the sixth floor, and headed for Gertrude's room. She had already been alerted that she had a visitor, and Gertrude was expecting Dr. Prine.

Prine walked in the small room with a fury in his eyes. Gertrude was lying in bed, with her mattress angled up in the back. She was in a gown, and had her long white hair tied tightly in a bun.

"Good morning Eximus," she said with a smile. "I was expecting you."

Prine was agitated by her act of innocence. "You won't be smiling for long, if what Jericho said was true."

Gertrude was concerned that her name was being slandered. "What did he say I was guilty of?" she asked.

"The life of my son, was jeopardized for the sake of saving your granddaughter. I know it was Jericho's idea, but did you agree to it?"

"Agree to what?"

"To letting my son be the guinea pig and giving Jericho money so that he could do it! To set Lexington up as bait, just to get me to fight!"

"Eximus," she said, "I don't have a great fortune. My wealth is meager by Jericho's standards. He did not ask for money, nor did I offer it. What you did was for me, not him! I will never forget. My granddaughter is recovering, and is doing fine. Who knows how many others are out there—how many Rameci had held in bondage? Well, they are all free now. I just hope they will realize that he will never return, before it is too late for them."

In a way Prine was relieved, he wondered if he could find the will to kill the old woman. But it did not have to come to that, the plan was all Jericho's idea. And Prine now knew Jericho had his motives, so it all made sense.

"Wait," Prine inquired, "how did you know Rameci was dead?"

"Jericho informed me that you had succeeded," said Gertrude. The news came as a surprise.

"And he also told me to tell you thanks," Gertrude continued, "for poking him in the chest with that sword. He said he feels better than ever. I don't know what it means, but I agreed to deliver the message."

Prine knew exactly what it meant! Jericho must have had some more serum hidden, and now he is back to full health. The news did not anger Prine at all. When he thought about it he was actually pleased. It was no fun cutting down someone who was halfway dead to begin with. Now he has the pleasure of hunting Jericho down while he is healthy.

And he might just be clever enough to discover the secret of Jericho's most treasured item. It was something Prine was actually looking forward to.

"Gertrude," said Prine, "it is time to hand over the journal."

Gertrude said plainly, "I cannot give it to you."

Prine was flabbergasted. "Dr. Clifford Bonney's journal—hand it over!"

"You don't need it," Gertrude yelled.

"It's mine, it is an account of my thoughts, my memories—it's mine!"

Gertrude pulled the bedcovers up to her chest, then slammed her open palms down on the bed. She was not going to give in. "Listen," she said, "what happened was exactly what the world needed—a guardian angel. A guardian to protect the world from evil. My father found the earth's guardian and cured him of his troubles. You are now free to do God's work as it was intended. That is what the journal was about. It was getting you in touch with what your purpose is. And now my father's work is complete, he will rest in peace and look down from the heavens. My father is looking down from Heaven right now, and he is proud."

Prine was stunned for about a half of a second. Then he smiled a discouraging smile. "There was never a journal was there? You lie. Let me tell you something—if the journal was real you would know that I am a fallen angel. I was one of Lucifer's own. You would know what this scar on my hand means. And you would realize that your father had managed to correct a condition, that was considered by the angels, a curse handed down by God himself. For that I regret to inform you that the place your father most likely is looking from—is Hell!"

Gertrude's face remained emotionless, she tapped her finger on the bed impatiently. Then, without warning…"Why did you think I had you followed for all those years Eximus? Do you think it was because I was crazy, and I just happened to luck out and find an angel? I had you followed because if my father's journal was right, and you somehow regained your old ways…if you believed it was necessary to resume your quest *to liberate Hell,* then I felt it was my responsibility to stop you! As his last living child, I wanted to know if I had to correct for the incredible mistakes of my father. I know who you are Morningstar, and I know what was in your mind. YOU DON'T NEED TO KNOW! You are a much better person now.

"As for my father, he *is* in Heaven! The devil is not the only angel you can sell your soul to. I bought my father's place in Heaven by turning the journal over. The archangel Raphael, in all his heavenly glory, stood in the very spot you stand and promised me, my father would be in Heaven, if I broke my promise to you, and handed the journal over to him."

When it was all said and done, Prine looked Gertrude in the eyes and said, "I don't believe a word of it! You are just a liar. No wonder you and Jericho get along. You are both cut from the same cloth."

Prine slowly made his way out of the room never to return again. Before he could clear the door, Elise, Cindy's mother, met him in the doorway. She grabbed Prine and hugged him, then kissed him on the cheek. "From the bottom of my heart, I thank you," she said. But Prine promptly pushed her aside and continued out the door. The ramblings of an old cantankerous woman could not be trusted. But, to Elise, for the one who saved her oldest child, Prine's past did not matter one bit.

There were many things on his mind, things Prine wanted to believe and things he did not. But of all things, he regrets not knowing his history, and his struggles. His triumphs, but most of all, the longing in his heart was for a place called Heaven. If his soul were eternally damned, he would at least like to have known what Heaven was like.

He will be forever denied of that experience.

On his way out, Prine walked by the door of Harold Franklin, the man he noticed on his first visit. Harold had no visitors in over six months, and he was at the end of his time on earth. Harold was extremely pale, he barely had the strength to move. The clock in his wrinkled and fragile body was winding down. Prine could sense the time was near, it was an angelic sense. The transitioning of a soul was something angels were attracted to.

Prine entered the room, closed the door, and pulled up a chair. He observed Harold. Prine said nothing and neither did Harold. They sat and watched each other for over an hour. Then Prine stepped close to Harold and spoke to him.

"You will die soon. I know you already accepted that. I will spend these last hours with you, but there is something I need from you. I have seen many people die in my lifetime and they all go the same way. In the final moments their eyes get real big, like they see something. This lasts for six seconds. I need for you to be strong. I don't know what is on the other side and I want you to tell me. For six seconds you will be at the gateway, between this world and the next. I want you to focus; I want you to be strong. And at the beginning of the six seconds I want you to tell me what you see."

The movement was so minute, Prine could barely see Harold's head nod in agreement. Over six hours had passed; Prine dozed to sleep in his chair, to the rhythmic beeps of Harold's heart monitor. When the pace quickened, Prine jumped from his chair. The time had arrived. Harold grabbed Prine's hand and squeezed, his body tensed. The beeping turned to an almost steady tone. Harold's eyes grew as big as saucers; the six seconds had begun.

"What do you see?" said Prine.

Harold's mouth opened, his lungs filled with air.

"What is it?" said Prine again.

Harold strained to look at Prine. His eyes wide open; his mouth agape. The words were on the tip of his quivering tongue.

"WE ARE RUNNING OUT OF TIME! SPEAK...SPEEAAAAK!!!"

The seconds ticked by,

Three...

Two...

One...

Harold's grip on Prine's hand softened, his body went limp. The word never got off the tip of Harold's tongue. But if Prine could read lips he would know...

It was *Heaven.*

0-595-23253-1